D0290075

FIREBUG

LISH McBRIDE

FIREBUG

HENRY HOLT AND COMPANY

NEW YORK

Henry Holt and Company, LLC
Publishers since 1866
175 Fifth Avenue
New York, New York 10010
macteenbooks.com

Henry Holt® is a registered trademark of Henry Holt and Company, LLC.
Copyright © 2014 by Lish McBride
All rights reserved.

Library of Congress Cataloging-in-Publication Data
McBride, Lish.
Firebug / Lish McBride.
pages   cm
Summary: Ava, a contracted hit man who can start fires with her mind, hits the road
with her friends, desperately trying to escape the Coterie, a magical mafia, while
keeping the murder to a minimum after she is asked to kill a family friend by Venus,
who killed Ava's mother.
ISBN 978-0-8050-9862-4 (hardback) — ISBN 978-1-62779-160-1 (e-book)
[1. Fantasy.   2. Magic—Fiction.   3. Organized crime—Fiction.   4. Assassins—
Fiction.   5. Fire—Fiction.   6. Adventure and adventurers—Fiction.]   I. Title.
PZ7.M478267Fir 2014   [Fic]—dc23   2014016089

Henry Holt books may be purchased for business or promotional use. For information on
bulk purchases please contact Macmillan Corporate and Premium Sales Department at
(800) 221-7945 x5442 or by e-mail at specialmarkets@macmillan.com.

First Edition—2014 / Designed by April Ward

Printed in the United States of America

1   3   5   7   9   10   8   6   4   2

To my brothers—
I couldn't have picked better ones if I tried.
(And believe me, I've tried.)

1

STOP, DROP, AND LET'S ROLL

RYAN SLAMMED the book shut and tipped his head back, sprawling on the bench and claiming it as his own. I looked down at my lap, his current pillow, and shook my head.

"It's cheating."

"I'm not asking you to write the paper for me, Ava. Just engage in a lively discussion about the book." His put on his best pleading face—eyebrows up, a wide smile that showed his teeth, his hands clasped in supplication and—the kicker—his hazel eyes begging. Say what you would about Ryan James, the boy had killer eyes. And he knew it too. It was almost impossible to say no to him. Almost.

"You want to discuss a book you haven't read so you can write a paper on it. So, yeah, totally cheating."

"You seemed way less concerned with moral fiber yesterday." His grin was so impish, there were probably imps nearby taking notes. Not that imps are native to Maine.

I could feel the flush creeping up my cheeks as memories

of yesterday, when I'd closed up the bookshop a little early so that Ryan and I could have a little, er, "quality time," started a conga line through my mind. I looked out at the harbor until my blush dulled.

"Illicit make-out sessions aren't even in the same league as skipping your required reading, hoss."

Ryan sighed. "Can't I just watch the movie?" Then he started laughing, no doubt at the scandalized look on my face.

"You did *not* just say that to me, Ryan James!" I sputtered, and shoved him off my lap. He hit the bricks with a thud but kept right on laughing. "*The Count of Monte Cristo* is a classic for a reason. I don't know what I see in you. Ugh. Such blasphemy."

He rejoined me on the bench, and I helped him brush some of the grass off his jacket. We were deep into mud season, or "early spring," as I'd heard it was called in other states, and Ryan was lucky that grass and twigs were all he was brushing off. The weather had warmed lately, the snow melting, for the most part, and what was left was more mud than a body knew what to do with.

Ryan leaned over, sweeping a kiss along my temple while putting his arm around me at the same time. "You're so mean. Why do I date you, again?"

"Because you like pain?" I made it sound like a joke, but really, I had no idea why Ryan dated me. Besides his killer eyes, Ryan had curly brown hair that always looked a little tousled, like he'd been doing something forbidden, a lean build, and these lips . . . man. He made me act like a mush-headed girl, which I hated, but it was hard to avoid his allure. He always had this sort of hand-in-the-cookie-jar look about him, just bad enough to be fun.

2

He pulled a cigarette out and placed it in those devil lips, using his free hand to pat his pockets for a lighter. I cupped my hand around my old-fashioned Zippo, flicking the cap open with my thumb, and lit his cigarette.

"You're always ready with a light—that's one thing in your favor." Ryan took a drag on his cigarette, the cherry flaring a bright red. I tucked the Zippo into my pocket with a tight-lipped grin.

The lighter was a prop, empty of fluid and flint. Since I was playing a regular human girl, props were necessary. I could set fire to the bench we were sitting on and every boat in the harbor if I put my mind to it, and that's all it would take: just my mind. But Ryan? He didn't know that. He was normal. He thought *I* was normal.

Ryan sighed, the smoke from his cigarette coming out in a *whoosh*. "I wish I was homeschooled. You didn't have to finish reading *Lord of the Flies* when you hated it."

"They were stuck on an island and no one even *tried* fishing or digging for clams? I understand the symbolism of the pig, but really."

"They were ignorant boarding-school kids. It's not like Woodland Foraging and Basic Survival Skills was a class."

"Whatever. Anyway, don't be jealous. I had to read two books to replace it and write a five-page essay clearly stating my reasons for protest." Then Sylvie and I did a dramatic reenactment of the essay using sock puppets we made to look like the main characters from *Lord of the Flies*, but I didn't tell him that. I think I can honestly say that was the day my little hyperactive coworker and I really became friends. She made a killer puppet that looked like an angry clam. Then she sang a song called

3

"Clams, the Better White Meat," which she accompanied on the mandolin. She's thinking of turning the whole thing into a full-length musical.

Ryan threw up his hands. "You win. I'll read the book."

I curled into him, kissing his cheek. "Good, because you would have failed if you went off the movie, anyway. They're different."

He turned into me, his face only a breath from mine, those damn hazel eyes going bedroom sleepy. "You couldn't have just said that?"

I shook my head. "Nope. Tell you what, though. I'll discuss it with you while you read it and go over your paper with you."

"You're a harsh mistress." Ryan was about to kiss me when I heard a disgusted scoffing noise behind us.

"Hey, Ryan. Hey, homeschool."

Aaaand enter Brittany, sullen bitch queen of Currant, Maine.

"Hey, Brittany."

"Orphan."

I rolled my eyes. "Get new material." Technically, I was not an orphan. My mother was dead, yeah, but my dad was probably still around. I just didn't know where, or who, he might be. I kissed Ryan on the cheek. "The sound of her mind cogs screeching as she tries to think up new insults is my cue to leave." I stood up and brushed my hands on my jeans.

Ryan grabbed my arm, glaring at Brittany. "You don't have to go."

My phone chirped and I shrugged. "Yeah, I do." It was maple sugaring day, and if I missed that, Cade would have my head.

———

CADE was my guardian. He was one of those family friends so entrenched that he transcended trivial things like genetics and blood. We weren't related, but we were family, even if the state labeled him differently. He was my mom's childhood sweetheart and, to be honest, her forever one as well. You could tell from the way she'd looked at him that Cade was my mom's true heart. Which sounds like a vomit-worthy line from a crap poem, but for them it had worked. They'd been epic poetry in motion.

Whatever the label, my guardian took his job as a parental figure seriously. Everything became a lesson, and being regular old human didn't stop him from training the firebug side of me one bit. Especially during maple syrup season.

I pulled the truck up to the cabin and wasn't surprised to see that we had company. I recognized Lock's car—which probably meant Ezra, too, since he would never turn down a free meal— and Duncan's beat-up Jeep. Apparently it was a party. Cade was fairly serious about his maple syrup, or really anything we could make or grow at home. He owned the used bookshop, Broken Spines, where Sylvie and I worked, and he didn't make oodles of money. So he planted gardens. He canned, pickled, jammed, traded, and did whatever he could to supplement his income. Some of the syrup from today's session would go to Duncan, and in return, we'd get some smelt and whatever else he pulled out of the water.

The guys were already settled in the shack, which was mostly just a roof and a concrete floor with a brick-lined hole in the center for the fire pit. The "walls" were a few structural timbers to hold the roof up, and that was it. Sugaring produces a lot of steam.

A game of cribbage was about to begin, snacks were on

the card table, and Duncan had brought some Allen's Coffee Brandy, according to tradition. And also according to tradition, Cade kept looking at it and shuddering.

"No true son of Maine can resist Allen's," Duncan said, pouring himself a small measure. Duncan also brought a case of Moxie for those of us not old enough for Allen's, but only Lock would drink it. Imagine Santa dressed in L.L. Bean, and you might have a good grasp on what Duncan looks like. He was, of course, whittling. Duncan was a golem maker, and I knew that the things he whittled were more than mere wood.

"Then I guess I'm no true son. I'm fine with a mugup, thanks." Cade poured coffee for the rest of us. If you put my guardian and me together, we're like opposing bookends. He's tall, blond, cheerful, and bespectacled. The thin gold wires frame blue eyes that are almost always in good humor. I'm surly, brown eyed, and have more curly dark brown hair than I know what to do with. My vision is perfect, my height is average, and if you look deeply into my eyes, you'll probably just see flames. If you look into Ezra's, you'll probably just see bullshit. Not so sure about Lock's.

I grabbed my mug and one-arm-hugged Cade. We may be opposites, but I love my guardian more than anything. I tousled Ezra's hair and took a seat by Lock.

"I know what you're doing," Ezra said, not glancing up from his cards. "You're trying to irritate me, thinking my vanity would howl at you messing up these glorious tresses." He moved a card on the end into the middle of his hand. "You should know by now, Ava my darling, that my hair will be fantastic *no matter what.*"

The thing is, Ezra was right. He seems like he's two steps

6

away from strutting down a runway or entering a photoshoot all the time. He's not handsome or pretty or good looking. Ezra Sagishi is nothing but time-stoppingly, heart-rendingly, sent-straight-from-temptation gorgeous. Good cheekbones, dark hair with deep russet tones, amber-golden eyes that look lined in kohl, and a smile that actually does stop traffic. I've seen it happen. Twice.

And he knows it too. Ezra is a fox, literally, and they don't believe in false modesty. Stealing everything that isn't nailed down, yes. But modesty? Not in their lexicon.

I nudged Lock. "I know Ezra's here for the free food—did his stomach drag you along?"

"You don't think I'm here for the sparkling conversation? The scenery? To watch Ezra lose spectacularly?"

"I do everything spectacularly." Ez moved another card. "What makes you think I'm going to lose?"

"Because we won't let you cheat. There goes everything in your favor."

Ezra gave a minute shrug. "Can't argue there. Anything you need to wait for isn't worth it."

"Whereas I am a creature of patience."

"Well, I'm not," I said. "And you didn't answer my question."

"What else would I be here for? You, cupcake. I'm here for you."

Cade smiled over his coffee mug. "Have you come to make me an offer? I'm almost positive my girl here is worth her weight in chickens, so let's start talking dowry."

"Chickens? Cade, you insult the girl."

"Thank you, Duncan." I leaned in and kissed him on the temple.

"Now, goats, that's getting closer. But not cattle. She's not worth large livestock anymore. Maybe when she was a little younger . . ."

"You're all jerks."

"My apartment building doesn't allow goats," Lock said. "So you're safe. For now. And since you asked: I'm here to keep the trees calm. For some odd reason, firebug, you make them nervous."

Ezra may be all fox, but Lock is half-dryad. Or as he puts it: half-dryad, all man.

I decided to ignore the rabble and get to work. Maple sugaring is a process. You tap the trees, collect the sap, and then boil it down. Sap has to be kept cold, and since the weather was warming up, this would be our last batch. It's a forty-to-one process, so if you have ten gallons of sap, you're going to get one quart of syrup. That makes storing the sap indoors difficult unless you have a lot of freezer space, so we kept ours outside.

It takes several hours to boil the stuff down, and that takes wood. Well, it usually takes wood. Using me to provide the fire, or at least part of it, kills two birds with one stone, which is Cade's favorite way to do things. He loves multitasking. It saves us wood for our woodstove, which is the main way our cabin is heated, and works on my endurance.

Cade stacked a few logs into the fire pit to give me a little fuel to work with, and I settled in for the long haul. With the wood and the abundant oxygen, it wasn't hard to get the fire going. All it took was a little concentration on my part.

My phone beeped, and a photo came through: Brittany with her arm around Ryan, her lips pressed to his cheek. Ryan bowed away from her, one eyebrow raised in question.

8

Wish U were here, homeschool. Ryan seems lonely, but what R friends 4? ;)

I thoroughly regretted ever giving Brittany my phone number. The flames shot up with a *whoosh*, the tips reaching like a tower to the ceiling. I pulled the fire back before anything was scorched, but the ceiling looked . . . *smoky*. I'd need to wash it.

Cade eyed the ceiling speculatively. "Lock, could you take her phone? Ava is apparently having concentration issues."

I mumbled an apology, my face flushing. A firebug without control is dangerous, and I'd let mine slip like an amateur. Lock took my phone, at the same time setting a bottle of water at my feet and a snack bowl to my right. Like the flames, I'd work better with a little fuel to keep me going. He squeezed my shoulder, and I instantly felt less embarrassed about making an ass of myself. Lock's good like that.

Cade was still examining the ceiling. "Maybe I should get the shack warded as well. Something to look into."

I doubted it would happen any time soon. It had cost a mint to fire-ward the cabin, and the shack didn't have the same level of priority. I'd read an article that said the average cost of raising a child is around $250,000. I bet that looked like a sweet deal to Cade after raising me the last few years.

We were a couple of hours into the syrup-making process, and I was taking a break, when my phone beeped again. When Lock's followed, I knew it wasn't Brittany this time. Ezra's phone, saying *Did we get up on the wrong side of the coffin this evening?* in the smooth, rolling voice of the actor Cleavon Little, confirmed that it was Venus. Ezra wouldn't assign that text tone to anyone else. We all grimaced, the joy draining from the room in a messed-up Pavlovian response. I grabbed

9

my water bottle and kissed Cade on the cheek. He hugged me tight.

Duncan got a kiss on the cheek too, and the same silent conversation we always had passed between us. *Take care of him*, my eyes said.

And his replied, *Will do*.

We never discussed whether that meant until I got back or in case I didn't. Probably for the best.

COMBAT BOOTS don't make the best running shoes. Of course, I hadn't been planning on joining a marathon. The file that Owen, Venus's pet firebug, had emailed us had said "ice elemental," not "god of sprinting." I'd expected the creature to throw icicles—and hadn't been disappointed—and I'd known to keep my hands to myself. Nothing like a quick hypothermic death to ruin my night. But nowhere in the file had anyone said, "Oh, and by the way, he runs like a gazelle with an espresso addiction." At least not in the parts I'd skimmed. I didn't read the files closely, because if I read too closely, they became real. And I desperately needed them to be statistics. I only wanted the bare minimum of information. I didn't want to humanize anyone I had to hunt—and I mean *humanize* in the loosest sense of the word. Most of the people I met on the job were about as human as string cheese.

I leapt over an overturned trash can, my feet sliding on the ice as I landed. A conveniently placed brick wall broke my momentum, bruising the hell out of my shoulder, but I kept going. My quarry was sprinting away from me, leaving the lacy pattern of hoarfrost twisting fernlike on the buildings and pavement in his wake.

The creature turned long enough to throw another jagged ice missile at my head. I ducked with a curse, only barely getting out of the way. He'd been doing that just often enough to keep me from getting within easy range, continually breaking my concentration. It's hard to dodge, run, *and* throw a fireball. And anyone who thinks icicles aren't dangerous hasn't spent a winter in the Northeast. But fire, well, that's another story, isn't it? Everything fears fire.

Calling this a job makes it sound like it involves a time card or a name tag, something that will lead to bigger and better things. A choice. I guess it is, sort of. I can choose to hunt down targets for the Coterie, or I can be "in violation of my blood pact." In the Coterie that means someone like me shows up and helps you into a pine box. No one turns them down twice. No one gets the chance to.

Why couldn't I work only at the bookstore or have one of those mindless summer jobs every other teen got to have, like scooping ice cream or washing dishes? I would have sold my soul for a crap paycheck and a little polyester uniform.

Instead, I got to be brass knuckles in human form. Worse, really. I was there to kill the creature I was chasing. Not warn, not smack around, but straight up end his existence. That's the fun of being Coterie owned. And I *was* owned. I was chattel to Venus, queen of the manor and head of the Coterie. Lock and Ezra at least had the illusion of hope. Since they were tithes, their blood pacts were over at age twenty-five. They donated a few years of service to the Coterie, and Venus left their families alone. My contract only ended with death—mine or Venus's. Oh, there was a line saying she could release me at any time of her choosing, but Venus doesn't give up her toys. I think that line is in there to give me false hope or leave her the option of trading me to someone else if I become too problematic. Lock's and Ezra's don't have all those clauses—they're not as valuable as I am—but on some level we all know they are the same pact. No one leaves the Coterie without enforcers on their tail, and no one knows that better than the enforcers themselves.

A stitch sliced into my side as I tried to catch the ice elemental. Now, he was hardly innocent. The file told me that. Ice men like ice, which makes sense. They create it wherever they go, and they don't differentiate between a tree and a human being when it comes to building materials. Then they build nests, like birds. In their enthusiasm to create ideal conditions for themselves, they often freeze people to death. Venus couldn't give a shaved yeti about the most recent victim being human, though. She only cared that this particular ice elemental had been poaching on her turf. I was the only one in this equation who cared about the humans. All creatures have a right to survive. I know that. But Ice Man could have built his nest somewhere else.

Kinda sucks, doesn't it? Most girls my age worry about prom dresses and SATs. I have to weigh the ethical nature of being an assassin against the value of human life and basic freedoms. Makes detention seem like cake.

"He saw me, and he's doubled back. I think he's headed for the park," I heard. Ezra's voice was so clear, it sounded like he was right next to me, whispering. My earpiece looked like it was part of a high-tech walkie-talkie. The idea was similar, only ours ran on a spell. Safer that way. Actual walkie-talkies run on radio waves, and those can be intercepted. Not a great idea when you're working for the Coterie. But ours? I could speak safely into the microphone attached to my watch and know that only Lock and Ezra heard me.

"As your eye in the sky, I feel I should inform you that there's a pond in the park." Ez and Lock had flipped a coin for roof duty. Lock won.

Cursing to myself—though the boys probably heard it—I doubled my speed and shot out of the alley I'd been running down and across a street into a play park. The night was so cold, my breath crystallized in front of me, so the park was understandably empty. The ice creature was closer to me now. He was getting tired and had been slowing down, but as soon as he saw the playground, he put on more speed, heading toward a small frozen duck pond ahead of him. The ice might be thinning, but it was still ice. It was still his element, and I had to keep him away from there. He stopped tossing ice missiles and focused on running. Which was his mistake. The only things keeping me at bay so far had been the distraction of dodging and attempting to close the distance between us.

"From the sound of your panting, I can tell we need to start jogging as a team again. Clearly you're not training on your own. Ezra, stop groaning. It will be good for you. By the way, Ava, Ez is in position and I don't see any cannon fodder about, so we're a go."

Owen would have started on the outside—enveloping the creature in a low flame until he melted slowly away, fully aware the whole time. The Coterie and Owen: a match made in heaven. Or, more realistically, a match made in much warmer and brimstone-y climates.

I am not Owen.

I concentrated on something small—the creature's frozen

heart. Ice elementals are made of snow and frost and other wintertime things. But deep in their chest lies a heart that looks like a Swarovski crystal about the size of an apple. It's hard and dense, and if I tried to do something pedestrian like hit it with a bullet, nothing much would happen. I mean, yeah, it would shatter, but after about three seconds the elemental would just fuse it back together. Magic.

But I wasn't going to shatter it—I was going to melt it. If this were a movie and I the action hero, this is where we'd have a dramatic standoff. The creature would ask me why, and I'd either apologize or give my tortured reasoning. But this wasn't a movie. The creature didn't care why I had to do it. And I'm not much of a hero. So before he could reach the ice, and without a single word, I concentrated until a white-hot flame erupted in the elemental's chest.

I stopped running, my hand glued to my side as I stood gasping, hoping the stitch there would go away soon. His heart gone in the smallest of seconds, the elemental probably didn't know what hit him. Or, at least, he hadn't had time to care. That was the most I could hope for.

Yanking my phone out of my pocket with half-frozen fingers, I took a picture of the melting elemental—the proof that would get the boss-monkey off my back for a little while.

We waited until he was a puddle. Lock tossed a handful of seeds from his pocket into the water. Green sprouts shot up, opening out into large, heart-shaped leaves. A sea of tiny blue flowers erupted between the leaves.

"Pretty," Ezra said.

"*Brunnera macrophylla*—a perennial forget-me-not." Lock looked up at the cold, clear night sky. Though we were an hour

14

from home, we were still far enough from Boston that there wasn't much light pollution. "It's an early riser, well suited for the season." He slipped an arm around me. "Ready to head out, Aves?"

I nodded.

"Wanna make Lock whip us up some late-night hot chocolate?" Ezra asked.

I nodded to that, too.

2

DREAMS AND OTHER THINGS THAT HURT

I WAS BACK in the hallway, which meant I was asleep and this was a nightmare. That's the only time I ever walked those particular halls. They were just as I remembered—dark, windowless, cavernous and yet claustrophobic at the same time. The wood was cold and unforgiving under my bare feet, and the air smelled like old smoke and bitter herbs. Two men stood next to me, sized for the hallway—gargantuan and hulking. I doubt they were actually human. They were too big for that, but since the cowls on their robes hid their faces, I couldn't begin to guess what they were. I wouldn't see their faces until after the ceremony. Not until I became one of them. And really, it didn't matter. They were Coterie. They were all monsters.

There are two levels to the Coterie organization. Inside those levels are all kinds of sublevels, but really only the main two are important: the Associates and the Elite—or as Ezra calls them, the Suckers and the Made. Associates work in Coterie nightclubs and businesses—they run around and help out, doing odds and ends, hoping for a little handout, a scrap of power. They thirst to be part of the Coterie machine. Suckers. They're hangers on, the remora fish to the Coterie's shark. They're useful and necessary, but when it comes right down to it, they don't matter. They aren't Elite, and therefore they aren't to be completely trusted. They certainly aren't special. The Elite are raw potential, sculpted and shaped by Venus's hands until they become something hideous and twisted. Not born that way but made. Created.

I had another word for it. Damned.

Once you go through the blood-pact ceremony, you're Elite, and that's it. You're Coterie until you die. If you don't like that idea and you complain, then Venus makes your wish come true the only way your contract allows: her death or yours. Guess which one she's going to pick?

I was barely thirteen when I stood in that hallway, Venus's goons flanking me so I didn't bolt. Cade wasn't allowed to attend, even though he was my legal guardian. He wasn't Coterie. He wasn't even an Associate. The goons latched on to my arms with grips that went beyond iron. Both were warded, and neither had much sympathy for me. There was no small talk, just two thugs holding a quaking firebug in their grips in front of large oak doors.

At some signal I neither saw nor heard, the thugs opened the doors and dragged me in. The room was dark and not as big as I'd thought it would be. Thirty people in robes of dark crimson, their deep cowls putting their faces into shadow, stood in a circle, parting only for me and my escorts. My bare feet left prints, outlines of sweat and heat, as they led me through the crowd. I couldn't see anyone's face. I'd known I wouldn't be able to, but it bothered me all the same. The only light was from a series of candles set on tall wrought-iron candelabras. It was a little over the top for my taste, but the scene did its job. I was terrified out of my wits.

The circle enclosed me; the thugs released my arms and disappeared back into the sea of red. Venus stood in the center with me, the only other person besides me not wearing red. Her robe was snow white and blinding. She stood there, silver dagger in hand, and said nothing. A small smile played on her lips, and even though I'd never gone further than kissing a boy, I remember thinking, *That's a lover's smile, and not the nice kind.* It was a smile of desire that had nothing to do with sex or love. Venus's smile was one of possession. The curve of her lips said that no matter what happened after this, first and foremost I was hers. I would always be hers. I swallowed hard, sparks appearing around my hands like tiny stars.

One of the red-robed figures came up and drew on me with oil. The hands were small and delicate, which made me think it was a woman, but that was the only evidence I had. She drew on my forehead, the palms of my hands, and the tops of my feet. I couldn't quite figure out what she was drawing, and before I could ask, she used an index finger to cover my lips in that same oil. The sharp smell coming off it was so strong that my mouth was filled with the taste. My throat constricted, and I had to choke down the saliva.

Someone handed the woman a brass bowl, and before I could wonder at its contents, she reached her hand in, settling a mound of ash into her open palm. I barely had time to close my eyes before she blew the ash onto the oil. The marks she had drawn sprang to life then, and it felt like fire, like the burn

18

of a blowtorch against my skin. I screamed and fell to my knees. Red robes tried to draw me back up, but I didn't make it easy on them. I hung like dead weight, my skin burning, a thunderous headache banging between my temples, and in my mouth now only the taste of ash.

With a distinct and unhelpful certainty, I knew those delicate hands belonged to a witch. I'd just been warded, and while it wasn't permanent, it certainly sucked. The robes finally got me on my feet, and Venus snatched my hand. She clasped it, her icy fingers prying open my balled fist.

"Ava Jane Sheppard," she said, raising the knife.

"Halloway," I said. "It's Halloway now." I had seen no reason to hold on to my name—no family to attach it to, and plenty of old Coterie baggage my mother's name might stir up. Taking Cade's name made sense to me.

"Halloway it is, then," Venus said, "Ava Jane Halloway"—and then she sliced my hand with that silver knife. Blood welled. I wanted to yank my hand back, instinctively cradle away the pain, but I couldn't extract it from her grip. She fixated on the wound, and for a split second I thought her vampiric nature would get the best of her. With her free hand, she lifted her ward, keeping the chain around her neck. She placed the ward in my palm, rune side up, the design for fire winking at me before the silver charm disappeared into the blood and ash.

"You belong to us now," she said. The room narrowed to her and me and my bloody palm. "The Coterie comes first, before all things. It is your family now. Your lifeblood." She put the hand still holding the blood-smeared knife over my heart. "Your heart beats only to please us." Her hand moved to my forehead. "Your only thoughts are for our well-being." Blue eyes dug into mine. "When you speak, you speak for us. When you move, you move for us. Where you walk, you do so at our will." Her fingers touched lips, palms, feet, and all I could do was stand there. She pressed a folded square of linen onto my wound, and I could feel it pulsing like a second heartbeat.

Venus never looked around. She only had eyes for me. The witch returned with another brass bowl, this one filled with hot coals. Venus used the linen to pick up her ward and dropped both items into the bowl. The linen caught and burned, but the ward remained untouched. Only my blood dried and flaked away from the heat. The witch put the bowl on a stand, and Venus finally let go of my hand. Before I could hold it to me, the witch grabbed it and squeezed. The wound responded with more blood, and the witch tipped it while holding a cold glass vial close underneath. The clear glass became clouded with blood and ash. She set it aside, and my hand was wrapped with fresh linen, then returned to me at last.

I hugged it to me while Venus used her dagger to remove her ward from the bowl. I knew better than to think that was her only ward, but a reckless part of me whispered that I should turn my powers on her anyway, to see how much of her I could burn. My fingers pressed harder into my bandage, and I knew there would be singe marks where they rested. For now I kept them covered.

Steam rose as the ward was dipped in cool water before Venus returned it to its usual resting place around her neck. The witch handed me an honest-to-goodness feather quill, and a parchment was unrolled before me. I signed my name with ink made of ash and my blood and knew it was mostly a formality. The real pact was in the ritual. That's where the magic lay. The witch in front of me was a blood witch—blood was her element as much as fire was mine. I was screwed. There was no getting out of my pact. That didn't mean I wouldn't try.

Venus put her lips on mine, then leaned back and her smile widened, growing with her feeling of possession. "You are mine, now, little firebug," she said. I trembled.

And then the cowls came down. I was allowed to see their faces now. I was Elite. I was Made. I was Damned, and there was no going back.

I BOLTED AWAKE, drenched in sweat and swearing like a sailor. I gulped in warm air and oriented myself. The ritual was over, past and done. I was home. I was safe. My breath came out in a relieved whoosh. Then I sat on the edge of my mattress.

I don't wake up well, even when I'm not having nightmares. I had almost kicked Lock when I climbed out of bed. He had started out curled by me but ended up on the floor, probably when he became tired of me elbowing him for snoring. Ezra was sleeping on the couch because he was too good for the floor, and too handsy in general for bed sharing. Not that he wanted to get handsy with me, specifically. His was more of a hands-on-anybody sort of thing.

I heard Cade whistling in the kitchen, accompanied by the occasional clink of dishes. Damn it, he was doing my chores again. I dug around the floor until I found my slippers. The idea of flopping back into bed was very tempting. After hearing the clink of another dish, though, I started searching around on my nightstand for a ponytail holder to pull my hair back and get it under control. Finding the elastic was harder than it

21

sounds. My room is small but messy, and I'm always losing things. It was even smaller with Lock sprawled out on my floor like a human rug.

I finally found a band behind a picture frame on my desk—me, Lock, and Ezra at Palace Playland last summer. In the photo, Lock and I are mugging for the camera, my dark hair wild from the sea spray, wind, and rides, Lock grinning like a mad person and squeezing me to him despite my rat's nest. Ezra looks like Ezra—pretty and too cool for school, his hair mussed but seeming like he meant it to be that way. Ez had wanted to stay at the beach but caved after I'd reminded him that the amusement park was full of marks. What can I say? I'm a fiend for Skee-Ball, and Ezra likes to pick pockets. Lock made him turn all the wallets in to the lost and found at the end of the day. Ezra didn't actually want the money, he just liked the challenge, and that challenge doubled when he had to find a way to get thirteen wallets into the lost and found without anyone noticing.

I smiled at the picture and went about the annoying process of taming my hair into a ponytail. I'd have to do some laundry soon or clean my room, I thought as I took in the mess around me. It was too small to not keep it in some sort of order. Though if I left Lock in it long, he'd clean it for me, which was enticing. *Room* isn't really the proper word for where I slept—it was just a small loft above the den. There was enough space for a single mattress and box spring, a nightstand, and a sorry excuse for a dresser. I think the loft was originally intended to create an office space in the one-bedroom cabin. Whatever its initial intention might have been, it was cozy, it was clean (sometimes), and it was mine. I'd never had my own room until I started living with Cade. Every once in a while, I would reach out to touch the wall, just to make sure it was real.

Cade had tried to give me the bedroom downstairs when I'd moved in, stating some nonsense about a teenage girl needing her own space, but I refused. Moving me into the house had been costly—the walls had had to be treated with fire-retardant sealers and paint, a sprinkler system was installed, and we were probably the only house in America that owned fifteen fire extinguishers. Cade rarely has to get them refilled anymore except for maintenance reasons, but he still checks them. Regularly. The couches and mattresses are routinely treated with a chemical that makes them fire resistant. And, hey, it makes them stain resistant too. We buy the stuff in bulk and keep it in the unattached shed, where Cade keeps anything even remotely flammable on lockdown. I'm not allowed within ten yards of the storage shed.

At least he wasn't making me do monthly fire drills anymore. I think after he'd forked over the cash to get the cabin spelled and warded against fire by a Coterie-sanctioned witch, he'd chilled out a bit. He would have felt better with an independent contractor, but there wasn't a witch within three hundred miles who would come near me without Venus's okay.

Wards aren't cheap, so we only had the witch do the house itself. Between the magic and the stuff we sprayed on the walls, we figured we were covered. The furniture and linens had to settle for human-made chemicals only. Except for my sheets. They sported a fine edging of warded embroidery. You think silk sheets are expensive? Not even close to how much warding

23

will set you back. I guess it's a good thing I can't go to college (as if Venus would allow anything that might cut into my time, or as she saw it, *her* time). Couldn't afford it anyway.

So I wouldn't take the only bedroom in the house. Cade did enough for me; I wasn't about to make him sleep in a loft.

I padded into the kitchen, my slippers making a soft scraping noise on the hardwood floors. As soon as it was warm enough, I'd go barefoot again, and I was looking forward to it.

Cade had the sleeves of his button-down shirt rolled haphazardly so he could scrub the dishes. I gave a small wave to our morning visitor, Duncan, who was sipping coffee at the kitchen table. He smiled back before I turned a glare on my guardian as I poured myself a cup of coffee.

"You're doing my chores again." If Ez were awake, he would shake his head in dismay at me for saying that. Ez spends his entire life doing his best to avoid work, and here I was asking for it. What he doesn't get is that chores are important. They are daily ritual. And normal teens do chores. After a night like the previous one, hunting the ice elemental, I wanted back into normal as quickly as possible. Duncan got it—I could tell by the way he looked at me. Not for the first time, I wondered what Duncan had done in his life that made it so easy for him to understand me. Cade probably thinks I do the chores just to repay his kindness.

He placed a wet plate into the drying rack. I set my coffee down and grabbed a dishcloth and the dripping silverware already in the drainer.

"You looked tuckered out, Rat."

I smacked him with my towel. "You turned off my alarm."

"I sure did," he said, completely unrepentant. He rinsed

24

some bowls and put them in front of me. "And nearly stepped on your friend in the process."

"How am I supposed to be a responsible adult if you let me sleep in and you do my work for me?"

He reached over and put a blob of suds on the end of my nose. "You have two jobs, you work really hard, and you help around the house. Everyone deserves a break, Rat. Besides, you're not eighteen yet."

"Soon."

"Soon doesn't mean now. It means later. Don't rush it on me."

Duncan chuckled into his coffee cup. "Rat" may not sound like the most endearing nickname in the world, but it was when it came from Cade. When I was little, before I lived with him, he used to call me Mouse—something to do with my squeaky little-girl voice, I think. But when I showed up on his doorstep about five years ago, drenched from rain and shaking with cold and grief over my dead mother, he'd said I looked like a half-drowned rat, before he ushered me in and wrapped me in a blanket. After that, he didn't call me Mouse anymore. I guess I was no longer small and squeaky.

Lock and Ezra came stumbling into the kitchen, Lock quietly taking a mug out of the cupboard and getting coffee and Ezra flopping in a chair, whining and waiting to be served, as usual. I grabbed a cup of coffee for Ez, holding it out of reach until he said "please."

Ezra cradled the mug in his hands. "What is it with you people and your hours? It's not even *noon* yet. That's hardly civilized behavior. Rising at the crack of dawn and getting up to who knows what—" Cade silenced him by slipping a plate of food in front of him. The only way to close Ezra's mouth was to put something in it. Lock leaned against the counter and didn't say anything, but I could tell he wanted to roll his eyes.

Ezra looked at his bacon and then stared at me. Ez likes his bacon hot, and crispier than Cade cooks it. I flicked my fingers and made it happen, a small spark wending its way toward the table.

Cade pinched it with wet fingers. "She's not a microwave," he said, but he was scrutinizing me.

"Why am I in trouble? And how is this any different from sugaring?" This argument was so old, it had grooves in it.

"Sugaring works on your endurance, and you benefit from the making of it. What does cooking Ezra's bacon teach you?"

"That Ezra likes his pork products crispy?"

"He just doesn't want people to use you. And I agree, Ava," Ezra said around a mouthful of bacon. "Except when it comes to me. It's not using if the person is your friend."

Cade shot him a withering look, one I knew well. It was friends you had to watch the closest. They were the hardest ones to say no to.

"When are you taking off?" I asked.

Cade put the last dish in the rack and let the water drain out of the sink. "In a few minutes. I want to get to the shop early and do some rearranging."

"I can be ready in five," I said.

He wiped what was left of the suds I'd forgotten off my nose. "No, you'll eat some breakfast and finish your coffee, and I'll see you in an hour."

"Besides," Duncan added, "evicting Ezra in under five minutes is hardly humane."

Ezra groaned. "I can't imagine how anything this morning could get less humane. It's so *bright* in here. Why do you people need so much light? It's freakish and unnatural."

"That's the sun, Ezra." Lock said, taking a sip of his coffee. "I'm told it comes up every morning."

"Well, it's trying to kill me. Someone do something."

Cade fished an old pair of sunglasses out of a drawer and handed them to Ezra, who put them on immediately. He looked ridiculous, but at least he stopped complaining.

I finished drying the dishes and hung up the towel neatly. I knew better than to try to argue with Cade about going in to work. We both knew I'd split the difference and show up in thirty minutes anyway. "Aye, aye, Cap'n," I said, surrendering.

Cade put a plate down in front of me—eggs, bacon, home fries, biscuits, a banana, and half a grapefruit. I ignored the grapefruit and started buttering biscuits. I scowled at the banana. Lock took the other half of the grapefruit to go with his coffee, because he's a damn hippie.

Duncan nudged a pot of jam closer to me. "To go with your butter," he said.

I slathered my biscuit with jam. "Do you hear that cheering? That's all the cholesterol in my arteries welcoming their new friends, butter and sugar. *Yaaay*, new friends."

Cade joined us at the table. "Don't ignore your banana, please, Ava. And thank Duncan for the eggs and jam—he brought them over for us this morning."

"Thank you, Duncan," I chorused with Lock, though my mouth was full of biscuit. I threw Cade a "sorry" before he could lecture me about table manners.

Duncan was always stopping by and bringing us things. When he went fishing, we got fish. When he made jam, he always brought us a jar. He also had a ton of chickens, so sometimes we got eggs. Duncan was one of the few people I ever saw in our kitchen. Cade didn't have any family that I knew of, except for parents that he didn't get along with, and because of me we didn't really have any friends.

My mom and I were on the run all the time I was growing up, and even though it put Cade in danger, sometimes my mom would sneak back to Currant. It was like staying away was a Herculean effort for her; she couldn't help running out of fuel, and the only way to fill up was to come home.

Even at the age of five I knew that home was where Cade was. That time, we'd snuck home for the holidays and ended up snowed in for the whole week. For one week my mom looked happy and I was totally spoiled. I ate candy and read books and drank homemade cider. Cade got me new pajamas and showed me how to string popcorn and cranberries for the tree. I'd never had my own Christmas tree before. Cade didn't own any ornaments, so we covered it in popcorn chains and paper snowflakes. It was the most beautiful thing I'd ever seen. Duncan came over, and I asked him if he was related to Santa, because they looked alike, and he told me yes. Then he handed me a present with a big, red ribbon. I tore into it.

Inside the box were four carved animals. The biggest was the pony, which stood five inches high. Then a dog, a cat, and a tiny wooden bird the size of Duncan's thumb. They looked so real, I thought any second one of them would breathe. Duncan sat cross-legged with me on the floor, and then he gave each one a little tap. The tiny wooden figures sprang to life and lined up, biggest to smallest. Duncan had me clap, giving them a marching beat, and then the creatures pranced, heads high, parading through the house. It was magic. Duncan was magic. When the parade ended, the figures froze in midprance. I squealed and made him do it again and again.

I fell asleep that day curled up in Duncan's lap, the wooden creatures held in a death grip in my little fists. I'd had to leave them behind at the end of the week. I tried not to cry, because I knew it would make my mom even sadder, but I couldn't help it.

Cade kept them for me. They're on a shelf in my room, and every once in a while I want to ask Duncan to make them dance, but I never do. I'm afraid that if I see them parade again, they'll lose their magic. Irrational, but there you go.

Duncan watched me devour my breakfast, a thoughtful look on his face. "Rough job last night?"

I nodded—an answer to his question and a cue that I didn't want to talk about it.

"They're all rough," Lock said.

Duncan didn't push for more detail. He just drank his coffee, sympathy muddying his eyes. When I couldn't take it anymore, I excused myself and went to take a shower.

But Lock made me finish my banana first.

BROKEN SPINES was my home away from home, and what I considered my real job. It wasn't huge, but it was packed to the gills with paperbacks, comfy chairs, and a shop cat named Horatio. We couldn't afford to get the store warded yet, so I had to be extra careful about losing my temper at work. In the meantime, we'd managed to get the chairs, curtains, floors, and walls sprayed down with the same stuff we used on the furniture at home. Basically, everything except Horatio and the books was covered.

Cade has a thing for taking in strays, be they feline or firebug. We found Horatio one morning, sick and half-starved outside the shop. We rushed him to the vet and, five hundred dollars later, we had a furry little tenant. Horatio keeps the mice down (mice are death to a used bookshop) and the fur up—one of my jobs is de-hairing the couches. Everyone thinks Cade named the cat after Horatio Hornblower, but he's really named after the character from Hamlet. In the play, Horatio lived to tell the tale. So did our cat. He's a survivor. Like me.

He greeted me with a purr when I walked into the store, his head stretched out for a scratch, but I was far from his favorite. At first he'd seen me as a competitor for Cade's attentions. I'd had to bribe him for weeks with kitty treats and catnip before he relented and decided to honor me with his approval. In Horatio's mind he was royalty and I was the lucky peasant who got to feed him. Huzzah.

I began dusting and organizing before opening the doors to the public. I heard Cade in the back, cleaning up a bunch of used hardcovers. I was not allowed near him during this process. He used lighter fluid—it's the best thing to remove sticky residue from old books—so . . . not a good place for me to be. You could say that about the entire store, I guess. Cade thought it was good for me to work there, though—practice in restraint and patience. Personally, I thought it was asking for trouble, but I liked my job, so I kept my mouth shut.

The bookstore was quiet; most of the people were friendly

or left you alone, and I got to read a lot. Oddly enough, it held some similarities to my Coterie job, with the solitude and people-leaving-me-alone thing, except Cade never ordered me to kill any of our customers. At least, not yet.

As I finished the tidying, the bell rang and I looked up to see Ryan sauntering over to me.

"Think I can take my favorite girl to lunch?"

"Favorite implies that there are others."

"My nest of love slaves is a mighty one, but you hold the spotlight."

"You're so gross."

He tossed me a small velvet box. I opened it and was greeted with earrings—three silver stars on a fine chain dangled from each post, like they were shooting through space.

"Thought they might go with that necklace you always wear."

I realized that my hand had unconsciously gone to the chain around my neck. A simple silver chain with an interlocking heart and star dangling from it. A gift from Cade to my mom, and all I had left of her.

"I love them. How did you—" My eyes narrowed. "You did *pay* for these, right?"

He leaned on the counter and grinned. "You ask so many questions. Just say thank you." When I kept glaring, his smile faltered a bit. "I paid for them, okay? Dearly. Can you just put them on now? For me?" He pushed an errant curl behind my ear.

I put them in, watching Ryan the whole time. He seemed happy that I was wearing his gift, but I couldn't shake the feeling

31

that he also seemed a little sad about it. Maybe he'd bought them for someone else originally? An ex? Stole them from his mom?

I tucked the same lock of hair that Ryan had just straightened behind my ear again and found paper. He'd snuck an origami flower behind my ear without me catching on. I could see that it had been refolded a few times, and it was a little lopsided. He'd obviously worked hard at it, and it was nice to see Ryan not be perfect. I grinned at him in thanks. It was easy to grin at Ryan. "Earrings and a flower? What did you do? Make out with a nun? Because that is some guilt you must be working off."

He ignored me and leaned in, planting a gentle kiss on my lips. "They look great. Now, lunch?"

"I'll ask Cade."

As I wound my way into the back room, I thought about how odd it was to get a present from a boyfriend. I'd never really had a boyfriend before. I barely had friends. Cade, Lock, Ezra, and Duncan, sure—but Cade is more family than friend, and Lock, Ezra, and Duncan fall into the same category as far as I'm concerned. Of course, Cade is always at the top of the list because he feeds me on a regular basis.

And I guess Sylvie is a friend, in some respects, though I have to keep a lot from her. She doesn't know there's anything different about me, Lock, and Ezra. It's safer that way.

Ryan is not my friend. We go on dates, we hold hands, and we've steamed up our fair share of car windows, but I wouldn't list him as my buddy. We would never sit in our pajamas and watch movies or get BFF bracelets. You can't be true friends with someone when you're lying to him all the time, not really. And I was one big walking secret. Our whole relationship was like a game to see how many times I could play the Sick Grandma card to cancel on a date when I was really out doing Venus's dirty work.

My mom had taught me what it meant to love a firebug. Everything was fine as long as you kept it light. No delving into major relationships. Avoid all complications, especially the pitter-patter of little feet. Once my mom figured out she was pregnant, she was vapor. If the Coterie found out, they'd have staked their claim on me. Best-case scenario, I would be a firebug and forced to work for the Coterie my entire life. Worst case, I was human and a bargaining chip, a walking weakness to be used against my mother. Mom had already spent most of her young life working for the Coterie. Working for Venus. One unplanned pregnancy was all it took for her to break free—the idea of me having to suffer the same fate was too much. So she shook her tail feathers and made for the hills.

But it wasn't just for me. My mother had worried that if I took after her, Venus would make life hell for my dad, too, forcing him to become a breeder. Venus the undead mafia kingpin (or queenpin, I suppose) would own him.

The firebug gene is recessive. So to produce a firebug, both parents need to carry the gene. My dad turned out to be a carrier—he had the gene but couldn't actually produce fire. Plain ol' human. That much my mom had told me. At first she hadn't known if he was a carrier or not, but she couldn't take the chance of waiting around to find out. If I had been born human, she would have brought me back to my dad so he could raise me. She wouldn't have been able to keep me or let the Coterie know I was her daughter—so she would have walked away. I have no doubt. Anything to protect the ones she loved.

33

It's sort of like a disease. My mom was full-blown, while my father had the potential lying dormant inside his DNA. If they'd had more kids, some could have been firebugs and some could have been carriers, seemingly human. Normal.

Lucky me, I won the genetic crapshoot. Full-blown, just like my mom. That's one reason that we're so rare: even if both parents possess the gene, the chances that their offspring will be firebugs aren't very high. The other reason we're rare is that we don't seem to have a very long life expectancy. We have the Coterie to thank for that, or groups like them. Poachers. The Coterie wanted us because they wanted to use us for their own ends. Living weapons. Mom told me Hitler tried his damnedest to track down our kind as weapons for the Third Reich. Too bad Owen wasn't alive then. Ol' Tiny Mustache would have loved him. Peas in a psychotic mass-murdering pod, those two.

So Venus would have looked at a pair that could definitely breed firebugs as Christmas in July. She could have built her own personal army out of us, breeding my parents like cattle. My mom couldn't wait around to find out if I was normal or not. So she did the impossible—she fled the Coterie. Which meant we had to be on the run, living under the radar. Not just for a little while, but forever.

I FOUND Cade seated at a desk, bent over an old leather-bound hardcover, running a finger up the spine to see how it was faring.

"Can I go to lunch?"

"With Sylvie, or the delinquent?"

"Right, because as an assassin, I should really watch who I'm seen with. Wouldn't want to impugn my own reputation." He grunted and I rolled my eyes, both of us winning the blue ribbon for maturity. "Besides, no one has ever proved that he's a delinquent."

Cade looked up from the book and stared at me over his glasses. "Don't you think it's a bad sign that your best argument for your beau is that nothing has been proved in court?"

"Don't you think open contempt is the best way to drive me into the arms of the aforementioned beau? I mean, really, this is textbook stuff when dealing with a rebellious teenager, Cade."

He put the book down and leaned his elbows onto his knees. "You don't get to be textbook, Rat. I wish you could. I wish that boy were the least of your worries. You have to be more careful than most, and that includes who you date."

"Exactly. It's a date, Cade. Not a betrothal. You don't have to start thinking of how many chickens and goats I'm worth yet."

He gave me the patented that's-not-funny-and-you-know-it look that every parent or guardian develops. Do they teach it in a class? Hand it out with the diapers?

"You have other options open to you—why this boy?"

"Why not this boy?"

"It's difficult for me to endorse any suitor you meet because he wandered into the bookstore while playing hooky." He took off his glasses and rubbed a hand over his eyes. "Didn't Lock ask you out to see a band or something?"

"So you'd rather I date the guy I met through my Coterie assassin gig than the one who was skipping school? That makes sense."

He put his glasses back on. "Not the same thing: Lock made a responsible decision to protect his family; Ryan is a bored kid with too much time on his hands and not enough life skills to make good choices."

"One class, Cade. Let's not blow this out of proportion. As for Lock taking me to see a show, he's my friend. Friends do things together. I know you're a bit out of the loop, but I hear that's how it's been done for centuries."

Cade sighed, and I could almost see him mentally throwing up his hands in frustration. He didn't actually do it, though. Instead he got up and kissed me on the forehead. "Sometimes I forget how young and new to the world you are."

Oooookay. "So . . . can I go?"

"Fine. Before you leave, call Sylvie and see if she can come in a little early today."

"Will do, boss-man." In the eyes of the law I was almost an adult, but neither Cade nor I cared about that. He knew I was capable of making my own decisions and blah blah blah-bitty-blah, but that didn't mean I'd ever stop seeking his approval. Cade was my only family, and when you only have one person chiming in on things, a negative vote hurts.

Ryan and I went to a café down the street for lunch. I picked at my hot Italian sausage grinder, and I was too bummed out after my conversation with Cade to even make any innuendo-laden comments about it. Which is just sad. With "hot Italian sausage" in the name, the jokes practically write themselves.

Maybe I was coming down with a cold. I needed to eat, but my stomach wasn't up for it. Ryan didn't seem to notice, babbling on about . . . well, I wasn't really paying attention to what he was babbling about. I was eyeing my pickle and wondering how horrific my breath would be after I ate it, and then wondering why that made me want to eat it even more. Are teenagers naturally contrary, or was it just the firebug in me, drawn to friction and heat?

"So, do you wanna go?"

Ryan's face was all pleading, hopeful puppy dog. I was tempted to just agree and figure it out later, but that could land me in something I hated or, worse, interfere with my Coterie life. How on earth did other people manage double lives? Batman must be tired *all the damn time*. Of course, Batman also has Alfred to keep his shit straight for him. I had a sudden image of Cade as Alfred and Sylvie as my hyperactive Robin, and almost choked on my soda.

I poked my sandwich with a sword-shaped toothpick. "Sorry, Ryan, I haven't been paying attention. I guess I'm a poor lunch companion today."

He grinned and swiped my pickle without asking. If it were anyone else, I'd have stabbed his hand with a fork—I like pickles. And manners.

Normal girls, however, do not stab their boyfriends with forks over a pickle—or cremate them with their supersecret mind powers, as I also considered doing—and since I was going for normal, no stabby-stabby or burny-burny. Some days are just no fun at all.

I made a mental note to tell Cade about this. *I didn't stab him when he stole my pickle! And you say I'm not gaga for him!* On second thought, that might earn me a lecture on violence. Or pickles.

"I asked if you wanted to go into Boston this weekend. Then I said I had amazing things lined up guaranteed to knock your socks completely off. And yet here you sit, socks still firmly on and mind totally not blown."

My immediate response wasn't just no, it was *hell, no.* Extreme no. No ad infinitum, ad nauseam, with trained No! dancers doing a routine in sequins on top. If the Coterie were a human body, then Boston would be its whole central nervous system. That's where Venus was based, for crying out loud. No way was I voluntarily going anywhere near her territory. I might not have had a choice in working for Venus, but that didn't mean I had to spend my downtime hanging out around her and her flying monkeys. But again, since I was playing a normal girl-friend, I couldn't just toss the table over and run screaming from the café. I would have to find something reasonable to calmly object to. What I needed was more information. Unfortunately Ryan didn't seem to have anything else to say on the subject. "To do what?" I asked.

"There's a theater doing a foreign horror movie marathon. Totally blood, guts, and gore, but with subtitles so we can pretend to be highbrow." His grin was all boyish charm, and he grabbed one of my hands with both of his. My heart gave a dramatic little swoon. My brain rolled its eyes in disgust. It was like my hormones wanted me to gush all my feelings for Ryan in some ridiculously overblown Bollywood-style dance montage, while my brain was leaning toward black-and-white art cinema. Problem.

I didn't know all of Boston, but I knew the area around the Inferno pretty well, and that was usually where Venus lounged about while she managed operations. It was a Coterie-owned, money-laundering, restaurant/dance club that also served as Venus's evil lair. To my knowledge, there were no movie theaters in the vicinity. As long as we didn't wander around the city, Ryan's outing might be safe. I still didn't want to go, but he'd get suspicious if I passed on it. That movie marathon had my name all over it.

"Well, you had me at blood, guts, and gore, but I have to check with Cade. What's our timeline look like?"

Ryan's face lit up in his trademark grin, the one that had most of the teenage girls in Currant swooning. I couldn't say no to someone so swoonworthy, right? Based on all the literature I'd consumed, girls swoon. Usually because of too-tight corsets or the sight of Elvis's gyrating hips, but it did happen.

"I'll pick you up, say, six on Friday? Bring you home Saturday morning?" I raised an eyebrow at that and received an overly innocent expression from Ryan in return. "The marathon runs late, so we can either stay the night in Boston and drive home in the morning, or, if that raises old Cadey's hackles, I can bring you home straightaway. But it will still be in the early hours of Saturday morning."

I hated it when Ryan called him Cadey. "I'll ask and let you know, okay?"

Ryan nodded and ate the last chip on his plate. He cast a hopeful glance at mine. "You going to eat that?" He pulled the rest of my sandwich toward him while I scowled.

He grabbed my hand and gave my fingertips a quick kiss. "You're cute when you do the mock-pissed thing." Then he started devouring my sandwich. I wasn't doing mock anything, of course. My hand twitched for my fork, and the corner of the paper napkin in my lap burst into flames. I knocked it to the floor and stomped it out with my boot.

"Do you smell something burning?" Ryan asked, taking a brief break from destroying my sandwich.

"Nope." I smiled tightly at him and shoved my hands into my warded pockets.

3

ESCAPADES IN FOWLNESS

AFTER MY LUNCH with Ryan, Lock and Ezra picked me up for another Coterie mission, at Venus's command. The boys showed me their wards automatically, knowing I wouldn't get into the car unless they had them on. It only took Ezra forgetting his once before that became standard practice. He'd had to go to a Coterie witch to get her to grow back his eyebrows for him, which had cost a pretty penny—meaning Ezra had to go out and steal more to get the cash back. He loves stealing, but hates extra work, and when he *has* to steal, suddenly it's work, and repugnant to him in every way. Ezra's mind is complicated.

So now Ezra and Lock hold out their chains and I make sure I see the rune for fire etched into the silver warding charms around their necks before we go anywhere. Though Ezra's only looked silver, since were-foxes weren't exempt from the silver sensitivity that plagued most of the were community. His was made out of platinum.

We drove for forty-five minutes before we reached our target.

"What is it?" Ezra asked, his head tilted to the side. The implied follow-up being "... and can I steal it?"

"No," Lock said.

"It's a Baba Yaga house." I couldn't keep the surprise out of my voice. I'd read about them, but I'd never actually seen one. A Baba Yaga house is a cabinlike structure situated on some big-ass chicken legs. It's like the architectural version of a mermaid, but instead of a woman/fish combo, it's a house/chicken combo.

Ezra scoffed. "As safe houses go, that's not the best choice. It looks like an avant-garde nightmare." He stepped forward. "Let's get this over with. What a waste of perfectly good nap time." He reached for the gate, and Lock and I both jumped forward at the same time, but we were too late. When Ezra opened the gate, it creaked. Loudly.

The house shuddered, its feathers ruffling as it lifted up from the ground. Dust and the occasional feather floated on the breeze as the house raised itself to its full height, revealing some really orange, somewhat bedraggled chicken legs. I swear, in the silence that followed, I heard a faint "Bu-kaw!"

Lock grabbed Ezra's shoulder and mine, holding us firmly in place. "At least it doesn't know we're here and we haven't spooked it or anything," he said. His words were even, but the expression he turned on Ezra was one hundred percent sarcasm.

A man's cracking voice drifted down to us. "Tell Venus she'll get her money! I just need more time."

Now it was Lock's turn to scoff. "He must be new. More time? Yeah, because the Coterie is in the kittens and hand-holding business."

I cupped my hands to my mouth as an impromptu megaphone. "I'm sure we can reach some sort of agreement, Mr. Monticello, but you have to tell your house to sit so we can talk it out like civilized—" That's as far as I got before he screeched. The house did an about-face and started loping through the woods. "Damn."

Ezra took off his shirt, folding it neatly before he draped it on the fence. "I've got this." After he finished stripping down, Ez shifted. I've never seen anyone else shift, but from what I've heard, fox shifters aren't the norm. Like the creature they turn into, their shift is quick and graceful. In a few steps, Ezra went from a human Adonis to a russet-colored fox. If I'd blinked, I might have missed it.

Ezra's amber eyes shone in the light as he hopped on his little black feet in front of us.

"Don't get distracted," Lock told him, shoving his hands into his pockets. "Now get going. We'll catch up in the car. If you can, steer him deeper into the woods." Ezra bounded off after the crashing sounds the Baba Yaga house made as it moved through the dense thickets of spruce and pine.

"How does he get so small?" I asked as I climbed into the passenger seat.

"Out of all the things we just saw, that's the one that your brain won't accept? Not the giant chicken house, but the size of our friend when he's a fox?"

I clicked my seat belt as Lock jerked the wheel and punched the gas. We tore off down the street.

"Sylvie explained conservation of mass to me, and it just doesn't make sense. How does he get smaller?"

"It's magic, cupcake, not science."

"But—"

"Science would also tell us that we couldn't possibly be chasing a house on chicken legs, you couldn't be a firebug, and I couldn't talk to trees, but we both know that all those things happen." Lock turned abruptly down a side road. "Now be quiet. I need to listen, and it's difficult from a moving vehicle."

We tracked the house using Lock's intel from the trees and Ezra's yips and barks. It got to the point where we couldn't drive anymore and we had to get out. Then we tracked it by the giant mounds of chicken poo. Lock stopped at one big pile with what was clearly a beanstalk growing out of it.

"The moron is feeding it magic beans."

"He's afraid," I said. Lock squeezed my hand. Fear of the Coterie, of Venus, was something we both knew well.

"You're going to have to burn these," he said after we'd had our moment. "They're an invasive species."

Then we heard what sounded like a woman screaming. No matter how many times I heard Ez make that sound, it gave me the willies. But it was a sound that carried well, so we used it as one of our signals.

Lock ran ahead to help him while I stopped at each beanstalk, put my hands on it, and vaporized it back into the ether. By the time I caught up, Lock had the house bound in a cage made of twisted tree limbs, a living chicken coop. Ezra was running around the house's feet, yipping excitedly. Everything is one big game to a fox. Lock was sweating from holding the house in place. Since the rest of my team was occupied, that left me to do the fun part. Venus didn't want a crispy fried-chicken house, so I couldn't burn it down, and Mr. Monticello was clearly not coming out. I buried my exasperation—before I

44

accidentally started a forest fire—and got ready to climb. Lock took my jacket and handed me my warded gloves. I slipped them on and began my ascent.

Mr. Monticello decided to take the express elevator down before I made it to the top. I can't say I blame him. The wet sound he made when he landed will show up in my nightmares for a long time.

I had to burn the clothes when we were done. The smell of charcoal and the eye-watering, acrid reek of chicken poop was never going to come out. I kept the warded gloves. They were too expensive to toss. Lock called Venus, and we had to wait until a recovery team came for the house. It was a long hike back to the car and a longer drive to the fence where Ez had left his clothes. Since he was the least exhausted, Ezra drove while Lock curled up in the back and I napped in the passenger seat. I was really looking forward to a hot shower.

THE BOYS dropped me off at home, and I took the longest shower in the history of long showers. Once I was clean and dressed, I sat down for dinner and asked Cade about Ryan's proposed road trip. Cade was less than enthused. Not for the reasons that most people raising a teenage girl would have— Cade trusted me and had no delusions in that arena. We'd always been honest with each other. Lock and Ezra stayed over all the time, and though Cade knew we were just friends, a lot of other parents would have said no. I'd brought that up once, and he'd laughed.

"My parents had that rule, and I've always thought that was funny," he'd said. "Like teenagers can only have sex at night in someone's house. If you were really dead set on it, I couldn't stop you. It certainly didn't stop me."

"Ew." I pretended to gag.

"Your face could freeze like that, you know."

"Totally worth it."

He rested his chin in his hand, an amused twist to his lips. "Despite current evidence to the contrary, I prefer to believe that I've raised you right and know where you are at night." He'd earned a hug for that.

So it wasn't illicit behavior that Cade was worried about. And he certainly wasn't worried about Ryan doing anything harmful toward my person. When your little princess can scorch an entire city block with her mind, you just don't have those kinds of fears. No, Cade had the same worries I'd had.

"Isn't that tempting fate?" he asked. "Might as well strap pork chops to your body and run into the lion's den." We were eating dinner at home. Cade had cooked, so my steak was tender and well-marinated and sitting next to some tasty roasted root veggies.

I can cook, since I'd been on my own with my mom for years and it wasn't a skill I could live without, but unlike Cade I tend to cook in a very utilitarian fashion. I eat so I don't die, and I can't seem to get beyond that. I create fuel. Cade creates a meal. I go for quantity, while he stresses quality. No one will starve in my presence, but I'm not a chef. Cade, though, is a foodie. He likes smelly cheeses and fresh herbs and shudders at my idea of cooking.

Firebugs have to be careful about two things: calories and potassium levels. We burn through both like mad when we light fires. Both are easy to maintain—eat a lot of bananas and make sure to keep electrolyte supplements handy. But I get seriously tired of bananas. There's really only so much you can do with them. When Cade's not around, I eat them plain and bitch *a lot*. When he is around, he bakes them into things, slices them into oatmeal, and sneaks them into desserts.

I glanced at the counter. Yup, a banana pie for dessert. I was starting to have an ingrained response to the color yellow. When I saw it, I wanted to vomit and light things on fire.

I sliced into my steak. "I realize that it's Venus's turf, but what am I supposed to tell him? He thinks I go to Boston all the time to see my sick grandma, so I can't say I'm not comfortable going there. Besides, I don't think there are any theaters around the Inferno, and it's not as if Venus and her crew are the art house theater types."

Cade had given up eating for the moment, focusing on the conversation at hand, his fork and knife held loosely in his fists. "Boston isn't *that* big—you might run into her or one of her minions . . . or some as-yet-unforeseen third misfortune." With me there always seemed to be an as-yet-unforeseen misfortune around the corner.

I stabbed a chunk of sweet potato with my fork, giving it the eye before I took a bite. Last time we'd had sweet potatoes, Cade had snuck plantains into the dish. Even though sweet potatoes are high in potassium, he didn't think it was enough.

"No plantains, Rat."

Says the plantain man. It could be a trap. I brought my glass of milk closer, just in case. I'd chug it if I hit plantain.

"Can you remember the last time I went out and did normal-teen activities? When I went to Boston to do something fun?

Not work, *fun*." I squished an errant chunk of what looked suspiciously like plantain with the tines of my fork.

"That's a turnip," Cade said, reaching for his wine. "Counterargument: It's not fun if you or your friends are injured at the end of it."

Oh, the temptation to roll my eyes. "Point, but you could say that about anything. I could walk down the street tomorrow and get hit by a bus. Does that mean I shouldn't walk anywhere?"

"Faulty argument. You're taking something that is extremely likely—Venus discovering you—and comparing it to something very unlikely—getting hit by a bus in a town that does not have a bus system. Try again."

"I want to do something normal," I whispered, suddenly tired and overwhelmed by a feeling of hopelessness. "If we went to school together, I'd have pictures of him in my locker. We'd hold hands while we walked down the hallway. I'd ask him to the Sadie Hawkins dance, and then we'd blow it off to go to the movies." I slumped in my chair. My next argument was going to hit a spot Cade felt bad about—me having to be homeschooled—but I used it anyway. Sometimes I am a grade-A jerk-a-tron. "I don't get to go to school, though. No walking hallways and no locker so covered in photos of us that students gag themselves with their fingers and pretend to vomit when they see it." I straightened up, suddenly angry. "I have *dreamed* of envy-induced vomit pantomimes, Cade. I want them. I deserve them."

Cade looked at me over the rims of his glasses. "If you went to high school, you'd be the one pantomiming vomit at the girls who wallpapered their lockers with pictures of their boyfriends. You'd tell them you didn't like the idea of giving over your personhood and identity to the worship of some

48

high school mouth-breather. Then you'd probably ditch class to go get coffee with a college boy in a leather jacket who writes bad poetry and loves Hemingway. If you were going for a cliché, that's what you would go for."

Gah, Cade knew me so well. It wasn't fair. "So I buy Ryan a leather jacket and we're almost there." I slumped farther into my chair. "I don't even like Hemingway," I grumbled. "And maybe just once I want the normal girl cliché." I waved him off before he got into his "What is normal?" diatribe. Because it didn't really matter. No matter what Cade would say next, we both understood that I'd never really know.

Well, I might have been missing out on the American teen experience, but I still got to kiss Ryan's lips, and that was nothing to complain about, let me tell you. There were a few other trade-offs as well. No curfew, a long leash, and I never needed a bonfire to make s'mores. It wasn't all a crap parade.

Cade wiped his mouth with his napkin before straightening the cloth and setting it back in his lap. "I won't lose you just so you can feel like every other girl on the planet. You aren't normal, Ava. You're *special*. Not because of what you can do, but because you're my little girl."

Ugh, how did you argue with that? This was why I always lost our debates. Cade was one of those guys who could talk about his feelings to no end, while just the mention of anything mushy made me squirm. Sometimes, when we were watching a movie and it got really emotional, I would go to the kitchen for a glass of water, even if I wasn't thirsty. That's how uncomfortable I got. But I wasn't going to fold this time. I steeled myself and brought out the big gun.

"Please. I don't ask for much, and you know it."

Cade studied me, and I could see him beginning to cave.

"I'll keep my phone on. I'll be careful." He grimaced and stared at his plate, and I knew that I'd won.

"All right," he said. "And don't just be careful, Rat. Be smart."

I clapped my hands. "I will," I said. We spent the rest of the meal discussing what we were reading and changes we were thinking about making to the bookstore. Happy thoughts. If only I were Peter Pan and happy thoughts were enough to help me fly away from the Coterie. Lock would have made an excellent Tinker Bell.

After dishes were washed and put away, we got into our pajamas and Cade made popcorn on the stove. It was movie night, and it was Cade's turn to pick. He used his turns to educate me, so the film was usually black and white—occasionally colorized—but always good.

I curled up in my favorite spot on the couch and snuggled deep down into an afghan. Cade brought me my own bowl of popcorn so I didn't steal all of his—not that it stopped me poaching from his bowl anyway—and we settled in for that night's selection, *Key Largo*. Humphrey Bogart, Lauren Bacall . . . I mean, what's not to love? All in all it was a pleasant evening, and I'm glad, because my evenings were about to get a whole lot more uncomfortable.

I DON'T know why I thought Ryan and I would be going by ourselves. When Friday night rolled around, I found myself squeezed into a Volvo with Brittany and her latest conquest. After a few minutes of stunted conversation, I fervently wished she'd remove his tags and release him back into the wild. Maybe if I'd tried harder we'd have had *loads* to discuss. Like when he was talking about Robbie's bitchin' party last week, I could have snuck in some charming anecdotes about how I burn creatures to death for a living.

The closest specimen in my life of what normal teen behavior might look like is Sylvie, and she likes *kaiju* movie marathons and cosplaying as obscure anime characters. I'm fairly sure she mastered Elvish and Klingon before she got her braces on, and she likes to read old chemistry books that come into the store. I'm afraid that if we were to leave her alone in the shop too long with normal household cleaners, she'd build a bomb. Or a spaceship. Or Godzilla. Any of those options seems equally likely. I might not know normal, but I'm certain that Sylvie is not the best barometer for it. Which just made Ryan's friends that much more perplexing. Surely they couldn't all be jerks, right?

"Interesting ensemble," Brittany said when I climbed in the car, her tone slow and lazy. "I hear hobo chic is really in this year. Wherever did you get such a lovely . . . shirt?"

She made the last word a question, obviously pointing out to the others that my shirt was of dubious origin and quality. I did most of my shopping at thrift stores, something Brittany would obviously never do. But my clothes got scorched, ripped, scuffed, and stained on a regular basis because of my job. It wasn't worth buying new stuff, especially since Cade was footing the bill.

What I wouldn't have given to be able to tell Brittany about the chicken house. Instead I smiled and told her I got my clothes secondhand. She smirked as if she'd scored a major point somehow. Like Ryan gave a crap where my clothes came from. "Besides, I just read an article saying something like eighty percent of designer clothing is made by children in sweat-shops. Small fingers make tiny stitches." She frowned at me, and I saw her unconsciously reach out and trace the seam on her jacket. I had no idea if what I'd just said was remotely true, but she didn't know that. I nodded sagely at her—a sort of *trust me* expression on my face. She looked away first.

Ryan turned his head so she wouldn't see his grin. "Play nice," he said when he got his expression back under control. "Don't make me turn this car around."

I was glad when Ryan cranked the music up too loud for any of us to try to talk. Brittany started sucking her boyfriend's face at some point, and after that I kept an eye on the scenery outside the window, thankful for the pounding music that most likely drowned out any slurping noises coming from the happy couple. I never thought I would be grateful to have my ears assaulted by uninspired whiny alterna-pop, so already the evening was bringing about more surprises than I cared for.

We stopped to get gas halfway through our drive.

"Does anyone want anything?" I asked, because that was how Cade had raised me, even though Brittany didn't deserve my good manners.

"Just a bottle of water. A girl's got to watch her figure," she replied, not so subtly eyeing my waistline.

"With that comment alone, you've set feminism back twenty years. Well done, Brittany." I needed to get away from the gas pumps before anything unfortunate happened.

I probably weighed a good twenty pounds more than she did, most of it muscle. If only she knew that I would kill for a muffin top. She might be aiming for anorexic, but I desperately needed the reserve those few extra pounds of fat could give me. My metabolism becomes turbocharged when I light fires. It's not safe being a skeleton in those situations. There'd been some nights when my fat ass had *saved* my ass (*ba-dum-tsh*).

Ryan snagged my belt loop and pulled me into him as we walked through the chiming doors. "Wow, she really doesn't like you."

"Remind me why you're friends with that rabid show poodle?"

Ryan grabbed a soda and some chips. "Our parents are friends. She's not that bad when you get to know her, really."

"She's not that bad when *you* get to know her. When I get to know her, the hate grows exponentially."

He laughed and went to pay for the gas while I picked up some beef jerky and something to drink. I considered poisoning Brittany's water, but I was fresh out of arsenic.

And the evening had only just begun.

An hour later, as we closed in on Boston, my mantra had become, *At least we can't talk in the theater*. Wait a minute. I surveyed my fellow passengers as Ryan looked for parking. This was not a subtitle crowd, even if half-naked girls and gore were involved.

I tapped Ryan's shoulder. He turned the music down so he could hear me.

"We're not going to a movie, are we."

Brittany made some noise between a scoff and a snort. It was a biological miracle. Human throats shouldn't be able to make that sound. She had to be an alien, or a genetic experiment that had gone horribly, terribly wrong.

"Does this look like a movie-theater outfit to you?" She opened her jacket to reveal a tiny skirt, heels, and what was either a sparkly handkerchief or a shirt. I honestly wasn't sure which one.

"Yes?" I crossed my arms and sank into my seat. As far as I could tell, Brittany dressed like that all the time. What, exactly, made this outfit a non-movie-theater outfit? The hoop earrings? The body glitter? Did she wear less or more to the movies? Was this her version of understated? It wasn't that warm yet. She was going to either get hypothermia or die of exposure. You kind of had to admire her commitment. I shrugged. "How should I know?"

She made that weird noise again and looked away from me, like I was dismissed from her presence. "Silly of me to ask as if you would."

That seemed to be as close to an apology as Brittany ever got. I glared at Ryan's profile. "Then where are we going?"

"It's a surprise."

Have I mentioned how much I love surprises? As Ryan backed into a spot, I really took in my surroundings. I have to admit I'd been too distracted to pay attention until then. Imagine my dismay when I recognized the streets around the Inferno. I desperately hoped there were other restaurants in that section of town. Boston is a big city. He wouldn't pick the one place in the great state of Massachusetts that I wanted to avoid, would he? I crossed my fingers and prayed that we were going anywhere else.

My silent entreaties belly flopped as soon as we walked around a corner and saw the neon-red sign. I'd waltzed straight into Cade's as-yet-unforeseen third misfortune. Neither of us had thought Ryan would actually take me directly into the lion's den.

As it was Friday night, the line twisted around the corner of the building. Not that there wasn't a line every night. There were three levels in the Inferno. The top floor, or Heaven, was a dance club and bar. I was only seventeen, so no Heaven for me, which suited me just fine. At ground level, Purgatory, a maître d' is there to take your name and seat you, whether you're in a nice suit or ripped jeans. You could get surf 'n' turf or a fancy burger in a nice candlelit atmosphere. Most places can't pull it off, but the restaurant managed to be fairly high end without being snooty. If the place had belonged to anyone but Venus, I would have loved it.

Below, as you might have guessed, was Hell, and while Purgatory was open to the general public, Heaven and Hell were VIP. It's easiest to think of the Coterie as a mob family, except what mattered was that you weren't human. Whether you had joined up through coercion (like Lock, Ezra, and me) or by choice, the one unifying factor of the Coterie was that back in your bloodline, something grew fangs, talked to trees, or had the ability to start fires, and those genes bred true. If you were in a Coterie establishment and you were human, odds were you were someone's sack lunch. Or Venus's juice box.

Duncan had once told me that some cities have a Council, a ruling body that kept this kind of thing from happening. Boston had one a long time ago, but not anymore. Maybe Venus ate them. So, personal reasons aside, I didn't exactly want to bring Venus three boxes of human takeout. Okay, fine, she could have Brittany and her paramour, but I wasn't handing over Ryan.

I couldn't think of a way to derail this train, though. Fake illness? They'd probably just go in without me. That was even worse. Ryan grabbed my hand and tugged me to his side. Since he was unsure as to whether the line was for the dance club or just to get in, Ryan led us to the front of the building.

I had to try something. "You know, I don't feel well, and this place looks really busy. I bet it's not up to code. Didn't I read somewhere that they were shut down for rats? And cockroaches. And cockroaches riding rats, like a rodeo. It's a bad scene."

"I'm sure if we slip them a twenty or something, Ava, they'll overlook you." Brittany examined me as she wrapped her boy-friend around her like a stole. "Maybe a fifty."

Ryan dropped my hand and made his way to one of the bouncers, but the bouncer didn't look like he was listening. His eyes tracked the crowd as Ryan talked, and he gave no indication that he was hearing any of it. The bouncer raised up his hands in an I-can't-help-you gesture, and my heart did the there's-hope dance. Then the bouncer looked over, and realization hit as he saw my face. I gave him a minute head shake, hoping he'd understand that I didn't want to be recognized. Amazingly, he got it, because without a twitch in my direction, he suddenly lifted the rope and motioned us in. What I really wanted to do was seize Ryan and his ridiculous friends and shove them down the sidewalk. I needed to take them somewhere safe—like a shark tank or a hungry-bear sanctuary. But they were already inside, and there was no way I could make them leave. If I didn't go in, they'd have no one to protect them. Defeated, I mouthed "thanks" to the bouncer as I passed him, even though I wished he'd thrown us out on our asses.

My luck held through the maître d' and all the way until we were seated. Or, at least, everyone was seated except me. I was about to climb into the booth next to Ryan when Ezra pounced. I suddenly felt myself lifted off my feet as Ezra gave a yip of joy, and if he hadn't yelled "Ava, my saucy dumpling! My curvy cherry blossom, how *are* you?" while he did it, I might have been able to pass it off as a case of mistaken identity.

When I found my feet again, I was blushing and Ryan looked ready to hit something, probably Ezra.

"Hey, Ez," I said with a sigh. "I'm fine."

He noticed Ryan's glower and snuggled in closer to me, kissing my cheek. "We're not working tonight, are we?" His voice was a soft murmur, and though I couldn't see his face, I knew what it looked like. Mischievous smile, eyes glinting, and warmth in his cheeks from the game. Foxes like to raid other people's henhouses. The phrase "Gentlemen, lock up your ladies" is a good one to use when Ez is around. ("Ladies, lock up your gentlemen" might also be useful. Ezra loves attention. He isn't about to let a little thing like gender get in his way.)

"What are you doing here? I didn't know you'd be in town tonight," Ezra said. He hadn't quite let me out of his grasp, something Ryan had definitely noticed, and when Ezra observed Ryan's rising blood pressure, he of course had to rub it in. He squeezed me closer. At least it wasn't Lock, I thought. That would have been way worse. Which was of course when Ezra said, "Hey, Lock, look who tumbled in."

Lock ambled over, a serving tray under his arm. His bleached-blond hair was spiked and reflected the candlelight as he approached. Lock is stockier than Ezra, and not a classic beauty like our foxy friend, but I knew for a fact that he went home with just as many numbers. Lock is a charmer, and unlike Ezra, he won't steal your wallet.

He didn't look charming now. He was hiding it well, but I could tell by the expression on his face as he scanned the people I was with that he was unhappy with my current life choices. His expression held both annoyance and hurt, if you knew how to read him right, and I knew how to read Lock. I felt instantly guilty.

"Paws off, Ezra," he said, leaning in to give me a chaste kiss on the temple, which for some reason I found more embarrassing than Ezra's manhandling. I felt my cheeks get hot. He slipped an arm around my waist, tugging me out of Ezra's grasp and tucking me in close. "So this is the elusive Ryan," he whispered into my ear. "I thought you'd skip the bad-boy phase."

"You knew?" I didn't whisper. It's rude.

Lock continued being rude. "When you didn't spill, we asked Cade. He was a little surprised that you hadn't told your *friends*. Besides, I saw your phone when you tried to burn down the sugaring shack." Ah, the photo Brittany had sent. Another thing to thank her for. Guess who's getting a box of angry vipers for her birthday.

Ezra patted my head in a way that managed to be both affectionate and condescending. "Please. Like you could hide things from us." He grinned. "We discussed it and decided that you were a big girl and we'd only step in if he broke your cold black heart."

"How thoughtful," I said through gritted teeth.

Ez looked Ryan up and down. "Lock, pay up."

Lock kept his arm around me while fishing money out of his apron. "I was sure he'd be taller." He shoved a ten into Ezra's open palm. It was bad enough having one guy manhandle me in front of my date, but to have Lock come in and steal me away with nothing more than a bit of possessive dialogue while money changed hands was worse. Ryan was frowning so hard, I thought his face might crack. Brittany looked like she was going to combust with sheer glee. Her boyfriend just needed some popcorn for the free show. I leaned away, but Lock squeezed me back in.

"Seriously," Ezra said, chirpy as usual. He was lapping up all the attention like a cat. "You almost never come to Boston. We always have to visit you."

Except that Ryan thought I went to Boston all the time, because that was the lie I'd told him to cover all my Coterie business. Crap.

Lock at least remembered my cover story and jumped in to save me. "Ez, you know when she comes to town it's all about visiting her sick grandma. She always puts loved ones first." I wasn't sure if that was a dig at me keeping Ryan to myself or not.

Lock aimed the next line at Ryan. "She's big on charity, but I bet you knew that already." He grinned, and I shoved his arm off me with a glare.

Ryan bristled at the insult, his jaw taking on a firm set, but he didn't say anything.

Ezra's raised brow was the only indication that anything was off. "Of course," he said, "I didn't mean to imply that Ava is anything other than a saint. A curvy, delicious, foul-mouthed saint."

Between the back and forth, the staring from the table, and all the affection, I was officially beet red all the way to my roots. I should have faked a stomachache when I had the chance. In fact, I actually did feel like barfing. I smacked Lock's arm as it moved to snake back around me, but that didn't take the smug look off his face as he stared at Ryan.

"By the way, if you're looking for your black jeans, they're at my place," Lock stage-whispered at me. "I put them with your spares and your toothbrush."

I glowered at my best friend. The bastard. On the occasions when I had to work close to the city and I was too tired or too weak after a job, I crashed at Ez and Lock's apartment, rather than take a room in one of the Coterie-owned hotels. Can you imagine their mini bar? Candy bars, vials of blood, raw meat, brains, maybe some bottled water . . . ew. I had a bag full of spare clothes and supplies at Lock's place, and he had just used that information to take Ryan's jealousy to code red. It looked like he was ready to shoot flames out of his ears. Which I did once, by the way, just to see if I could. It took months for my hair to grow back properly.

"Ava," Brittany drawled, her eyes now fixed onto the snug way Lock's T-shirt fit. I didn't care for the way she was examining him, like she was eyeing a choice steak at a butcher shop. Unlike Ryan, her boyfriend didn't seem to care much about what his date was up to. He was actually trying to read the menu. The menu didn't have pictures, so someone would have to help him. "Why don't you introduce us to your friends?" Brittany emphasized the word *friends* like she didn't believe that was all they were. Ryan didn't miss the implication either. She smirked, knowing full well she was throwing nitroglycerin onto the flames.

There was really nothing else I could do. "Everybody, this is Ezra and Lock. Guys, this is everybody."

Most people would have left it at that, but not the unstoppable blonde from the black lagoon. "Ava, I swear, you have the comportment of a farm animal." She leaned over the table, oh so subtly displaying her bountiful (and probably stuffed) cleavage as she did so. "Hi, boys. I'm Brittany."

I should have given her a blistering retort, but honestly, I was just impressed that she knew the word *comportment*.

"This is Jeff and—of course—Ryan." The little blond she-devil grinned savagely as she introduced him.

Ryan stuck his hand out. "Ava's *boyfriend*," he added.

Ezra feigned surprise. "Why, Ava, you sly dog." He slid into the seat next to Ryan, ignoring his outstretched hand. Instead, he slid his arm around the back of the booth and got up close and personal. "Well, aren't you the looker." He grabbed Ryan's chin. "Isn't he just the end, Lock? So very pretty."

"He *is* pretty," Lock said. "Would you say eyelashes to die for, Aves?"

Ezra gave Ryan's chin a little shake. "I could just eat you up." The light caught Ezra's eyes, and they shone. He suddenly became very serious. "I really could." Ryan shrank away from him, and I could tell he'd caught the oddly implied threat. Then he realized what he was doing and straightened his shoulders, chest out.

By then, bouncy Ezra was back. "You simply must tell us all about yourself."

"Aves hasn't mentioned a boyfriend," Lock chimed in, "and we're just dying to hear all about you." Liar. My friends were filthy lying sadists. Lock grabbed Ryan's hand off the table and shook it, winking at him conspiratorially. "She's fond of her

61

little secrets, aren't you, cupcake?" He chucked me on the chin. He actually took his knuckles and gave my chin an affectionate little push. Between that and the use of "cupcake," I think Ryan was experiencing some sort of aneurysm. I know I was.

Dead. The bastard was dead. I didn't care how pissed Lock was that I'd tried to keep Ryan a secret.

Ryan looked thrown by the whole thing. He was used to being the one who started the trouble, who stirred things up. What he didn't know was that he was a small-town amateur next to Ezra. On some level, he recognized that he was out-classed, and he didn't know what to do.

Why had I kept him from my friends? I'd tried to tell them once, but it had felt strangely like I was betraying Lock. I wasn't supposed to keep secrets, though, not from him, and he was hurt, so he was pushing me into hot water with Ryan. Ezra was just in it for the fun.

Mostly I'd kept Ryan to myself because it was nice to have one corner of my life not touched by the Coterie. So much for that. Besides, it felt weird and almost juvenile to call up Lock and gush about my boyfriend. I wasn't that kind of girl and he knew it.

Apparently neither of us was being terribly understanding about the other's foibles at the moment, if our mutual glare was any indication. I briefly considered setting Lock's hair on fire just to teach him a lesson. There was enough product in there that it would only take a spark. I put my closed fist up by my forehead and pushed my fingers out like an explosion. "Snap, crackle, pop," I sang softly.

"Don't you dare."

All the fun must have left the situation for Ezra because he was no longer doing his part of the flirting. In fact, he appeared slightly alarmed. "Where are my manners?" He surged out of the booth and damn near shoved me into it. "You guys must be ready to gnaw the leg off a buffalo, am I right?" He laughed a little hysterically. Before I could reply, he'd called over some waiters and told the group that it was, of course, on the house. The last was meant to mollify my companions, but all it did was take me from hot water to molten lava. Now I was going to have to explain why I was getting star treatment in a restaurant that no one at the table had ever been in and that I had tried to avoid. This is why I hate surprises.

I should have feigned Ebola and stayed home.

4

FOR SAFETY'S SAKE, HIDE THE CUTLERY

I MET LOCK and Ezra about a year after I showed up on
Cade's doorstep. That's the time the Coterie gave me, and it
wasn't out of softheartedness. It wasn't for mourning purposes
either. They wanted my powers to finish developing. You could
almost choke on their goodwill, right? Venus showed up at our
cabin, all glamour and manicured nails, to tell us how lucky I
was to be joining her organization.

During the conversation, two things became evident. First,
my mom hadn't been exaggerating when she said firebugs are
rare. I've met a handful during my lifetime, but then again, we
wandered all over the fifty states and occasionally had to seek
help from other supernaturals. Statistically speaking, we were
bound to trip over a few of them. But as Venus sat at our table
and shoved her deal down my throat, it clarified for me how
valuable I was to her. Venus was the head of the Coterie. For
her to do this personally was like the president showing up at
an army recruitment office in Dingle, Idaho.

I slouched in my chair and looked at her. Venus's face was friendly, unlike the stony faces of her guards outside, or the creepy face of her sidekick, who'd been introduced as Owen. She wasn't taking any chances on losing me by sending henchmen. The way she'd lost my mother. I interrupted her spiel about the benefits of Coterie life (protection, safety, power, and cement shoes for anyone who tries to leave) with a question. Well, it was more of a statement, really.

"You killed my mother." I said it matter-of-factly, because everyone there knew it was true. I wanted to get it out into the open air, to test it and see how it felt.

Venus assessed me with her emotionless eyes. I've seen warmer expressions in the eyeballs of *carp*. I'm not sure what she saw; I certainly wasn't intimidating at the age of fourteen. Almost fourteen. I was all elbows and knees and big hair, but for whatever reason, she decided to go with the truth.

"Yes," she said simply. "Though her death was not my intention."

Nope, just garden-variety kidnapping and enforced labor. "Still your fault," I said. The anger in my voice didn't even touch her. We could have been discussing my shoes or the annual rainfall in Switzerland.

"That little snafu cost me greatly. I appreciate your saving me the trouble of executing my team by doing so yourself." Venus pulled out a cigarette in one of those long holders you see in pictures from the 1920s. She placed the stem between her lips and waited only the slimmest of seconds before the tip lit. Behind her, Owen smiled. "Ava, I'm going to cut right to the thick of things, since you seem to be a girl who appreciates honesty. My offer? Not really an offer. It is, however, a choice.

You may go through the blood-pact ceremony and join the Coterie, or start buying burial plots for any humans or pets you hold dear. 'No' *is* an option, but it's a terrible one." The cherry of her cigarette brightened as she inhaled. "I will destroy everything and everyone you've ever loved. I will raze this whole town if need be. I will salt the earth so that nothing, not even the smallest weed, can come back, and I will not lose any sleep over it."

She meant it too. That much was clear. Under the table I reached over and grabbed Cade's hand. He wrapped his fingers around mine and held tight.

"Or," she continued, "you can live a relatively normal existence. Happy in your"—she looked around the cabin, her amusement at our provincial life evident—"home. You work for me on an as-needed basis. I keep you safe, because believe me when I say there are others who want your services, and they won't be nearly as concerned with your happiness and welfare as I am."

So my choice was death for anyone in a twenty-mile radius, or life under her thumb. Cade squeezed my hand again, and I knew he'd support any decision I made. He would go on the run with me if I wanted. I felt the gentle warmth of his hand and knew that wasn't going to work this time. I thought the world of Cade, but he was human. Fragile. And to Venus, expendable. He'd be dead in six months. If we stayed in Currant, at least I could keep an eye on Venus and the Coterie. I could keep Cade safe. I desperately needed to do that. He was the only person left who loved me, and I would do anything to protect him. Even if it meant working for the person who killed my mother.

There really wasn't enough therapy in the world to make the situation okay.

AT FIRST Venus tried to schedule training sessions with Owen at the Inferno. I like to think of Venus and Owen's relationship as akin to that between sea anemones and clown fish. Apart, they don't amount to much. Together, they form a perfect symbiotic relationship. The anemone provides a safe home for the clown fish, which is immune to its stinging barbs. In return, the clown fish chases away butterfly fish, which would eat the anemone. The clown fish's poo also feeds the sea anemone. Nature—it's both amazingly complex and totally disgusting. Just like Owen and Venus. They protect each other, they benefit from each other, and there's a lot of crap involved, metaphorically speaking.

Owen's training sessions were a disaster, much like the Chernobyl accident was "a bit of a spill." The end result was someone pulling a shrieking ball of me off of Owen while somebody else hit me with the spray from a fire extinguisher. The cold white foam did nothing to stop my spot-on banshee impression. Owen was laughing, which made me kick at him again before they removed me completely. I connected with a meaty *thunk*, but he just laughed harder. Totally not gratifying.

I was still screaming curses and verbal bile while I was carried out of the room by my waist. I must have been a charming sight—spit flying from my mouth, my face red, snot dripping from my nose, and the rest of me completely covered in whatever that flame-retardant stuff is that comes out of fire extinguishers. Whoever had me didn't speak, and I was too out of it to care until I was bumped through the kitchen door and thrown into the area where the big rubber kitchen mats were hosed down. Then the hose was turned on me. The tile smelled, the water was ice cold, but I sat there until I was thoroughly drenched. Gone were the snot, white foam, and my red face. I was a Popsicle, but a calm one.

A skinny dark-haired guy serenely coiled up the hose and replaced it on the wall hook. He seemed to be only a few years older than I was, and while his manner was cool, he looked pretty dorky. Too much floppy emo hair and overtly hipster clothing to do him any good, and I'm not even going to get into the ironic mustache. It should, in fact, never be mentioned. Ever.

The other guy, the one still holding a fire extinguisher, looked like an angel had decided to slum it here on earth. His features had an Asian cast to them, but his hair was full of strange russet highlights and his whiskey-amber eyes looked lined in kohl. Somehow, through the whole ordeal, he'd managed to stay clean. Hipster Mustache, however, hadn't.

"Feel better?" Mustache said, leaning against the wall.

I nodded, shivering.

"Good. Let's get you a towel, then." He got me dried off as best he could while I was still in drenched clothes, and then they took me back to Owen. Of the two of us, Owen definitely seemed to have come out better in the fight. When I entered, Venus was—I kid you not—stroking his hair like he was a dog. Owen, sitting in front of her divan, didn't seem to mind.

Venus gave him a final pat, then rose and sauntered toward me. Her perfect mouth quirked as if trying to restrain a smile, and her eyes damn near twinkled. As I got older I'd learn that when Venus was like this, she was to be feared more than usual. She was at her most dangerous when she was feeling whimsical.

Leaning close, she whispered in my ear, "You're dripping all over my nice carpet, my lovely."

"Sorry," I mumbled. I didn't feel particularly sorry, but I said it anyway.

"Yes, you are," she said, her hand lovingly caressing my face. "Take them off."

I blinked at her. "What?"

"Your clothes," she said. "Take them off. I don't want your wet rags saturating my wonderful things."

"Fine," I said through clenched teeth. "Show me where to—"

She cut me off and pointed down. "I'm not letting you puddle down my hallways just to give you the gift of privacy. And it is a gift, Ava. Every basic right you enjoy is a present from me." She patted my cheek.

The fight and the hose-down had been bad enough. No way was I stripping down just to please her majesty. "No."

I don't even remember her hitting me. I just went from standing to on the floor in an instant. The scrawny emo kid was looming over me, gently nudging me awake. His gray eyes were clouded, and his brow was knitted so tightly that his eyebrows could have reached out and high-fived each other. He helped me up carefully, and I was very proud that I only swayed a little as I wiped the blood from the corner of my mouth. I noticed the other guy was still with us too, on my other side.

My vision blurred as I tried to get a lock on Venus. She was back on the divan, lounging like Cleopatra, Owen standing behind her. There were more people now, her entourage having swelled while I was unconscious. Fifteen or so total, all seemingly completely at ease. I'm sure some of them were brought in as punishment and were just faking their composure. I eventually learned that when it came to torture, Venus was a multitasker.

"I believe I gave you an order."

I knew better than to argue again. If I did, next time I woke up, the audience would have tripled. So I pulled off my cold, wet jacket and let it drop to the floor. My face was blank, my movements unhurried. I knew that the more I reacted, the more pleased Venus would be, and the last thing I wanted to do was make that twisted harpy happy.

My fingers were frozen, and I was shaking too much to undo my shirt buttons. The emo kid touched my shoulder gently until I looked up and gave him a nod. My useless hands at my sides, I let a strange boy undress me in front of other strangers and felt only relief. At least with his help it would be over quickly.

The pants were the hardest. They were stuck, so I had to hold on to the pretty boy's shoulders while the emo one yanked the soaked jeans off my shaking legs. By the time my underwear hit the carpet I wasn't even embarrassed anymore. Just tired and cold and ready to go home.

I refused to give Venus the satisfaction of seeing my embarrassment, so I didn't try to cover myself with my arms but held them loosely around my waist, my hip cocked, waiting for her next command. Apparently appeased, she made a flitting motion with her hand, and the pretty boy fetched me a robe.

Once I was wrapped in fluffy white cotton, Venus shooed me away, done with me and my antics for the day. "That will be the end of your lessons. From now on you train alone in your spare time. You start work next week."

When I didn't instantly move to leave, she returned her attention to me, her eyebrows raised in question.

"How do you expect me to get to my ... jobs?" She still looked perplexed, so I made little wheel-turning motions with my hands. "I'm too young to drive." And there was no way on earth I was letting Cade drive me around. I couldn't help what I had to do, but I could keep him from seeing it. Keep him from witnessing me doing something so monstrous.

Venus pursed her lips. "You," she said, waving airily at Hipster Mustache. "What is your name?"

"Lock," he said.

"And you, lovely one, what is yours?"

"Ezra."

"You will be her team. Go together or work out a driving schedule. I care not. Now leave. You tire me." And with that we were ushered out of the room.

DINNER WAS AWKWARD. Ryan would hardly make eye contact with me, and Brittany was eating it up. Which is about all she was eating. She took only three bites of her entrée. I counted. After that, she just pushed her food around. And it was a freaking *salad*. Jeff talked, but nobody listened.

By the time dessert came, Ryan's cold shoulder and Brittany's barbs were getting to be too much for me, and I had to do something I hadn't done in months. I snuck into the bathroom, checked under the doors for feet, and when I saw the coast was clear locked myself into a stall. With my back pressed against the door, I raised my hands and aimed at the calm water in the toilet bowl. The water gave a satisfying hiss each time I hit it with an egg-size fireball. The stall began to fill with steam.

Fireballs take concentration and focus, and I needed that grip right now. Shooting them into the toilet instead of at Brittany's stupid face gave me a safe vent for my anger and kept me from committing a felonious and disfiguring act on the stuck-up ice princess.

I heard a whoosh and the click of heels as the door to the restroom opened, but it was too late to stop the fireball I'd already sent. There was nothing I could do but enjoy the resulting *hiss* and the small billow of steam that came up as the fireball made contact with the water in the toilet bowl.

The heels stopped, and I heard a hesitant "Everything all right in there?"

"It's the steak," I answered. "Never sits well with me, you know?" She didn't reply. I guess she didn't know. I heard more heels clicking and the sudden burst of restaurant clatter as she left. Apparently she just didn't have to pee as bad as she thought she did.

I felt better when I got back to the table, sticking my fork into my dessert with rapturous joy despite Brittany making *oink oink* noises under her breath. I knew Ryan had other friends, and statistics told me that at least a few of them must be decent people. But Brittany was a she-beast from beyond the stars, and Jeff had obviously crawled out from some primordial slime and decided to stop evolving soon after.

Brittany passed on dessert, choosing to sip her diet soda instead. I guess she was cool with malnutrition as long as she stayed a size negative two. Jeff also skipped dessert and went straight for sucking on Brittany's neck. At the table. Gross.

Have I mentioned how much I loved the whole double-dating thing?

I offered Brittany a spoon. "Are you sure you don't want any? Their desserts are award winning—supposed to be the best in the city." I lifted up the plate and watched as Brittany's eyes followed the movement. It might have been the light, but I swear a slight dew of sweat had broken out on her upper lip. Her self-control was straining, I could tell.

"No, thank you," she said, another plastic smile on her face. "I need to fit into my prom dress. I guess you don't have to worry about that, homeschool." Her grin widened, an obvious score mark appearing on her side of the board. I continued to eat out of pure stubbornness; I couldn't help but notice that Ryan hadn't argued with her. I guess he wasn't planning on taking me. Not that I wanted to spend my evening watching Brittany dry-humping the Neanderthals at her school and calling it dancing, but it would have been nice to put my arms around Ryan's neck, that awkward little corsage getting in the way while we slow-danced under cheap streamers and a disco ball.

As I took the last bite of my strawberry cheesecake, I felt pretty miserable, and when I saw who was approaching the table, I knew it was only going to get worse. I considered stabbing myself with my steak knife and getting it over with.

Venus was wearing an ultrachic off-the-shoulder number that probably came straight from a runway. Every guy in the vicinity stopped midbite, and Brittany instantly became grumpy from the lack of attention. I guess that was at least one positive outcome of Venus's arrival.

My boss always reminded me of someone you might see

on a Swiss Miss package, or an advertisement for Norway or Sweden: blond and milky skinned, with high cheekbones, and if her look had stayed like the ads, I might have felt cozy and welcome. I didn't. The difference between the two was simple: The advertisements were inviting and Venus wasn't. She possessed a cold and haughty kind of beauty. If I had to guess her age based on sight alone, I'd say she was just striding into her early thirties. But if Venus was thirty, I was a penguin.

Venus paused and smiled down at us. It was a dazzling smile, to be sure, but it looked wolfish, like she'd just spotted some fluffy sheep to gnaw upon. Baaa.

"Ava, you didn't tell me you'd be bringing in your lovely friends this evening."

I stared at her, trying to not betray all the anger that I felt. It was never good to let Venus know how you felt about anything. Once she found a weakness, she'd stick a small knife in it over and over again and then watch as you bled out slowly.

"It was a surprise," I said.

"I bet it was," she replied, all glitter and sunshine. There wasn't a day that went by when I didn't want to burn her slowly until nothing was left but ash. Unfortunately, Venus always wore her ward, and it made other wards look like useless trash. Her ward was roughly the size and shape of a Scrabble tile, and it hung out of her dress as she stood over me. The rune was set in platinum that glinted in the candlelight, mocking me. If only she'd forget that damn thing just once. And whatever other secondary runes she had stashed on her body. She'd need to forget her guards, too, and Owen, I suppose. But *then* we'd see what was what.

She rested a hand on my shoulder like we were bosom pals.

"We can't let friends of Ava's leave after dinner. That would be a waste of an evening. How about some passes into Heaven?"

"We're not twenty-one," I told her happily, earning me some dagger-eyed glares from my companions, plus a kick under the table from Brittany. Please, like a kick from her little high-heeled foot could do anything to me. I was used to way worse, and if we went up into Heaven, I was positive we'd *see* way worse.

Venus waved my response away, like the law was something to be considered only by insects and puny mortals. Which shouldn't have been a surprise. After all, Lock and Ezra worked Purgatory's bar, and they weren't of legal age either. "Let me worry about that," she said with a flash of teeth.

Everyone thanked her, even me, though my face probably looked more stiff than full of gratitude as I said it. As if on cue, a waiter brought over a tray, the passes spread out and ready to grab. "I believe Ezra informed you that the meal was on the house, which I do insist upon. If you don't mind, I'm going to steal Ava for a brief moment. I'm sure she won't object if you wish to go upstairs and enjoy yourselves in the meantime."

No one minded. Shocking. Venus gracefully left the table, and Brittany looked at me with reluctant awe. Of course, Ryan wouldn't look at me at all. Yay for our romantic date.

Though I didn't spend much time in groups of my peers, even I knew better than to try to dissuade them from taking Venus up on her offer. There was no way on earth I was going to keep them out of Heaven. It would have been easier to teach Horatio to salsa dance on his hind legs while playing tiny kitty maracas. The best I could do was try to keep them out of trouble. Things could easily go wrong in Heaven.

I got up and followed Venus. She was long gone, but I knew where she was going. No one tried to stop me.

I wasn't sure of the details, but I could guess why Venus wanted to see me. In the human world, if you want someone taken out remotely, you hire a sniper. In my world, you hire a firebug. Occasionally we have to call in a cleaning crew, but not as frequently as a vampire would. A burned-up body, if done right, is a lot easier to explain away than a body drained of blood. Even the most unimaginative cop, when faced with an exsanguinated corpse, will think the word *vampire*. They may not say it, but they will at least entertain the idea. When they find someone burned to death, they think electrical fire, they think arson, they may even think spontaneous combustion, but not a single one will say, *Hey, chief, think some girl burned this guy up with her mind?* Maybe we don't get sexy TV shows about us, but there are a lot of good things about being under the human radar.

Behind the maître d's podium was a bank of elevators for staff use. They were a tad ostentatious, all gold Art Deco design, but they were pretty. I showed my ID to the guard even though he knew damn well who I was, swiped my key card, and went down. At the bottom I'd have to go through another set of guards and a pat-down. If I carried a purse, which I didn't, it would have been searched.

Hell is plushly carpeted. It is also, probably out of stubborn perversity, decorated almost entirely in white. Venus loves white. The carpet is ivory, the walls are a paint color called Arctic Chill, and the couches and chairs are the color of fresh snow. Rather hard on the eyes, really. And considering the general goings-on, rather stupid, in my opinion. Blood shows on white things. But only a suicidal person would point that out to Venus. More than once, I had tracked mud onto the bright white carpet. Each time, I'd spent an hour chained and hanging from a wall. Venus owns this nifty set of manacles built especially for me, a present she picked up from some necromancer on the other coast. When the manacles are on, I'm separated from my power. I can't use it, and my entire body feels asleep. It's uncomfortable and disorienting. Getting mud on that carpet was worth it, though.

As I navigated through twisting hallways, I wondered what life without the Coterie would be like. My mom once told me that organizations like the Coterie used to be more prevalent. Before phones and cars and all those modern conveniences that make communication and quick travel possible, creatures needed a local force in place, scarier than they were, to keep them in check. Even monsters needed monsters, it seems. They were vicious, bloodthirsty organizations that would have made Vlad the Impaler shake with envy. Survival of the fittest doesn't even begin to explain it.

Over the last century or so, most of these groups either died out, went underground, or were supplanted by a Council. We'd evolved past our need for our own personal nightmare. But instead of following along with the rest of them, Venus seemed to take it as a challenge. Give up? Not her. No way. To her it was an excuse to step up her game and be the biggest baddie she could be. Right now she was content with ruling Boston, but for how long? Creatures like Venus never stayed satisfied. That's the thing about being the biggest baddie. You have to keep finding other baddies to challenge just to prove you're number one.

There were a few times in our travels where my mom would seek temporary asylum with a local Council. One time, it almost got us killed. Someone on the Council ratted us out to the Coterie, and we had to sneak out a bathroom window in the middle of the night to avoid capture. We never contacted a Council again. The closest one to Currant is in Portsmouth, New Hampshire. If the rumor mill is true, though, they're in the Coterie's pocket—totally useless.

I went down a set of stairs and through a door, back to where Venus usually held court. Walking through the lower level can be a bit like walking through a Hollywood extras lot, at first. Or, at least, what I imagine it would look like. Lots of people dressed to impress, mingling and making small talk. Not all the women are classic beauties, and not all the guys are ruggedly handsome, but there's an old-Hollywood sense of glamour about the place.

As I approached Venus, I saw that she was lounging on a divan, elegantly decked out in a skimpy beaded gown that probably cost more than everything I owned, and, as usual, smoking a cigarette stuck in a long, slim holder, like she was Cruella de Vil—a comparison that wasn't too far off, when I thought about it. Venus loved her wardrobe changes. I bet she'd kill puppies to make a jacket too.

"Ah, Ava," she said smoothly. "There's my other little firebug." Owen stood behind her. I did my best not to snarl at him.

"We need to talk about the ice elemental the other night. A text message?" She shook her head, saying *tsk-tsk*, cigarette smoke billowing around her face as she did. "We've discussed this. Within a certain range, you're supposed to report in person. At the very least, I expect a phone call."

"Phone call, text message—what's the difference? The job's done, and lucky you, I didn't have to call in the cleaning crew." Mick's Sparkle-Time Cleaners consisted of Mick and a few surly workers. They showed up in dirty coveralls, grunted a lot, and made you wonder if you could count on them to clean themselves, let alone whatever actually needed cleaning. Meeting Mick also made you wonder how an overweight, grizzled, churlish beast of a man who spoke mostly in monosyllables came up with a name like Sparkle-Time. That is, until you saw his little girl, who liked to dress up like a ballerina and needed everything she owned to be in various shades of purple. With glitter, if she could get her adorable little hands on some. I once saw Mick pummel an enraged troll with a metal fender after it stumbled and dented his truck. A troll that could easily have *eaten* his truck. After a few minutes of red-faced screaming, fender-wielding, and general assault, that troll skulked away completely cowed, its tail held contritely in its hands. But Mick say no to his little princess? Not happening.

Venus always preferred it when we didn't need to call in Mick—he was expensive, for one. Those purple tutus don't pay for themselves. Venus also detested having Mick in her white-carpeted kingdom. You didn't entertain the help, and she certainly didn't want him to smudge something in her underground lair. Knowing Mick, he'd charge her to clean it up after he did.

"It matters because I say it matters," Venus answered, a touch of ice in her voice. Owen grinned behind her, a chilling specter.

My mouth went dry. A smiling Owen is a portent of bad things to come.

"Sorry," I said. "Won't happen again." Yeah, right. Of course

I would do it again. Punishment would follow, but as long as I didn't push her too far, it would be manageable.

Venus tossed her hair like she was stalking down a runway in Paris instead of reclining on a divan in a basement in Massachusetts. "If you would move closer like I keep telling you to do, then you wouldn't have to worry about this kind of thing. You could just pop in and report on your way home." She curled out of the chair, slow like a cat, and sauntered over to me on bare feet. "I'm sure your *guardian* could keep just as good of an eye on you here." She smiled, mockingly using the legal term for Cade as a reminder that he couldn't really guard me at all. Cade was amazing—he could cook a steak like nobody's business, he homeschooled me without complaint, and he'd even learned to sew when I'd moved in so he could replace plastic buttons with more heat-resistant material. You melt the buttons on one blouse and suddenly it's a hazard.

Cade always took that kind of precaution because he wanted to keep me safe, but what he couldn't do was protect me from Venus. Not really. He was wonderful but also totally, completely, ordinarily human. He didn't have the know-how, the connections, or the power my mom had.

Venus's cold, pale hand touched my jaw, turning my face this way and that as she inspected me like I was livestock—which was precisely how she saw me.

I dug my hands into my jacket pockets, my fingers sliding along the fire-resistant cloth Cade had sewn in, but didn't speak. This was an old argument, one she knew I wasn't going to budge on. When your life is mostly engineered by others, you don't give up the few choices you have a say in. Like where you live.

"If I didn't live far out, Owen would have to travel more,

80

wouldn't you, Owen?" A bare twitch of an eyebrow was the only answer I got from him. And it was creepy, at that. My fellow firebug was pasty pale, having mostly converted his schedule to match Venus's. Despite popular folklore, vampires can go out in the sun, they just prefer not to. They are substantially weakened by it, and they do about as well as any other nocturnal creature in the daylight, but with enough sunblock and a parasol or umbrella, they can manage for short periods. Though Owen was no vampire, he clung so tightly to Venus that he might as well have been.

Owen pulled a hand out of his jacket pocket and blew me a kiss. I flipped him off, but in a very ladylike fashion (I batted my eyelashes and smiled), because that's the type of girl I am. Classy.

Owen wagged a finger at me slowly, his black curls shining in the light. Venus ignored us and handed me a file. My next job, and coming a little too fast on the heels of the other two, as far as I was concerned.

I opened up the file and, when I saw what was inside it, immediately tried to put it back in her hand. She wouldn't take it, so the file dropped to the floor, the papers scattering across the pristine carpet. One of her flunkies darted over and scrambled to put the pages back together. He handed it to Venus and scuttled away again. She kept her eyes on me the whole time, holding the file out for me again when it was placed in her hand.

"No," I said. The room stilled. I swear I could hear the air move. Venus froze, her hand in the air like she'd been paused while conducting an orchestra. She was in stasis—a fly stuck forever in amber. Then I saw her pupils shrink and the tiny muscles around her mouth tighten. I felt a squeeze in my gut and a chill run down my spine. I was in it now. Licking my suddenly dry lips, I continued. "I don't care what beef you have with Duncan. He's off limits."

I have a rule: I don't kill people who hang out in my kitchen. If I did that, no one would ever visit.

DUNCAN is the closest thing I'll ever have to a grandpa, and I hang on like hell to family. I never knew my dad, I lost my mom, and I'm not losing anyone else. Even if I didn't care, Cade loves Duncan, and that's enough for me.

Cade was never close to his parents. From the stories he tells me, it sounds like he has what Lock calls pod-baby syndrome. It's like someone stole the baby his parents were supposed to have and left Cade in its place. They weren't evil, they just didn't get along with their kid. Still, they managed to go through the motions, until Cade met my mom. Cade's parents didn't like Lilia because they thought her parents were, and I quote, "ne'er-do-wells." (They weren't entirely wrong—Lilia's parents were Coterie, so they certainly weren't up to any good most days, but I wouldn't say they *never* did well. A bit of an exaggeration there, I think.) Cade's parents forbade the friendship. Cade ignored them. The die was cast, so to speak.

By the time he turned sixteen, he'd packed a bag and decided to live in his car—a car bought with his own money. That lasted all of one week before Duncan found him camping out in the woods. After that, Cade lived with Duncan until he was old enough to get his own place. Cade's parents didn't seem to mind. They moved to Vermont shortly after their son walked out. He gets a card every year on Christmas. They sign it with their names, not "Mom and Dad" or anything. No mention of love or missing him or even best wishes. Just their names. I don't think they even know about me. Every year he gets the card, reads it out loud, and then, with much pomp and ceremony, turns it into a paper airplane that he throws and I incinerate midflight. Tradition—it's important in a family.

Duncan always seemed to know when Cade heard from his parents. I guess it wasn't hard to gauge—one card on his birthday and another on Christmas, but still. We'd get the card, and then Duncan would show up. At Cade's birthday, he'd arrive with a bottle of stout, and during the winter holidays he'd appear with mulled cider and whiskey. Then he'd sit by the fire and whittle, and I'd make him tell stories about Cade as a teenager. Even though he'd run away from home, Cade really didn't get into much trouble when he was young. Well, unless my mother was involved.

Venus knew I wouldn't take this contract, with Duncan as the target. She had to. So why push me on this? She was usually more careful, which meant she wanted him bad enough to risk losing me as an asset, or it was a trick somehow. I kept turning it around in my head and couldn't figure out my angle.

"Why him? Why now?" Everyone subtly moved back a few steps. Questioning Venus led to punishment unless she was in a good mood. Since she wasn't in a good mood until after she punished you, retribution was pretty much guaranteed.

Owen stayed where he was. Venus didn't scare him.

Venus looked at her nails, either admiring her manicure or wondering what damage her nails could do. It could have been either one. "I have reports that he's building his own little army. Well-substantiated reports. I can't have that happening practically on my doorstep, now, can I?"

Duncan amassing an army? For what, overthrowing the Coterie? That would interfere with his fishing. "You mean, like, a golem army?"

"What is an army of wood to my Owen?" She stroked Owen's arm, and I wanted to vomit a little.

"So, you think he's . . . recruiting people or something?"

"What I know is not really your concern. All you need to worry about is you. Never make me question your loyalty, Ava. Remember that." She ran her fingers down the chain that held her ward. Logically, I knew there was no way any traces of my blood were still on it. My blood-pact ceremony was too long ago. But it felt like the connection was still there, one touch and my blood was hers. I shivered.

None of this made any sense. I kept waiting for her to threaten me, shove Duncan's folder back in my hand, or . . . something. Instead, she stood there, watching me. Okay, then.

"I'm not doing it. That's final." I scowled at Owen, my chin jutted out and defiant. "And if I catch you within burn range of him, I'll roast you myself."

A soft smile played across Owen's lips as he made a lick of flame dance across his knuckles, the glow flickering as it wove its way from index to pinkie and back again. "You mean you'll try," he said lightly. His finesse was amazing, I had to give him that.

"If I'd meant *try*, I would have said so." I was angry, tired from all the politics of the evening, and ready to go. In my book, Owen was long overdue for a smackdown.

Venus clucked at us. "Sometimes you two are worse than children. You don't want me to make you behave, do you? I didn't think so." She had a strange look on her face; it made my heartbeat quicken and my palms sweat. It wasn't a good idea to say no to Venus. And I certainly didn't have any grounds to refuse her order. According to my blood pact, she owned me. Up until now, I'd contented myself with tiny rebellions, things that annoyed her but certainly didn't do a whole lot. But this— well, I was being stupid. Was Duncan worth it? I thought about last winter when he'd stopped into the bookshop and given Cade and me an ornament he'd hand whittled—it was a very Horatio-looking cat relaxing on a book. Cade had loved it so much that it stayed up well after Christmas on our counter. Yes, Duncan was worth it.

"Can't blame me for trying." Venus never took her eyes off me. Her tone told me that she absolutely *could* blame *me*. "Surprising, though, you of all people defending Duncan. Yes, *very* interesting." She smiled then, in a cat-eating-a-whole-aviary-of-canaries kind of way. I didn't like that smile.

"He's not part of Coterie business," I said. "Leave him be. Please." I wanted to look away but knew I shouldn't. It had hurt to say "please." "I don't ask for many favors. Whoever gave you your information, they're wrong."

"You appear to know very little about what is or is not part of Coterie business, my little bug." She stepped closer to me. "Even if what you said were true, it doesn't matter. My business *is* Coterie business. Understand?"

I held her gaze, though my eyes were starting to water from not blinking. What did she mean, "if what you said were true"? I may not have known every single person in the Coterie, but I knew that Duncan wasn't involved. Was she hinting at things I didn't know, or was she just messing with my head?

"Yes," I finally said, when it was clear she was waiting for me to respond.

"You need to sleep more," she said. Her hand caressed my temple, then pulled back slowly. In a blink, she'd slapped me, thankfully not into unconsciousness. Enough to sting and remind me who was boss, though. Enough to draw blood where the inside of my cheek met teeth. I didn't pass out, but I fell to my knees, my hand cupping my cheek as my vision tunneled. Venus leaned over me, her ward swinging. I had a flash of memory, an image of her ward in my blood. Even though it dangled in my face, I couldn't reach out and tear it off her neck. The pact forbade it.

Constructed by Coterie lawyers, signed in my blood, and sealed by a blood witch—there was no way I was wiggling out of the pact safely. Unless Venus died, or—much more likely—I died, I wasn't getting out. Oh, and the incredibly likely option of her setting me free was always there. Yeah, right. I could always track down the blood witch and ask her to undo it, but since that would result in a quick and messy execution for both of us, it wasn't really an option. I had to face it. I was bound to Venus. It was the only way she allowed me to live. Let Cade live. The platinum of the swinging charm taunted me, and I couldn't so much as reach out to it. *Stuck*, it said. *You're stuck with the rest of us.*

Hmm. If I thought the necklace was talking to me, maybe she'd hit me harder than I thought.

My head complained about me standing so soon, but I didn't want to stay on the floor. Venus handed me the file again. I used it to wipe off the blood that had dribbled from the corner of my mouth. Then I handed it back to her with a tight-lipped smile. It felt like the temperature in the room dipped about ten degrees, and I heard a few audible gasps from our audience. Venus could kill me right now and be within her rights granted by the pact. I had disobeyed her, and I'd done it openly and flagrantly. I was banking my continued health on the fact that she needed me—that I was worth too much. If the bet had Vegas odds, I wouldn't have staked money on it. Even with my worth, the outcome did not look good. Would Cade be safe with me gone? Or would Venus track him down out of some perverse sense of vengeance? I could only hope that Duncan would take care of him.

She stared at me for a few breaths while we all waited to see which way she would swing. A sudden image of her as a Roman emperor filled my mind. Venus in the Colosseum, watching gladiators battle for her, waiting for her to give a sign as to whether they lived or died. Would it be thumbs up or down? Cheery. She finally shooed me away with one hand. "Go, rejoin your friends, then."

A light dip of the head—as close to a bow as she was going to get from me—and I was out the door. Even though I walked at a normal pace, I couldn't get out of Hell fast enough.

5

AIN'T NO PARTY LIKE A COTERIE PARTY, 'CAUSE A COTERIE PARTY HAS A BODY COUNT

THERE ARE SEVERAL bars in the Inferno, but the Purgatory bar is the smallest and has only one or two bartenders working. The bar, like the restaurant, is dimly lit, mostly by candles and chandeliers made to look like they're full of candles. There's some red backlighting that reflects off the burnished copper set into the wall.

I went to check on my two favorite bartenders—and despite their earlier behavior, they still were my favorites—behind the Purgatory bar. I slid onto the stool behind Lock, winking at Ezra. He solemnly held up one finger in a shushing fashion, then went back to wiping down a pint glass.

Lock's spiked, bleached hair appeared magenta in the bar's light. He wore his black Purgatory T-shirt and black pants well, judging from the way the women seated at the bar were staring, and by the amount of drool Brittany had produced at the table earlier. Not that I was sizing up one of my best friends. That would be weird.

I leaned forward and pinched him on the ass. I thought he'd leap or startle, as most people would when receiving an unexpected goose, but Lock simply spun around, grabbing my hand.

"Let go," I said.

He shook his head slowly, eyes twinkling in the candlelight, then pulled me forward so he could lean over the bar and kiss me on the cheek. I felt the collective death stare of every girl seated at the bar.

"You're not supposed to be over here," he said into my ear. "Especially since I'm full of wrath toward you right now. Never visit a wrathful bartender. We can do terrible things to your beverages."

"You're full of something," I said, leaning away from him and yanking my hand back as I did. "But I'm not sure it's wrath. Besides, you love me too much to poison me or kick me out for being underage." Especially since I knew for a fact that neither Lock nor Ezra was twenty-one either. One of the perks of working for the Coterie? Best fake IDs ever. Venus had even made *me* take one. She didn't want my age to get in the way of my job, should I ever have to go after someone in a bar or voting booth. But just because I had one didn't mean I wanted to use it to go into a Coterie bar unless it was to see my friends or carry out an assignment.

Lock rolled his eyes theatrically at Ezra and pulled me a Coke from the bar, topping it with a cherry before he handed it over, but he didn't argue. When I was in Purgatory, the only two people who were allowed to give me food or beverages were Lock and Ezra. It was one of their rules. The Inferno had a large staff, and since I'd been one of Venus's enforcers for years now and a lot of the creatures held a grudge, we didn't know what one of them might pull. People don't care that you hurt them or their loved ones because someone else told you to—they just care that you did it. I thought Ezra and Lock were being overly cautious most days, but after my little meeting with Venus I was willing to go along with their paranoia.

"How did it go?" Lock asked, handing off a set of martinis to a waitress.

"I turned down a job."

Ezra and Lock both stilled.

"I'm sorry," Ezra said, "could you repeat that last part? I couldn't hear it over the sound of you losing your damn mind."

Lock tossed his bar rag on the counter. "Funny, you don't *look* dead." He poked me with his index finger. "And you certainly don't feel dead. Maybe I need to feel you more to double-check."

"Piss off." He reached to poke me again, and I batted his hand away. "It was Duncan. What was I supposed to do?"

Ezra came around to my side of the bar, completely ignoring the customers who'd just approached to order, forcing Lock to walk away for a second and deal with them.

"Duncan? Beardy, food-bringing Duncan? I like him. We can't kill him. He brings us fish."

"I know," I said.

"Also, because it would be wrong," Lock said, walking back over to us. "Still, Ava. You told her no? Flat out? No attempts at negotiation?" He rubbed the back of his neck. "What am I saying? Of course you didn't negotiate. You probably yelled 'no' and then spit on her shoes."

"I'm not that bad. I know better than to spit. But I *am* a little worried about her lack of instant torture and/or murder. At the very least I should be hanging from warded manacles while starved weasels nibble at my toes."

Lock rested his elbows on the bar. "See, you kid, but that really is where you should be right now. What did she do?"

"She slapped me." We all knew that the slap was almost a nonpunishment. I mean, Venus slapped when she was feeling playful. I gave them a brief sketch of the meeting, and Lock went back to wiping the counter, but he did it slowly, his face creased in thought. Ezra left his stool to drape over my back and steal the cherry out of my drink, because touching reassured him, which is how I knew that he was worried even if he was acting like his usual carefree self.

After a few seconds like that, Lock shook his head. "I don't like it, Aves. You need—no, we all need—to watch our step for a while. She has to be planning something. No way she'd let you walk away with just a slap." He grabbed a few dollars that someone had left as a tip and shoved them into his apron. "There's talk lately that she's been even more . . . interesting than usual. I know we always try to tiptoe, but now might be the time to add padded slippers and a noise machine into the act. Know what I mean?"

I stared down at my soda, stirring it with my straw. "I'm worried, Lock." Ezra stroked my hair, and I caught a few people staring daggers at me. It didn't matter that we were just friends. All they knew was that I'd walked in and stolen Ezra's attention.

"You spoke for all of us," Lock said. "Which means that, if she wants, Venus could terminate Ez and me as well."

"I'm sorry," I said. "I should have brought it to you first—"

Lock cut me off. "Why? Our answer would have been the same."

A new drink ticket flashed on the screen behind Lock, and he started pulling some beers from the tap to fill the order. "Ezra and I can handle ourselves, but maybe you should go check on the friends you came with."

"They aren't really my friends," I said.

"Really? But you have so much in common."

I knew that tone. It meant that the subject would come up again later, in much more detail. I squirmed in my seat and whined. "You're not going to make me talk about my feelings, are you? I hate that. Sometimes being friends with you is like having a girlfriend. If we X-ray you, will we find an errant uterus?"

"You can always strip-search me and find out." Lock leaned against the bar and gave me a mock smolder. It always made me smile, but secretly, I found it a little thrilling. Not that I would say so to Lock.

"Uteruses are found on the inside, Lock. *Inside.* You have met women, right?"

That earned me another grunt. "You have no idea." There was no leer when he said it, just an honest response. "Okay," he said. "Playtime is over." Ezra took his place behind the counter, and Lock walked me to the elevators.

"What, you think ninjas are going to jump out and attack me in the fifteen feet between the bar and the elevators?" I looped my arm in his.

"The way tonight has gone, I would follow you into the bathroom right now."

92

My throat went dry as he brushed my hair back from my face, staring at me for a moment before he turned to the elevators and shoved his hands into his pockets. "I can't follow you up there—I'm still on shift, and Venus would kill me. Well, she's probably going to kill me anyway, but I'm not going to go out of my way to give her extra reasons. Be careful, though, Aves, okay? Stay safe?"

I agreed, even though we both knew that it was an impossible promise. The only way to stay safe in a Coterie bar was to leave it.

A SECURITY GUARD waved me into an elevator. There are stairs going up to the top floor, but they're used only for emergencies and staff. Venus thought the elevators were much more dramatic. For once, Venus and I agreed on something.

The doors dinged open, and my first impression was that the place was on fire. Maybe that was just the firebug in me, though. Smoke rolled over the floor, so you could only see the dancers from about thighs up. The seats that lined the dance floor were done in deep purple velvet, and everything was hazily lit, making the scene ethereal and dreamlike. I had expected a disco ball. Don't ask me why. Apparently I pictured Heaven as a grand seventies-style disco party. And I wouldn't have said no to some roller-skating dancers. A sudden image of my mom in bell-bottoms and an Afro made me smile, even though it hurt.

I felt bad for the waiters, who were all wearing scanty outfits. The guys had on short, Grecian-looking, white linen skirts that somehow emphasized rather than took away from their masculinity, and oh boy were these guys masculine. You could have made a "Men of the Inferno" calendar—you know, the kind where guys are half-naked in waterfalls for no apparent reason, or chopping wood, even though it's clear they've never even held an ax before? Dreamy, every single one of them, and they were wearing nothing but those tiny skirts and the leather straps that held on their long white wings. I kid you not. The staff up top was winged. And the ladies, all voluptuous curves and sultry looks, were wearing the same thing, except they had an additional, if minuscule, piece of linen to go across their chests. How did anyone stay with their date?

As I watched, a feather drifted down from one of the wings and disappeared into the smoke. Everything was so realistic. So beautiful. But it was too much. Like anything that Venus touched, it was over the top—too pretty, too luxurious, too *everything*. There was no heart in it. The dancers were gorgeous, but their expressions left me cold. It was like computer-generated music—sure, the notes were right and hit everywhere they should, but there was no passion.

I noticed something else that the dancers were wearing. Tiny silver squares dangled on the ends of chains around necks, wrists, and ankles, all winking at me while they moved. But I was betting they weren't for fire. They were for glamour. Illusion. How many of the dancers had *real* wings? When they took off their jewelry, how many of those wings turned leathery? How many of those straight white teeth became fangs or something else? I shuddered. Maybe they were the kinds of creatures who considered humans to be in the same category as food. Or maybe the feathers were real and all the creatures actually were soft, delicate, made of spun sugar and not muscle and sinew.

Pawns slaving for protection and safety, creatures with no power of their own. That was the problem with the Coterie. It could be damn difficult telling the victims apart from the perpetrators.

Still, I hoped the staff was extremely well paid. You'd have to offer me a hell of a lot of cash to get me in that outfit. I now understood why Lock preferred downstairs—this was way too much of a scene for him. And for Ezra it was too much competition.

After scanning the crowd a few times, I found Brittany gyrating around her boyfriend on the dance floor. She was clearly eyeing the winged dancers, hoping someone would cut in. Jeff didn't appear to notice. He was too busy having what appeared to be some sort of epileptic seizure. Or he was dancing. It was hard to tell.

Ryan was perched on a stool, looking sullen, a half-full drink in his hands, with several empty glasses next to him on the table. I went up behind him and snuggled his back. No response. I could have been air.

"Thinking about trying on the uniform?" I asked. "You'd look good with wings." He shrugged. "C'mon," I said, tightening my grip. "I'm a sucker for a man in a skirt. Eh? No?" He drained the rest of his glass in one gulp, turning so he could give me a partial stink eye, since I could see only half his face from where I was standing.

I stepped in front of him and gently removed the glass from his grip. Then I dragged him out on the floor. Ryan enjoyed dancing, and he was good at it—it was one of the things I liked about him. A lot of guys our age do the awkward dance-floor shuffle . . . or they dance like Jeff. Ryan could really move when he got into it, though. So maybe if I could get him into it and reassure him that I was there with him, he might get over the whole evening. Surely two months together meant he could shrug off one bumpy night. I just had to help him change the gears of his mood.

The song switched to something slower, and the lights dimmed. I slid up close to him and kissed his chin. He smelled like harsh juniper and lime, and I wondered how many gin and tonics he'd had. Ryan pulled me closer, but it was an automatic gesture. His eyes were anywhere but on me, and his body was so stiff, I was surprised he could move.

I enjoy shaking my booty. I'm not great at it, but it's fun, and I don't get the opportunity to do it often. Unless you count my solo dance parties in my living room that always end with me sliding around in my socks, which I don't. Official booty shaking is less enjoyable when your partner won't even look at you, though. Gently, I ran my fingers along Ryan's jawline and tried to maneuver his gaze onto me. For a tiny breath, his eyes were on mine and I could feel the heat between us, despite the wounded look he was giving me. Then he jerked his head away.

I made what was probably a really charming *erghk* noise, a sound born of pure frustration, and dropped my hands. I'd had enough of his pouty behavior. I walked away, leaving him alone on the dance floor, even though I knew it wouldn't last. Some enterprising girl or guy would hop into my empty space before it even got cold. But still, seriously, enough was enough. They could have him.

All the seats were taken, so I leaned against the wall and tried to calm down. To my surprise, the wall was padded, which brought to mind more of an insane-asylum aesthetic than anything celestial. I changed position slightly so my skin wasn't touching the cloth padding. The last thing I needed was a scorched outline of me on the wall. How would I explain that one? Since I was angry, my control wouldn't be at its peak, so I took the extra precaution and moved.

Ryan joined me, his pout still in full swing. I hate it when people do that. If someone wants to be mad at me, fine. I probably earned it. When they go out of their way to sulk in my presence, however, then it's more about hurting me than it is about their own hurt. It's a revenge move, and I'm not a big fan of those. You know, unless I'm the one committing them. Then it's revenge all the way.

Silence was heavy between us even though the DJ was filling the air with various overly processed Eurocrap, what I consider to be the Velveeta of the music industry.

"Did you just come over here to sulk some more?" I asked when the beat slowed again.

"I'm not sulking," he said, his brow furrowed and his arms crossed.

"The hell you aren't."

"Well, what do you expect?" He threw up his arms, exasperated. "I take you to a restaurant to surprise you, only to find out you're, like, a VIP here and you've got another boyfriend—possibly two—on the side. Or am I the boyfriend on the side?" The glower had returned by the time he stopped talking.

"You got me. I've been sneaking off to Boston to build my harem. Your billowy pants and diamond collar are in the mail."

He laughed despite himself. Grabbing my waist, he maneuvered me into the corner of the alcove and bent close. Suddenly the world was just Ryan and me. His lips were hot, demanding, like he was trying to reclaim me with a kiss. My body was all for it, and I automatically leaned in, my hands sliding up his back and over his neck to twist into his curls.

We stayed tangled into each other when he pulled back, resting his forehead against mine. "It's so easy when it's just me and you," he said, rubbing my cheeks with his thumbs. "I wish we could stay in our own little bubble. Just you and me against the world. Tonight . . ." He stared off into the smoke on the dance floor. "It just didn't go as planned."

"We could leave," I said. "Get Meathead and Queen Awful and hit some other club. Start over."

"Naw," he said, still watching the dancers twist and move. "It wouldn't work." I'm not sure what he saw out there, but when he looked back at me, his eyes shone in the dim light. Then I blinked, and he was back to the Ryan I was used to seeing—one big devil-may-care grin.

"Not fair to Brittany and Jeff, you know?" He ran his fingers down my arms. "What say I get you something to drink?" Before I could answer, he was dragging me to the bar. He rolled his eyes when I told him I wanted soda, but he leaned over, yelling into the bartender's ear in order to be heard over the music.

Ryan got yet another gin and tonic. Apparently I'd be driving us home. A waitress brought us a plate of appetizers, and I tried to pass, but Ryan made such a fuss over how good they were that I had to try at least one.

My taste buds exploded, or at least they felt like it. I made the hand-wave/face-pant sign for "my mouth is on fire" and I swear my vision tunneled for a minute. I downed my soda, and Ryan handed me another one.

Between gulps, I thanked the bartender, another beautiful nameless angel whom I didn't know. He smiled politely before he went to help someone else. I continued to melt into the floor. Ryan handed me another drink, and it took several gulps before I realized it was his. All I could taste was burning. I handed back his drink, and he laughed at the scowl that came with it.

Ryan led me into the gyrating bodies of the sweaty crowd, and Velveeta music or not, I started to have fun. I did what seems to happen only when I'm in Ryan's sphere: I let go. I forgot about everything else and just concentrated on being with him. I forgot about Lock's warnings and the impending doom. In the crowd I felt safe. What could Venus do to us here? On that floor I was just another girl dancing, and it felt amazing. Like magic. The crowd pulsed and we went with it, a single organism moving to the same beat.

The magic didn't last. It never does. I guess if it stayed around forever, it wouldn't be magic, would it?

The dancing and the stress of the evening, plus the music and the smoke, began to take their toll. "Can we go?" I asked. "I'm not feeling very well."

Ryan made a face. "But we just got here. C'mon, Ava. You've been trying to drag me home all night. I know you get to do this all the time, but we don't. If you make us leave, well, that's kind of selfish, don't you think?"

Selfish? Trying to be a *normal* girl out with her *normal* boyfriend was harder than I'd thought it would be. It meant I had to bite back my nasty response and be good. I also had to resist the urge to set fire to *everything*. Relax. Deep breath. Don't burn down Boston. Clearly Ryan didn't understand how poorly I was feeling.

I pulled him so close, we were almost kissing again. "It's going to be a lot less fun if I pass out and you all have to dance over my unconscious body." Ryan sighed and reluctantly dragged me over to the corner where Brittany and Jeff were making out.

"Ava's not feeling well. She wants to go."

"So let her go," Brittany said, barely glancing over at me.

"We came here together," I reminded her.

She traced Jeff's bottom lip with the tip of her index finger. "I'm sure one of those nice boys downstairs will give you a ride." Jeff started nuzzling her neck, oblivious to everything around him. "They're probably used to it." She waved me off. "There's a couch in the ladies' room. Why don't you go lie down or something? It will pass. Now go away. I'm busy."

I waited for Ryan to call her selfish, but nothing happened. My stomach bubbled, and I decided to take Brittany's suggestion, even though all I wanted to do was leave. Going without them wasn't really an option. You don't leave your friends—even when you wish all their hair would fall out and they'd all be turned into hamsters and they're not really your friends anyway when you stop to think about it—alone in a Coterie bar. Especially when they don't know it's a Coterie bar.

I wove through the crowd, Ryan shouting my name behind me. He finally caught up when I was outside the restroom. I whirled on him, an action I instantly regretted. The room tilted a little on its axis.

"Why do I have to perform the nice-nice dance all night while Brittany and that brain slug she calls a boyfriend are allowed to be complete and utter bastards? I have to bite my tongue while everyone gets to call me a whore? What the hell, Ryan?"

100

His hands dropped to his sides, fisted in frustration. "No one called you a whore."

"Roll back the conversation, Ryan, because you accused me earlier of having multiple secret boyfriends, and Brittany just did the same. That mouth-breather of hers is the only one who's bordered on polite the whole night, and that's just because he clearly has a rudimentary grasp of the English language *at best*. And by the way, Ezra and Lock are my friends. *Friends*, not boyfriends."

Ryan shook his head, his curls swaying back and forth. "I want to believe that. But I saw how they were with you. Especially Lock. We all have eyes, Ava. Maybe Brittany's just calling it like she sees it." The anger gave way to a kicked-puppy expression. "I thought I was important to you."

Stars and sparks, I wasn't even going to touch that last part. "I'm sorry, did I miss the section of the evening where I started making out with another guy in front of you? Was I licking faces and stripping down or something? No. The only girl panting at the table was Brittany."

"Leave Brittany alone for once. She's my friend. Get over it."

"Brittany is not your friend. She's an evil robot from the moon bent on making teen life hell. If you can't see that she was *this close* to ripping off her panties and throwing those manky things at *my* friends, then you're freaking delusional. And if you can bring my friends into it, why are yours off-limits? That's totally ridiculous and—"

"You think I can't see what was right in my face? I'm not stupid, Ava. You're jealous of Brittany, fine. But making fun of her to make yourself look better right now? Pathetic." He looked furious and crushed, but to be honest I was having a hard time feeling sympathetic. Just keeping my jaw from dropping to the floor was proving difficult. Why would he think I was jealous of someone like Brittany? Ryan should have known me better than that. A tiny voice piped up in the back of my head, asking how Ryan could possibly know me better than that, seeing as he didn't know me at all, and whose fault was that? I told that voice to shut up.

I watched the lights play off his cheekbones. How could anyone that good-looking be so insecure? This was new territory, and I didn't know how to navigate it. We were both hurt, but hurt or not, that didn't give him license to treat me like this.

I dug my hands into my pockets in frustration. My hands were always the first part of my body to spark when I lost my temper. I could feel the heat spilling from them as they rested against my thighs. The fire-resistant material Cade used to line my pockets is the same stuff they make firefighter suits out of, and it serves its purpose well, but it's pretty heavy material and makes you sweat, so pockets were about all we could do. I'd need to have the spelled reinforcement stitching redone soon. I put it off once and ended up burning up a perfectly good pair of jeans. We were out at the time, so I had to hide in the truck while Cade ran into a store and bought me new pants.

Warded pockets wouldn't hold things off forever, but they bought me a few precious seconds to rein things in. I had to get control. Ryan might have the luxury of throwing a tantrum, but I did not. When I went nuclear, I could really go, well, nuclear. So I very calmly marshaled my thoughts, lining them up like little tin soldiers.

"I am not dating anyone else, nor am I sleeping with

anyone here." I pushed the words through clenched teeth. "And I'm not jealous of Brittany."

"So you're sleeping with someone not here?"

I threw my hands up in the air, an errant spark wending its way into the fog. Ryan didn't notice. "Seriously? You know what? Fine. Either you believe me or you don't." I jabbed my finger toward the bathroom. "I'll be in there when you figure it out and decide to apologize."

The door swung as I pushed my way in, and I expected Ryan to follow me, even though this was a ladies-only zone. But he didn't, and I collapsed onto a stained and beat-up settee and tried not to vomit or set anything on fire.

6

SHOOT THE MOON

AT SOME POINT, I tried to check on my companions. I made it all the way to the wall outside the bathroom. My surroundings spun and twirled, and everything felt heavy. Lights flashed, whirled, and danced like mad dervishes. I slumped against the wall. I tried to text Lock or Ezra or even call Cade, but I couldn't seem to manage to use my phone properly.

Then Lock was there, dragging me back into the bathroom, my boots skidding on the polished floors. He held me as I got noisily sick into the garbage can. Or at least mostly into the garbage can. My aim wasn't perfect. Once I was done, he pulled me back onto that nasty settee in the corner and held me cradled in his lap. I felt hot and tired, and I just wanted to go back to sleep. Lock shook me awake.

"You need to work with me here, Aves. C'mon." He pulled back my eyelid. "Bloody hell." I felt the world shift as Lock heaved up from the chair and carried me out of the bathroom. We couldn't leave yet. I remembered that much.

"Ryan." It took a lot more effort to get that out than it should have. I could actually feel the word slurring as it left my lips.

"They're long gone, cupcake, and we're getting you away from here." Lock carried me into the pounding music, the smoke and flashing lights making me even dizzier. I was having a hard time keeping my eyes open. What I needed was something to focus on, and since Lock's face was right in my view I decided to go with that. The muscles in his jaw were tight and twitching. Lock was clearly pissed. He was cute when he was pissed. I giggled. Oh, sweet monkeys in the trees, I had giggled! I am not a giggler. Then the word *giggler* made me giggle more. I was in trouble for sure.

Lock glanced down at me. "C'mon, Aves. Hold it together."

My giggle turned into a hiccup. "No wonder Ryan thinks we're sleeping together." I tried to sit up in his arms, but the result was more of a flail. "Ryan! I have to make sure he's all right."

Lock's jaw tightened even more. "Like I said, look around. Long gone."

My head apparently had a mind of its own, so it took some coaxing to get my body to do what I wanted. When I did convince it to comply, I realized that Lock was right. Though the floor was far from deserted, there weren't as many people dancing. None of the faces were familiar. "Crap on toast."

"I'd rather not."

I batted at his chin. "Pretty face." Then I rested my head against his shoulder. He swore under his breath, but his arms tightened around me anyway.

The next few hours were a hazy blur. Someone pulled back

my eyelids and flashed a light into my eyes. It hurt like hell. Then Ezra and Lock made me drink something that tasted like rotten leaves, and, rather unfortunately, I remember vomiting all over whatever back room I was stashed in. There's a last hazy memory of Lock tucking me in on a couch somewhere as I patted his head in thanks and then burst into more giggles at the feel of his spiky hair. I might or might not have said, "Good night, hedgehog." Then, thankfully, I passed out.

THERE ARE LOTS of reasons why I don't drink. Heavily, I mean. Cade lets me have the occasional glass of wine with him at dinner on special occasions, but nothing much beyond that. Besides the obvious fire-related control reasons I had to deal with, when you drink a lot, things tend to come out. I've seen drunk girls throw themselves at guys they wouldn't normally give the time of day to, cry over ancient troubles, and generally place themselves in dangerous situations with questionable people. I've seen drunk guys act just as bad. This is not to say every drunk person I've ever seen is a train wreck, but when you mix a depressant with hormone-crazed kids who are already depressed most of the time, the mess gets worse.

I've spent my whole life watching parties from the outside. Until my mom died, I never stayed anywhere long enough to make friends. When we were on the run, I had to watch people to survive. To blend in. To act normal. You know what I learned? Human nature sucks. And drunken human nature sucks more.

Needless to say, for various and fairly obvious reasons, it's a really bad idea for me to go out and get blitzed. I tried it. Once. I was only twelve, but I had told everyone else I was fifteen. The result was a melted kiddie pool, some kids who needed therapy after a night of what they thought was some really bad acid, and a rather hasty exit out of Lickskillet, Ohio, for yours truly.

Not to downplay the life struggles of my peers, but I don't have skeletons in my closet so much as a whole underground cavern of terra-cotta warriors like the ones that were found in China. They are ready to come to life and start some shit, given the slightest provocation.

And I have enough problems, thank you *very* much.

I DIDN'T sleep well after my visit to Heaven. It wasn't the deep and blessed sleep I needed, but restless and even more nightmare filled than normal. And I have plenty of memories to create nightmares from. No embellishment necessary. Unfortunately my brain picked the worst one.

I'm twelve, and I'm eating dinner. We're in Florida, at a safe house that Mom's friend Benny had found for us, and the air is thick and hot, even though it's nighttime. The bugs are making a racket, and having just come from a desert climate, I'm not used to it yet. I'll acclimate quickly, though. We never stay anywhere longer than a few months. When you're hunted by the Coterie, you don't get the luxury of putting down roots. I'm used to it.

I'm eating dinner with Benny and my mom. Her dark brown hair is pinned up so a breeze can find her neck and I'm thinking that my mom is the most beautiful woman in the world, and wishing I looked more like her. Oh, I have some of her features and her hair, but I'm stockier and not as graceful. I assume these other traits come from my father, and if I'd ever gotten to meet him, I'd know. He didn't leave us—we left him, or so my mom tells me. For his safety.

I'd had this explained to me at a very young age. I needed to know, my mom had said. My dad would have loved me, given the chance. But he wasn't given the chance, and I was in Florida with loud insects, eating dinner with my beautiful mother and Benny.

Benny was nice enough, but more important, Benny was like us—a firebug. He had gone underground after some friction with an organization out in Texas. Benny was hazy on the details, and since we were often around other people in hiding, I'd learned not to ask. We were in Florida with him for now, but that was temporary. Benny was part of a network that moved creatures like us away from groups like the Coterie. He had scars down his back and a slight limp because of this, though he wouldn't tell me exactly where he'd gotten them. He only showed me these things to firmly underline that what he did was very dangerous work. Like he needed to underline it. As if I didn't live it every damn day. I had to bite my tongue to stop myself from telling him that being a kid doesn't mean you're a moron.

My mom met up with Benny every so often to hear news and find out what was going on with the Coterie. We'd split up in a few days, but for now I had someone else to learn from and to play cards with.

I hadn't come into my own yet. As my mom told me, I was just beginning to spark. The ability doesn't fully manifest until puberty. Until then, I was like a box of wet matches. There were occasional flare-ups, like I'd had in Lickskillet, but they weren't dependable. The potential was there, but I needed more time for it to be useful. So I was sputtering along and Benny was helping out. We'd spent the morning reviewing distance, his weathered hand using a charred stick to draw lines in the sand, each scratch marking off ten feet from a burnt-out tree trunk. I can still hear his patient explanations about our limitations—we can only be so far from our targets or the fire goes out. Or worse, we lose control of it. Benny had great control and excellent distance. He could almost give my mom a run for her money. Almost. I'd had a few lessons with my mom, and she outstripped Benny, but we didn't tell him that.

I didn't always like the appraising looks he gave my mother, but Benny was a nice-enough guy. Too nice to get the end he got.

We'd set our empty plates in the sink after dinner so we could play hearts. I was always attempting to shoot the moon, though I lacked the skill to pull it off.

"You need to play a more conservative game, hoss," Benny said, the words stretched out by his slight drawl.

"What's a hoss?"

"You're a hoss. Now stop being flashy or you're going to lose again."

"I can't," I said, shifting my cards. "I want the glory of the slaughter."

My mom laughed and shook her head, and Benny couldn't help joining in.

Benny had just started to go over his strategy again when there was a knock at the door—*thunk, thunk, thunk*—and we all went silent. It was too late for a casual caller; the neighbors weren't very close by and kept to themselves.

The snap of a twig by the back door—where we'd piled them for this exact reason, so we'd have some warning—told us that there would be no sneaking out that way either. And the only windows that opened were in the back bedrooms, which would put us out by the back door. The side windows were nailed shut, and breaking one would loudly declare what we were up to. There was nothing to do but open the front door and see who'd come a-callin'.

My mom gestured for me to hide, but I was used to this game, and I was already halfway into the broom closet, my cards held loosely in my fist. If I'd left out my hand, it would have been too easy for someone to spot that a third person had been at the table. I thought absently as I left the door open a sliver that I was getting too big to hide, and that pretty soon I wouldn't fit easily into closets like this anymore.

There were three of them at the front door. Two guys and a girl. I can't remember exactly what was said or what they looked like. All I heard was the blood pumping in my ears. But I could tell the conversation wasn't going well. Soon Benny was tossed into a wall like a crash-test dummy. He lay still. I watched for the rise and fall of his back, something to show he was alive. Nothing. Whoever had sent these goons would be pissed. You don't damage valuable assets. I'd already begun to see us that way. As merchandise. Which meant either this group was stupid or they hadn't known that Benny was a firebug.

The girl had my mom up by her throat now, and she was squeezing. Not too hard, but hard enough. I shook in my closet, wanting to help but knowing my mom wanted me to stay hidden.

One of the guys broke my mom's fingers. I heard each bone crack, but she wasn't giving them whatever they wanted. I closed my eyes for a second, trying to wish the situation away. My eyes opened just as the girl smacked my mom into the wall. Blood flowed quickly, but since I couldn't see the actual gash, I had to hope it was just an over-enthusiastic head wound.

My mom had told me all about recovery teams. They were my childhood bogeymen, the long arm of the Coterie. I knew that when the Coterie sends a recovery team out, the leaders are vamps chosen by Venus and two strong backups—my guess was some kind of were-creature. Whatever these thugs were, the blood was distracting them and they weren't handling the situation well.

The female vampire hadn't fed—that much was obvious—and the smell was going to throw her into a frenzy, like I'd seen happen with sharks on TV. If that happened, I doubted her helpers would stay out of it. A blood frenzy was dangerous, but it was also helpful. It meant that they weren't paying attention to me as I slipped out of the closet and clobbered one guy with a chair. While they were focused on him, I grabbed the necklace off the other man, praying that his ward was attached to it. It was.

Baby firebugs are kind of like baby snakes. When a juvenile snake bites you, the bite itself isn't as bad and they have less venom, but nature makes up for that by concentrating what they've got for emergency situations. I'd rather be bitten by a full-grown viper than by a baby. It's hard to fight survival instinct. Since I hadn't grown fully into my power yet, my spark didn't always listen and my control was incredibly shaky, but the adrenaline built into the fight-or-flight response overrides everything else. So while I wasn't trained and had limited control, in times of extreme stress my ability worked just fine. In fact, it worked better than fine. And I was in a situation of extreme stress.

I flicked my hands out, and the were I'd stolen the ward from burst into flame. No slow burn, no trickle of smoke, nothing but quick combustion. He screamed and tried to roll, but that doesn't work when I'm around. Every flame he beat down, I encouraged.

The guy I'd hit with the chair was down, and I could see his ward plainly pinned to his jacket, which really only protects the jacket. Moron. So I set his pants on fire. Either someone had told him that wearing it on his jacket would be just as good and he'd been duped like the meat that he was, or he hadn't really believed we were a threat. Weres got so used to being stronger and faster than everyone else that they started to think they were invincible. Skin contact was ideal when it came to wards, but the one on the pin had probably been cheaper. It was my experience that you shouldn't skimp on something that kept you alive. It didn't really matter why he wasn't well protected, though—whether it was ignorance, stupidity, or thriftiness. All were fatal flaws for members of a recovery team, especially when they were hunting firebugs.

Fire-pants, clearly mad about the chair and his trousers, threw me back. I bounced off a cabinet and slid down, but it was too late, and he burned as quickly as his friend.

The girl still held my mother pinned to the wall. The chipped white paint that Mom's head rested on was smeared with her blood, and it looked like a lot. Head wounds can do that, bleed so much that you think it's worse than it is, but from the panicky flutter in my gut, I had a feeling that it was just as bad as it looked. Her eyes flickered, and I was pretty sure she'd lost consciousness.

The female vamp and I stood locked in a stare. She was

stuck and she knew it—she couldn't let go of my mom, and she couldn't come after me without letting go. Her companions couldn't help her anymore. She was a lower-ranking minion, I was positive. She'd been sent to do a job, and she'd totally botched it.

In fact, I couldn't think of any way she could have screwed this job up more than she had. I was out of control, and her compatriots were dead. If she got out alive and made it back to the Coterie, she would be punished, probably fatally so. If she stayed and tried to handle us, she was just as dead. Stuck in every way. It was almost enough to make me pity her, except she was trying to either kill us or capture us, which kind of obliterated any sympathy.

"Walk away," I told her. "Go back to your master and tell her to leave us alone. That's all we want."

She sneered at me. "You know I can't do that."

I shrugged and the movement hurt. I'd whacked my head pretty good against that cabinet. "Then stay and burn." I said it like it didn't matter to me what she decided, and it didn't. I knew she was already a walking, talking corpse. She just hadn't gotten the memo yet.

The sneer turned into a grin. "Big words, little bug. We both know I'm warded."

I cocked my head then, just a slight nonchalant tilt to the side. "Are you sure? I mean, your buddies thought they were safe too."

Her eyes strayed to her friends, who were now turning into charcoal briquettes on the cabin floor. They'd stopped moving except for the crackle of the flame, and the smell was turning my stomach. Burning flesh and hair weren't among my top-ten favorite smells, and I doubted she was enjoying them either. I could see the doubt as it passed over her pinched features. I did my best to look calm, to continue to chip away at her confidence, but it was hard. I was scared, and I was worried, and my body wanted to respond. It wanted to burn, and it was all I could do to keep it in check.

The vampire kept one arm crushing my mother's windpipe while the other dipped into the neckline of her shirt and pulled out a long silvery chain. She waved it in front of me, and sure enough a delicate silver ward hung at the end of the chain. Her face was triumphant as she turned away, deciding I was no longer a threat.

Poor decision, that.

As she went back to snarling at my mother, I slid over to the left. The fire was starting to spread to the cabin now, and I let it, encouraged it, using the crackle and snap of the flames to cover the sounds I made as I reached for the hatchet we'd hidden in the thin space between the pantry and the cupboards. It was rusty and dull, but that didn't matter. I just had to use a little more force when I slammed the blade into the back of the vampire's neck.

She turned on me, the blade still stuck into her spine like the fin of the shark she'd reminded me of earlier. One hand continued to hold my mom against the wall while her other hand whipped out and grabbed the front of my shirt, pulling me close to her. The sneer was back as my face came within kissing distance.

"Aw, the little baby has some claws." Her pupils dilated as she caught my scent. "I bet you'll be a tasty little thing. Maybe I'll tell Venus you didn't make it out of the fire? Too bad, so sad, boo hoo." She grinned, and I could see her fangs, sharp and extended. She breathed me in, bloodlust clouding her eyes. "Did you really think the ax was going to kill me, little bug?" Her words were a soft exhalation against my cheek.

"No," I said, my voice just as breathy as hers from the grip she had on me. "I didn't."

She pursed her lips, which was difficult because of her fangs. "Then why did you do it?"

I didn't answer her and she shook me, the movement followed by the chime of her necklace hitting the floor, her motion finally dislodging the broken thing onto the ground. She looked at the shining chain as it puddled at her feet.

"That's why." And as she gaped at the severed chain of her ward, sliced cleanly by the dull blade of the ax, I grabbed onto her arms and let her burn. Overconfidence, according to my mother, is the vampire's Achilles' heel. Fire may kill them, but it's often their hubris that opens the door. I guess when you've been an apex predator for so long, you forget that you aren't indestructible.

The vamp screamed and dropped both my mother and me, yanking her arm out of my grasp. It didn't matter. I didn't need to touch her to keep the flames going. I ran for my mom, grabbing underneath her arms and dragging her out of the building. The cabin was starting to catch now. I didn't stop it. Once I had my mother at a safe distance, I ran to check on Benny. He hadn't moved, and I wasn't surprised to find no pulse. I used the side of my hand to close his eyes, told him good-bye, and then got out before the building collapsed on me.

The night air, so muggy and hot before, was cool on my

skin now. We'd been using Benny's truck to get around, since our old station wagon had had its death throes somewhere in Tennessee. The truck was a gas guzzler, not to mention a stick shift, which I wasn't very good at, so I did a quick search for the car the Coterie flunkies had used. I found it parked just around the bend in our driveway, keys hanging from the ignition. Shaking my head once again at their freakish self-assurance, I was at least glad that it was working in my favor.

They had been driving a nice nondescript sedan, far better suited to my needs than the truck. I was, of course, way too young to drive legally, but knowing how to do something and being allowed to do it by law are two different things. I drove the car up to the cabin and pulled my mom into the back seat. She wasn't looking very good. My shirt was covered in her blood by the time I got her settled.

Someone had left a jacket in the passenger seat, which I handed to my mom to staunch the blood. She held it, but her grip was limp and she'd lost most of the color in her face. That flutter of panic came back and I ignored it. Wouldn't do me any good. Still, I was crying as I got back in and threw the car into reverse.

It took me about ten minutes of driving to find a sign for a hospital. I pulled up to the ER, parking the car in the ambulance lane as I ran to get a nurse, a doctor, a janitor—anyone.

Things got blurry after that.

I remember white coats running around, and white floors, white bandages—that's what I remember, an overall impression of white. White, and the red of my mother's blood on my hands. On my shirt.

The doctors did what they could, but the damage was too

extensive. I nodded at them numbly when they told me. I wasn't feeling much of anything; it was like all that running, spinning whiteness had seeped inside me. My brain wasn't working and my heart was gone. It had slipped away with my mother, following her into her coma, then death.

Things remained hazy as the people at the hospital talked to me and I stared at my hands. I finally snapped back to reality when they asked me if I had someone to call, someone who could come get me. The nurses were staring at me expectantly, sympathy on their faces.

Did I have someone to call? Yes, I did, the only person I trusted, but I also knew I couldn't hang around here waiting for him to play fetch. I was a sitting duck for not only the Coterie but Social Services as well. I nodded at the nice nurses and pretended to call a made-up relative. After I told them that a fictional aunt was on her way, they let me say good-bye to my mother. They didn't want me to—they said I should remember her the way she'd been. Like anything could make me forget her. As if seeing her now, peaceful and asleep, was worse than watching her bleed to death in the rearview mirror as I drove. Adults say the stupidest things sometimes.

I took her necklace and slipped it around my own neck. It wasn't much, a little silver heart with an interlocking star given to her by Cade when they weren't much older than I was then. He'd had to mow lawns, wash cars, and chop firewood to get it. It was the only thing my mom valued besides me.

I kissed her good-bye. A kind hospital employee brought me a clean scrub shirt to change into. The dried blood in my shirt stuck to my skin as I yanked it off. It was beyond redemption, but I couldn't just toss it. Leaving evidence for human

117

police was a bad idea. Leaving it for the Coterie to find was even worse. If the next tracking team had a blood witch on hand, it would be disastrous. I'd never met one, but my mom had told me about them. They work with blood the way green witches work with plants. The smallest drop of blood was enough for them to track with, even if it was just from a close relation. Like my mom. If I left my shirt, I might as well stay put and wrap a big bow around myself.

The pale blue scrub top was way too big for me. It looked weird with my jeans. I wrapped the old shirt in paper towels and shoved it into my waistband for the moment. I cleaned up as best I could in the sink, trying to think how I was going to slip out of the hospital. It was only a matter of time until someone called the cops or Social Services and I really only had one option: run. I was so tired of that being my only choice.

The nurse popped her head in and asked if I was okay on my own for a few minutes. She had a patient or something to get to, and I told her I would go back up to the front desk when I was done.

Every once in a while, things go your way.

I slipped out of the hospital and found the sedan pushed off to the side. Without the keys, which were safely in my pocket, that had been about all they could do until someone got around to calling a tow truck. After making sure no one was looking, I started the car and drove slowly away.

I drove until the car almost ran out of gas. Maybe I could have found a station to fill up at, but twelve-year-olds driving cars tend to attract attention, and I couldn't risk that. Plus, the back seat looked like a horror movie.

The scrub shirt had to go as well. I searched the car for anything that would help. There were a few roller bags and a backpack filled with clothes and a little bit of cash—probably travel money. I put on a shirt that must have belonged to the girl, which was a tad too big, but less conspicuous than the scrub shirt. Then I emptied the backpack and filled it with someone's hooded sweatshirt, the cash, a map, and a flashlight I'd found in the glove box.

I backed that car into the trees and got out, then set it on fire, making sure that my bloodied shirt was at the heart of the blaze. As the flames ate away the interior, I egged them on, amazed at the control I had over them. This wasn't like at the cabin—gut-reaction survival instinct fed by fear and adrenaline. No, this was something else. Like when you have a growth spurt and suddenly you fit into that jacket you really liked. For a split second you think it's the jacket—that it's shrunk. But then it hits you. You're the thing that's changed.

It was then that I realized I hadn't eaten since dinner. I should have sweet-talked the nurses into a candy bar or a soda or something, but I hadn't been thinking straight.

Ignoring my weakened condition, I kept the car blazing until the flames could go on their own. Too much evidence to just leave it.

I walked in the trees for a short time, not daring to come out until I found a service station. I bought the biggest Gatorade they had (for the electrolytes), several candy bars, and a better local map, one that had a bus station clearly marked on it. I was far enough from the hospital that I hoped no one would be looking for me. I bought a baseball hat anyway, pulled my hair back into a low ponytail, and tucked it under. With the hood up on the sweatshirt, you couldn't see my long hair. It would have to do.

I didn't have enough money to get a bus ticket all the way to Cade's, but I got pretty close. After that, I walked and sneaked the occasional ride. Dangerous, I know, but not as dangerous as waiting for the Coterie to finish me off.

By the time I got to Cade's door, I was soaked to the bone, exhausted, half-starved, and riddled with grief. He opened the door and I collapsed into him, glad I could finally let go and stop being in charge of myself. He didn't get a chance to ask what happened, but I think he figured it out from my sobbing.

He pulled me into his arms and let me cry. Once my sobs became hiccups, he deposited me on the couch under some blankets and went about the task of finding me dry clothes and warm food.

He didn't break down until he saw the necklace. That tiny silver heart and star. Though he tried to hide it, I could see the echoes of his own heart fracturing in his eyes. But he didn't let his grief stop him from taking care of me. From loving me.

Not then.

Not now.

Not ever.

7

SHOCK AND AWE

I WOKE UP sputtering. Ezra stood over me, an empty bottle of what had been ice-cold water held in his fist.

"Oh, good," he said. "You're awake. We wouldn't want to go to the party without you."

I loved Ezra, but sometimes I wanted to choke the damn life out of him. "Party?" My voice was a parched croak.

Lock handed me a full bottle of water and I drank greedily. "Yeah, while you were unconscious and vomiting, Owen popped in. Apparently Venus needs to talk to you again. Somehow he was unsurprised to find us all still here even though our shifts were over and your friends were gone."

"You think we were set up?" Ezra asked, handing me a rough hand towel, probably filched from the kitchens.

"No, I think the world is full of wonderful coincidences," Lock said, taking the finished bottle from me.

"So Venus knew I was going to get drunk and planned around it? Seems a little convoluted to me."

"You don't drink, Aves," Lock said, pointing at a spot I'd apparently missed. When I didn't get it, Ezra snatched my towel and wiped my chin.

"I had some of Ryan's drink by accident. Gin and tonic."

Lock shook his head. "Even if you had two G&Ts, they wouldn't affect you like this. Someone slipped you something. Who was near your drink?"

"Ryan, of course, and the bartender. Maybe some of the waitstaff..."

"Is that what you call careful?" Lock said. "Would it be faster for you to list who isn't a suspect?"

"Don't yell at me!" I shot back, shouting even though it made my head throb. "I've had a crappy night!"

"I'm not yelling!" Though even he seemed to figure out that he was, in fact, doing exactly that. Ezra grabbed him by the shoulders and pushed him into a corner like Lock was a naughty child. Then he thrust the towel into my hands and sat alongside me on the couch.

"I think what our friend is trying to say is that you scared us to death and we were extremely worried about you."

"Ezra, when you say things like that, totally serious and without a single come-on or innuendo, I have a hard time taking you seriously."

"Fine: We were worried about you, baby. Is that better?"

"That was actually kind of weak," Lock said, coming out of his corner and joining us on the couch. "How are you feeling, Aves?"

"Remember that time Venus threw a mandatory pool party and we played Marco Polo with the nixies, and we won and they got so mad they tried to drown me and I puked water up all over the floor?"

"It sounds familiar, yes."

"And the time we tried to subdue that Valkyrie who was sauced up on mead and we all ended up with concussions?"

"That's ringing a bell," said Ezra.

"Combine those two feelings and multiply them by ten."

"Excellent," said Lock. "Then you're in just the right condition to deal with Venus. Ezra, tie your shoes and let's go."

I HAD to admit that Lock looked more badass than I did, in his leather jacket, his dark jeans, and his Purgatory shirt. Between the scorches, my tears, the combat boots I was wearing, and what was probably a little dried vomit—though I chose not to examine it closely enough to be sure—I resembled something out of a paramilitary group made up entirely of bedraggled orphans. Ezra, for some reason, was wearing a tailored black three-piece suit, a bright red carnation sticking out of the buttonhole. Apparently he'd had the suit in his locker. I don't know why, nor do I know where he procured a carnation at that hour. We flashed our passes and were let into the ostentatious elevators that descended into Hell. The doors closed with a soft hiss, and we were left staring at our reflections. Lock openly checked himself out, but I pretended not to.

"Not bad," he said. "They will tremble before our badassery."

"Yeah," I said, checking my pockets for the fifth time, "because with all their strength and weaponry, they're going to get weak-kneed at the sight of your leather jacket."

"Never underestimate a nice jacket," Ezra said.

"And why are you wearing a suit, again?" I asked.

"Because I look spectacular," he said. "Besides, no fox responds to a formal invitation looking like a common vagabond." He ran his hands down his chest, smoothing the fabric. "No offense."

"How could I possibly be offended by that?" I said.

"Good," he said, patting my shoulder. "Glad we're on the same page."

I can never tell if Ezra misses some of my sarcasm or if he simply chooses to ignore it.

Then the doors slid open. I wasn't sure what to expect. Maybe more guards, or Venus waiting for us by the elevator— something a little different from the usual, I guess. But everything was normal. I was so keyed up, I forgot that for Venus and her goons this was just another day at work. Clock in, launder some money, plan some assassinations, drink some blood, clock out.

A guard escorted us into a small lounge. "Wait here," he said, adjusting his tie. It must be hard to get a good tie when you have no neck. It was like his head sprouted directly from his shoulders.

"For how long?" I asked. "It's just that I have a dentist appointment after this. I can't be late."

The second guard, who looked like a very thin, stretched-out version of the first guard, frowned at me. "It takes as long as it takes."

I dropped the joking tone. "Let me make this very clear: I will wait only so long before I start lighting things on fire. I'll start with your underwear and move to the drapes. Got it?"

They both moved a step away, obviously uneasy, but not

ready to bolt. I was scary, but I couldn't hold a candle to Venus.

After a surprisingly short time, we were led into a... ballroom? You'd think this building would stop surprising me. Small tables, all covered in white tablecloths and linen napkins. Chandeliers, vases of roses on every table, everyone in black tie. A string quartet played softly in the corner. The walls were all draped in thick red velvet. It was not unlike being inside a Goth music box.

There had to be at least a hundred people there. And they were all staring at us. I guess we were a trifle underdressed, except for Ezra. I gave a little wave. No one waved back. Venus, naturally, was seated at the middle of a long table in the front. Her table was raised up on a small dais, rather theatrically, I thought.

As I looked around the room, I noticed that there was no food on the plates. Hungry predators, even ones that don't like their meals in human packaging, might lack impulse control. If any of the creatures in this room didn't know who we were, we would appear to be walking, talking Happy Meals without the toy. Or maybe it was a two-for-one deal and we were also the toys.

I approached the dais where Venus was waiting, her hand trailing though Owen's hair, a close-lipped smile on her face. Her side of the table was full of lesser minions, but the side facing the audience was empty. Wouldn't want the audience to miss out on seeing those pretty, bloodthirsty faces.

I stopped at the table and waited. It seemed silly to make demands—Venus knew what I wanted, just like I knew what she wanted. Silence stretched out because Venus was trying to not talk first. Me standing there with my arms crossed, patiently waiting, was not exactly giving her the image she wanted. But of course she couldn't break the silence either, so Owen had to speak.

"You know why you're here, I'm sure," he said before snapping his fingers so the wine steward would refill his champagne flute. Sloppy, to be drinking like that. If I'd liked Owen, I might have explained to him how alcohol affects coordination and control and how bad it is for folks like us. Or I could watch him drink his way to destruction. Maybe I could bribe the steward into bringing him a bigger glass.

"Yes," I said. "Though I'm not sure what this meeting will accomplish."

"Compliance," Venus said slowly, like she was savoring the word. "You need a reminder as to what it means."

I cocked my head at her. "Oh?" Lock shifted on his feet slightly, his shoulder brushing mine in a silent *be careful here.* Ezra examined his nails, a nonchalant expression on his face, but I knew he was taking in the room, cataloging exits and people. If I'd asked him right then what color tie the violinist was wearing, he'd have known.

"If you recall, I offered you a job earlier. You refused."

The Duncan contract. What had Duncan done, exactly? Maybe he'd put plastic wrap on her toilet seat or something. Do vampires pee? Now was probably not the time to ask.

"I do recall," I said. Then I stood there and smiled. There's nothing more irritating than someone who refuses to argue with you. I could tell this was aggravating her. A bit like yanking on a hungry lion's tail, but I never claimed to be wise. If I didn't act normal, if I toned down my usual insolence, then she'd know she had me.

Venus sat there primly, her back straight, her blue eyes on me and only me. "I've decided to do you a favor."

Unlikely. Venus didn't do nice things. Ever. So if she was offering a little goodwill, I knew it was anything but. I didn't respond. I just kept staring at her until she continued.

"I've decided to offer you the job again."

"I politely decline. Again." The answer popped out before I had a chance to think about it. Not that I was going to say yes, anyway, but still.

Venus shook her head, playing up to her audience. "My naïve little firebug. I was hoping you wouldn't say that." Some very large men moved up to flank us. I wasn't worried about them as much as I was worried about the shorter, skinnier guy who came with them. If your hired tough is small, that means he makes up for it in other ways. In a street fight in the human world, that might mean he has a knife, or maybe he's a ninja or something. In my world it could mean, well, anything. Maybe he secretes a lethal poison or has chain saws for hands. You just couldn't know. Except about the chain saw thing. That one wasn't very probable.

"You've been growing too . . . comfortable lately," Venus continued, running one finger down the side of her empty champagne flute. "And you're beginning to set a bad example." She looked out at all the people sitting quietly at the tables. The quartet kept playing, but the dulcet tones did nothing to soothe the tense atmosphere. They just didn't go together. It was like harp music at a NASCAR race. "After all, monkey see, monkey do." Some of the diners began to fidget.

We were going to be made into examples. Yay. I reached out and took Lock and Ezra's hands. It would make us look weak, but at this point I didn't think it mattered. The toughs kept us in place as we watched a man in a tux pull back one of the red curtains to reveal what looked like a transformer box. He opened it and hit a button. There was a loud grating noise and the floor started to move. People jumped up from their tables, scattering place settings and wine glasses everywhere. They flocked to the edges of the room, where the floor actually managed to stay in the same spot. It was only the middle that was sliding back, opening up to reveal an Olympic-size swimming pool that was—thankfully?—empty. I've never seen a pool so deep. It had to be twenty feet down at least. We scrambled up onto Venus's dais, our burly handlers right behind us. I watched as table after table crashed down into the pool, creating a floor of broken wood and shattered glass. That was Venus all over. She enjoyed creating a spectacle.

The small tough who'd climbed up next to us on the raised dais ran his delicate hands alongside my body, never touching. It didn't hurt. It was just weird. He did the same to Lock and Ezra. When he was done, he indicated points on each of us quickly, and his large companions proceeded to rip our wards off us with absolute precision. Interesting. So he *was* deadly to us, just not in the way I imagined. Once we were naked of protection, he pointed at the ladder. "You can either climb down that or we can throw you in." He said it like he was a bored flight attendant offering us pretzels or peanuts.

I picked the ladder. We made it down the rungs in silence. Once I reached the ground, the sound of broken glass and wood met me with every footstep, and I was grateful for my boots. There were a lot of nails down there, too, and I didn't fancy getting a tetanus shot if I survived whatever Venus had in mind. I looked up and saw the faces of the diners, including Venus, peering over the edge of the pool.

"I feel," Lock said, leaning close to me, "that this could have gone better."

"I feel," Ezra said, smoothing his suit again, "that I look like James Bond. Tell me I'm not killing it in this suit." His smile was strained as he turned to us. Though he was obviously as terrified as we were, he was still trying to make us feel better.

"Well, you're certainly killing me," Lock said.

I kept my mouth shut, watching as two people came down the ladder at the other end of the pool. One, I could see quite clearly, was Owen. Even if I couldn't tell him by his clothes, his cocky walk would have given him away.

The other person, a younger guy of about medium build, was new to me. Faces continued to peek over the edge at us as the crowd grew. Venus looked incredibly smug. There were three of us and two of them. She should have been concerned, but she wasn't. Which meant we were in for a nasty surprise.

Owen was bad enough, but at least I knew what he was capable of—he was a known factor. This new person at the end of the pool was not. Venus wouldn't have thrown the new guy in here if she didn't have a damn good reason. But what was that reason? Was it to punish me or him?

"Who's with Owen?" Lock whispered.

"No clue."

"Great."

That was the other thing I was worried about. I'd dragged

the boys into this mess. Venus would probably kill us all, but there was a small chance that she might let me live. Break every bone in my body several times, yeah, but that slight chance existed. Ezra and Lock were, at least to Venus, expendable. Replacing a firebug? Not easy. Hiring new bartenders? Not really a problem.

My thoughts were interrupted by what can only be described as a fireball the size of a pony. My friends and I dove to our respective sides, making it out of the way before we got singed, but we landed in sharp, jagged rubble. Apparently it wasn't as hard as I thought to find new firebugs, because Venus obviously had. Big and flashy, oddly enough, was not Owen's style. When he threw flame, it was tightly controlled, small, and superhot. Despite all his other faults, Owen was a professional. He knew how to pace himself, something this newbie obviously hadn't learned yet. Though with that kind of power, he probably wasn't too worried about finesse.

"What the hell was that?" Ezra yipped. "Can you do that? I've never seen you do that!"

It had been impressive. I was hoping that the new kid was all flash, but Venus had been too confident for that. No, he was just that powerful. Great.

I could only cross my fingers and wish that that he didn't know how to pace himself and his body would start pulling from essentials—the energy usually used to run automatic systems like the heart, lungs, and so on. If he wore himself out, we could have a chance.

The fact that Venus had found a prospective replacement for me changed the game. Of course she'd rather have three firebugs over two, but then again, replacing me with a lap dog might be enough for her. Doing so before he was fully trained, though, would be like trading a Jedi for a young Padawan. Darth Venus might not enjoy my lip, but at least I hit what I was aiming for.

After picking myself up from where I'd fallen, I threw a few short bursts of flame, more to keep our opponents busy than anything else. What I needed was a precious second to think. If the Coterie had been training this kid, it hadn't been for very long. People gossip, and even if it had been kept under wraps, the secret would probably have leaked. I was reluctant to hurt anyone who didn't deserve it, and who knew why the kid was in the pool with us. Maybe he wanted to join the Coterie and we were looking at his initiation. Possibly he was like us—forced. Owen I would happily roast over a spit with an apple in his mouth while coating him in a glaze every thirty minutes, but the kid was a different story.

He threw another fireball, this time the size of a Volkswagen bus. Hard to dodge that. I hit the ground again, slicing my hand on a piece of broken glass. Lock also tried to move to the side but didn't quite make it, though his leather jacket took the brunt of the assault. Smart wardrobe choice. Note to self: Wear more leather. Bikers might be on to something.

Ezra appeared to be snapping open a small collapsible crossbow. How had he hidden that in his tailored suit?

I couldn't play dodge-the-fireball forever. The kid would probably get tired soon, but that left Owen. And if I avoided Owen, then Venus would send someone—or something—else in, because I needed to be taught a lesson.

A wave of fire arched toward me, like something out of a flamethrower. I got hit this time—not bad, but there was definitely a smell of burnt hair about me. Lock wasn't as lucky. He was stopping, dropping, and rolling. It shouldn't have worked with a firebug flame, but it did. The kid either had no endurance or didn't care about seeing it through. He probably wasn't used to killing with flame, like I was. Lock writhed on the ground, his jacket smoldering.

I watched a wisp of smoke dissipate, and my high and lofty morals went with it. You don't mess with my friends. Newbie was going to have to crawl out of this pool after I was done with him. I sent a volley of flaming orbs at Owen and the kid. I hit them both, but nothing happened, of course. Venus may have had our wards removed, but she had no qualms about giving her side a leg up.

I watched a bolt fly from Ezra's crossbow, but the shot went too far to the side. Lock was kneeling now, digging through the wood, his leather sleeve pulled down over his hand so he didn't slice his fingers open on the glass.

"What are you doing?" I yelled.

"Looking for wood!"

"Um, try looking down?"

He shook his head. "Most of it's treated with chemicals."

I shot another volley, this one at debris around our opponents' feet. If I couldn't hurt them directly, I'd try another way. The debris wasn't warded.

Lock stood up, his hands holding shards of wood that apparently met his standards. As I watched from the corner of my eye, he did something to the shards and then started hurling them across the pool. They fell far short but Lock didn't seem bothered by this. He shouted, raising his arms as he did. There was a loud cracking sound, and the floor shuddered. A blur of brown and green shot toward the ceiling, moving almost too quickly for me to follow.

Trees. Lock was growing entire trees out of pieces of wood. Not seeds, *wood*. If we hadn't been fighting for our lives, I would have high-fived him. Even I hadn't known he could do that. I bet Venus didn't know he could do that either. Giant trunks split the ground. They started to break through the ceiling before Lock stopped them with a slashing motion of his hand. Then they grew outward, widening until we'd have had to all join hands to circle them.

Ezra dropped his bow and ripped off his suit. Leave it to Ezra to have a high-end suit made into a tearaway. He hit the ground on four paws, scooped up the tiny bow with his mouth, and took off. I could barely track him as he dove in and out of debris, moving around the trees.

Owen was coming closer, smiling, his sidekick following in his wake. I could tell their attacks were going to get more serious. The new kid was powerful and flashy, which would please Venus and the crowd, but he wasn't very effective. A few years of intense training and he would probably light circles around Owen and me. But Owen had decades of experience—he was the one to watch now. He would get creative. What I really needed to do was get creative first, and shut things down fast. Jumping into a firefight after my disastrous night in Heaven wasn't the best idea. I could feel my energy flagging, and when I moved my head too quickly, I got a little dizzy.

Owen raised his right hand in a fist, palm up. With a smirk, he splayed his fingers. One of the trees blew up at the base. It just *exploded*. I turned and dropped to the ground, trying to avoid the worst of the shrapnel. The air smelled like burnt sap. Owen had used a little too much force, though. Without the base, the tree toppled, and it fell in his direction. For the first time our enemies had to scramble out of the way.

The ground trembled when the tree came down. I took a moment to glance at Lock, who was on the floor with me. I motioned to the trees. "Can you do more?" He shook his head with a grimace. I didn't know how much energy it took to grow trees out of dead wood, but it had to be a lot. Well, I couldn't stay balled up on the floor forever.

I looked around. Jeering faces looked down at us from above. Someone yelled, "Play 'Free Bird'!" and I wasn't sure if he was yelling at me or the now-silent quartet. One drunk asshole threw his drink at us—the whole drink, glass and all. It shattered at my feet. The drink thrower waggled his ward from the end of a long chain, taunting me. He reached out to grab a martini from a waiter's tray, but I set the alcohol on fire before he could touch it. He jumped back with a yelp.

The crowd laughed. So many people. A few enterprising souls were exchanging money, taking bets on the outcome. I wondered if they all had wards. Then I wondered if it mattered. I ducked, dodging another wildly thrown fireball from the new firebug. A flash of russet fur at the far end of the pool caught my eye. I didn't know what Ezra was planning exactly, but we'd worked together so long that I knew what he needed from us.

"Lock," I hissed. "Distraction."

Instead of answering, he took off, leaping over debris,

running full tilt at the younger guy. Surprised, his target didn't move. No one ran *at* firebugs. That was just crazy. And while everyone was watching the crazy guy, I got to work.

The debris was getting in our way—I had to turn it into an asset. The tables had been made of wood and the linens were, well, linen. I set patches of them ablaze, the treated wood giving off toxic-smelling smoke, the flames lighting up the floor of the pool around Owen and the new firebug. Lock tussled with the newbie. Owen was trying to turn my sea of fire against me, not paying attention to his sidekick. That's the funny thing about fire—it's so hardwired into us as threat that we concentrate on it and ignore other dangers. So Lock was able to pick up the new kid and toss him well away from Owen, who was intent on my flames.

The young firebug got up slowly, clearly injured. His eyes were on Lock. He seemed to have forgotten that there were three of us. And that was his downfall. Ezra stepped out from behind a tree, naked as a jaybird, his crossbow a flash in the light. He unloaded it with three quick taps, the sound so quiet, I might have been imagining it. The kid just stared at the bolts sprouting in a cluster around his heart. Then he fell to his knees.

They'd been prepared for fire. Everyone had been so worried about me, so used to the firebug being the big gun, that they'd discounted my backup. But I worked with Lock and Ezra all the time. I knew better.

The kid screamed. And then he totally lost control. Things in the room started to burst into flames. That fancy red curtain. Venus's table. I knew what was coming next—I could feel it.

"Lock! Ezra!" I shouted. "Hit the deck!" I threw myself down, heedless of the broken glass and nails, my jacket pulled over my head. I heard chunks of the wall start to explode as if someone had laced the pool with tiny detonators. The walls were getting hit with such intensity that they were becoming unstable and collapsing. As soon as I could, I got up, my jacket still draped over my head, and ran for Lock. Ezra was a red blur through the rubble, his tiny fox form darting here and there. We had to get out before the new guy went completely supernova. The crowd panicked above us.

The onlookers may have been warded, but wards don't protect your mind. Fear of fire is instinctual. It takes a lot of willpower to repress that response. Unless you've had intense training, like firefighters, the urge to bolt always prevails. Suddenly the jeering crowd was standing in a flaming box and everyone reacted like I thought they would—they panicked and flew for the exits. All at once. If someone got in their way, well, that was what a right hook was made for. Clearly Venus had thought she didn't need to safeguard the drapes. She was used to people in control of their powers—Venus knows I'm careful not to risk unnecessary injury, and Owen wasn't stupid enough to set fire to the room—unlike the kid she'd thrown at me. She'd made a mistake, and if she'd had more experience with firebugs other than just my family and Owen, she would have known better. She'd have realized too much can go wrong in a situation like this, too many people can get hurt. But Venus always thinks she knows best.

Right now, Venus was shouting and trying to maintain order. She'd get it too. Eventually. Already, a few level heads were breaking out fire extinguishers. The sprinklers came on, adding to the chaos. That was fine with me—I didn't actually want the building to burn down, at least not while I was in it. Besides, there were a lot of people upstairs whose only crime was wanting a fun night. My main goal had been a chance to get out of there. So I encouraged the dying firebug's flame, keeping it controlled but burning. I shouted to Lock as I got closer. At my shout, he tossed part of a smoldering chair at Owen. Then he started running like I was.

We climbed the ladder quickly, a naked Ezra trailing behind. I paused halfway to blow up the rest of the trees, creating more confusion.

Once at the top, the three of us tried to go in different directions. Lock grabbed on to Ezra and me. "Don't just bolt like spooked cattle. Think. Best way to get out of here?"

"What about the way we came?" I shouted over the din. The sprinklers were doing their job, but I was fighting them. Keeping fires going, starting new ones, trying to maximize the pandemonium. I wouldn't be able to keep it up forever. When I moved my head, the emergency lights left a trail and things blurred. My mouth was dry and I was getting a major headache. It had taken a lot out of me to blow up the trees. Good to know.

Lock shook his head. "Elevators automatically stop working during a fire alarm."

"Back hallway," Ezra said, pointing to the other side of the room. "There are stairs."

"We go for the stairs." Lock let go of Ezra but shifted his grip on me, sliding his hand down my arm until he had a hold of my hand, pulling me close. Lock took point while Ez went behind me, putting one hand on my shoulder to keep from getting separated.

"Venus is going to shut down the building, if she hasn't already." Lock swerved around a table that was miraculously still standing. "We've got to get while the getting is still possible."

"Any chance Ryan and his friends are still here? Maybe they didn't leave-leave but came down here instead?"

"If that's the case, I'm especially not going to take the risk of seeking them out," Lock said, dragging me through the crowd.

"Comeuppance," Ezra said, shaking off the water from the sprinklers.

"Guys, they're in totally over their heads, and they don't even know—"

Lock cut me off. "Look, I understand you don't want to believe that Ryan had anything to do with tonight's misery, but if we stay, we're not going to get anyone out of here. We'll just be stuck under Venus's very unhappy boot. If we escape, we have possibilities."

I didn't like it, but he was right. Still, the idea of leaving Ryan behind . . .

"I'll carry you out of here if I have to. Toss you over my shoulder and run." Lock's features were stern, the water from the sprinklers running down his face, flattening his bleached hair against his skull. It would have been comical if we hadn't been in danger. Okay, it was still comical.

I nodded at him in defeat because I didn't relish being carried out of there like a sack of flour, and I knew Lock would do just that. He hauled me toward one of the exits, Ezra behind us like a naked caboose.

The various doorways were packed with people stampeding their way out. It wasn't going to be easy. Lock leaned his head back so I could hear him shout, "I think you're going to need to intervene."

It's hard to aim accurately while you're running, and the crowd was making me slow down anyway, so I stopped in my tracks, yanking Lock back. I concentrated, making two throwing gestures with my hand. Strictly speaking, the gestures weren't necessary, but they helped with focus and aim. Two large fireballs shot out—one enveloped the door we were headed for, which exploded noisily, leaving a gaping hole. The other one did something similar to the opposite wall, creating a door where there wasn't one before. I didn't want it to be immediately obvious which way we were going. This way, either Venus would have to pick between the two or divide her forces. It might buy us a little time. Sometimes a few more minutes could make the difference between survival and ruin.

Lock grabbed my hand again. "This building is going to have serious structural issues when we're done." Ezra gave a yip, pushing us along, obviously anxious to get out of there.

After the explosions, people either jumped out of the way and hit the ground or they ran back in the other direction. The path was now clear enough that we were able to push our way through and into the outer hallway.

Lock, his hand still firmly gripping mine, led me down a series of corridors. I was already lost.

"Is there an exit this way?" I asked, gasping for breath. Between the sprinting, the adrenaline, and all the fires, I was feeling shaky, my headache now a raging monster. My mouth was so dry, I was this close to licking Ezra just to get some moisture. But I didn't, because I knew where he'd been.

"You think Venus would spend her time somewhere that didn't have escape routes?" Ezra asked.

Of course she wouldn't. If I had been thinking clearly, I would have realized that, but my brain was feeling foggy. I was keeping the flames in the ballroom going as long as I could, which was hard without being in there. Soon I would be far enough removed that the connection would break on its own. In the meantime I had to try to maintain it.

Lock pulled me through a door that led to some stairs. He headed up, and as I tried to follow, missing a few steps as I did, I suddenly wondered why no one was on our tail.

"We need to stop by the locker room so I can get some clothes," Ezra said, examining the hall behind us. "Eventually, we'll have to go outside, and the last thing we need is people dropping to their knees out of devotion. We don't want to draw that much attention."

"I'd say we could just shove you in a locker and call it a day, but I don't think your ego would fit."

Lock motioned us both to be quiet. "The locker room is a good idea. We also need your car keys. My car is probably being watched, so yours is the better bet."

Ezra didn't trust the open lot by the Inferno, so he always parked a block away at a garage with an attendant. Nothing was too good for his "baby." Since Lock usually drove us around, I wasn't sure anyone at the Inferno would remember that Ez even had a car.

We headed for the employee area. With the kind of costume changes Venus required, people had to have somewhere to put their regular clothing and swap out their wards if they were for physical glamour. Can you imagine the staff from Heaven trying to ride the bus to work in their uniforms?

We ran, following corridors, going through doors, down passageways, up stairs. I quickly lost all track again of what was going on. We needed to get to a safe place soon, somewhere I could rest. I wasn't holding up too well.

We dashed into the locker room. It was the men's, but Lock didn't want to separate just for convention's sake. Ezra popped open his locker and grabbed a set of clothes. Inside was a brief window into my vain friend. A bottle of mouthwash, a hairbrush, a mirror, what appeared to be a Ping-Pong paddle, and a mango resting on a rather battered copy of *Little Women*.

"Huh," I said, reaching for the book. "I didn't know you could read, Ezra."

"He mostly looks at the pictures," Lock said absently as he pawed through Ezra's jacket, looking for the keys.

"Oh. My copy wasn't illustrated."

"It was a joke, cupcake." Suddenly Lock pulled me between him and the lockers, his body pressing into mine as he leaned in so close, I could smell the leather of his jacket. I just stood there, paralyzed.

I heard a voice off to the side, someone past the door of the locker room and out of my line of vision. "Hey, she can't be in here."

Lock gave him a sheepish grin. "Sorry, but it's my girl, you know? Hates to be left alone." He shrugged his shoulders in a "silly girls, but what you gonna do?" kind of way before reaching over my head and pulling Ezra's keys out of the locker. "Ready to go, sweetheart?" I nodded, and he waved a good-bye to the interloper. Ezra grabbed his jacket from the locker and slipped it on. I don't know anyone who can dress faster than Ezra. Lock guided me to his side as he slipped an arm around me protectively. With his free arm, he shut the locker door before whisking me out of the locker room.

"If that hand gets anywhere near my ass, I'll bite it off," I whispered.

"That's my girl," he said, pulling me close again for a quick peck on my forehead. "Thought I'd lost you there for a moment."

I mumbled something and let him drag me down yet another hallway. I was stumbling now and losing energy fast. I could feel the fires getting away from me, pulling from my control. They would probably die without me to egg them on. I tried to hold them as best I could, but it was like grabbing handfuls of sand. A sudden blast of cool air hit me in the face. We were outside. Ezra held the door, slowing its close so it made only a muted *click* when it shut. Then we moved quickly along the wall, slipping around cars, finally sliding behind some Dumpsters. We watched as a patrol of security guards went past, people already looking for us.

As we hid in the shadows, another group of guards went by, coming from the other direction. We saw more off along the edges of the lot. There were too many for us to conceivably make it past without detection. They were walking in small groups of two to four, circling like sharks. My adrenaline was gone, and without it I was fading fast. The cold didn't help, either; I could feel the night air nipping at my fingertips and turning my wet clothes into ice. We needed something to draw the patrolling groups to one place. And perhaps something to bring the customers out, to add to the confusion—something that would get the human authorities involved as well.

And what brings people together more than a cheery bonfire? I squeezed Lock's hand. He turned his face toward me, just enough so he could see me, but not enough to take his eyes off the people looking for us.

"Where's your car?" I whispered.

He frowned. "I'm not going to want to answer that, am I?"

"You have insurance," I said. "And I'd feel bad destroying a stranger's car."

"That's by far one of the weirdest things to come out of your mouth. You feel better about destroying your friend's car? How does that make sense?"

"You'll be fine. But what if I blow up someone's car and they have no insurance, or they need it to . . . I don't know, transport gruel to homeless puppies or something?"

"You're insane, you know that?"

"Shut up and tell me where your car is."

Of course it wasn't close to us. That would have been too easy. We had to go back toward the building and slide around the side of a particularly ugly van so I could see Lock's car. I was still feeling shaky, so I kept telling myself that I just had to do this—one more thing—and then I could rest. I'd often mocked Owen for not practicing his long-distance game, but I was just as guilty. I hadn't trained enough, and now my endurance was shot. No use crying over spilt milk and all that.

I held my hands out, slightly cupped, but kept my elbows

tucked tight against me. My hands shook a little, though that could have been from exhaustion or the cold.

"Are you okay?" Concern filled Lock's face.

"Yeah," I said. "Fine. You worry too much."

Lock said nothing, but he didn't look any less anxious when he glanced over at Ez, so I wasn't certain either of them entirely bought my reassurance. They didn't argue, though. Finally, Lock just sighed and leaned against the van, next to me. Ezra stood on the other side, keeping watch from that end of things. A hand wave from Lock told me to proceed, even though it was obvious he wasn't keen on what I was about to do.

I'd set fire to cars before, though I couldn't say I was an expert at it, which I guess was a good thing. I didn't have to do it frequently, but it was necessary at times, like when I had to burn the Coterie car after my mom died. This time I needed more than a burn to be really impressive. I wanted a solid distraction—I needed to light up the sky. In the end I decided to go with a two-pronged assault. First, I set the interior to smoldering. This was harder than it sounds because people prefer that their cars not blow up. So newer car upholstery is flame retardant. Plus, I didn't want to use any more energy than I had to, because I was going to need it for the second part of my plan.

I kept raising the heat until I had a nice friendly blaze going. Then, after a few heads had turned toward it, I continued with part two. I quickly expanded a giant ball of flame in the gas tank. Of course, Lock didn't have that much fuel in the car, nor do things blow up quite the way they do in the movies, but that didn't really matter, since I was there to help it along. There was no way in hell a car could do that naturally. It was straight-up theatrics on my part, but people would buy it. They wouldn't know any better.

So I created a column of flame that would have made Prometheus blush.

Then I passed out.

8

THIS IS WHY WE CAN'T HAVE NICE THINGS

I WOKE UP in Ezra's car. I could tell it was his because it was ostentatious, it was immaculately clean, and the warm leather seats smelled like Ez—a combination of vanilla and smug vanity. If a peacock could drive, this was the car it would pick. Lock's leather jacket was draped over me even though the car was warm and I had my own jacket on. Ezra was curled up, asleep, in the back seat. All the shifting between forms had worn him out. I peeked over the collar of Lock's jacket and saw the telltale fluorescents of a minimart.

Had I felt like my normal not-exactly-perky-but-at-least-healthy self, I would have hopped out of my seat and gone in search of Lock. As I felt now, it was pretty much all I could do to keep my eyes open. The world was still a bit wobbly. I'd overdone it. Hello, firebug hangover.

I had a stash of electrolyte pills, and I tried to get them, but my hands were shaking too hard to even open my pocket. Stupid buttons. Note to self—get a jacket with Velcro. After the night we had, I wasn't even sure I could wake Ezra, and if Lock hadn't been around for me to rely on, I could have been in some serious trouble, all because I couldn't manage a damn button. But I did have Lock. So I nestled farther under his jacket and waited for him.

With the jacket up over my nose, Lock's smell overpowered Ezra's. He'd had this leather jacket as long as I'd known him, and his scent had really seeped into it. If Ez smelled like vanilla and smugness, Lock smelled like green things and warm days. And sweat. I couldn't smell deodorant—he used some natural unscented hippie crap. So yeah, sweat, but not bad. Not like a locker room or anything. No, Lock's scent reminded me of spring buds and the way the earth smells when it just starts to get warm. Lock smelled like promise. I found it comforting—which, when I stopped to think about it, made me uncomfortable.

Moments later, Lock pushed open the minimart door with his back, his arms laden with bags. He looked singed and haggard.

Bags stashed in the trunk, he slid into the front seat.

"You look like an extra from *Escape from New York* or something," I said, my throat scratchy from breathing so much smoke at the Inferno.

"You look worse." He popped the lid off a generic sports drink, apparently feeling that the electrolytes in my pills were not enough, and glared at me. "Now is not the time for idle jaw flappery."

Since his fingers weren't shaking, he had no problem digging a few of the electrolyte capsules out of my pocket and popping them into my mouth. He held the bottle so I could drink and not spill all over myself as I washed them down.

147

Once he was satisfied that I'd managed to get enough of the liquid in me, he started the car and drove to a different gas station. After filling up our tank, he came out with the keys to the bathroom and dragged me in with him. We left Ezra asleep in the car. His clothes had been put on postbattle, so they weren't burned, torn, and wrinkled like mine and Lock's. And they were, I'd noticed jealously, completely dry.

"Romantic," I said as Lock flicked on the lights and bolted the bathroom door. "I was kinda hoping for dinner first."

"Please, even if I took you on a date in a gas station bathroom, it would still be the best date you've ever had," he said as he started digging through one of the bags he'd brought with him. He was joking, probably to distract me, but unfortunately he was probably right.

"Ryan once took me to—"

"*Ehhhh*," he said, making a harsh buzzer sound. "You started that sentence with 'Ryan,' and therefore I already know that the date wouldn't live up to one with me. That's not arrogance, it's fact. Here." He pulled out a bright yellow T-shirt and threw it at me. I unrolled it, finding a few rows of bold text that read IF YOU ARE WHAT YOU EAT, I MUST BE FAST, CHEAP & EASY.

"Classy. Are we picking up souvenirs?"

Lock took off his own shirt and tossed it in the trash. "As you've pointed out, we look like hell. If we get pulled over by the cops, they're going to ask questions. I can't do anything about the fact that we smell like the main course at a poorly handled luau, but we can at least ditch the charred clothing and make ourselves semi-passable."

My fuzzy brain managed to grasp this logic. I nodded and tried to shrug out of my jacket. I wasn't very successful. Lock helped me out of it and then out of my shirt with a gentlemanly efficiency, or as gentlemanly as he could manage. He only wiggled his eyebrows at me once. For Lock that was remarkable restraint.

"Any extra supplies and clothes we had stashed in my car are gone, and we can't go back to my apartment, so gas station fare is all we've got." There were no paper towels, of course, so he wet the mess that was my old shirt and used it to clean off my face. His movements were quick and capable, but I could tell he was trying to be as gentle as he could.

I wasn't able to stand very well on my own yet, so Lock held me with one arm while helping me shuck off my burnt jeans and boots with the other. "You're pretty skilled at this, Casanova."

"I told you I could make a gas station bathroom the place to be, and I'm not even trying. Think of what I could do if I actually set my mind to it."

I grinned at him. "Yeah, some candles, a little mood music . . ."

He stared at me for a moment like he wasn't quite sure how to respond, and in the silence I realized how close he was, and how little I was wearing. Outside, an engine roared and the weird spell broke. My cheeks flushed and I looked at my socks, the only thing between me and the disgusting floor.

"Reminds me a little bit of the day we met. Wasn't I taking off your wet pants then, too? Apparently we're not making any progress in life." Lock leaned away, balling up my jeans and tossing them in the trash but keeping one arm tight around me. "So of course I'm getting good at this—practice makes perfect. I mean, c'mon, Aves, first roofies, now this. If I didn't know any better, I'd say you were making a pass at me."

"Yeah, well, I wanted to play hard to get. And how would me being roofied be a pass at you?"

He grunted and used his free hand to pull out a pair of the ugliest sweats I've ever seen, and that was saying something. They were a sickly pastel green and they had GOT CLAMS? tastefully printed on the back, in an outline of the state of Massachusetts. Nice.

"I think I'd rather just stay in my underpants. Got clams? Really?"

"The condition this bathroom is in, I'd be more worried about crabs."

"Is that supposed to reassure me or make things worse?"

"Both. Look, gas stations aren't generally known for their haute couture. It was the best I could do, though after seeing your underwear, I'm not sure your fashion opinions are valid."

"What, a girl can't wear Incredible Hulk Underoos?" I stuck a foot into the hideous sweats. "Hulk smash, Lock. Hulk smash."

"Only you would wear underwear with a catchphrase. What do you say when you wear the Spider-Man pair?"

I grinned. "My spidey sense is tingling."

He looked up at me, smirking. "Fantastic Four?"

"Flame on," I said. "Those are my favorite, obviously." Growing up, I had a big interest in Johnny Storm. He was the closest thing to a media-based firebug role model I could get. I used to think that if he could be a firebug and a hero, maybe I could be one too. That particular dream had gone poof, but I still had a soft spot for him.

"I figured," Lock said, pulling the sweats up all the way. "At least it wasn't Clobberin' Time." He picked me up at the waist and set me on the bathroom counter so he could help me get my boots back on more easily. Combat boots and gas station T-shirt and sweats. Oh, if Brittany could see me now.

Lock leaned back and took a good look at me. Once I passed inspection, he started on himself. I tried my best not to admire my friend as he stripped to his skivvies, but I mean, honestly, he spends a lot of time in the gym. He's not disgustingly overdeveloped, but he was, for lack of a better word, *defined.* It would be unkind not to admire something he obviously put so much effort into. I mean, when someone works hard, it's polite to acknowledge that, right? It's just good manners.

His gas station ensemble was better than mine, as it wasn't a violent yellow and pastel green. His shirt was an understated gray, though the lettering was no less saucy. I NEED SOMEONE *REALLY* BAD—ARE YOU REALLY BAD? was etched in black lettering across Lock's chest. He got off light on the sweats, too. They were black with an embroidered lobster on the leg.

"You sure they didn't have those in my size?"

"Best I could do, Aves."

I leaned my head against the questionable tile and waited for Lock to be done. "Why didn't we just do this at the last place?"

"Because I walked in there looking like an arson victim, and sometimes people call the cops on people who look the way we do. The guy who gave me the bathroom key here didn't even look up from his comic book, which means we have a few minutes to fix our appearance. I figured, you know, better safe than sorry."

"That makes sense." I closed my eyes.

"Huh-uh, none of that." I felt Lock take my arm and pull

151

me to my feet. "Just make it back into the car, and then you can go right back into nighty-night land." He helped me walk to the car and into my seat, brushing my hands away so he could fasten my seat belt. Then he tucked his jacket back around me and ordered me to rest. Sometimes I appreciate Lock's mother-hen tendencies, even if I don't tell him that.

WHEN I woke up again, we were parked at the end of a long dirt driveway, the driver's seat empty. The engine was ticking and the interior of the car still toasty, so we hadn't been parked long. Lock was just climbing back into the car, letting in a gust of cold air with him.

"Summer home," he said. "It's empty. I checked."

"You just happened upon this?" I said groggily.

"Looked it up online on one of those rental sites." He turned the car back on and eased it up the driveway, pulling into the carport so it would look like we belonged. Lock roused Ezra with a gentle poke, followed by a less gentle one.

"Wake up, sunshine. We need your skills."

"Which ones?" Ez mumbled. "My charm? My devastating good looks?"

"All of those, but mostly your ability to break into a house."

"Ah."

Ez unfolded himself slowly, and I could tell he was stiff and sore. But he climbed out of the car and disappeared. Predawn was already upon us. What a long-ass night. I pulled out my phone, dropping it as I did. Even with the nap, I was tired and my brain felt thick. Lock saved the phone from the floor and held it out to me.

"Can you call Cade?" I asked. He dialed the number and

held the phone up to my ear so I could stay snuggled under his jacket. It went to voice mail. The message I left was short: "We're safe for now. You're not. Call me."

When I was done, Lock used my phone to text Duncan. I stretched so I could see the message. *Contract on you. We're seeking cover for now. Get some eyes on Cade?* Then we sat and waited for Ez.

It took Ezra maybe five minutes to break in, but that was much longer than usual, which made me worry. Maybe he was still tired, or maybe it was something else. Lock got us all into the house along with the bags of supplies from the gas station. We sat at a small, battered kitchen table while Lock disappeared into the rest of the house and Ezra and I dug out some snacks. It was dark and cold, and the kitchen was a faded pastel nightmare, but at least there were tiny chocolate donuts. I drank some more sports drink and popped a few more electrolyte pills and began to feel like myself again.

"Where did our forest-loving friend flit off to?" Ezra asked, swiping a donut.

"He's probably doing what he can to make things a little more comfortable," I said. "This is a summer cabin, so it's most likely been winterized. Water turned off. Maybe power."

"He's like a punk-rock mama bear. I love it." He stole the last donut. "Let's face it. Someone has to keep us from falling apart."

The lights came on, and a few seconds later Lock's footsteps thumped up from the basement. "We've got power and water. Luckily they didn't shut things off completely." He looked weary as he rested against the cabinets, dark circles under his eyes. Lock had probably driven for hours before, exhausted, he'd been forced to pull over and find this place. We shouldn't have stopped, but then again, we hadn't had much choice. It's not like I was in a position to take my turn at the wheel, and neither was Ez. My mind flashed to the giant trees Lock had grown last night. He probably wasn't in great shape either.

He rubbed a hand over his face. "Woodstove for heat. I'll get some wood from the pile on the side of the house, but after that I'm afraid it's up to you, Aves. I know you're tired, but . . ."

I shrugged. "A little fire like that isn't going to kill me." We left Ez at the table and went to work. Lock filled the stove with logs, stacking the rest off to the side. He didn't bother with kindling or paper. I lit it up, jump-starting it until it was blazing merrily on its own.

The room was just beginning to get cozy when Ezra joined us. Lock patted Ez's back, and though Ez tried to cover it, we both saw him wince. Without a word, Lock rolled up Ezra's shirt. Like every other part of him, Ezra's back is usually something fit for an art exhibit. Not now. It was lumpy and misshapen. I ran a finger lightly over one protrusion, and Ez's eye twitched.

"What happened?"

I knew that tone in Lock's voice. I caused it, more often than not. Punk-rock mama bear in full effect.

"I had to drop and roll in the pool. Lots of glass and things, and I guess a few cut deeper than I thought."

"And your body healed over them?" Lock asked. Ezra nodded.

Lock released Ezra's shirt. "I'll see what I can dig up. We'd better go back in the kitchen." The linoleum floor would be easier to clean.

154

Lock found a razor blade in the toolbox, but not much in the way of medical supplies in the house. No bandages, and only an expired bottle of hydrogen peroxide. We didn't need much, not with Ezra's healing ability, but it wouldn't do to have him bleed all over the place either. Once his shirt was off, Lock tucked a towel into the back of Ez's pants to catch anything that dripped. Then we went to work, Lock with the razor, me with the peroxide and a smaller rag.

Lock placed his hand on Ezra's back, the blade hovering just below the biggest lump. "Sorry," he said. And then he cut.

Ezra let out a sharp hiss. It turned into a shout when Lock pressed gently down next to the glass until it slid out of Ezra's body. Then I poured peroxide and dabbed at the gash with a rag. It took only a few seconds maybe, but they felt like long glimpses into forever. I counted the other distorted shapes on my friend's back. Eight. I hoped they all came out that easily.

They didn't. The last one was a chunk of wood that had broken into large pieces. Ez's grip on the countertop was white-knuckled as Lock pulled them out, but he was quiet. Lock caught my eye and nodded. We were done. Even though a few of the gashes were deep, we wouldn't bother to stitch them. Weres heal too fast to bother. I had to place a hand on Ezra's cheek to rouse him from whatever self-induced trance he was in. Lock placed the razor blade carefully on the counter right before he turned and walked out the back door, letting it close softly. Lock was not a door slammer. That was usually my role. I curled one arm around Ezra, not caring if he bled all over my gas station T-shirt.

"He just needs a minute. Tonight was hard for him." Says the guy covered in gashes and fresh blood. "I don't know if you've realized this, but between the two of us, we're kind of a hot mess. Emphasis on the hot." He gave me a ghost of his usual grin. "It's difficult for him to watch."

As I stared at the door and thought about all the messes Lock had cleaned up and how many times he'd kept our act together, I had to agree with Ezra. We were a hot mess.

Ezra kissed my forehead and unwound himself from me. "I'm taking first shower."

The bathroom was only a short jaunt down the hallway from the living room. I sat in front of the fire and looked at the dried blood on my hands, going over the night in my head. I heard the shower start. Normally Ez sang in the shower. Not this time.

"Ava?" Ezra's voice was muffled by the door and all the noise from the water.

Steam billowed as I opened the bathroom door and turned on the fan. "Don't tell me that, even wounded and demoralized, you're going to try to invite me into your shower." I expected my friend to peek out, a lascivious grin in place. Instead, Ez's hand popped out from behind the curtain, the trembling fingers gripping an already bloodstained washcloth.

"I can't reach my back."

It was his voice that really punched me in the gut. Impromptu surgery in the kitchen? No problem. But Ezra's shaking voice? I was used to Ez sounding like a lot of things—cocky, brash, sly, arrogant—but never, in the entire tenure of our friendship, had I heard him sound *small*. I stripped out of my clothing and grabbed the washcloth. The shower wasn't huge, but luckily it wasn't tiny, either. The wounds were already looking knit together, the skin still pink and raw. Most of the blood was gone off Ezra's back. The water had done the work, really. But the problem was, he could still feel the weight of it there. Until someone washed him and double-checked, Ez would feel dirty. So I lathered up the washcloth in soap that smelled like oranges and spice, and I scrubbed the hell out of his back. Then I grabbed the cheap shampoo that had been left behind by the owners and set to work on his hair. He had to lean back so I could reach. While foxes don't have packs like wolves do, they aren't entirely solitary, either. Mates, family— they groom each other. Ezra's family was no different. They might squabble like a bunch of spoiled brats sometimes, but if anything happens, they circle the wagons and anything not inside that circle gets destroyed. Besides, were-creature or not, there's something soothing and reassuring about someone else taking care of you.

I pretended to not notice the slight jerk of Ezra's shoulders as he cried. Until he turned around and buried his face in the crook of my neck. Then I held him until he pulled away.

"If anyone asks about this later, tell them I made a hell of a pass at you," he said. "I have a reputation to protect."

"Of course. Now rinse that shampoo out of your hair and do me." I handed him the washcloth.

The leering grin that spread across his face lit him up from inside, and my old friend was back. "I'm going to tell everyone you said that."

"I meant wash my back, you perv."

"Sure you did."

———

I WAS TUCKED under a light quilt that smelled like cedar, probably from the trunk it had been stored in. Someone had shoved a chair under the knob of the flimsy door as a last-ditch precaution. Lock was passed out next to me on the bed; Ezra was on the other side of him. They hadn't even made it under the covers. Even as he slept, Lock's face looked pinched and worried, dark circles under his eyes.

I slipped out of bed slowly, trying not to wake my friends. They barely stirred when I put the quilt over them. After chugging some water, I dug my cell phone out of my pocket. The battery was almost dead. No messages. Not from Cade, not from Ryan. Not even a mocking one from Brittany.

I called home, and when I didn't get an answer, I tried Cade at work. I was hoping Glen was working instead of Sylvie. No such luck.

Glen was an older retired gentleman who filled in at the shop occasionally and took his pay in paperbacks. I was hoping for him because he'd be easier to handle than Sylvie. Sylvie is my friend, and she would want to talk, and right now I desperately needed to hear Cade's voice and know that he was okay. So naturally it was Sylvie who greeted me with a chirpy "hello" and then immediately asked if Lock was with me.

I hadn't actually caught her doing it, but I'm pretty sure she named all her gaming avatars "Mrs. Sylvia Lock." (Yes, I know, it should be his last name, but Sylvie doesn't know it's Treadwell. Lock generally goes by one name, like Cher.) Actually, she was probably a hyphen type of girl—Mrs. Sylvia Martin-Lock. Maybe she'd just give him her last name—Mr. Lock Martin had a good ring to it. It made him sound like a brand of boot.

As long as Sylvie didn't teeter into obsession and show up with an I ♥ LOCK tattoo on her chest, I was okay with her crush.

"You are so lucky to be traveling with that hotness all the time."

"Ezra?" I asked, pretending I didn't know what she meant.

"No way. Ezra is one hundred percent dreamy, but he's totally a ramblin' man. If you want a whirlwind romance, he's your guy, so long as you don't expect him to be there the next day. But I bet Lock would write poetry and hold doors open. He'd stay home with the kids while I get my PhD, probably in one of the sciences. I haven't picked my major yet, but he would be supportive during the process. Progressive, but totally a gentleman."

"Wow, you really have this planned. Is Cade around?"

"*Yeaaaah*, he is."

"I don't like the way you dragged that out. He's mad at me, isn't he? Has he said 'I told her so' at all today?"

"I think he feels that it didn't need to be said, considering the situation. Or maybe he's been saving it for when you called to check in."

I searched through the bags on the counter to see if there were any donuts left. None. Damn it. "Please. You don't even know the situation."

"No, but I know you and Cade, and I'm pretty sure the setup was him giving you advice and you ignoring it and nose-diving outstandingly."

"Naturally."

"So how does my boyfriend look today? Rumpled bed head? You know that just-tousled-enough look with sleepy eyes..." She actually sighed. I kid you not—an honest-to-goodness he's-so-dreamy *sigh*. Gross.

"Earth to Sylvie. Come down from your strange planet and get Cade for me." Though I couldn't see her, I knew she was scrunching her cute nose at me. Everything about Sylvie was cute. She was just one of those girls. I bet even when she vomited, it was adorable. It probably came out rainbow and smelled like sunshine. If it didn't already, she could figure out the chemical compounds to make it happen.

"You wish you could live on my planet," she said. "It's only terraformed for extremely awesome alien species though."

"Yes, I do wish I could live there. Boss-man, please."

"Fine, I'll get him. He's in the back room pouting. What did you do? He only pouts like this when you did something. Stop making him sad, Ava! I hate it when he's sad. I tried to show him pictures of kittens on the Internet, but he said that didn't work for him, so I tried to switch to otters, because c'mon, *otters*, they're like the kittens of the sea, but he just looked at me like I was a crazy person, so I showed him my list—"

"List?" Sometimes Sylvie talks so fast, there aren't any spaces between her words.

"The one where I compare kittens and otters. It's a good list. There are illustrations and infographics."

"Sylvie. Cade, please."

"I wouldn't talk to him if I were you," she said in a little singsong voice. "You are in danger of being trampled like a teeny Asian person underneath the rampaging feet of *Grouchasaurus rex*.

"Sylvie."

"It's your funeral," she said, handing the phone over. In the background, I could still hear her yelling. "Remember, Grouchasaurs have poor vision and minimal turning capacity! I recommend running in a serpentine pattern!"

Cade grunted into the phone. The grunt might have been the word *hello*. I'm not sure. "I hear you're on the rampage, Bosszilla," I said.

He grunted. "Sylvie exaggerates."

It was so good to hear his voice, I almost cried. "Yeah. I left you a message. You didn't call me back."

"Was it on my cell? You know the cabin can be kind of a dead zone. Sometimes I get bars, sometimes I don't. Let me check." There was a pause, and I could almost see him unearthing things from his pockets. "Ah. There it is—a message." The phone went quiet for a moment. "I'm not going to want to listen to the message, am I?"

"Probably not."

Cade is not a yeller. When I mess up, he likes to take his time and think it through before he punishes me. We've been through the process many, many, many times. This might seem like a soft approach, but by the time Cade gets around to talking to me, I usually feel pretty crappy about whatever it was I did and I'm also ready to listen to what he has to say by then. Sometimes I think it might actually be less painful if he'd just let loose and scream.

Not that I didn't yell at him sometimes, but I tried not to, and honestly it was pretty hard to get mad at Cade. His criticisms were usually well thought out and difficult to argue with. Or there were times like this, when I was so grateful to be talking to him that I wouldn't have cared if he *was* screaming the whole time.

So I went over the night, telling him what had happened, smoothing over some of the more embarrassing points. He'd probably guess the embarrassing bits anyway. At least I knew he wouldn't interrupt me until I was finished.

"Duncan's okay?"

"As far as I know. I don't think she's ready to confront him on her own."

The line went quiet while Cade thought over what I'd said. "Why'd you eat the appetizers? You don't eat anything at the Inferno that wasn't handed to you by Lock or Ezra."

"Ryan made a big fuss."

"Why?"

"I honestly can't tell you why boys do anything."

"Then tell me why you caved."

I thought for a moment. "I felt bad. We'd been arguing, the evening was a disaster, and he was already sensitive about Lock and Ezra. It seemed to mean a lot to him, so I ate one. Why?"

"What happened after you ate it?"

I shrugged, then realized he couldn't see that. "I got thirsty?"

"Exactly," Cade said. "They were spicy. You drank whatever you were given next, and you were even less likely to ask questions about that because your mouth was on fire. If it tasted weird, you would just dismiss it because your sense of taste would be off."

Cade's logic was dead on, as usual. In retrospect, I'd been incredibly stupid. I knew better than to accept food at a Coterie establishment unless it came from someone I trusted. It should have passed directly from Lock's or Ezra's hands to mine before I took a bite. I should have turned down those appetizers.

"But how would they know I was going to eat them? It's not like I ordered them."

"But Ryan did," Cade said. "And he guilted you into eating one. Then he handed you his drink. He took you to the Inferno in the first place and then made sure you didn't leave."

I hadn't thought it was possible to feel worse than I already did. You'd think by then I'd have known I could always feel worse. "You can't be saying what I think you're saying." My gut felt leaden, and I worried for a second that the donuts from earlier were going to make an encore performance.

"But he's human," I said. "Normal. How would he even . . . why would he?"

"I'm human," Cade said. "And yet I know all about the Coterie. How do you know he doesn't? How do you even know he's human? Do you really know that much about him besides what he's told you?"

"You think he tricked me?"

"I don't know," Cade said, the connection crackling as he breathed into the phone. "All I know is everything is pointing back to him, and I don't like that one bit. Heaven is a dance club, Ava. I bet drugs are easy to come by. I don't know what was planned, or if anything was planned at all. Maybe he was trying to get back at you because of Lock and Ezra, or maybe he was acting on Venus's orders. We don't know, and I'm not sure it matters. But what would have happened if Lock hadn't gotten there first? Would Ryan have taken you to Venus as an offering?

You were unconscious in a public bathroom. Anything could have happened."

I didn't have an answer for him. I wasn't sure I wanted one.

Cade sighed. "Have you checked on your little friends today?"

I felt my blood chill. I told Cade I'd call him back, but I didn't wait for the response. The text I sent Brittany was short, just asking if they'd made it home okay. It was even polite.

The response I got was not. An image of Ryan appeared on my screen. I couldn't see his face, but I knew Ryan's back. I couldn't see his face because he was being led away by Venus, her arm around him possessively. She probably hadn't even known the picture was taken.

After the image came the text part of the message. *Ryan didn't make it home last night. Who knew he was into mature women?* ☺ *Didn't take him long to forget you, homeschool. Lol.*

My hands burst into flame, and I dropped my phone on the counter. I turned on the faucet by hitting the lever with my elbow, then thrust my hands under the icy-cold running water. The water hissed and steamed, but I felt better doing this than trying to clamp down on my rage. When I'd finally calmed down, I toweled off my hands and texted Brittany back.

I hope you get chlamydia. Lol. ☺

I called Ryan's cell, and it went right to voice mail. Then I called his house. I'd never actually called there before.

The phone rang a few times before someone picked up. "Hello, James residence." A lady's voice, probably his mother. Or sister. An aunt? It could be a maid for all I knew. Did they have a maid?

My pulse started doing hurdles and my palms began to sweat. "Um, hi." I swallowed, trying to get my body to calm the fuck down. Sparks danced around my fingertips, and I shoved them into someone's half-drunk glass of water from last night. "Is, uh, Ryan around?"

"No," she said. "I think he's still in Boston with his friends." Her tone had that you-know-how-boys-can-be kind of air about it. I noticed she didn't say that he was with his girl-friend. I wasn't sure if it was comforting or upsetting that she didn't seem to know about me. Probably a little of both.

"Oh, okay. Thanks." I hung up before she could ask who was calling. I put my phone on the table, afraid the sparks swirling around my hands might damage it. Eyes closed, I took deep breaths, pulling as much air into my lungs as I could, and tried to settle my nerves. When I finally opened my eyes again, the sparks were gone.

I filled the stove with more wood and got a blaze going, trying to burn off my energy in a constructive manner before I called Cade back and melted my phone in the process.

I'd wrapped myself in a blanket by the fire and was doing my best to not dwell on things when I heard a twig snap. It was a small sound, but one that put me in mind of my time with my mom, and traps we set to warn us of intruders. In my mind I saw Benny's face as he looked at the window, and I almost edged back to the broom closet. Except I was too big now. That startled me out of my memory. The hairs on the back of my neck stood at attention, and my body was on full alert. I'd spent too much time living off my gut instinct to ignore it. I bolted upstairs to wake the boys.

The good thing about being a teenage assassin? Your

friends know what you mean when you wake them with one hand pressed over their mouths and a meaningful look in your eye. I pulled my hand away from Lock's face. "How many?" he mouthed. I shrugged. He poked Ezra awake and we relayed the info.

Short of Cade, no one knew me better than Lock and Ez did. Venus hadn't intended for it to happen when she'd put us together, but we'd become a well-oiled machine.

I shoved the chair back under the door as Ezra opened a window. We pulled on boots and jackets and slipped out onto the lower roof. Lock closed the window after we were all out. We sat. We listened. Of the members of the Coterie recovery team—and clearly that's what they were—only one had been left to walk the perimeter of the house. Ezra dropped to the ground. There was a muffled shout from the man as Ezra quickly took care of him. The man's chest was rising and falling while Ez pulled him into the bushes, so I knew he'd live. Lock coaxed a root to curl and twist around our would-be assailant. It wouldn't last forever, but it would slow him down.

Once we were all off the roof, Lock and I worked in tandem to take care of the others. He encouraged some vines to wind their way over the windows while I set fire to all the exits. We didn't even have to discuss it.

I felt bad for the recovery team, I guess, and I definitely felt bad for the owners of the summer home I was burning to the ground, but not enough to actually stop. We got into Ezra's car and sped down the driveway. The fire would go out soon, and if the recovery team was smart, they would probably get out alive. I hoped they would, sort of, but I was hoping for our getaway more.

We drove aimlessly in silence, Lock turning the car this way and that, going more for confusion than distance.

"How did they find us?" I asked finally. "The car?"

"They found us yesterday, too," Lock said. "I shrugged it off because we were still in the Inferno, but now she's found us again. One of us is bugged."

"Then why couldn't she find us after I torched the Inferno?" I asked. "Teams were scouting and couldn't locate us."

"It was a madhouse. Whoever had the tracker probably had their hands full," Lock said.

Ezra turned in the passenger seat so he could see both of us. "Well, all my clothes are from after our little pool party, so it's not me. It's probably not the car, but I guess we should get rid of it anyway." He sighed and ran his hand along the dash. "My poor baby."

"All my stuff is new, except for my jacket and my shoes," Lock said. "I don't think they're the problem, but I can discard them if you guys are worried." Lock's eyes met mine in the rearview mirror. "What about you, Aves? Any clothes the same?"

I thought on it. "My underwear, but we would have seen something if that was bugged, right? My jacket."

"And your boots, right?" The car was silent for a moment before he asked, "Did Ryan give you anything recently? Anything you keep on your person?"

"No," I said. "Everything is . . . wait." I reached up and felt my new earrings, the shooting stars he'd given me. That he'd insisted I wear. I quickly tore them out, not looking at them as my vision blurred and I handed them to Ezra. He didn't even examine them before he threw them out the window. I began

167

to protest, but Ez just looked at me and said, "I don't care if you want to believe he's innocent. I refuse to take the risk."

And I got it, I did. My mouth snapped shut with a click of teeth and we drove for an hour in silence. While my brain used logic to tell me that the boys were right, I mourned those earrings. They were the first present given to me by a boyfriend and they hadn't even made it a week.

The town we stopped in wasn't very big, but it had a small used-clothing place, which was what we needed. I had some cash sewn into the lining of my jacket, but not much, and I wasn't sure when I could get more. The Coterie would be checking our accounts. We bought backpacks and two changes of clothes. The underwear I bought new. I just couldn't quite bring myself to put on someone's used knickers. I didn't want "Got Crabs?" to become my official motto.

That handled, we hit a convenience store. I purchased three use-and-toss cell phones, even though cell service could be anywhere from spotty to nonexistent in that area. I also bought some maps. I knew we wouldn't find any in the Ezramobile. Ez thought the glove compartment was for condoms only.

We stopped at a diner and grabbed breakfast, and I can honestly say it was probably the most depressing breakfast I'd ever had.

Lock tore into a biscuit. He'd ordered biscuits and gravy, which shows just how grave the situation was. If Lock was reaching for comfort food, we were all doomed. "So, now what? Go into hiding? Change our names? Join the circus?"

"The circus?" I reached across the table and stole half his biscuit. Someone had to look out for his health. "That is so passé.

We can do better than that. It's high-class grifting in Rio, or it's nothing." I took a sip of orange juice. "I need to call Cade back. Maybe he can help us with an actual plan. I was about to call him back when they found us."

Lock dug his phone out of his jacket pocket, or what was left of it, anyway. At some point, he must have landed on it. He sighed.

"No, that's good," I said. "In fact, we should have tossed them last night. GPS. I bought us new phones, but I need to contact Cade from a different one. I'd rather not use my burner phone yet."

After some arguing, we piled into the car and headed for the nearest train station. We abandoned Ezra's car a few blocks away. I didn't want any video cameras at the train station catching us ditching the car.

While I wiped it down for prints, Lock found a few pickup trucks to toss our cell phones into. I made him erase all the information first, of course. I wanted to give the Coterie something to chase on the GPS, but I didn't want to give them the phone numbers of our friends.

Lock tried to find trucks with out-of-state plates in hopes that they'd lead the trackers on a merry chase. I silently hoped that no harm would come to the drivers of those trucks. I'd have hated for someone to get hurt because they unwittingly helped us. If it had just been me, I wouldn't have risked it. Unfortunately we weren't just discussing my safety. So: sorry if our cell phones get you in trouble, mysterious truck-driving folk, but I'm a selfish jerk who wants to keep her loved ones alive.

Once Ezra said good-bye to his car, we started walking

toward the train station. We hit an ATM on the way, and we all pulled out our maximum allowable amounts. Since we were leaving this place soon and we wanted to give them a spot to focus on, it wouldn't matter. At least, I was hoping that, with all the precautions we were taking, it wouldn't matter.

I actually managed to find a functioning pay phone to call Cade. I didn't have much time, but then, I didn't need much either.

"Sorry," I said as Cade answered. "We were interrupted before I could call you back."

"You're never, ever, going on a date again."

I could hear the strain in his voice when he made that joke. "That's cool. I was thinking of joining a nunnery. I hear they're all the rage these days." The line went quiet as we both thought the things that were too hard to say on the phone.

"Your grandpa has suggested I close up shop for a few days. I'm thinking he might be right. I'm just going to pack a few things from home and head there."

"Grandpa"? Cade never talked to his parents. "Grandpa" could only mean Duncan, which meant he was headed there and wanted us to go as well but didn't want to say that over the phone. You can never be too paranoid when dealing with Venus.

"Sounds like a plan," I said. "I'll check in later."

"Love you, Rat."

"Love you, too, legal guardian. At least until I'm eighteen. Then it's splitsville."

He huffed into the phone. "You're not as cute as you think you are."

"Even if I'm half as cute as I think I am, I'm still pretty adorable."

"I'm hanging up now."

"That might be for the best."

WE DECIDED to follow Cade's advice. If we could take a train to the coast, then we could catch a bus from there. Once a day there's an old school bus that runs down the coast. Surely we had enough money for that.

At the train station, we used my card to purchase tickets to two drastically different locations. Ezra turned around and hocked those tickets while Lock bought tickets to our real destination in cash. Maybe we were being too paranoid, but history had taught me to take any precaution possible when the Coterie was involved. I remember my mom doing similar things, and she managed to avoid the Coterie for twelve years.

The train left in twenty minutes. When he'd bought the tickets, Lock deliberately chose one that didn't have a long wait time. No reason to sit like cliché duckies if we didn't have to.

We huddled in a corner of the station, our paranoia and overvigilance bloating the minutes until the wait seemed like hours. It was like we had giant bull's-eyes painted on our backs, and everyone who walked by looked like an enemy.

9

NEW FRIENDS

THE TRAIN RIDE was uneventful. We tried to get Ezra to wear a cap or pull his hood up, anything to tone down his pretty. People remember Ezra. It made being on the lam difficult. He finally caved and raised his hood. Since it would do less damage to his hair than a hat, it was the lesser of the two evils in his mind.

We left the train and managed to get a taxi to take us to the bus stop. The bus was old and smelled a bit like feet and desperation—and, yes, desperation has a smell. It's not pleasant. I took a seat next to Lock, Ezra choosing to take up an entire bench in front of us. Lock breathed on the window and fogged it up, using his index finger to draw little hearts and arrows in the moisture.

"You're such a girl."

"I can't help it—I was raised by a bevy of women." He added tiny broken hearts around the arrowed ones. "There, is that better?"

"Yes." I snuggled into his side. "Do you think we're being stupid?"

He wrapped his arm around my shoulders and pulled me closer. "Most people run out of a burning building. It's common sense. But firefighters run back in, because they're brave. And most people would run from the Coterie—that's common sense too."

"We're running back toward it. So are you saying we're brave?"

He sighed. "No, I think we're stupid, but I can't think of anything better." He gave me a squeeze. "You should rest while you can." Before I could protest, he said, "You need it more than I do, and one of us should keep watch. Ezra is already napping, so sleep."

I could tell Lock wasn't going to let me win on this one. Some battles just weren't worth fighting. I shut my eyes. The smell of desperation was even stronger with my eyes closed. I wondered idly if that was because it was coming from me.

WE COULDN'T just take the bus directly to Duncan's. We got within thirty miles, which was the best we could do. I'd napped for a lot of the ride, but the rest of the time was spent in a state of frustration and fear. Even though every inch brought me closer to Cade, it also brought me closer to the worry that he wouldn't be there. I had to keep my hands in my pockets in case I sparked. What I wanted to do was run home and pretend none of this had happened. I desperately needed the sight of the bookshop, or the sound of Sylvie psychoanalyzing the newest arrival of bodice rippers (though she always read them anyway), or even to be on the receiving end of Horatio's disdain.

I wanted to slip back into my life and forget Ryan and the Coterie. I pressed my forehead against the rough weave of the seatback in front of me. Lock nudged my arm, indicating that it was time to get off. The second he stepped off the bus, he started walking—quite resolutely—in the wrong direction. Well, it was the right direction, just not the one I wanted to go in. I jogged to catch up to him.

"I've been thinking maybe I heard wrong. Cade might have been telling us to stay away from Duncan's. We should stop by the shop or something—you know, just to check." Lock didn't slow down. When he grimaced and looked away, I knew he wasn't going to play along with me.

"We're not going home, Ava. We're going to Duncan's."

Loose gravel rolled along the asphalt as I jerked to a stop. "I need—"

"No, Ava," he said, cutting me off. "You *want* to go home." He stopped in front of me, his hands fidgeting in agitation along the straps of the backpack. "But what you need is to go to Duncan's."

"Bullshit."

He cut me off again. "Shut up and listen. You didn't just thumb your nose at Venus last night—you told her off in front of witnesses, then Ezra crushed her new firebug right before you *burned down part of her business*. You turned my car into a fountain of flame, lighting up the entire city, no doubt, which means she had to deal with the human police force. She *hates* that. Then you escaped. As an encore, we slipped away from a recovery team. We got away, Ava. She's probably spitting nails and pissing fury right now." He took a deep breath and softened his voice, which had been growing more tense as he'd talked.

"She can't just let last night slide. If she finds you and gets to do whatever she has planned, you're going to look back with nostalgia at the time she hit you and made you strip." Lock looked out into the trees, over the road, anywhere but my face. "She likes it, Aves. She enjoys making people twist. But more than that, if she doesn't publicly bring us in hand, she'll have a mutiny."

I bit down on any argument I might have had. Sparks popped in the air around me, and I let them. Something had to give, and sparks didn't seem so bad. Lock was right. And I hated it. He grabbed my chin gently and turned my head until I had to look at him. His expression was pity-filled, which just made it worse. "If you go home right now, you're endangering us and your house, and you're delivering yourself right into her hands. Might as well tie a big-ass bow around your waist while you're at it."

Frustration and anger are good when you need to throw a fireball at someone's head—emotion is a very powerful fuel. When your best friend is trying to keep you from doing something idiotic, these emotions aren't ideal. If Lock had let go of my face, allowing me to look down, I'd probably have seen flames licking my fingers. I either needed somewhere safe to send the fire or a really quick emotional shift.

Lock did the next best thing—he shoved me into a puddle. A very muddy puddle, and an extremely cold one. There was a crunch as I fell through the thin layer of ice on top of it.

"You asshole!" I shouted. Steam billowed around me as my flames dissipated. I hated to admit it, but despite now being soggy, cold, and muddy, I felt better.

"You were on fire, cupcake. It was the first thing I could think of."

175

"Mom and Dad are fighting!" Ezra sang as he pushed his hood back. "Part of me wants you to kiss and make up, but most of me is hoping for two Christmases."

Lock reached down to pull me up, and I took the opportunity to smear mud down the side of his jacket. He glared at me. I grinned back. Then Lock pulled me to him and kissed me on the cheek.

"You're my favorite," he said before letting me go.

I stomped over to a tree so I could scrape more mud off onto its bark, and so Lock wouldn't see that I was blushing. "Can the sarcasm. It was a shitty thing to do."

"Better than starting a forest fire." He passed me, his strides clipped like he was angry. "And it wasn't sarcasm. We'd better get a move on."

We walked in silence, and I mused on all the stuff Lock had said before our one-sided mud-wrestling match. He was right, of course. I couldn't go home. Everything I loved would be in danger if I did. Venus would have people watching my house, the bookshop, wherever she thought I might go.

The silence was starting to get to me. Fighting with Lock was like fighting with Cade: I hated having either of them mad at me. It wasn't like I had so many friends that I could just ignore him and go hang out with someone else until one of us cooled off. I quickened my step until I caught up with him. Ezra trailed behind, staring up into the tops of trees, looking for birds' nests.

"You're still a jerk," I said, lacing my arm through Lock's. "But I need to talk to you, so can we call a truce?"

"That is quite possibly the worst apology I've ever heard."

"That's because it wasn't one. For the sake of time can we just skip to the end where neither of us apologizes, or possibly both of us do, and move on to the part where we're talking to each other again?"

Lock ran a hand through his hair and closed his eyes. I knew that look—it was the look of a man battling for patience. I was very familiar with it. "You can't always just skip to the end, Aves. Sometimes you have to actually do the hard stuff."

"Yeah. Bo-ring."

I could almost see Lock counting to ten. "Okay, fine," he said. "For now."

"What are we going to do after Duncan's?"

"I don't know yet, but we need some answers, and Venus isn't exactly going to be forthcoming. Duncan must know why she wants him dead so badly. If we knew what was driving this, maybe we could figure out our next step. Get ahead of the game. Maybe we can even get him on our side. We need some backup, Aves. This on-the-lam thing is going to work for only so long." He kicked a rock. "Besides, that's all I can come up with. I'm tired, I'm cold, I'm hungry, and last night Ezra started licking me in his sleep. I think it's a grooming thing, but it's creepy and it can't be hygienic."

"Better you than me," I said, giving Ezra the side eye.

Shortly after that, we hitched a ride in a pickup truck. We didn't have a car and couldn't rent one without ID and—let's be honest here—if there was any sort of hinky business, I could set the truck on fire. If that didn't work, well, then I could light the driver up brighter than the Vegas strip.

We gave the driver gas money and rode in the covered

bed of his truck. The front seat was full of the biggest dog I'd ever seen, and he didn't like Ezra one bit. The ride was cold, but uneventful, for which I was grateful.

The driver let us off on the side of the road about two miles from where Duncan lived. We hitched up our backpacks and started walking through the woods. There was a bumpy country road about a quarter of a mile up that would have saved us a lot of time in the long run, but we didn't want to broadcast our presence.

Duncan kept his land on the natural side, which meant carving our way through bushes and passing between the trunks of overgrown pines and oaks. The sun was starting to edge farther down on the horizon, and the temperature was dropping. Little green buds peeked at me from branches. It wouldn't be cold for much longer.

Lock was muttering softly to himself—I couldn't catch much of it beyond getting the general idea that he didn't like being there.

"I thought you would enjoy being out in the trees," I said with a smirk. "Back among your tribe, so to speak."

He glared at me. "They're not my tribe. I like the city. It's quiet."

"You know, most people go to the country for the quiet."

He shook his head as he helped me over a fallen log. "I can block out city noise, but not the sounds here. The trees haven't seen someone like me in a while, and they all want to chat."

"So? They're just being friendly."

Lock made a scoffing noise. "Yeah, you try talking to a tree sometime and see how scintillating you find the conversation."

"I start F-I-R-E-S, remember? Trees aren't exactly lining up to be my pen pals."

Lock slowed and cast his eyes up at the branches. "About that—I'd keep your powers to yourself here. There's an old feel to these trees, and I get the idea that there's a lot out here we can't see. If the Coterie wasn't looking for us, I'd head for the road, but things being the way they are . . ."

I nodded, unhitching myself from a branch that had snagged my jacket. "Best take our chances with the unknown danger. I get it."

What with the terrain and all, we weren't making very good time. Though it was better than being stuck on a bus, I could still feel the frustration building in my chest. I was afraid this whole trip might come to nothing. What if Duncan couldn't help us and we'd just wasted valuable time? Worse, what if Cade wasn't there? What if Venus had gotten to him? My chest tightened.

I wondered, as we walked, if it was possible that Ryan had really sold me out. Had he been in league with Venus all along? I couldn't quite see it, but then again, when I put all the puzzle pieces together, the only picture I could make out was that he was a traitor. No matter what the truth was, I wouldn't be happy with it.

Lock's arm shot out, interrupting my vision of Ryan feeding Venus strawberries while I sat on the sidelines dressed as a nun. Lock kept his arm against me as he held a finger to his lips and then tapped his ear. Obviously, he'd heard something. I think Lock was really enjoying the cloak-and-dagger part of our adventure. Not that he wasn't taking things seriously, but still.

Ez sniffed the air but couldn't seem to make anything out. "It just smells like food," he whispered.

"Food? Like what, fried chicken?" I whispered back. He shrugged.

I didn't hear anything beyond an owl and a few other evening noises. But Lock was a nature spirit—well, half nature spirit, and if he gave me advice in the woods, I was damn well going to take it.

He frowned, and I could tell he didn't hear anything anymore either. Whatever had stopped him wasn't repeating itself. Finally he shrugged and we started to move again, but stepping quietly this time. We didn't have to caution Ez. He moved through the woods like a ghost.

That's when we saw them.

They melted out of the trees, slow and fluid like shadow. And they were everywhere. We'd been surrounded and we hadn't even known it. Men and women, all dressed in biker-chic leather and denim. Despite their obvious affinity with the forest, they looked out of place.

We bolted. Even though we knew we were surrounded, we hoped to catch them off guard long enough to get away. But everywhere we ran, new faces appeared—popping out from behind trees and bushes and out of the darkness. Lock threw a punch, but he missed. That's when the rangy biker he'd swung at tackled him and took him to the ground. No one else piled on, apparently thinking that the lanky guy could handle things on his own.

Four of them surrounded Ezra, who was yipping and bouncing on his toes. If he'd had a tail in human form, it would have been twitching in anticipation. Whatever these people were, Ez found them very entertaining, but they were keeping their distance and not engaging him. That didn't stop him from hopping about and enjoying the game.

I guess they expected me to stand on the sidelines as well, patiently waiting for the outcome. And, I don't know, biting my nails or crying into my skirts or wringing my hands or something. Boy, were they wrong. I kicked Lock's attacker in the ribs, knocking him off of my friend. I pulled Lock up. Even in the low light, I could see bruises forming on his cheek and a smear of blood around his mouth. I felt the anger boiling up from my gut. I put myself in front of Lock, glared at our attackers, and lit a fireball about the size of a grapefruit between my hands. The trees weren't going to like it, but since they weren't the immediate threat, they'd have to suck it up.

The rangy one jumped back with a hiss, but one of the other bikers pushed forward and inspected the flame, a look of careful consideration on his bearded face. He was shorter than his lean friend, built wide more than anything. As he leaned close to the fireball, I could see a fine tracery of scars on his neck, curling up into his stubble and behind his ears. Ouch.

The rest of the group came closer, either keeping their eyes on us or watching the man in front of me intently. Obviously, he was in charge. He leaned back from the ball and turned his gaze on me.

"I think it's time to state your business," he said. His tone was conversational, light, but I knew better than to relax. Just because he sounded friendly didn't mean he was.

"I don't see how my business is any of yours," I said. Lock put a hand on my hip and squeezed gently, telling me to be careful.

But the big man wasn't offended. He simply nodded and said, "Well, you're cutting across Duncan's lands, so that makes it our business." He raised one of his meaty hands and scratched his beard. "So let me rephrase—you have thirty seconds to convince me that you're the people we're out here to meet so I don't break your necks and dig a shallow hole."

The rangy one leaned in to add, "Or we can always string you and your boyfriends up from the trees. We'll make it bloody. A nice warning to any other trespassers."

"No need to be melodramatic, Sid. I think they understand things fine, don'tcha, girly?"

"Yeah," I said, looking closely at the group, "I think I do." I let the ball dim down to the size of a tennis ball. "We're here to see Duncan. It's a friendly visit, I promise. He knows me—take a photo with your phone and send it to him. Tell him Ava's here to have a chat about Venus." I grinned at him, and my fireball flared briefly. "And if you call me 'girly' again, I'll melt your boots to your feet."

The leader nodded, and one of the group peeled off to make a call after taking several photos of us with his phone. He talked to someone—I assumed Duncan—for several minutes before I was handed the phone and made to answer several questions Duncan thought only I would know. It was the only way to make sure. Someone could put on a ward to look like me, but they wouldn't be able to tell Duncan about the time when I was nine and he took me to a carnival and I ate so much junk food that I threw up. Once I'd gotten to the part about how my vomit was fluorescent pink because of the cotton candy, Duncan told me I could hand the phone back. The guy I gave it to listened and did some nodding before he finally hung up.

After he signaled to his boss, the group's demeanor changed and the big man offered his hand. I hesitated, then realized that if he wanted to beat me up, he could do it whether I shook his hand or not, so I took it after I extinguished my fireball.

"Just doing my job, you understand."

"Of course," Lock said smoothly. "But do you think you could take us to the house now? I'd hate to keep bleeding all over Duncan's nice forest."

The big guy chuckled. "C'mon." He turned and gave orders for the majority of the group to stay behind. They were gone in an instant, seeping back into the trees like they'd never been there. Sid and a few others remained, our guards until we got into the house. Probably after that, too.

Lock grabbed my arm, and our eyes met. I could tell we were both thinking the same thing. If Duncan wasn't building an army, then what were all these secretive and violent people doing running through his woods?

Sid handed Lock a handkerchief. "No hard feelings, yeah?"

"I think being noble would be easier if the pummeling had been more in my favor."

Sid grinned. "Ain't that always the way?" He bowed and swept his arm out. "Ladies first." We walked toward the house, the big guy leading the way. I guess it was only ladies first up to a point.

It turned out that Sid was quite talkative and cheerful now that he was done threatening us. I learned that I should call the big guy Les, which Sid informed us was short for Lesley—a family name—but that if we used the full name, someone would probably punch our teeth out, and that someone was probably Les. I was smart enough not to snicker, and Lock was too busy trying to stop bleeding to do so. Ezra was still bouncing around, our captors giving him a wide berth. He was grinning like a mad thing.

"What is up with you?" I asked.

"Can't say," he said. "You have to guess. This is too good." His grin got even wider, if that was possible.

As we walked, I noticed that our guards all had the same patch on the backs of their jackets or vests—a cartoon jackrabbit that looked like he'd seen a few bar brawls. By the look of the grin and the cigar butt jutting out of his mouth, he seemed to have enjoyed them.

"Interesting mascot. Don't bikers usually favor things like eagles or stallions or something? You know, tough stuff?"

Les snorted. "You ever try to catch a wild hare?"

I shook my head.

"They're fast, they're wily, and if you manage to get a hold of one, it will scratch you to bits."

Sid leaned in with a smile. "I would think you'd appreciate small, fierce creatures."

"I'm not small," I said with a glare.

"You're smaller than me," he said.

I kept my mouth shut after that.

DUNCAN lived in a cabin on Maine's rocky coast. I saw a few motorcycles huddled under the carport next to Duncan's ancient 4×4 and an old black van. I counted only a handful of bikes, so I guessed that most of his entourage had set up camp elsewhere on the grounds.

Duncan greeted me at the door with a big hug and the offer of a hot meal. I accepted both. Though Duncan looked like a woodland Santa, there was a presence about him—not a feeling of power exactly, just, well, when he walked into a room you felt it. Almost a sense of command. I don't know how to explain it. Whatever it was, it made me want to tiptoe around him more than anyone else I knew who wasn't Coterie. I didn't actually succumb to the feeling and tiptoe, but it was there. I usually managed to ignore it. I went to change out of my muddy jeans before I sat down to eat. I would like to say that I was ruining clothes faster than I usually did, but that would be pants-on-fire-level fibbing.

When I emerged, Lock and Ezra were sitting at a large table with Les, Duncan, and a tall dark-haired woman. Sid stood loosely behind my friends, but I could see past the nonchalance. One quick move, and he'd spring, I was sure of it.

The woman was sewing, but she had the look of someone who should be sharpening knives and spitting nails. Despite her hard look, she was smiling at us.

"Hope Sid didn't talk you to death," she said, continuing to sew. She paused to push a basket of what turned out to be fresh bread toward us. "He doesn't know when to shut up."

"You're a cruel woman, Ikka, cutting a man to the quick like that."

"I see no man, only my brother." She nudged a tomato-shaped pincushion at him so he could take up another mending project. It looked like a kid's shirt. Though Sid thought he needed to guard us, she clearly thought our threat level was low.

"Ikka?" I asked.

"Short for Veronica," she said, tying off her stitch. "Sid couldn't say my name when he was a kit, only Ikka. It stuck." She shrugged. "Better than Ronnie."

Les grabbed a bowl and dished himself some chili from the stove before joining us. "I would say I think you both talk too much, but I'm afraid of what Ikka would do with that needle."

She started a new stitch, smiling. "I would be more likely to poison your food. Speaking of which, help yourself, guys."

Nothing like the mention of poison to sharpen one's appetite. I got up and took a bowl. I stirred the chili with the metal ladle, noting absently that Ikka's chili was different from Cade's. And that's when I realized something had been bugging me since we walked in the door.

"Duncan, where's Cade?"

10

HEART BURN

"WE'VE BEEN TRAVELING for hours," I said, my throat tightening. I didn't realize that the ladle had turned a molten red until Lock took it with an oven mitt. "He only had to cross town. Where is he?"

"He's not here yet," Duncan said. "I offered him an escort, but he said it was unnecessary. I was about to send out a scouting party when you showed up."

I had to take several deep breaths. Now was the time to concentrate, control, and calm down. I looked around Duncan's cabin, which was big and open beamed, made of a honey-colored wood. Upstairs was a loft where he slept. At least, that's where he used to sleep. I hadn't been out to the cabin in a while. The kitchen held a large, beat-up table—the one we were parked at. There was no real divide between the kitchen and the living room, which held a big fireplace built out of river stones. There was a hallway off the living area where I could see a few doors—probably a bathroom and a guest room or two. All the furniture was worn and the rugs were frayed, but it looked more lived in and homey than run down. It was all I could do not to turn every last stitch and whorl into ash.

I felt sick. Lock took my empty bowl and returned it full of chili, putting one in front of Ezra as well before he sat down with his. It smelled delicious, but I had no desire to eat it. "Duncan, you know why Venus offered me your contract, right?"

"I surely do," he said, leaning back in his chair, resting his folded hands on his gut.

"Because I can get close to you, like I am now. You knew that, but you let me up here anyway. I have an enraged Venus claiming you're building an army, and when I get here, I find one. You've offered us sanctuary, but Cade isn't here. All this smacks of a trap." It's possible that I was feeling a little sensitive after Ryan's betrayal, but I couldn't ignore the coincidences.

In the span of a breath, the guards in the room changed. Just a subtle shift of their bodies—a tightening of muscle, a knife in Sid's hand where there'd been none.

"Down, boy," Lock said, holding up his hands. "No need to be jumpy."

Ezra snickered but just shook his head when I stared at him. Well, at least someone was having fun.

In a flash the knife was at Lock's throat. "That supposed to be funny?"

Lock looked at him in bemusement, but I could see the sweat beading on his brow. "No. Did it come out funny?"

Les gave the table an odd thump with his fist. "Take a breather, Sid. He meant no offense." Sid gave a little bob, the knife disappeared, and just as quickly he slipped outside.

"What did I say?" Lock asked. "I'd rather not say it again, whatever it was."

"Some of the young bucks are more sensitive than others. That might lead them to . . . overcompensate on occasion."

Ikka snorted. "On occasion?"

"Bucks?" I asked, putting my hands to my head and making little antlers.

Lock slid down in his chair, smacking his forehead at the same time. He has a tendency toward the melodramatic. "Stupid, stupid, stupid. Their jackets!"

I looked at Les's leather vest. I certainly didn't notice anything spectacular about it. "They're . . . cows?" I ventured.

Now it was Lock's turn to put his hands up by his head, only instead of antlers, he made little rabbit ears.

Ezra made little whiskers with his fingers. Then he laughed so hard, tears shone in his eyes.

I stared at Les and Ikka, my mouth all but hanging open. "You guys are *bunnies*? But . . . you look so badass."

"Hares," they both corrected automatically.

"Oh, man," Lock said, sliding even deeper into his chair. "That's even worse. Were-hares. It *rhymes*. I thought were-bears had it rough, but no one's going to laugh at someone who turns into a grizzly." He shook his head. "You're wrong—a knife isn't overcompensating. If I was Sid, I'd carry a damn machete everywhere I went."

"Please," I said, pushing my bowl away. "You're part tree. So let's not start throwing stones." I'd never heard of were-bunnies before. In fact . . . "Wait, aren't all weres predators? I mean, you always hear of werewolves and stuff, but I've never—"

"Nonsense," Sid said, gliding back in the door. "That's part of the therianthropic conspiracy, isn't it? Putting wolves and bears at the top, like we're nothing. Let me ask you, lady—you ever catch a wild hare with your hands?" He didn't wait for me to shake my head. "You can't. They're too fast. Even if you managed it, they'd scratch and bite. Powerful hind legs, that's what they've got. A five-pound hare can do a lot of damage."

"Oh, leave it, Sid," Ikka said, tying off her thread.

"No," Sid said emphatically. "Look, you think we don't get shit from other weres? Of course we do. They think because we turn into hares that we're going to be gentle and cute." He jabbed the air with his index finger. "There's a difference between domesticated rabbits and *hares*."

"Not to mention that we're half-human," Les said softly. "Everyone always forgets that. Is there a more bloodthirsty predator than humans?" His fingers traced the fine lines on his neck. How did a were get scars, anyway?

"We aren't an army. We needed a place to winter, and Duncan offered us one. As a trade-off, we're acting as extra security." He looked at the three of us. "Which he clearly needs. Security, Ava. Nothing else. We didn't take Cade."

Duncan lit his pipe. "That's enough, I think, children." He gave the pipe a puff as he studied me. "I know you're not here to kill me, Ava, because I know *you*. That's why I offered you sanctuary."

I looked at my hands in my lap. "What if the Coterie had convinced me?"

"That would take some leverage," he said. "It would take Cade. Last I checked, they didn't have him. But you're right, he should be here by now."

Les pulled a phone out of his pocket and handed it to me. My throat tight, I dialed the numbers, only to get voice mail. My stomach fluttered at the sound of Cade's voice telling me to leave a message. What if something had happened to him and this message was the last time I'd hear his voice? I quietly handed the phone back to Les.

"Someone will run you into town," Duncan said. "Just in case."

"That could put them in danger," I said, but I was already putting my jacket back on.

Duncan puffed his pipe. "You're not going to stay. If it was just you and Lock and Ezra, I'd be concerned about your safety, but with backup you should be fine. We need more information; it's as simple as that. Cade isn't answering, so we need to go there and see what's keeping him from the phone and from here."

"Shotgun," Sid said, peeling himself away from the wall.

"What, you're not going to try to drive?" Ikka asked, putting her sewing away.

"You always win on that, so I thought I'd save us both some time and just go for shotgun."

"Aw," Ikka said, tousling her brother's hair. "You're learning."

He batted her hand away. "Let's not leap to conclusions, now." Ezra got up, and Sid shoved him back down. "Not you. You stay."

Ez didn't argue. A sly grin split his face, and he put his elbows on the table, his hands cupping his face. Horatio gets that look sometimes when he's mousing. I was about to argue, but Lock put a hand on my elbow.

"We brought a fox into the rabbit warren," he said. "They want him where they can keep an eye on him. Honestly, I can't say I blame them."

"You'd think they'd want him out."

"We've found," Ikka said, eyeing Ezra, "that it's better to keep trouble in sight. Especially when that trouble is a fox."

Five minutes later, we were bouncing along in Duncan's Jeep. We went to the bookstore first because it was on the way and Cade spent most of his time there. Well, we went to where the bookstore used to be, at any rate.

I stared at the charred ruin. There wasn't much left. It looked like the fire department had at least been able to get to it before the flames spread to other buildings. No doubt all our precautions and sprays had slowed the flames, but even those gave out eventually.

Even though I had no proof that Owen and, ultimately, Venus, were to thank for this mess, it had Coterie written all over it. I'd like to say that I stood there stoically, taking it all in and making a vow of revenge. Everyone wants to believe that they're strong, that they'll take things like this in stride. The truth is, I totally broke down. The bookstore was my safe place. And it was ruined.

One minute I was looking at the building, the next I was a sobbing wreck being held up only by Sid's lucky catch. At first I thought he was Lock. Both smelled like leather, both were strong, though Lock has wider shoulders. And I guess I was really only used to being hugged by three people—Lock, Ezra, and Cade. Sid made soft shushing sounds and stroked my hair.

That's actually what snapped me back into reality. Lock never did that. I heard Sid say, "Not that I mind, but could you

192

take her for a minute?" And then I was transferred into Lock's arms while Sid dropped to the ground and rolled.

"Sorry," I mumbled into Lock's chest. I mentally reached out to Sid and extinguished the sparks.

"It's okay," Sid replied, getting up and patting his jacket. "What's a little smolder between acquaintances?"

"I don't—" My voice broke and I had to start over. "Usually I have better control." I'd been out of it a lot lately. This was the third or fourth time in as many days that I'd lost my handle on my power. Sloppy.

"Where are we?" Ikka asked, casting her eyes around the wreckage.

"Cade's bookstore," I said, leaning back from Lock. His features were bent in concern as he wiped my cheeks. From the look in his eyes, I knew he was as heartbroken as I was. "Kind of a second home."

"There's no 'kind of' about it," Lock said, his voice firm. He hugged me tighter.

Ikka touched my shoulder—just a gentle feather of pressure, and then her hand was gone. "We shouldn't linger."

I straightened up suddenly. "No, we can't go. Not yet. We need to find Horatio. And Sylvie. What if Sylvie was in there?"

"Cade was planning on heading up to Duncan's. Which means he got off the phone with us and closed up shop. The place was probably empty when this happened," Lock said. "He wouldn't have left Horatio here if he wasn't sure when he was coming back. Call Sylvie."

I jogged down to the corner gas station to see if there was a pay phone about. There was, but it had obviously been broken for a long time. I cursed and felt the overwhelming need

193

to kick something. While I wanted to call to check in with Sylvie, I didn't want to use my disposable cell yet. After a short fuming fit in the booth, during which I may or may not have melted the receiver into a lump of plastic, I slumped back to the van. Sid tapped my shoulder and handed me his phone.

"This should be clean," he said. "You took off before I could offer it to you."

I dialed Sylvie's cell number from memory, getting a very excited—and squealy, but certainly relieved—"Ava!" for my efforts. She started babbling about how terrible the fire was.

"And I'm not just saying that because I don't like looking for a job and I'm worried I'll end up at some lobster place and stink like crustaceans forever—unless you think Lock would like that?—it's just I really *liked* the bookstore and it would be such a shame to lose it and I think that something like that would be a real loss to the community. I mean, the closest bookstore is two towns over and they don't even have used books and not everyone wants to search through the stacks at Goodwill, because they don't even organize. Plus, it has this smell? You know? I have to wash everything I get from there twice. They use this chemical—I wanted to analyze it but my science teacher said I'm not allowed to use the equipment unsupervised anymore."

The car was moving and well away from the gas station before I could break in. Sylvie talked more when she was nervous, worried, or upset, and she had obviously worked herself into a proper tizzy.

"Sylvie!" I yelled into the phone.

"What? You don't need to shout. Geez, gimme palpitations, Ava."

I rested my head against the dashboard, resisting the urge to crack open my skull on the hard plastic. "Syl, I just need to know if you've talked to the boss-man."

"He's not with you? Weird. I guess I just assumed he would be. I haven't seen him since he dropped Horatio off."

I straightened up suddenly. "You have Horatio?"

"Well, yeah. Cade brought him by, said he was going to be busy or something, and gave me some money for food and kitty-sitting since the shop was going to be closed for a few days. I guess it'll be longer now." There was a brief pause—the barest of seconds—but for Sylvie it was the equivalent of a vow of silence. "Come to think of it, he didn't say when he was coming back, and he gave me kind of a lot for food. . . . Are you guys okay?" The last part was quiet and said in a very un-Sylvie-like tone.

"Yeah, I think so. Look, just . . . be careful. Don't tell anyone you talked to me, especially people you don't know. Cade and I will be back as soon as we can."

"Okay." Another pause. "I know something's going on. Some kind of trouble. You don't have to tell me what it is, but don't try to deny it. Just be safe and come back. I won't forgive you if you don't. I don't want to get a job at the pharmacy. I'd gain a million pounds being that close to the frappé counter. My dad says its not good for me to have all that sugar, anyway. And I don't want to work at the lobster place and get nick-named something putrid like Crustacean Queen."

Despite my worry, I couldn't help but smile. Sylvie has that effect. "I promise to do the best I can, Crustacean Queen."

"Great!" she chirped, back to her normal self. "Is Lock there? He is, isn't he? I know he is, because you guys are, like, joined

195

at the hip or something stupid like my mom would say. Put him on the phone." Knowing better than to argue, I handed the phone to Lock, making a few kissy noises as I did. "Your girlfriend," I mouthed.

He flipped me off, but he took the phone.

AS THE CAR got farther away from the mutilated husk of Broken Spines, I felt my heart crumble at the edges. Just one more thing I needed to take the Coterie to task for. Too much of my life had been a reaction to the things they'd done, to what they wanted. They would answer for it, come hell or high water. But that was for later. For now I just curled up in my seat and tried not to cry.

My fear that I'd find the cabin in the same state was unfounded. The windows were dark and empty, but it was intact. A quick search of the inside yielded very little in the way of information, but I had to see for myself that Cade wasn't there. That he was really missing. Ikka was able to tell me there had been someone about who wasn't human—she'd smelled different scent trails, but no blood. So if someone had been hurt, it hadn't happened in this cabin. Unless it was poison, but that wasn't really Venus's style.

Why couldn't the Coterie have been thoughtful enough to leave a dagger planted in my kitchen table with a detailed note outlining their plans? At the very least, some sort of threat or something for me to go on. A nice theatrical clue would have been good just then—of course, burning the bookstore was a pretty clear signal, but they could deny that they did it. I could see Venus sitting on her divan, her blue eyes wide and innocent, her voice full of sincerity as she talked about humans and arson and the state of the world these days. In this scenario Ryan was painting her toenails for some reason, while she sat and pointed fingers at anyone but the Coterie. Sure, we both knew who did it, but what could I do? Nothing.

I went to my room and packed. Lock rapped on the wall as he entered.

"We should go."

I nodded. "Just a few things, then we're gone." I sat down on my bed. "Lock? Can I ask you something?"

"You're asking permission? It must be a very awkward question."

I materialized a small ball of fire between my hands, tossing it idly back and forth. While other kids were playing video games and complaining about braces, my mom was teaching me to juggle fire, just like I was doing now. It was something I did when I was thinking or nervous. "How come you and Ezra are willing to do all this?"

He dropped down into a crouch in front of me. The fireball lit his face while it passed, leaving one half in shadow as it flicked back and forth. He studied me for a second, his elbows resting on his knees. I tried to ignore him and keep the flame ball bouncing. Suddenly he stuck his hand up right in its path. I quickly extinguished it, but it was very close to his skin when I did.

"*What the hell do you think you're doing?*" I think I spit a little when I yelled.

"Proving a damn point. I'm not scared of you, Ava. We're friends. That means if you're going to duck march into the maws of hell, I'm going to be right behind you carrying the marsh-mallows and roasting sticks."

I kept my head tilted away, not wanting Lock to see me tearing up. I hate crying in front of people. Lock, of course, wasn't about to let me get away with it. He gently grabbed my chin and pulled it until I was looking at him. "I know you didn't really have any friends growing up, that you couldn't," he said softly. "But this is kind of how it works. You're going in, then I'm going in right behind you, whether you like it or not. And we couldn't lose Ezra if we tried."

"We should really try harder."

Lock dropped my chin and rested his arms on my knees. "Remember that time he was chasing wild turkeys through someone's field and we tried to make it back to the car before he spotted us leaving?"

"I still say we would have made it if my phone hadn't gone off."

I don't know how long we sat there lost in our happy memory before I felt his mood shift. He traced a pattern on my leg with his thumb, and I knew he was trying to figure out how to say something. "Spit it out," I said with a sigh.

"Cade would have left a note if he'd changed his plans."

"He would have left something, yes."

Lock dropped out of his crouch and sat on the floor. "He probably never made it back here to pack."

A curt shake of my head, just enough to convey a no without completely collapsing into tears. Cade. They had kidnapped Cade. I couldn't handle losing him. Venus wouldn't kill him, at least not at first. She needed him for now. But she would hurt him. Lock had said she'd seemed extra unhinged lately. She didn't have the best restraint on good days. If she hurt Cade, would she know when to stop? Venus wasn't used to dealing with humans except for lunch. They were fragile compared with the rest of us. My whole body quaked at the thought of it. I took a deep breath. I hadn't lost him yet. No matter what, I needed to remember that. He was just temporarily misplaced.

"What do we do next?" Lock asked. I didn't know. But when we rejoined Sid in the kitchen, he gave us an answer.

"We go back to the drove," Sid said from his seat on the counter. "To Les and Duncan. That's what we do."

I scowled at him until he jumped down. "Drove?"

"That's what you call a group of rab—I mean hares," Lock said. When I looked at him, one eyebrow raised, he shrugged. "My mom's a dryad, remember? I know a thing or two about nature."

"I thought your grandma raised you."

"During the school year. But the summers were all Mom."

I heard a muffled thump from outside the door, presumably from Ikka since that was where I'd last seen her. Sid cocked his head. "We'd better get going."

"To the drove," I said, flinging my bag over my shoulder. Hopefully, Les and Duncan had some ideas. Because I was about out.

11

IT'S HARD TO FIGHT
IN PAJAMAS

B Y THE TIME we pulled back into Duncan's, I was feeling a little more hopeful. Sylvie had Horatio, and the cabin was okay. We could rebuild the bookstore. It was insured. Not quite the same as hearing that Cade was safe, but at that point any positive news was welcome.

Duncan was sitting by the fire when I got in, his big body huddled over a small piece of wood. He held a whittling knife in his hand, but right then he was running a thumb over the half-carved piece as if he were trying to decide what he wanted it to be. A handful of Les's drove were sitting here and there, even a kid curled up on the fireplace rug like a dog.

Lock brought everyone up to speed as I collapsed into a chair, moodily staring at the flames. Every once in a while, I'd glance at Duncan, who was still staring at that damn piece of wood, his occasional nod the only sign that he was listening. For some reason his inattention made me furious. There I was, miserable, tired, and in deep shit, and he was fucking *whittling*.

Like the situation had nothing to do with him, like it wasn't at least partially his fault that I was in this mess. If I had just taken the damn contract on him and burned this stupid cabin to the ground, then I'd have been home in front of *my* fire probably eating a damn steak while Cade talked about . . . well, anything at all, really.

"You look about ready to pop," Duncan drawled, keeping his gaze on his project. At least he'd finally started carving it again.

I glared at him.

Sid bristled, but Duncan just laughed. "I bet you're thinking how nice and simple things would have been if you'd just taken the contract on me, hmm?"

I nodded glumly, and before my chin even finished bobbing, the mood in the room took another one of those mercurial shifts. All eyes were on me, hostile and wary, and the little kid by the fire had rolled to his feet and pulled a blade on me before I could blink. It was a decent-size hunting knife too, and placed rather skillfully at my throat. This seemed to be a favorite move amongst the were-hares. I wondered where the kid had been hiding the knife.

Now that I looked, I realized I'd made an error—the knife wielder was a girl of about eleven, maybe twelve at most. Her brown hair was shaved short in the back, the top and the front kept longer and brushed forward so that it swept down to her nose. Despite the smudges on her face and the punk-rock hair, there was an almost angelic quality to her, probably something to do with the big brown eyes and ghostly skin. She was one tubercular cough away from being a perfect Dickensian orphan.

Of course, she'd have looked a lot more angelic without the knife. But then again, what did I know about angels?

"Olive," Duncan said drily, "while I commend your speed and dedication, that is hardly necessary."

I eyed the young girl. "You know I could barbecue you, right?"

She stared right back at me. "But could you do it before I finished the job?" With a flick the knife was gone, back to her mystery hiding spot. "And are you really willing to find out?"

"No," I said. "But if I'd really wanted to kill Duncan, I wouldn't have waited this long. Why come to the house and get mixed up with you guys?"

Olive continued to stare at me, calm and barely blinking. "Maybe you knew you couldn't get close enough if you didn't. Maybe you're just careless or stupid. How should I know?"

Lock leaned in, all charm and smiles. "We made it this far because Duncan is Ava's friend. He let us get close. We'd be idiots to think otherwise. Just like we both know that we'll be guarded tonight, friends or not friends, because Duncan isn't stupid, either."

The little girl seemed impervious to Lock's charm but assented to his logic soon enough. "Fine. Whatever." She turned to Les. "Can I have a cookie?" Les gave an almost imperceptible nod, and the girl was off like a shot.

"Just one!" Sid shouted after her. I'd only known Olive for about a minute, but even I knew she was going to take as many cookies as she thought she should have, and it was going to be more than one.

I turned to Duncan. "May I ask you a question? And please don't do that smart-ass thing where you tell me I've already asked one. I hate that."

"You may ask," Duncan said. "But that doesn't mean I'm going to answer it."

"Why does Venus want you so bad?" Venus liked to show that she was in charge, but she didn't usually force a confrontation unless she could guarantee she was going to like the outcome. She had to have known that I was going to say no to Duncan's contract. She couldn't offer it to Owen, since he wouldn't have been able to get close enough, but she must have wanted it pretty bad if she forced the issue with me. Twice. In public. She was hungry for Duncan's death in a way I'd never seen before.

Duncan contemplated the fire as Ikka put another log on, stoking the flames with an old iron poker as she did so. "What do you know about the Coterie?" he asked, finally.

"That it sucks," I said promptly.

He laughed. "Anything else?"

"That it sucks a lot."

Les gave me a small smile. "I see you don't put much store by the adage 'Know thine enemy.'" He helped Olive up onto his knee as he spoke. She was holding only one cookie, but the crumbs on her face told me she'd had several before she came back into the living room. I noticed that her pants were cargo style, with lots of pockets, and I'd have bet there were some cookies stashed in at least one of them, too.

"Knowing more about it isn't going to change anything. Snow is cold, water is wet, the Coterie sucks. Some truths are immutable." They were responsible for my mom's death and my current misery, and they probably stole candy from babies. What else did I need to know?

Duncan leaned back in his chair, his whittling forgotten for the moment. "Okay, let me ask you another question. Do you know who was in charge before Venus?"

I didn't. To me, Venus *was* the Coterie; it started and ended with her. Venus was old—really old. I knew that, in theory, there had been someone before her, I just didn't care. What came before wasn't my problem. Venus was. I said as much.

"That's exactly what Venus wants you to believe," Duncan answered, "that there is no Coterie without her, and that you can't get away from them. She likes to believe that everything is owned by the Coterie. But that's not true. In some areas, there's a Council in place. They look out for the weak and keep groups like the Coterie out."

"In my experience they're not much better than the Coterie."

"They aren't all like that," Lock said. "What about the one in Portsmouth? Are the rumors true?"

Although we'd heard they were on the Coterie payroll, that morsel of information had come from people associated with the Coterie. I leaned closer, excited. An official team of toughs at my back would be nice. The idea of a quick trip to Portsmouth solving my problems appealed to me, I'm not gonna lie.

Duncan shook his head. "Oh, you can go there, ask for their help, but it won't do you any good. The Portsmouth Council is weak—too much infighting and petty squabbles to be of any real use. Venus has at least half of them in her pocket. And we don't know which half. The other half is probably in someone else's pocket. You can only trust them as far as their own personal agendas go. Hopelessly corrupt."

"I guess if the Council was functioning properly, there'd be no Coterie, huh?" I tapped Lock's knee with mine, trying to soften the blow.

"If we were actually in Portsmouth, on their turf, then that'd be a different story," Les said, the firelight casting ruddy shadows on his face.

Well, so much for that. "Okay," I said. "I'm on my own—got it. Now can we get back to the history lesson?" Olive glared at me until I added a "please."

"Venus's predecessor died rather suddenly, as people in their position tend to do. Usually there's a lieutenant ready to step up and take over. That time, the situation aligned itself so that there was no clear successor. Venus was pushing for the position, but she was unpopular with a few of the other higher-ups, and she was new—she'd only been with the Coterie for a year or two. A couple of those higher-ups sought me out and asked me to step in."

"No offense, but you don't really seem to be a likely candidate," Lock said, leaning forward, his elbows resting on his thighs.

"It was different then. I'm not saying it was a benevolent organization, but it wasn't as . . . lethal. With the right leadership, it could have become something close to a new Council. Venus took it in the other direction, I'm afraid."

He paused there, letting it sink in. The information still didn't make any sense. "They wanted you to take over the Coterie?" I asked. "Why you? And, more important, why didn't you do it? You'd have been a damn sight less psychotic than Venus. You would have steered it right, I know you would've." Duncan as the head of the Coterie would have been a dream.

If Duncan had taken over the Coterie, I probably would have had a lot less work. In fact, I might not have had any work. If he'd stepped in, we wouldn't even be here. No one would have kidnapped Cade, no burnt store . . . and then I took it even farther back. "When was this?" I asked.

Duncan shrugged. "Twenty years ago? Twenty-five? Not sure, but about then, I guess. Time is a funny thing."

"Yes, funny," I said hollowly. Before my mom . . . My heart twisted and my stomach roiled. "Why didn't you accept?"

"Didn't want it, I guess. I'm old, Ava. I was old *then*. Tired. I want to live in my cabin, fish when I feel like it, and enjoy the simple things. Coterie isn't simple."

Fishing. My mom was dead because he wanted to go *fishing*. Yes, the voice of cold logic was telling me that there was no way he could have known. He didn't send the goon squad after us. It was listing all kinds of reasons why it wasn't Duncan's fault, but that cold voice was being overpowered by another, stronger voice—one hell-bent on hurt and destruction. And that voice was whispering that Duncan wouldn't have ordered my mother captured . . . even if he had, Duncan wouldn't have sent such a piss-poor recovery team. He would have sent professionals who wouldn't have botched the damn job. She wouldn't be dead, that voice jeered, and you know it.

I felt sick, raw, and I was trying to control it. Hissy fits, when thrown by a firebug, can be incredibly nasty. I gripped the armrests and tried not to scream. "Why you, Duncan? Why offer the job to you?"

"Because," Duncan said, his eyes back on the fire, "I was Coterie before I retired."

Stars and sparks—the only surprising thing was that Venus

had waited this long to make a move on Duncan. They'd offered the job to him. Which meant that, until he was eliminated, she'd continue to see him as competition. As a threat.

"What if they offered you the job now?" I asked.

"I'm still tired, Ava. Still old." He examined the half-finished carving in his lap. "I have no desire to rule." With one thumb he brushed away a tiny curl of wood from his project. "Go to bed. There's nothing more you can do tonight. The drove will keep an eye on your cabin and what's left of Broken Spines. They'll do what they can to run down some information. They're good like that."

Though he didn't so much as glance at us, I knew we'd been dismissed.

We were ushered into a guest room—and, yes, guards were put on the doors. I would be bunking with the boys again. The room held a queen bed and a fold-out cot. The boys settled in, Ezra flopping onto the cot and stretching out, but I was too busy sitting on the bed and being entirely incoherent to really pay attention. Duncan had been Coterie. I just couldn't believe it. He looked like Santa; he fished and whittled. People like that don't work for crime syndicates. They sit around and drink beer and talk about their arthritic knees and the weather.

Lock didn't respond right away when I presented this argument. I glared at him. "Why do I think I'm not going to like what's about to come out of your mouth?"

He pulled some of Cade's pajama pants out of the bag I'd packed for him, along with a toothbrush. "Look, Ava, I know how you think. Coterie is evil. Evil should be punished. Hulk smash, remember?" I narrowed my eyes at him, which was usually enough to make Lock hold up his hands in surrender. This time, all I saw was his jaw tighten as he stuffed the rest of his gear back in his bag.

"And you think what, they're all rainbows and glitter? If you thought that, why did you help me?"

"I helped you because I agree that Venus is one homemade shiv and a tinfoil hat away from being absolutely and psychotically bonkers." He finally met my eyes, crossing his arms and trying to look defiant, which was kind of hard to do while holding pajamas and a toothbrush. "But I hesitate on absolutes, cupcake. The Coterie can be good for some, especially when there's no Council to rely on."

"Bullshit."

"Fine," he said. "Don't listen. Be a fucking child. But the way you think sometimes, Aves? It's dangerous. Black and white. There's a whole lot of gray in this world. You need to be open to it."

"I don't understand."

"You wouldn't," he said hotly. "We're not all firebugs. Not every creature in the Coterie is rare or powerful. Some are weak. They need the protection. They need certain resources to survive that they couldn't afford or wouldn't have access to without the Coterie."

I opened my mouth to argue with him, but he waved at me to wait. "I'm not saying you've had it easy, but you at least have some leverage. You're not disposable like some of the other supernaturals I know. Why am I here, Ava? Why am I Coterie?"

I looked down at my socks. "You're a tithe."

"Right, a tithe. And what is Ezra?"

I couldn't remember the last time Lock had yelled at me. "He's a tithe too."

Lock splayed his hand on his chest. "I put in my time, an entire forest of dryads gets left alone. Ezra's here so his little sisters can go to school. Be normal. Be protected. Without the Coterie, who's going to protect us? The training we have, the skills we have now—that's all Coterie."

"Except my lock picking and general sneaking skills," Ezra put in. "Those are all fox."

"I would protect you guys," I said, softly, my arms crossed over my stomach.

Lock rested his hands on my shoulders. "Would you? Or would you be too busy fighting off all the poachers and ne'er-do-wells who wanted you for their own? You'd want to protect us. We'd want to protect you, but it's just not enough."

He hadn't moved his hands. "I get it."

"I don't think you do. I mean, you look normal, to boot. You can pass as human. Do you know how great that is?"

I didn't answer, but he wasn't waiting for me to. "We have a troll at the Inferno who manages the dish-pit staff. He has to have all kinds of wards to pass as human, just so he can do things like own a home and go to the store, things you and I take for granted. He has three kids. Three kids delivered by Coterie doctors. You think he could have taken his wife to a human hospital? What if her wards fell off? What if something went wrong and they had to do some tests? You think anything in his life would be possible without the Coterie? It's easy for you to pass judgment because you're in a position that makes it possible."

"Couldn't a Council do that? They might even do it without blackmail and treachery."

"You want to tell Luther to wait it out until that magical day happens? I'm not saying the Coterie is a pile of awesome, I'm just saying that they aren't all evil."

Lock's words hit me like a slap. I knew Luther. We chatted sometimes. I'd seen pictures of his kids. I hadn't known he was a troll and warded to the hilt just so he could work. But I didn't know how to reconcile what Lock was saying with my vision of the Coterie. It was easier to just get angry and yell at him while I figured it out, so that's what I did. "Are you saying I should go back to the Inferno and throw myself at Venus's feet and beg forgiveness? Is that what you want? And really, is this the best time? They have *Cade*! Doesn't that bother you at all?"

"Of course it bothers me!" He ran a hand through his hair. "You think we're not both worried? That he isn't family to us, too? It's just . . . there's no good time to talk about this stuff, Aves."

"I don't like it when Mom and Dad fight," Ezra said watching us from the cot. "Never mind about the two Christmases."

"Ezra, be quiet. Lock, I feel bad for all these people, but I'm not the villain. It's not my fault that I am what I am. It's not like it didn't land me in the same place as you, strength of powers or not."

Lock threw his arms up in the air in frustration, the legs from the pajama pants whirling about him. "Forget it—you're impossible to talk to when you're like this." Then he stomped out of the room. I grabbed the only thing handy—my pillow—and chucked it at the door. It was entirely unsatisfying.

I whirled on Ezra, but he merely held up his toothbrush. "I

was just going to brush my teeth. Hygiene is important." He edged around me but stopped before he got to the door. "We're as freaked out as you, you know?" He rested one hand on the doorknob. "I called home. With all this . . . I wanted to check on them. Did you know my mom is making Cade a sweater?"

I frowned. "Your mom makes things?"

"Making, stealing, whatever. The thing is, she's getting him a sweater. She thought about someone she isn't related to by blood. That's huge."

"She's met him only, what, three times?"

"I talk about him. And you. And Lock. What I'm trying to say is, you're not alone. He's family to us, too." He slipped out the door before I could respond.

While they were gone, I changed angrily into my pajamas. Which is totally possible—it involves a lot of air punching and feet stomping and, on occasion, fury-filled buttoning. The whole time, my brain was flitting from thought to emotion, which was hard because it was such a tangled mess. What the hell was I going to do? Laying siege to the Coterie walls would be next to useless. We were completely outnumbered. Plus, now I was imagining Luther's body in the wreckage, and his wife and children sobbing over him while accusing me of murder. Not good.

According to just about everyone, seeking out the Council in Portsmouth was equally useless. My angry buttoning slowed. Or was it? What if I could present the Council with something—in exchange for some backup, I'd wipe out the Coterie. Hand them this area on a silver platter, so to speak. If they were weak, this would only strengthen their position. Then again, if they were weak, how much would their backup be worth?

I dug my toothbrush out of my bag and sat on the bed, thinking. Normally I'd run something like this by Cade. Only, Cade wasn't here. Going to Portsmouth to talk to the Council would eat up half a day. More if they made me wait around for a few days to talk to them. And all the waiting would mean extra time for the Coterie to do terrible things to Cade. I tried really hard to not imagine what those terrible things might be.

I was pretty sure they wouldn't kill him, since dead people make terrible leverage, but Venus had plenty of torturous tricks up her sleeve.

Lock took his sweet-ass time brushing his teeth. I think he wanted to let me cool off. His plan worked, a little. By the time I got back from brushing my own teeth, I only wanted to hurt him a bit instead of tons.

"I'm tempted to make you sleep on the floor."

Lock eyed me carefully. "It might be safer, considering what you did to Duncan's ladle."

I deflated onto the bed. "You be a gentleman," I said, "and I promise I won't turn you into cinders."

"Of course," he said with a huff. "I'm not *Ezra*."

"I am a perfect gentleman," Ezra said. "It's not my fault that no one can resist me." He lifted up his shirt. "I mean, have you seen these abs? Who can blame them?"

"And that's why you're getting the cot," I said, rolling my eyes. "Because there's no way we'll be able to sleep if we're constantly touching your *abs*."

Lock and I curled into the bed, tossing and turning until we both got comfortable. I was exhausted. I needed to sleep. But my brain kept whirling—a frenetic spinning top of motion.

"What are we going to do?" I whispered to Lock. He took

so long to answer, I thought maybe he'd already drifted off to sleep.

"I'm not sure," he finally whispered back. "I know you want to ride in there all avenging-savior style—"

"Suicide."

"Yes, exactly. Sneaking in with a small team would be as stupid as the avenging-savior plan."

"What we need to do is draw them out."

We both considered that. The cabin creaked around us as the drove moved around. I heard the clinking of dishes, probably being washed and dried, and Ikka's laughter. If we hadn't been in our current situation, I'd have found it soothing, a nice change. I'd never lived in a place with a lot of people, and the background noise was kind of comforting. At first it had been mostly just Mom and me. Then Cade and me. If I wasn't smart, and if I wasn't careful, soon it would just be me.

"We should go see the Council."

I rolled over and stared at Lock, though I couldn't see much in the dark room. "I thought they were next to useless."

"They are," he said. "But we know they're weak, right? And we're pretty sure at least one of them has been bought off by Venus, yeah?"

"Yes," I said, still unsure where he was going with this.

"Well, what better way to draw Venus out? I mean, it's not like we can call her up and say, 'Meet us here at high noon.' She calls the shots at the moment, and she knows it. Eventually she'd drive us back into her territory, so we'd start off at a disadvantage. But if we go to the Council and ask them for help and, I don't know, let it slip where we're going to be at a certain time..."

"Then we can make her come to us at a place of our choosing. She'll think it's a sneak attack when really it's an ambush."

"Exactly!" I could hear the excited giddiness in his voice.

"Lock, that's brilliant."

"No need to sound so surprised."

"I'm not—it's just—I could kiss you right now." The air between us flooded with tension, and Lock took a split second too long to respond.

"Psh, I see how you are. First you tell me to be a gentleman, then you offer up your affections. Way to send mixed signals, Aves."

I punched his shoulder. "Its an expression, you ass." And just like that, things felt back to normal.

"Is it, Ava? I mean, really?" His voice was teasing, pure Lock. And yet there was a tone in there I couldn't quite identify.

"You're a jerk," I said. "You're like an entire fiesta of assness. Why are we friends, again?"

"Because I'm the only one who'll put up with you, that's why."

"Did I say fiesta? More like spring break. You're the Miami Beach of jackass behavior."

"Sure, you say that now, but I'm going to wake up with you smelling my hair, I just know it."

I couldn't dignify that with a response, so I settled for hitting him with my pillow. It was much more satisfying than throwing it at the door.

12

MEETINGS AND POORLY EXECUTED IMPROMPTU BARBECUES

SUNLIGHT POURED into the room, but I held my eyelids shut in firm denial. Then my stomach, the traitor, growled and I knew it was no use. I had to get up and face the world.

Ezra was still burrowed into his blankets, but Lock was already up and gone, so I grabbed my clothes and went to join him. Things would look better after food and coffee, surely.

Duncan seemed less than enthusiastic about our Portsmouth Council plan when we told him about it over breakfast. But he couldn't think of anything better, either. After some discussion and hashing out of details, it was decided that we would indeed go to Portsmouth, but Ikka and Sid would go with us and drive us there in the van. Duncan would call ahead and pull some strings to set up the meeting.

Les handed me a bag of food for the trip. It was enormous. "Um, we're only going to be gone for, like, five hours or so. You know that, right?"

He shrugged. "We eat a lot. And Duncan says that with your . . . uh . . . condition, you probably need to eat a lot too."

"My condition? It's not a disease, Les."

Duncan came up and patted my shoulder kind of awkwardly. "You sure about this?"

Staring down at the bag of food, I wondered if he really needed me to answer that question. I decided it was rhetorical, or at least it should have been, so I just handed the food off to Sid.

"We'll keep looking for Cade," Les said. At the look on my face, he added, "I'll get someone to buzz by the cabin. A few times. If he shows up anywhere in a fifty-mile radius, we'll find him."

I looked around at the assembled were-hares, a term I still couldn't think without mentally giggling a little, and was surprised to see them all smiling, all . . . happy.

"This really isn't your fight," I said, "even if your moving here has set some of it into motion. You've known me less than twenty-four hours. I'm not sure if you're helping me for Duncan or what, but I'm more concerned with why you all seem so excited about it."

Duncan snorted. "Thing you need to know about werehares—they're always spoiling for a fight."

THE FIRST HOUR of the trip was uneventful. Sid drove, Lock played with the radio, Ikka read. Ezra and I tried to think of what we were going to say to the Council, but then we gave up and started playing the alphabet game. After about an hour, though, a high-pitched but firm little voice piped up from the back.

"When are we going to stop? I have to pee."

Ikka smacked the back of Sid's headrest. "See? I told you I smelled Olive!"

He scowled at the road. "And I told you she was crawling all over the place before we drove off. Even I thought Olive was too smart to stow away in the van."

Olive leaned on the back of the seat, between Ikka and me. "I am smart. I waited until we were too far away for you to drive me home, didn't I?"

Ikka twisted in her seat. "You realize you're going to get the worst chore duties for at least a month, right? Not to mention a tongue lashing from Les."

"And you realize that I'm already *on* latrine duty, dish duty, and diaper duty?"

Sid snickered. Ikka sighed. "You're snickering because she said 'duty' aren't you? Never mind—don't answer that." She returned her attention to Olive. "I didn't know you were on diaper patrol."

When I raised an eyebrow, Olive said, "It means I have to gather and wash all the cloth diapers for the drove—and we have a ton of leverets right now." At my blank look she said, "Baby hares."

"Well, you're going to be on it forever now," Ikka said.

Olive just shrugged. "So? Washing diapers ain't no big deal. Don't see why people bitch about it all the time."

Ikka rubbed her face with one hand. "Don't say 'ain't,' and watch your mouth. And buckle up." Olive climbed over the seat and buckled up between us while Ikka pulled out her cell and texted someone to let them know we had Olive. "You're just lucky we're somewhere with cell service," she muttered.

THE ADDRESS the Council gave Duncan took us to a yacht club in New Castle. We parked in a lot behind a church. Our van would be hidden from the road by trees and the back of the building—I didn't want to park at the yacht club and let the Council see us coming. If they planned to follow the van afterward, they were going to have to follow on foot first, which would make them easier to spot.

We had to take Olive with us. It wasn't safe to leave her in the van—for her or the van. Olive struck me as the kind of kid who knew how to hotwire.

We walked to the boathouse, curving around the yacht club and trying to get down to the water. At the docks, there was a speedboat waiting for us among all the beautiful sailboats. A man leaned against its polished aerodynamic glory, his face a tribute to boredom. Without a word he ushered us on. When I asked if this would take us to the Council—just to make sure—he merely nodded and unhitched the mooring lines.

The boat cut through the water like a welding torch through cotton candy. Like it was nothing. It might have been a really enjoyable trip if I hadn't been a bundle of nerves. Once we were out in the harbor, we pulled up to a yacht. You know the kind you always see rappers on in music videos, usually accompanied by scantily clad models who could really use a sandwich? This yacht made those look like something you'd play with in a bathtub.

We climbed a rope ladder up onto the dock before being led into the cabin by a butler. Do you still call them butlers when they're on a ship? Because he looked like a nautical butler. The cabin smelled subtly of fresh flowers, which were everywhere, and I got an overwhelming impression of delicate but uncomfortable furniture. A big basket of fruit rested in the middle of the table, and a group of rather bored-looking people posed around the room.

There were seven total, all of them lounging in such a way that I expected a boy with palm fronds and a linen tunic to jump out from a closet and start fanning people at any moment.

A voluptuous woman off to my left sat by the window and drank a martini. Her red dress barely contained her curves—the fabric had to be magic to keep from straining, I swear, and she managed to look sultry while sipping her drink. I guessed that she was some manner of succubus. She stared at Ezra in open admiration. Close by, a wraithlike couple perched on stools while they drank from brandy snifters. With long limbs and gaunt faces, they looked like they'd crawled out of some deep sea crevice.

A humongous man in a rumpled L.L. Bean flannel and stained Carhartt pants leaned against the wall, an air of hopelessness about him. I couldn't say what it was, but something about him just seemed . . . I don't know, *broken*. He stared at us. I had to look away.

A petite—and slightly green—woman sat on a couch next to a guy who looked more like a longshoreman than anything else. The small woman smiled at me when she noticed my gaze resting on her, and I caught a glimpse of some very pointy little teeth. I shuddered. She was the only one who struck me as openly frightening.

A man in an overstuffed armchair addressed us. He didn't look like he should be part of the Council. He looked like he should be at a Harvard mixer or trying out for a crew team.

Someone who would do a lot of glad handing but not a great deal of actual work. "You must be Duncan's people."

"We are," I said.

"All right," he said. "You've dragged us away from important matters, so get on with it." No one else spoke—a few of them didn't even look up from their drinks. Apparently they were content to let the yuppie god do all the talking.

"You're scowling," Lock whispered.

Immediately I let my face relax. "Thank you for taking time out of your . . . busy schedules. I've come to make you an offer."

"Indeed?" Yuppie said with a mocking smile. "And what could you possibly have to offer us?"

"The Coterie off your doorstep." That got the attention of everyone in the room. I explained what I needed and why— and I kept it simple, giving them only the barest bones of things.

"These are grave charges," Yuppie said, steepling his fingers. "Kidnapping, murder, extortion."

"Do you have proof?" the green woman asked, but she was already waving me away with her hand. "You do not. I know this. There is no proof to have. The Inferno is a nightclub, nothing more. For whatever reason you wish to sling the mud at your boss, eh? With your fanciful tales of the money washing and the extortion. More like she denied you a raise, yes? Yes. You go away now."

"It's money laundering, poppet, not washing," the longshoremen said to her, amusement in his tone. Clearly he found her charming. Ew.

I shook my head. Had I not gotten rid of my phone, I would've been able to show them the many, many texts I'd sent Venus to let them know I'd finished a job. Not that

220

those would paint me in a great light either. "No proof. Just my word."

"Yes, the word of a stranger. Very convincing. Alistair," the green woman said to the yuppie god, "this is ridiculous. Make them leave."

A flicker of annoyance crossed Alistair's face. "No one asked you, Martinique." He eyed us levelly. "She has a point, though. You are strangers to us, and you make serious accusations." He held up a hand when he saw Lock about to protest. "Duncan vouches for you, but that goes only so far. You must see that we can't just go charging in there based solely on your testimony." His face was unreadable as he stared at us. "Naturally, we will investigate, but these things do take time. You can't waltz in here and expect us to drop everything and come running."

I wanted to choke him with his own Windsor knot. Come running was exactly what he should have done.

One of the gaunt people spoke then, though I wasn't sure which one. They weren't facing me. The voice was dry and quiet, like the rubbing together of insect legs. "There are others in front of you—people who have approached us through the proper channels. Not cutting ahead because of important friends. Naturally, they should be helped first, before we start investigating your claims."

I nodded. "I see."

Alistair rose, his trim frame unwinding from the chair. His light brown hair remained fixed in place, even when he moved to show us out. "I'm sorry you had to come so far to hear this—my apologies. Should you ever have proof, feel free to call on us again, during normal meeting hours, of course." He grinned, and I was reminded of Venus's predatory smile. "We are here to serve our people."

"Yeah, up on a platter," I mumbled.

Lock coughed and gave me a look, reminding me to watch it. I handed over a piece of paper with my temporary cell phone number and my address, since that was where we had chosen to direct Venus for our little showdown. "Just in case you change your mind," I said. "I'll be there."

WE DIDN'T say anything until we got back to the parking lot. A drive and a boat ride—all that time wasted.

"Ugh, what a colossal time suck," Olive said, her words echoing my thoughts. She glared at me accusingly. "Why didn't you burn the yacht?"

"Do you think that would have been very smart—you know, what with us being on board at the time?" I asked. "They did exactly what we wanted them to do." Olive gave me a look that said she clearly didn't believe me.

"We knew they wouldn't help us," Ikka explained quietly, her mouth tucked in close to Olive's ear. If I hadn't been right next to them, I wouldn't have been able to hear any of it. "The important thing is, they know where Ava will be now. That means whoever is working for Venus will pass on the information."

"So?"

"You can't attack the hare in its warren. You have to draw it out to where it's vulnerable. That's what we're doing with Venus. She knows where we'll be and thinks she can surprise us, but to get us, she'll have to leave her safe and cozy den."

"Why couldn't you've just called the Council?" Olive asked.

222

I noticed that her eyes roamed everywhere, just like Sid's, even while she talked to us. Ever on the lookout.

"We had to make sure we saw the whole Council," Sid said, keeping his voice low. "We don't know which ones are in Venus's pocket, so we had to make sure all of them heard our message."

"They certainly don't make it easy on people," I muttered. "Down to that dock to take a boat to the harbor. Why not bring the ship in closer? Why have us meet out there at all? It must be damn difficult for the locals to get a meeting with them." I stopped. "Oh. I guess that's the point. Answered my own question."

Olive was still digesting what Sid had told her. "So we're setting a trap. Still," she said with a sniff, "you should have set *something* on fire so they knew you meant business."

"Remind me never to cross you," I said.

Ezra stopped, reaching an arm out for me. "I don't like the way it smells here. It's off, somehow." That was the only warning we got.

They stepped out from around the van. Our assailants didn't melt out of the shadows the way the drove had. They clearly lacked that skill. Instead, their movements were jerky, like an action figure whose limbs have all been removed and put in backwards. They didn't move *right*.

They approached us in a V formation, and as they got closer I caught sight of green-tinged skin and scraggly hair. I counted nine of them total. They were small, and they were dressed—what the hell?—like 1920s newspaper boys. They wore suspenders. And those little caps. If they hadn't radiated malevolence, I'd have been afraid they were going to bust into some sort of tap-dance extravaganza.

"What the fuck are those?" Sid asked.

A light breeze drifted our way, and Ezra gagged. "There's that smell. Like toxic rotting fish." He gagged again.

"Vodyanoy," Lock said, coming to a halt. "Or something similar. They're mostly aquatic, that's why they're moving so strangely. But let's make sure they're unfriendly before we do anything rash. Maybe they just need—"

I never found out what Lock was going to suggest, because at that point the creatures stopped their jerky, slow advance and came at us in a sprint. Though they moved awkwardly when they walked, the same could not be said of when they ran—they were like cheetahs on speed.

Two of them were on Lock before anyone could react. Sid tackled another. Ikka aimed a kick at one, but it wheeled away, just out of reach. Two slowed as they neared Ezra, circling him carefully. I don't think they liked the way he smelled either. Olive had her knife in her hand and was crouching low, one of the snarling green creatures orbiting around her. I could see its pointy sharp teeth, and I was reminded of Martinique on the yacht. We seemed to be meeting her friends.

I didn't have much time to reflect on that, though, because I had to deal with the two approaching me. Hissing noises escaped their mouths as they came close, and judging from the color of the drool, I was guessing that their bite did something nasty.

"Avoid their teeth!" I yelled. Twin fireballs, one for each hand, materialized above my palms. The two creatures approaching me backed off a little. Fire has that effect.

"No shit," Lock said, kicking one away and sliding out from

under the other. The creature sliced the back of his leather jacket to ribbons, but hopefully that was all it got.

"Well, I was going to," Sid said, hurling one of the green men into a Volvo. "But now that you've mentioned it . . ." Just then, one of Lock's attackers leaped onto Sid's back and bit into his shoulder. He screamed, reaching back, but he couldn't get a grip. Ezra grabbed the newsie and chucked him onto the one Sid had thrown earlier. Its head snapped against the metal door, knocking it unconscious. I hoped the owner of that Volvo had really good insurance.

"That's what you get for being a smart-ass," Ikka said. She was eyeing her opponent warily as they glided around each other. I started hurling fireballs at mine, tired of the fight already. It dodged them, and the fireballs hit concrete, leaving scorch marks on the floor. Out of the corner of my eye, I saw the flash of Olive's arm as she sliced with her blade. She was the closest to their size, but that seemed to be working to her advantage. We had to stoop and aim lower than we usually did, but Olive was right at eye level. From the look of it, she'd already landed a few good hits. Her creature was oozing a blackish ichor from several slashes.

I kept throwing fireballs, and they kept dodging. Fast little buggers. The two on the Volvo hadn't moved, but we still had plenty to deal with. Sid and Ikka fought with speed and precision, but so did the little green newsies.

Lock was wrestling an adversary on the ground. He rolled into a concrete curb, and as I watched, he barely missed getting a blow to the shoulder. The creature's next swipe landed, though, and blood blossomed on Lock's shirt. I could have screamed—I felt like it. Instead, I stopped, ignored the two demented newsies circling me, and focused on the figure on top of Lock. Stuck in a wrestling maneuver, it wasn't moving around like the others. I was able to concentrate and imagine a tiny fireball in its chest, right where I guessed its heart should be.

Its heart wasn't flammable like a vampire's or melty like the ice elemental's. But all that meant was I had to work a little harder. The creature screamed and its chest exploded, covering Lock in some sort of . . . goo.

Lock lay there sputtering, knocking what was left of the creature off of him. He rolled over and spit a chunk of something out. Then he started gagging and heaving, his face covered in slime.

Sid was bleeding pretty freely from his shoulder, but he turned to take on another opponent while Ikka kicked hers into a windshield. Safety glass cracked, long fissures spider-webbing to the edges, but the newsie got up and went back to her, though he was moving slowly now.

I threw more fire, but the creature tracking me bobbed and weaved, inspired by his exploded friend to keep moving. Out of the corner of my eye, I checked on Olive. She had some scratches but seemed to be doing better than the rest of us. Her knife was covered with the vodyanoy's dark blood, and from the wheezing and the jagged gash her blade had caused, I could see her opponent was on his last leg. He gave her a greasy smile, and I felt my stomach clench.

That's when he spit. A mass of thick saliva hit Olive, covering most of her face. She screamed. A high-pitched, terrible sound that made me cover my ears. The newsies had an even

226

worse reaction, dropping on the spot and curling their arms over their heads. Olive clawed at her face and continued to wail. That sound caused a rage to build in me—something so quick and hot that it felt like my whole body went nova.

Everything tunneled until all I saw was fire and vodyanoy. I didn't stop until the newsies were nothing but a twitching mess. They were covered in cuts, bruises, and contusions— marks lovingly heaped on them by my group. And what wasn't bruised and bleeding was blackened and burned. A whole mess of minions cooked medium well.

None of them would survive. I didn't care.

We piled into the van, Ikka at the wheel. Lock cradled Olive in the back seat while Sid used his undamaged arm to pour a bottle of water over Olive's ruined face. Ezra offered up his shirt to be used as a rag to wipe the toxic slime off. Olive whimpered, and I didn't blame her. What wasn't bleeding was turning green and oozing. Sid's shoulder looked the same way.

I tore apart the van looking for bandages. I found a small first-aid kit, the packages inside yellow with age, and I knew it wouldn't be enough. Ezra brushed Olive's face with his water-soaked shirt, and her scream hit so high it could have shattered glass. I held the bandages in my hands and knew I couldn't do anything. I was suddenly overwhelmed—all I could see was blood, all I could hear was Olive screaming, and all I wanted to do was burn. But it wouldn't help. All these powers, all these gifts, and we couldn't help one hurt little girl. It made me wonder what good we were.

13

FAMILY REUNIONS AND OTHER PAINFUL THINGS

IKKA DROVE LIKE nothing was wrong, though I could see the panic on her face. I held what was left of Sid's shirt to his shoulder, trying to staunch the bleeding. It wasn't working very well. Olive had passed out from the pain and lay unconscious in Lock's arms. Ezra held her hand, rubbing the pressure points and doing what he could to add comfort.

"Please tell me you heal," I whispered. I didn't have much contact with weres besides Ez, but I knew that there were some differences between each kind. I was hoping the speed-healing thing was one of the were-hares' gifts.

"Yeah," Sid growled as I pushed harder on his wound. "But something tells me this whatever-it-is will fight us."

"Head toward Bradbury Mountain," Lock said as he shifted Olive in his arms.

Ikka looked at him through the rearview mirror. "But Duncan's cabin is—"

"I know," Lock said with a sigh. "Just trust me, okay?"

The glance Ikka gave him was doubtful, but whatever she saw in him convinced her to head in the direction he asked. It went unspoken that, should Lock be wrong, and should the delay worsen Olive's condition, he would pay. I could feel it in the air—heavy and weighted.

Bradbury Mountain is exactly what it sounds like: mountain, woods, trees. About eight hundred forested acres of national parkland, according to Lock. We didn't go through any marked trailhead but instead headed up some sort of access road. After a short drive, the road turned into two glorified ruts. Then we hit a point where Ikka couldn't drive anymore. She turned to Lock for directions.

"Come on," he said, edging awkwardly toward the door, thrown off balance by the still-unconscious Olive. "We have to walk the rest of the way." We all hobbled our way out of the van, ducking branches.

"If you have any lighters, leave them here," Lock said. "Whatever you do, don't so much as pull a leaf off any of the trees. Keep to the path, be careful of the plants, and for the love of all that you hold dear, Ava, *absolutely no fires*." He turned on Ezra. "You. Don't chase anything. Leave the squirrels alone. No porcupines, groundhogs, or birds. And keep it in your pants. That goes for both of you," he added, looking at Sid.

Sid turned to Ezra. "Are those two thoughts connected? Does he think we're harboring romantic interests in woodland creatures?"

Ez pursed his lips. "I assume that part referred to his family. We can ask for clarification if you think you actually need it."

"I do not," Sid said, and I could tell he wasn't sure if Ez was serious.

Lock had started walking up a barely visible footpath as he talked. I fell in behind him, a wary Sid and Ikka sliding in behind me.

"I mean it, Aves. Even if we're attacked or threatened—no fire."

"I got it, I got it. Geez."

He sighed like he didn't quite believe me, but he kept walking.

It was cold in the forest, especially under the branches of some of the bigger pines. Still, it was fairly sunny and the air was crisp. I could hear birds calling back and forth. It would have been really pleasant if half of us weren't bleeding to death.

I'd duct taped the wadded-up T-shirt to Sid's shoulder, but as I glanced back at him, I could see that the shirt was soaked. He smiled at me anyway. Ikka and Ezra appeared to be the best off, with only a few scratches and bruises. Except me. I was unharmed. I felt a little stab at that.

Olive whimpered as Lock hopped over a fallen branch. I winced at the sound. I hadn't known Olive long, but I knew it would take a lot to get her to make that noise. She was the stoic type. And she wouldn't be in this state if her drove hadn't been trying to protect me. First Ezra and Lock, then Cade, and now Olive—how many people were going to have to pay for me? When was it going to be enough for the Coterie? I pushed my guilt aside, concentrating on my feet as I walked. I could feel guilty later. Right now I had to pay attention to where I was stepping.

We arrived at a clearing and Lock stopped. It wasn't a big clearing, maybe just large enough to park our van in. Old-growth trees ringed us, and here, at least, the forest was silent. I wasn't sure why Lock had brought us here or why he'd halted. The clearing was empty.

He stood there quietly, staring at the trees, and though the rest of us exchanged curious glances, none of us said anything. After what seemed like forever, Lock cleared his throat.

"We're in a bit of a hurry, here," he said. I don't know who he said it to, but it wasn't to us, I was certain of that.

A throaty voice came out from the underbrush, "Aren't you always? That's humans for you—always rushing about, never staying anywhere long enough to really learn anything."

"Yes, well, that happens when you don't live for hundreds of years—you tend to feel a bit of pressure to do something." The conversation had the air of an old argument. The voice laughed, and then a girl came out from behind a tree. She looked maybe seventeen and way too young for a voice like that. That kind of voice belonged with nightclubs and sultry evenings by the river. Not coming out of a tiny slip of a girl.

She had long brown hair pulled back into a ponytail and the biggest brown eyes I'd ever seen outside of a cow barn. She was short, only coming up to Lock's chin, but she was perfect. Not movie-star beautiful, exactly. Her beauty was closer to seeing the first flower in spring, or a bubbling waterfall after the curve of a trail—natural, well-made, and for a second, overwhelming.

I bet she woke up looking that way too. What a jerk.

Lock leaned over and kissed her on the forehead as the girl examined the rest of us. "What have you brought us this time, my love?" She said the last part while she looked at me, as if to gauge my reaction. I raised an eyebrow, but she didn't respond. Could she tell I was a firebug, or was this some weird protective thing over Lock?

"I'll explain later. Can you take me to her?"

The girl gave a little bob, almost a curtsy, and said, "Of course."

"Thanks, Auntie Mar." She didn't look like an auntie. How big was Lock's family, exactly? I hate meeting families. It never goes well.

She patted his cheek and turned, leading us back into the forest. "Anything for my favorite nephew."

BIG FAMILIES make me a little uncomfortable. It's not hard to guess why. My family has stayed at a pretty constant me plus one my whole life. So when I meet people with cousins and aunties and siblings and what have you, I'm never quite sure how to act. What do you do with so many people?

We soon entered a more open forest area. There were still tons of spruce and pine trees, but the undergrowth was thin and seemed to want to keep out of the way. One giant maple dominated the center, its branches reaching out over us like an umbrella.

And then there were the girls. They were everywhere. In the branches, sitting on rocks, leaning against tree trunks, and they swarmed Lock. There was a lot of cooing and hugging, and they all addressed him as their nephew, though the tone they used was better suited for a young boy than for a guy with a five o'clock shadow who towered over them.

Some of the girls looked over Olive and tutted in sympathy.

Ezra also had a constant swarm. A few admired Sid, making him straighten up and then yelp as the duct tape pulled on his wound. "Serves you right," Ikka whispered. As for Ikka and myself, we were either examined as if we were something stinky that Lock had tracked in, or ignored completely.

The group included every type of girl imaginable—thin and wispy, short and squat, birch white and walnut brown. It was like a woodland sorority convention. Despite the cold, none of them were dressed in very much clothing. And there was nary a goose bump among them. The only other thing they seemed to have in common—besides Lock—was that striking natural beauty that Mar possessed. There was a sense of proportion about them—of rightness. Like they were exactly how they were meant to be, and the effect was beautiful.

It was kind of weird.

"What are they?" Ikka asked me under her breath.

I looked around at the girls, the trees, and Lock. "Dryads," I said. "They have to be dryads."

"Where are all the guys?" she asked.

I could only shrug. I didn't know a whole hell of a lot about Lock's relatives, except that he was raised by his grandma, and that when he talked about his summers with his mom, I didn't remember him mentioning any guys.

"I need to see her," Lock said firmly to one of his aunts. "It's important." He nodded at Olive.

A few of the girls nodded and ran off. It wasn't long before the group parted and a woman, obviously their leader, walked through. She was maybe in her twenties, with hair mostly the crimson red of fall leaves. She had part of it pulled back, and as she moved I could see locks of shimmering green, yellow, and rich brown in the light. Even in the khaki shorts and shirt of a forest ranger, she was a knockout.

She faced Lock and crossed her arms, eyeing the bundle in his arms. "Don't tell me you finally relented and brought me a grandchild?"

Our heads swiveled toward Lock with what I think was a combination of curiosity and shock. Well, except for Sid. He was staring at the redhead with open lust.

Lock rolled his eyes. "Mom, she's about eleven. I'm pretty sure it would have been biologically impossible for me to father a child while I was in elementary school."

The woman pouted in acceptance. "I see. Well, one can hope. Don't just stand there, then. Let's get her looked at."

The dryads disbanded, or at least lost interest in us, though a few trailed after Sid, lightly brushing their fingers through his hair or down his arm while they made eyes at him, and Ezra remained in the center of his personal horde. Ikka and I followed Lock and the redhead. "That's your *mom*?" I whispered. He nodded. "How old was she when she had you? Three?"

"I can hear you, you know," the woman said over her shoulder. "And your astonishment is very complimentary—I'll be eighty-four this spring."

I stopped short; Ikka bumped into me, and Sid bumped into her. We were one stooge away from a comedy act. "Eighty-four?"

"You don't look a day over twenty," Sid said, his tone fawning.

"Put your tongue back in your mouth," his sister snarled.

But Lock's mom just smiled. "We live as the trees live, dear."

234

She led us to a small glade, the kind you see in paintings in cheap hotel rooms—picturesque and vaguely unreal. A small cottage was nestled at the end of it.

Ikka bent close to me. "Am I the only one who thinks that thing should be made of gingerbread and frosting?" I didn't answer her, but then, I didn't have to. It looked exactly like a gingerbread house. Where, exactly, was Lock taking us? And were we going to be a side dish when we got there?

"Don't get into any pots filled with chopped veggies and boiling water—just in case," I said.

Lock paused in front of me, readjusting Olive's weight.

"You should let someone else hold her," I said.

He shook his head. "Sid can't because of his shoulder. Ikka's banged up pretty good too. And Ezra is ... distracted."

"I can take her," I said.

"Trust me, things will go more smoothly if I carry her in. Besides, we're almost there."

A gnarled old lady greeted us at the door. She squinted at us, and when that didn't seem to help, she grabbed a chain around her neck, pulling up a pair of battered eyeglasses. "What have you brought me today, Angela?"

"You remember my son, Lock?"

The old woman's glasses were now perched on the bridge of her nose, and she blinked owlishly at Lock. "You used to hide in my broom cupboard."

"It was the only place the girls wouldn't look for me."

"Hmm, yes, well." She waved us into the house. "Generally the saplings stay where they're supposed to. I suppose it was difficult being the only boy, though, eh?" She didn't wait for an answer. "Of course, I also remember that you used to sweep

235

my floor once you came out of the cupboard. Who are your friends?"

"This is Sid, Ikka, Ava, Ezra, and the little one is Olive. We got into a bit of a scrape earlier and could use some help. Everyone, this is Rose MacArthur. We call her Grandma Rose."

Grandma Rose shooed away the last of the dryads except for Lock's mom before she had Lock lay Olive down on what looked suspiciously like a medical table. It was padded, but also vinyl—easy to wipe down. "Pertinents, dear," Rose said as she examined Olive's face.

"The girl is a were-hare—she usually has fast healing abilities but we met up with some sort of vodyanoy. I'd never seen ones like these. They spit acid or poison or something. It seems to be interfering."

"Yes, it does look rather corrosive, doesn't it?" She checked the girl's pulse and listened to her heart with a stethoscope. "Sit her up, please."

Lock pulled Olive up gently and carefully grasped her chin, pulling her mouth open. Grandma Rose helped Olive drink a thick liquid that we were informed was for the pain. After most of it had made it down, Olive gagging and choking out the rest, Lock laid her back on the table. Grandma Rose had Lock hold Olive on one side while Ikka took the other.

"I've got to clean the wound. The corrosive is inhibiting her natural abilities. But if I clean it and salve it, she'll be right as rain in the morning."

"In the morning?" I asked before I could stop myself, which earned me a hard glare from the old woman.

"You have something more important than healing this little one, missy?"

My first impulse was to say yes, because Cade was the center of my wobbly universe, and we were hemorrhaging time. But there was nothing I could do for Cade right now. The drove was looking for him, our message was delivered—if Venus showed up at my home in the meantime, the drove would let us know. I had to put my fear aside and help Olive.

I shook my head. "No, ma'am. I just need to warn some friends is all." That seemed to pacify her for the moment. She got everything ready—various liquids and ointments and gauze, then she gave everyone one last look. "Now, this is going to hurt, even with what I gave her. But I have to do it, understand?" Ikka and Sid nodded, though Ikka bit her lip as she did so. "Okay, then. Hold her steady."

I don't know what she used to clean the wound, but Olive screamed. Lock and Ikka fought to hold the little girl down as her body twisted and jumped underneath them. Ezra pinned her ankles, trying to keep her from moving. Sid took one of Olive's hands, then squatted down so he could be closer to her ear and started murmuring reassurances to her. She calmed, though it was obvious she was still hurting.

I wanted to help. Everyone else was helping. But what could I do? I'd never spent much time around children. Okay, barring a few following their parents into the bookstore, I'd never spent *any* time with children. But I liked Olive, and she was hurt because of me. I reached for her hand, hesitated, and moved back. Angela watched me, and I was reminded of a cat keeping an eye on a mouse to see what it would do next. Grandma Rose snorted, grabbed my hand, and set it on top of Olive's. "It helps more than you know," she murmured, but it had the ring of a reprimand.

After the wound was cleaned, Grandma Rose applied a thick ointment to Olive's face. Sid eyed it warily. "That looks like Neosporin, but with . . . things in it."

The old woman shrugged. "Similar, I suppose. It will keep the skin pliant while she heals." Grandma Rose started putting away her tools, some of them going into a sink for cleaning. "Rest—that's what she needs now." She ordered Lock to carry the girl into a small guest room. The room held several cots and was painted a soft lilac color. The sheets were clean, and the blankets were cozy-looking quilts, but I knew a hospital room when I saw one. After Olive was tucked in and Ikka promised to stay with her until she was asleep, Rose ordered us back into her operating room. Sid and Lock still needed attention, now that Olive was taken care of.

Grandma Rose cleaned, then sutured in Lock's case and bandaged in Sid's, talking only when she needed to order one of the boys to stop moving or when she needed me to fetch something. I don't like being ordered about, but it felt good to be helpful. It felt good to heal for once.

When everything was done, Sid went outside to call in and report—and to tell Les that we weren't going to be at my house until the next day. Hopefully Venus wouldn't rush to take our bait. Lock went to bring our stuff in, since we'd be bunking with Rose for the night. When he got back, we realized that Ezra had disappeared.

Lock was pissed. "I specifically told him not to. Stupid fox—"

Angela cut him off. "You brought a fox into his habitat and told him not to be a fox? Who are you calling stupid, exactly?"

"But—"

Angela patted his cheek, smiling at his expression of cha-grin. "I will tell the girls to keep an eye on him. We'll keep him out of trouble."

"Or get him into it," Lock mumbled after she left. Then he carried our stuff deeper into the cottage without another word.

I stayed behind in the workroom to see if there was any-thing more I could help with.

Grandma Rose gave me some natural disinfectant, water, and a cloth. Everything had to be cleaned, but the dryads wouldn't let her bring bleach into the forest. The silence stretched between us as I worked, the bite of the cleaner waft-ing its way into my nose.

"Are they going to be okay?" I finally asked.

"Yes, if they can manage to keep their noses out of mis-chief for ten seconds. The weres heal well, but they don't always listen." She opened a drawer full of bandages, needles, and assorted medical stock so she could put away the items she hadn't used.

I handed her the bottle of cleaner and the cloth, and she handed me a mop and a bucket of water. From the smell of it, the water contained the same stuff. "'Trouble' meaning me?"

Grandma Rose harrumphed. "Hares will make trouble. Love to tussle, those ones. Foxes? Worse." She dumped her rinsed tools into a plastic tub to soak before they went into a small whirring machine that she'd informed me was an auto-clave. Then she turned my way, assessing me as she dried her hands on a towel. "But you need to be careful what opportuni-ties you present to them. Always think what you ask of people, what you're *really* asking them to do for you, before you tempt them with it. That goes for weres, and for others, too."

I knew she meant Lock. If Grandma Rose had known any-thing about me, she'd have known that I didn't really need a lecture on collateral damage. I was an expert. Or was I? I looked at the soaking tools, the water slightly pink from blood, at the crimson pile of used gauze already turning brown from time and oxygen. Had I really thought about what I was asking of Lock? Of the drove? No, I hadn't. Just like I hadn't really thought of what I was asking of Ryan merely by spending time with him. Suddenly it was too much. I managed to get the mop in the vicinity of the bucket before I rushed outside, away from Rose's suffocating accusations.

14

IF I'M GOING TO GO THROUGH HELL, THERE SHOULD AT LEAST BE SOME BACON

I'D LIKE TO SAY I just needed a breath of fresh air and some time to collect myself. That would have been nice. I would have enjoyed being calm and collected when Lock eventually found me—a pretty picture amongst a few brave fireflies willing to shake their stuff that evening. Maybe I could have been sitting underneath some sort of weeping willow looking every inch a brave, though conflicted, heroine. Instead, Lock found me sobbing uncontrollably into the mossy floor around a rather gnarled oak tree, and I'm almost positive that my swollen eyes and runny nose did not a pretty picture make. Plus, I had dirt on my face.

Lock nudged me until I was mostly propped up against the trunk. He handed me a handkerchief, which I immediately befouled by blowing my nose. "How did you know to bring a handkerchief?" I asked with a hiccup. Even though I wasn't crying anymore, my body wasn't quite done with the whole sobbing/spasming thing yet.

"Grandma Rose has that effect on people," he said, lowering himself down to join me under the tree.

"She's right," I said. "I'm endangering all of you, and it's not okay. This should be my battle—not yours. Not Olive's. That girl should be at home playing with dolls and, I don't know, making cookies or something."

"Please, it's Olive. She'd be home picking pockets and sharpening her knife collection."

I laughed, suddenly and surprised, spitting a little. So attractive. Since Lock's handkerchief was absolutely disgusting, I had to use the edge of my shirt to finish cleaning off my face. I supposed I should have been embarrassed, but really, Lock had seen me at my absolute worst. What was a little dirt and mucus?

"What, exactly, did Rose say?"

I recited the short conversation for him. He considered it, watching the fireflies in front of him. They liked Lock and kept swooping closer, until I could see his face in the flashes of their light. "She's both right and wrong, you know. Yes, it's your fight, but please don't try to tell me it's not mine, too. How many nights have I joined you guys for movie night? I spend more time with Cade than I do with my mom, Aves. He's family. I'm going to be part of this whether you want me to or not. So deal with it."

"But—"

He shushed me with a wave of his hand. "As for the drove, c'mon—Venus put a hit out on Duncan. Even if they didn't like you, they'd damn well fight to get Venus back for that. They can't just let her come in and kill the guy they're protecting. Besides what it would do to their reputation, I think they

242

consider Duncan to be one of their own. No way they're sitting idly by, especially since they'd lose their home if they lost Duncan. As for Ez, I'm sure if anyone but us asked him, he'd lie and say he was doing it for kicks. But we both know that's all show. We're a team. We're family. It doesn't really matter what title you put on it, the meaning is the same. You're in trouble, we're all in trouble. If the situation were reversed, you'd be doing the exact same thing. So, I'm sorry if it interrupts your grand guilt fest, but this isn't just about you. It's about all of us. Get over yourself."

"You can be such an asshole sometimes," I said, leaning my head on his shoulder. "I love you."

"Who doesn't?"

I smacked him, one-handed, but didn't move from my position. Being closer to Lock meant being closer to the fireflies—an unexpected but wonderful consequence. A rather enterprising one landed in Lock's hair, where it continued to shine like it had landed on a small outcropping of grass.

I was overcome with fits of giggles, and the startled bug flew off.

"Now what's wrong with you?" he asked, frowning.

"Nothing," I said, wiping away another tear, this one coming from happier origins. "It's just that I realized I could mostly see you because of the fireflies—because you were surrounded by butt lights. For some reason I found that to be very funny."

"I can't imagine why," he said drily. More fireflies floated around him, and I flew into another fit of laughter. Lock sighed and put an arm around me, drawing my giggle-twitching body closer to his. "I love you, too," he said.

"Of course you do," I said.

"Now who's the asshole?"

I SPENT a restless night on a cot. Every time Olive whimpered in her sleep or Sid snored—or Ikka cursed at Sid for snoring—I woke up. Ezra was still roaming about the forest, as far as I knew. The hares seemed to be used to sleeping so many in a room. Ikka barely woke to swear and hit Sid, and his eyes didn't open when he smacked her with a pillow in retaliation. But I wasn't used to it. I was used to quiet night sounds and maybe the sound of Cade getting up for a drink of water. It could get so quiet in our cabin that it was almost disruptive—like you could feel the weight of that silence pressing in on your ears.

I've lived in tons of places, and I've had to get used to lots of different kinds of night noises—the chatter of cicadas when we lived in the South, the honk of cars in a big city—but the lack of sound in Currant had been the hardest for me to grow accustomed to.

And now I missed it.

My nightmares alternated between Cade being tortured then locked in a cell and Ryan taking me on our first date. We were on top of a hill. He'd picked up food from the deli, packed it into his parents' wicker picnic basket, and brought an old sheet. From up on the hill we could watch the sailboats go by as we stretched out on the thin sheet and talked. I'd thought the date might be awkward, but Ryan was easy to talk to, and I didn't usually have the chance to get to know someone new. When I'd prepared for the evening, I was sure I was going to come home early, disenchanted after the first thirty minutes.

But we'd stayed out late, and I'd spent most of the time smiling. I'd had fun. I didn't often get to have fun.

In my dream Ryan leaned back on the sheet, his elbows digging into the ground beneath, and in a voice pitched husky and soft, he told me it had all been an act and how stupid I was to fall for it. I woke up, sweaty and shaking.

By dawn I decided I'd rather be tired than see those images anymore. I changed my clothes in Rose's bathroom, the walls of which were covered in hand-painted butterflies, with mats and towels in a bright purple jewel tone. A claw-footed tub took up most of the space, and it tempted me like all get-out. I wanted nothing more than a hot bath and a good night's sleep. I sighed and turned my back on the tub.

In the kitchen, Grandma Rose was already up. Like the not-all-together-sweet angel of mercy that she was, she handed me a steaming cup of coffee and a bowl of oatmeal. Something must have shown on my face, because she laughed as she sat down across from me.

"No doubt you're wondering why I'm not handing you a proper breakfast—eggs, bacon, whatnot?"

I grimaced. "I'm that transparent, huh?" And presumptuous, apparently. "I didn't mean to insult your hospitality."

She blew on her coffee, the steam parting and framing her wrinkled face. "I wish for the same thing every morning. But it's the dryads, you see."

I didn't.

She leaned forward with a conspirator's air. "Think about it, dear. You're in the middle of a forest. One must think of one's hosts."

"So—no bacon?"

"Limited fire, and a practically vegan lifestyle." She pushed a honey pot my way, gesturing toward the porridge. "They allow me some honey, and they look the other way for cheese. I love cheese."

"Don't we all?" I dropped a liberal amount of honey into my oatmeal.

"And they pretend not to notice when I go into town and come back smelling of lobster rolls." She sighed happily.

I couldn't help smiling back at her. Despite her criticism last night, I liked Grandma Rose. In fact, I think I liked her more for saying those things. I value people who care enough to give you the truth, who make you examine the dark and nasty sides of yourself. It shows heart.

I took a long swig of my coffee, the warmth going down to my toes and making me feel almost human. I tucked into my food. "Thank you," I said between mouthfuls. "For everything."

"It's my job, dear." She took the honey pot back, drizzling some into her coffee. I'd never thought to do that, so I repeated her action and found that I liked it. "I am a healer—I can be nothing else. Did you think about what I said last night?"

"I did."

"And?"

I thought for a moment, my oatmeal spoon hovering between bowl and mouth. Finally, I jabbed the air with it. "It's just . . ." I shrugged, dripping a smidgen of oatmeal onto the table. "I'm a firebug—I can't be anything else. The drove is the drove—it can't be anything else either. And Lock and Ezra are my team, and where one of us goes, the others follow. We can't turn away. For very different reasons, we have to see this through." I tapped my spoon on the side of my bowl. "Does that make sense? Or am I only justifying my actions?"

Rose leaned forward with a napkin and wiped up the blob of oatmeal. "I think as long as everyone is aware of the mess and willing to help clean it up, then you're being about as honest as you can be."

I nodded. "I think that's where we're at."

"Good. Now eat your food before it gets cold."

AFTER the rest of the group stumbled in and ate a ridiculous amount of food, Rose examined everyone. Due to her expert care and their own natural healing abilities, the bandages all came off. Olive and Sid both had some shiny red scar tissue, but I was told that would be gone soon enough. Lock was left to heal his stitches on his own, and his bandages were replaced with new ones. His few sutures would dissolve in a week or so. I was given a jar of the ointment and told to keep an eye on my friend or I'd suffer some dire consequences. Hearing those words from the mouth of the wizened old woman, her eyes blinking at me from behind glasses, I found myself believing her.

Ezra stumbled in halfway through the examination progress. There were twigs and bits of leaves in his hair, and he had no shirt on. In fact, he'd lost everything except for his pants, and he was pretty dirty. He was also looking rather smug.

Lock grabbed a washcloth and ran it under warm water, handing it to our friend. "You had that same smile when I found you passed out in that gas station parking lot, half-naked and covered in glitter."

Ezra looked wistful for a second as he washed. "That was a pretty great night. What I remember of it, anyway."

"I don't want to know," Lock said.

"Still?" Ezra asked.

"Still. I want you to take that story to your grave."

Ezra went back to washing and let the subject drop.

After a long and tearful good-bye for the boys and Olive—Ikka and I were still largely ignored by the dryads—we were finally ready to go. Most of the dryads dissolved back into the forest, but Lock's mother, Angela, stayed. She reached out, her strong hands holding the jacket the dryads had found for him to wear. We really were going through a lot of clothing lately.

"I wish you'd stay," she said, not looking him in the eyes.

"I know."

She let go of the jacket. "And while we're at it, I wish you'd stop wearing dead animals, putting chemicals in your hair, and not fathering any babies."

"Yes, Mom, I know."

"I'll let the rest of it go if you make some babies." He didn't roll his eyes, even though I would have. "I'm serious, Lock. We could use some fresh blood out there. We can hardly keep up with these humans destroying the trees as quickly as they do." She gave me the stink eye like I was to answer for all the humans everywhere.

"So get on it—meet a nice girl and knock her up. In fact, I'd like you to meet several."

Lock put his hands on her shoulders and looked down—he was more than a few inches taller than his mother. "Mom, I'm too young. I'm not ready to become the oak version of Johnny Appleseed."

"Too young," she muttered. "Your cousin started having children at thirteen. You've been ready for years. Years! You must be lazy. That's the only thing I can think of. You're handsome enough." She stared me down. "You. Girl. Isn't my son handsome?"

"Yes?" I said, looking at Lock helplessly. From his expression I could guess that this was not a new conversation. Well, it was new to me. Some help would be welcome.

"Then why aren't you pregnant yet?"

"Don't answer that, Ava," Lock said.

Like I was planning on it.

He squeezed his mother's shoulders. "Mom, my cousins are all dryads—of course they're having babies at thirteen. But I'm half-human. And partly raised by a human. And I can tell you quite honestly that teen pregnancy is generally frowned upon in this country. I'm not capable of handling rug rats right now. You'll just have to accept that."

She pouted. "It's not like you'd have to raise them. Just bring the baby here. The mother could come too, I guess."

He leaned in and kissed her on the forehead. "No."

She sighed, and the trees sighed with her. "Fine. For now. I'm not giving up."

"Oh, how I know," he said. Then he let her go and we made our way toward the van.

We managed to get back onto the main access road before Sid opened his mouth to make a crack. Lock, his arms crossed and his brows furrowed, growled at him. "Not a word. Not a damn word."

Sid closed his mouth, but I could tell it was an effort for him to do so.

Olive, however, completely ignored Lock's demands. "You should knock up a nice drove girl. We put out babies like nobody's business." She gave an exaggerated wink, even though it pulled the shiny scar tissue taut and probably hurt. "We're hares, remember? They have sayings about us and babies."

Lock glowered at her, but I could tell he was trying not to laugh.

I couldn't stop checking out Olive's face, the skin puffy and pink with scar tissue—though even that was fading as I watched, melting as if it had never been. Fascinated, I couldn't not look. Well, until Olive glared at me and very pointedly said, "It's rude to stare, you know." I stumbled over an apology, and Lock busted up laughing. I kicked him, but he didn't stop. He just tucked his legs to the side so I couldn't reach. Jerk.

The phone in my pocket buzzed and my heart leapt with it. I'd handed this number out to only three people. Cade, Duncan, and the Council. I wished I'd been able to give it to Ryan so I could tell him what an utter bastard he was, but my focus was really on Cade. I could track Ryan down later and scream at him to my heart's content.

I didn't recognize the number, but I hit answer anyway. "Hello?"

"Ava, so wonderful to hear your voice."

Owen.

"You have a lovely home, Ava. Charmingly quaint. Like something out of a catalog. I helped myself to some tea. I hope you don't mind."

I could picture Owen sitting at my table, his fingers slowly drumming across the top, a soft *tap tap, tap tap*. Pause. *Tap tap, tap tap*. "You didn't come home last night." His words caressed my ears in a hum. "I heard a motorcycle drive by a few times. Was someone supposed to be watching the house? For me? I'm touched."

My breath was a harsh scrape in my ear as it rasped over the phone. I couldn't think of anything to say. Owen had that effect on me.

"Then again, maybe they were looking for someone else? Your guardian, perhaps? Such a gentle man. You know his eye does this little twitch when he tries to not scream? Simply adorable." He paused, and I heard him swallow. He really had raided our tea stash. "So where did you rest your little head, firebug? Hmm?"

When was the last time I'd heard Owen speak this much? I couldn't remember. He was something to be avoided—a filthy puddle in the road, a pile of rusty nails and broken boards, thong underwear made of scratchy lace. Thong underwear period.

"A friend's," I said, my voice coming out thick.

"I told Venus you would come back here. She said you were too smart for that. It looks like I lost the bet. I rather dislike losing."

"Oh?" I asked.

"You've given us a merry chase, but its time to face the music," Owen said.

"I've never really understood that saying," I said, nervously. "How exactly does one face music?" I knew what he was offering. Return to the Inferno. Take my lashings and everything would slide back into normal. Only it was a big ol' stack of lies covered in maple syrup. Venus wouldn't let anything slide back to normal. I'd cost her too much, both financially and politically. She had to save face and restore order to her blood-thirsty little kingdom.

"You're obviously too untrustworthy to work in the field anymore," Owen said, and I was terrified by the joy in his voice. "Pity, really. Still, you have your uses. We were hoping to wait until you were a little older, but your defiance has sped things up a bit. You'll have to live under lock and key of course, but at least Venus will let you live. Maybe if you're really good, Venus will let you name one of our children after your mother."

Stars and sparks—a breeding program. All those years my mom talked about it, but I hadn't actually seen any evidence of one since I'd been at the Coterie. The idea of Owen touching me made bile rise in my throat.

"Why now?" I managed to whisper. "Why not as soon as . . ." I couldn't even finish the sentence. I was going to be sick.

"We would have lost a valuable field operative. What sense would that have made? Now, however, you've made it quite impossible for us to use you for anything else."

I know people throw around the phrase "I'd rather be dead" a great deal, but I'd rather be dead. As usual, all my options were shit. And overlying all of these was the fact that, if I wasn't careful with how I handled the situation, Cade might get hurt. Owen certainly wouldn't lose any sleep over burning him to death.

We were at an impasse, which I hated. It meant delicate treading, and let's face it, I'm crap at that.

I cleared my throat. "We both know I can't go back."

252

"And we both know I can't let you go."

My mind whirred, flitting about here and there, desperately trying to come up with any way out. A few of my fingers sparked, and I cursed.

"Language, Ava. Can't have you saying such things in front of our children, now, can we?" He had me spooked and he knew it. Damn.

Unless . . . wait. I could use this. Let Owen think I was scared out of my mind—overwound and frantic. It didn't really matter that I was all of those things. I could spin it to my advantage.

"Maybe we can make some sort of deal," I said, my voice intentionally high and breathy. "Venus wants me back in, right? And I don't want anyone hurt. So why not initiate some sort of trade? Me for Cade." I stumbled over my guardian's name. "Ryan, too. I don't know what Venus has planned for him, or what he thinks he's getting into, but if he wants to walk away, he can." If only so I could beat the tar out of him myself. "Me for two lowly humans," I said, wiping my sweaty palms on my jeans. "No muss, no fuss. Venus can even bring an audience." She would like that last bit. Venus loved humiliation and abasement.

I could almost hear him thinking it over. "Yes, it has potential." I heard the clink of Owen putting his mug in the sink. My sink. We might be twitching with fear and anxiety, but Owen was tidying up. "I'll run it by Venus and see what she has to say. Keep your phone handy. If we call, *you'd* better answer," he said. Then the line went dead.

15

NOTHING LIKE A FRIENDLY INVASION

THERE WAS NOTHING to do but comply. Sid called the drove and reported in while Ikka steered the van back to Duncan's. The drive was quiet after that except for Ez and Olive's heated discussion about the best pickpocket techniques.

"It's plain to see that I'm just going to have to take over your training," Ezra said, scrutinizing his nails. He had dirt under them, which was probably driving him mad.

"What's wrong with my training? I'm the best pickpocket we have!" Olive said. Sid grunted. "Except for Sid." Ikka cleared her throat. "And Ikka."

"Best of the fuzzy bunnies? Please. What do they know about being tricky?" There were several noises of protest, but Ez ignored them. "No. It won't do. We'll start immediately."

"Shouldn't we wait until we're out of danger?" Olive asked.

"See? That's rabbit thinking—you can't think like prey. *They* are the prey. You're the mighty hunter. Besides, you're always in danger, so you have to learn how to twist it to your advantage.

During some trouble is the best time. People are distracted." He held up a few crumpled bills with a flourish and handed them back to her. "See? You didn't even know this was missing."

Olive took the money with a look of irritation on her face. Then she shoved the cash into one of her many pockets and took a wallet out of the pocket under it. "Since you gave mine back, it's only fair."

Ezra took back his wallet, his eyebrows arched in appreciation. "Yes, I will train you now. Ignore the rabbits." He shoved his wallet into his back pocket. "You're obviously part fox anyway." Sid and Ikka took offense at that and started arguing with him, but I tuned them out for the rest of the drive.

When we got back to Duncan's, I took a hot shower. The great thing about showers? You can't tell if you're crying. I let the hot water roll off me and worried about Cade and fumed at Ryan and told myself it was just regular water on my face. I hate crying. It makes me feel helpless.

Once I was done, Lock took his turn. I vacated to my temporary room. I noticed that Ezra had swiped a few framed photos from my cabin. One of us, and another of me, Mom, and Cade. How old was I in that photo? Nine, maybe. I couldn't tell. There weren't any for me to compare it with. Life in hiding meant I didn't have many photos. No school pictures, no family vacation footage. In fact, the only ones I'd seen belonged to Duncan and Cade. In this picture my mom and Cade were laughing and holding me up. We were outside, and I recognized the fire pit in Duncan's backyard. I loved that photo when I was younger. I could look at it and pretend we were a real family. Now it hurt just to see it.

Ezra had set the frames on a shelf, shoving aside the photos that were already there. A young Cade next to Duncan, both of them holding up the fish they'd caught. Another of Cade and my mom, dressed up and clearly going to prom, or something like it. My chest constricted.

Ikka found me on the edge of my bed, trying in vain to get my hair to behave. When I was younger, my mom used to help me braid it. I had a lot of hair, and it was too unmanageable for me. After she died, Cade took over. I'd tried to do it myself the last few years but, to be honest, I'd never quite mastered it. Whatever Ikka had been planning on saying when she walked in, I'll never know. She took one look at me and grabbed the brush away from me.

"Here, let me do it. You're just making a nest."

I held up my hands in surrender. Half-assed ponytails I can manage, but not braids. I'm not so proud that I can't admit when I'm licked.

We didn't talk while Ikka climbed onto the bed behind me and unsnarled the mess I'd made. She hummed a tune I didn't recognize, and I closed my eyes and for a second—a guilty, heartrending second—I pretended my mom was still alive. That Ikka's soft song and gentle hands belonged to an impossible someone.

It made it hurt that much more when I opened my eyes.

"Ta-da," Ikka said, handing me the brush.

"You're fast."

She stood up and examined the new photos Ezra had brought. "The drove goes with the 'it takes a village' approach to child rearing. I've braided a lot of hair over the years." She picked up the photo of me, Lock, and Ez. "You look happy here."

Ikka didn't seem to be expecting a response, so I said

nothing as she peeked into my life. She held up another photo, this one in a smaller frame that had been tucked in behind the one of Cade and my mom. I peered over her shoulder and realized it was another of Lock, Ezra, and me, this one from soon after we met.

"Is this . . . ?"

I nodded. "Yes, and if you think that's bad, you should've seen the mustache."

Ikka shuddered. "You're all so *scrawny.*"

"Are you saying I'm fat now?" I asked with a straight face.

Ikka gave me a flat look, then went back to the photo. "Ugh, he looks like the great god Hipster threw up and made a person."

I leaned over her shoulder. There I was: frail, awkward, and way too skinny, but too depressed and growing too fast to really put weight on. And there was Lock, floppy black hair, eyeliner—an underfed puppy. Ezra didn't even have the decency to look awkward in his younger years. It looked like he was posing with misfits he'd taken pity on. "I kind of miss the eyeliner."

Ikka traced our faces in the photo with the tip of her finger. "You all look so young and innocent. What happened?"

"The Coterie happened," I said, sighing. "Lock had to get further up in the chain—for protection. He isn't . . ." I waffled, trying to think of a good way to phrase it.

"He's not scary," she said.

"They didn't think so at the time." After the pool incident, I bet Venus was reassessing my friend. "They know better now."

I sat down on the bed, unable to look at the photo any longer. "He volunteered himself as a tithe so that Venus would leave the dryads alone. Since he was supporting himself, he

257

needed to get one of the better-paying positions. There was no way they were going to let him onto the Purgatory floor looking like a half-starved Ichabod Crane. He started lifting weights, swimming, eating more. Ezra helped him change his wardrobe. And then they started sending him out with me." I could feel my voice hardening. "That's what really did it. He changed because of the Coterie. They made him change." One more thing stolen, one more thing to punish them for.

Ikka looked at the photo again before setting it back onto the shelf. "He had to grow up, Ava, that's all. It looks good on him."

I wanted to argue with her, to say that growing up had nothing to do with it, but she changed the subject before I could.

"Everyone's coming back," she said, picking up a paperback and flipping it over in her hands.

"Everyone? Who's everyone?"

She turned and blinked at me, more owl than hare. "The drove. Duncan. You know, everyone."

I wasn't used to having help or functioning in a group— especially not like Ikka was. "Oh," I said, pulling an old sweater over my head while I considered this. "Should I . . . do anything?"

Ikka seemed to understand what I was asking. Small-unit work, like with Ez and Lock, I was used to, but for the most part I was more sniper than general. You wouldn't come to me for ideas on how to lead the troops.

Ikka leaned against my dresser, her arms folded. "Not really. Sid has some snacks going. Lock is handling the logistics of where we'll put everyone since we're not used to having the entire drove all in once place like this. Ezra is showering finally, and Olive is checking the cabin's defenses."

"Olive? Isn't that kind of . . . you know, something one of you guys should be handling?"

Ikka laughed. "Oh, I'll double-check her findings because it's customary—two pairs of eyes, and all that—but you won't find anyone more thorough than Olive. Or more vicious."

I remembered how quickly she'd held a knife to my throat. Nope, couldn't really argue with Ikka there.

Her face brightened. "How about you start a fire? That would save us all the time of mucking about with kindling."

I HAD NEVER seen so many people in Duncan's kitchen. The drove had taken over the cabin. They moved in like a swarm of locusts—which, considering the way they ate, wasn't far off. The outside of the cabin, usually serene with its dirt driveway and surrounding trees, suddenly became a seething mass of movement. Hares were setting up tents, pulling up in campers, and parking motorcycles in clumps. Big camouflage nets were thrown over the larger objects, hiding them from immediate view. Small groups of patrols disappeared into the surrounding wood.

"We've been invaded," Lock whispered, nudging me.

I watched two of the were patrols motion to each other, their hands flicking quickly through several signals before they disappeared back into the brush. "You think they're saying anything important, or just trading dirty jokes?" I whispered back.

Les rubbed his chin, his fingers tracing the fine webbing of scar tissue at his neck. I desperately wanted to ask how it was that he had scars when I'd seen Olive and Sid heal up without a scratch. "Dirty jokes are important," he said. "They raise morale." Then he got back down to business, making me go over, for a second time, everything that had happened since we left.

All the talking and waiting was making me anxious. If Venus didn't call soon, I'd explode. My mom would have told me not to joke like that. A firebug going supernova isn't funny. I shuddered and grabbed a sandwich off of the platter Sid had put out. The last thing I wanted was to turn into a human meteor.

Les leaned back in his chair, thinking, and I could feel every hare in the room go still, all chatter and motion coming to a stop as they waited to see what their leader would say. "Not much to do now," Les said, staring at Duncan. "We can't plan until she calls."

Duncan agreed with a grunt. He was whittling again, this time a tiny fox, by the look of things. I wanted to smack the figure right out of his meaty paws. Was now really a good time for that? What was a tiny wooden fox going to do to help us?

He threw me a questioning look, even though his fingers kept moving, never once stopping their glide as he shaped the wood. Our eyes met, held. I turned away, my jaw clenched tight. I felt Lock's knee touch mine, and despite my best efforts to hold on to my anger like a comfortable old blankie, I felt my muscles relax, the fire in my gut dim and sputter. Lock always had that effect on me. Sometimes I hated him for it. Sometimes I needed that anger.

Duncan put the wooden fox down on the table and the hares eyed it warily, like it might come off the table and nip

260

at them. Since it could fit in the palm of my hand, I didn't see why they all leaned minutely away from it. Even if Duncan made it come to life, wouldn't it still be too small to do any harm? Maybe it was an ingrained survival thing—must beware of foxes, even tiny ones. I squished down a smile.

"We'll just have to wait," Duncan said, pulling a new chunk of wood from a bin by his chair. I was beginning to think he had a problem, an addiction to whittling. Was that a thing? Could we find him a support group when this was all over?

Les slumped, his eyes on the tiny fox, seemingly more as something to rest his gaze on than anything else. "Maybe we should go over Venus again—her strengths and weaknesses. Try to plan our attack."

I got up from the table, stretching, knowing this discussion would be fruitless.

"Nothing to add, Ava?" There was a sarcastic note in Les's voice, an accusation I didn't care for.

"I want her gone as much as you do," I said, wrapping my arms around my waist, suddenly bone weary of it all. "More, probably. But speculation is useless. Besides, I know what her weak spot is, I just don't know if we'll manage to exploit it."

"If you have something to share with the class . . ." Duncan said, not looking up from his work.

"Hubris," I said, holding myself tighter. "With vamps like her, it always comes down to that." Then I stomped out of the room, refusing to explain myself further. I didn't owe anyone explanations, least of all Duncan.

MY MOM and I were somewhere in Colorado. The air was cold and dry, and the sudden shift up into higher elevation wasn't going well for me. My mom was making me drink tons of water. She was also keeping a hawk eye on me, since I'd start to spark at random times. When that happened, I could never quite tell if she was worried or proud, so I'd made up a new emotion—I called it *woud*, or sometimes *porried*—to describe the welter that seemed to overtake her whenever I made the slightest flame.

We'd holed up in a snug cabin somewhere at the edge of a tiny town. There was no electricity, and I would cozy up on the bench seat by one of the cabin windows, where I'd read and watch the snow fall. I loved the quiet and the sense of safety. My mom must have felt the same way—she didn't look over her shoulder as much when we were there. She'd relaxed a fraction. I watched her from my seat as she sat by the fireplace, humming a tune and doing her best to mend the torn sleeve on my jacket. It was quite an undertaking—the sleeve tore when I'd thrown the jacket over some barbed wire that topped a fence I was climbing. We were running from Coterie men—they'd come close to getting us, and there hadn't been time to be careful. I made it over the fence, but in yanking my jacket, I'd torn the sleeve.

I could have left it, but I knew better. Short term, leaving the jacket would have bought me a few more seconds of running time. Long term, I could have frozen to death, not to mention the importance of all the things I had sewn into the lining—things I needed. Things that might have helped them track us again, or worse, confirm what I was.

A flare of anger over my jacket—and the scratches on my mom's forearms from the same climb—caused sparks to jump from my fingers onto the blankets. I yelped and she sighed as she watched me swat at the tiny spots of singed wool.

"Really, Ava."

"Sorry, Mom," I mumbled, rearranging the blanket so the scorched bits were at my feet.

"If you keep this up, I'll have to take your books away. I'm afraid of your fingers on all those flammable pages," her voice was stern, but I could see a half smile on her lips.

I clutched my paperback to my chest. "You wouldn't dare," I said, cradling the book protectively.

Her tiny smile flared and then dimmed before she looked away from me, suddenly sad. I padded over to her, resting my hand on her shoulder. "I'm sorry, Mom. Don't be sad, okay?"

She smiled up at me then, but her eyes were wet and shining in the firelight. "You don't need to apologize to me, sweetheart. It's nothing. You just..." She turned back to the fire. "You reminded me of Cade just then, somehow. The expression on your face. And the book."

The comparison made my chest squeeze, but in a good way. There was no greater compliment from my mom. I would hold on to these moments in my mind, squirrel them away. And sometimes, when things got really bad, I'd bring them out and pretend, just for a second, that Cade was my dad. I knew he wasn't. The math didn't add up. I'd seen photos of the first time he'd met me, when I was two, and he hadn't seen my mom in almost three and a half years before that. The time line just didn't work. Still, I could dream. It was better than trying to imagine a stranger.

I shoved my mom's mending away and flopped on her lap, which I knew would cheer her up.

"Get off, you big whale." She pushed me gently. "You can't be my child—you're too big. I gave birth to an adorable little girl, not some sort of giant."

"I can't get up. My legs are broken."

She laughed and hugged me close, her cheek resting against my hair. When I felt like she was out of her slump, and when I knew it was safe to, I asked when we'd get to visit Cade again. Besides my mom, he was the only thing even remotely consistent in my life. And he made my mom light up in a way that nothing and no one else did.

"I don't know," she said, her voice a whisper.

I knew better than to ask, and I already knew the answer, but I couldn't help asking anyway. "Why can't we live with him? I'll be careful, Mom. I can hide. I know I can."

My mom squeezed me. "He practically lives at that bookstore of his, and even if he didn't, his cabin is full of books too. Books are paper, dear. Paper burns really well. It seems like a terrible place for a bug."

I sat up and play punched her arm. "Be serious."

"I am," she said; then, seeing that I wasn't going to give it up, she gave me a real response. "It wouldn't work, sweetheart. Even if we were careful. Even if we hid. Cade wouldn't be safe—we wouldn't be safe." I could hear the brittle pain in her voice. "Cade deserves to live his life fully. It wouldn't be fair to put him in danger simply so we could be happier." I saw her reach unconsciously for her necklace, her fingers gripping that tiny silver heart and star.

"I think Cade would risk it," I said softly, looking down at my hands. "You should let him choose."

"Sometimes," my mother said, her voice suddenly firm and taking no nonsense from me, "you have to protect people from their own choices. Without us he's out of harm's way. Our occasional visits are risky enough."

I did my best preteen sulk, and the flames in the fireplace sputtered in reaction. My mom pulled me close again, stroking the top of my head before she kissed it. "Nothing lasts forever, Ava. Not even the Coterie. That includes Venus. Who knows," she said, the last bit having a wistful air about it, "maybe someday we can stop running."

"And live with Cade?" I couldn't help asking, just like I couldn't help the flicker of hope in my chest. It was a child's question—I knew it even then. It was built from cobwebs and air. Fragile. And reality was a big, fat spider, ready to tear it to shreds to get what it wanted.

"Yes, and live with Cade."

I wished for that future on everything in the room. With every tiny molecule in my being. I would regret that wish later. It was a faerie wish—it came true, but the cost was too high.

My mom complained that her legs were going to sleep, so I slid to the floor, my head resting on her knee. I must have had a hopeful cast to my face, because my mom continued to reassure me.

"I don't know if it will be in our lifetimes, but eventually Venus will be defeated, sweetheart. Empires fall, and so do their emperors."

"I hope it does happen," I said. "Soon. But she seems so . . . invincible." Because of the stories my mother had told me, Venus loomed large above my life, an overwhelming shadow. Bedtime stories take a different tone when the bogeyman is real.

"Even Venus has her flaws," my mom said.

"She'll never take her wards off, though," I said. "You told me that."

My mom shook her head. "That's not what I meant. Don't get so stuck on your gifts that you don't think around them, dear. I was talking about hubris. Her overweening pride. She thinks of herself like you think of her—like she's indestructible. It will be the death of her someday."

16

THE WINDS OF CHANGE KIND OF BLOW

WHEN THE PHONE call finally came, it was Owen's voice on the line. He gave me coordinates and a few hours for travel, putting us at our destination after nightfall, which was probably the reason we were given so much time—Venus wouldn't want the disadvantage of sunlight against her.

I repeated Owen's instructions out loud, and in response there was a flurry of movement as the weres behind me pulled out a map and spread it on the table. As if seeing this, Owen chuckled.

"And let me add one little thing. You know how they always say 'and come alone' in the movies?"

"I didn't know you watched movies," I said. I had a hard time picturing Owen doing anything that didn't involve following Venus around or killing things. Did he secretly knit? Make mosaics or dioramas? Owen with downtime—what a frightening thought. "What's your point, Owen?"

"My point is that, while most people would go through

the charade, we have no need to. You may bring anyone you wish. But while we'd like to keep you alive, at least for our own needs, we have no real interest in doing the same for your friends. So go ahead. Pick those you want to see die a terrible and painful death. And it will be painful, I can assure you." Owen was clearly enjoying himself. "Toodle-oo," he sang, and then the line went dead.

I stared at the phone in my hand until Sid took it from me and hung it up. "Sick little puppy, isn't he?" Then he barked like a dog.

I couldn't help grinning at him. Apparently his cheering powers extended beyond Olive.

Everything became a flurry of movement then. Phone calls were made, bags packed, and all the general chaos of a mass exodus was in evidence. I seemed to be in the way, so I went to my room to prepare myself. Which basically meant stuffing my pockets, getting warm clothes together, and—my personal favorite—eating another sandwich. I was going to need it.

There was a quick rap at the door, and then Sid popped in. First Ikka, earlier, now her brother. If I kept entertaining like this, I would have to ask Duncan for a bigger room.

"Good sandwich," I said, still chewing. "What is it?"

Sid leaned down and sniffed. "Venison. We've got company."

I stopped chewing. "I'm eating Bambi?"

"No, Bambi was a cartoon. The deer you're eating is completely real. Now get your butt downstairs. You're not going to believe who's here, so I'm not going to bother telling you." And with that cryptic comment, he left. Ooo-kay.

I don't know what I expected, but even with no expectations, I was surprised. Alistair, his elegant frame folded into a chair, his fingers steepled, and his face smug as hell, sat at the head of Duncan's table. There were two more people with him—a dainty little blonde who looked like she'd be more at home in an artist loft somewhere, maybe wearing a beret and discussing Nietzsche, and the superhuge guy from the Portsmouth Council.

The only thing that kept me from casting a flame ball into their faces was the way the drove was lounging about. If the new people were a threat, they'd all have been on alert. I had faith enough in their commitment to keeping Duncan safe that I took my cues from their behavior. Still, I wasn't happy.

"Last time I saw you," I drawled, resting my palms on the table, "a group of vodyanoys tried to kill us. So please tell me why I shouldn't return the favor right now."

Alistair's expression was sunny but cold, like a clear winter morning. Beautiful, but if you stayed too long in it, something was going to get frostbite and fall off. "Ava, please. We are pressed for time, so let us forgo the pissing contest. If your little friends here had the slightest inkling that I'd been part of any such fiasco, they would have eaten my liver by now. I still have all my organs; therefore, they don't believe me to have been involved. So let's discuss why we're all gathered together today instead of rehashing nonsense. Sound peachy?"

I grabbed a chair and flipped it around before I sat on it. Cade hated when I did that. He said it was bad for the chair, but I've never figured out how. "Fine," I said. "I'm game. I suppose your minions would have been better dressed and less green."

His arctic grin widened. "I wouldn't send minions. In my experience, they fail. I would have gone myself."

"Touché. So why are you here? Last I heard, the Council wasn't going to stretch out its neck for us."

There was a grumble, but it was smooth, like a stampede off in the distance. This was from the giant heap of a man next to Alistair. I didn't understand the grumble, but Alistair obviously did, because he responded with "I don't know if it's so much cowardice as greed. Our fellow members have been bribed so many times that the only action which won't land them in hot water with someone is complete inaction." Then he turned his attention back to me. "You're right—but we're not here as Council. We're here as . . . an interested party."

"You just want to help out of the kindness of your heart, right?"

"My, my, no. Do I look like a philanthropist to you?"

"You look like a model for *Elitist & Wealthy* magazine," Lock said as he walked into the room. He rested a reassuring hand on my shoulder. Ezra slipped in behind him, coming to my other side.

"Thanks," Alistair said, buffing his nails on his sweater vest. "I want to make this clear, Ava. I am not joining your loveable band of misfits because my heart bleeds for you—any of you—or your position. I'm here entirely for my own advantage. Duncan and I have been in contact for some time about bringing in a regime change. Until now, he has turned me down. So I wish to offer you a proposition. You need help; can we agree there? It certainly appears to be an all-hands-on-deck situation. Well, we're here to offer that assistance."

"And in exchange?" I asked.

"In the simplest of terms, I will help you remove Venus, and then I'll help you avoid the inevitable power struggle by stepping into her place."

Lock gave a low whistle. I was glad he did it so I didn't have to. Alistair was certainly aiming high. "And if we want to disband the Coterie entirely?"

Alistair leaned forward, his fingers splayed on the table. "I would say I thought you were smarter than that. Something else will spring up in its place, Ava. And while that's happening, this area will become a war zone. I'm giving you the chance to remove your enemy and have the smoothest transition possible."

"Who says you won't be worse than she is?" I asked.

"Duncan could vouch for me, I suppose, though he'll tell you that he doesn't know me very well. He trusts me to a point. The rest of my character references you don't know, so I doubt they will hold much water for you. You'll just have to manage a little faith."

Oh, good. Because that always works out.

Duncan, who up until then had stayed quiet, obnoxiously whittling away as usual, piped up. "It's the best offer you're going to get, Ava."

I knew he was right, but I wanted to at least think about it. "If I may ask: what, exactly, do you three bring to the table? All you have right now is your status as ineffectual Council members and"—I stared at the new girl—"whatever."

"Fair enough," Alistair said, holding his arms out. With seemingly little effort, a tiny storm cloud gathered over each of his hands.

Sid scoffed. "That's it? What are you going to do, get their clothes wet?"

Alistair didn't respond as the clouds continued to grow. The air in the kitchen stirred as a sudden wind sprang up from nowhere. Clothes flapped and the papers attached to the fridge with magnets rustled. I could feel the crackle of electricity as it danced along my skin. There was a clap of thunder before a lightning bolt leapt from one of the clouds and sizzled to a stop at Sid's feet. He yelped and jumped back. Then, as quickly as it started, it was over, and the kitchen went back to normal.

Alistair showed us his palms, as if to proclaim his innocence or wash his hands of the situation.

Duncan huffed, a singular sound of disapproval. "Show-off."

"I'm almost afraid to ask what you other two can do," I said.

The giant mass next to me introduced himself as Parkin, though he had to say it twice for me to get it, and Alistair had to ask him to speak up. It wasn't enough to say he was large—it was like everything about him was on a bigger scale than the rest of humanity. There was a general air of rumpledness about him, as if he'd slept in his clothes his whole life and somehow that had permeated his very personality. He didn't put me on guard like Alistair did, though, and he didn't instantly annoy me like the girl did.

"I'm not going to demonstrate," Parkin said in that rough, tumbling voice of his. "Let's just say I get big."

There was a general sniggering amongst the drove at that, but my reaction was more surprise than anything. "You *get* big? I already want to call you Paul Bunyan."

"I am small now."

I held up my hands in surrender. "You're right—don't demonstrate. This kitchen is too full as it is."

The girl's name was Bianca, and with the exception of her

clothes, which were all black, she was a study in petite and pale. What I could see of her hair peeking out of her watch cap was closer to white than yellow, her bangs hanging in a jagged cut to her chin. I couldn't tell if it was natural or not. She'd lined her eyes heavily in thick black liner so that you were instantly drawn to the gray of them—the color of the sea when it reflects storm clouds, like at any minute there might be rain. Her elfin features were twisted in disdain.

"Bianca," Alistair said, a warning in his voice.

"I'm not a trained monkey," she said. "And I don't perform."

Alistair leaned back, hands folded in his lap, and waited.

"Ugh, okay, fine." She blew her bangs out of her eyes. "I'm a caulbearer," she said, scowling at us like we'd bullied her instead of Alistair.

I must not have been the only person looking at her blankly, because she curled her lip and then just disappeared. There were a lot of surprised noises and people withdrawing from her empty chair. Except Sid, who moved closer, his nose twitching as he sniffed the air. "I can't even smell her. Where did she go?"

Bianca reappeared, her face so close to his that too deep a breath would've caused them to collide. A strangled noise escaped Sid as he scrambled back from her. Her laughter was a whispering thing as she watched him skitter away.

Olive, who had snuck in when no one was looking, was eyeing her like she was livestock. If she'd reached out and checked Bianca's teeth, I wouldn't have been surprised. "I thought a caulbearer was when babies were born with stuff on their faces."

"Some people refer to the amniotic membrane as a caul," Ikka explained. "Either way, it's not 'stuff.' At least act like we educate you."

"*Caul* means 'veil,'" I said, getting it at last. Bianca didn't exactly throw me a grateful look so much as tone down her open contempt before she gave me a slight nod.

"Like the kind brides wear?" Olive said, her features arranged in the pinched tilt of skepticism.

"More like a covering."

Duncan set down his newest whittled creation, this time a hulking bear, with the earlier fox. He was really churning them out. "I've seen bearers who can throw a caul over themselves, but never one that tricked more than one sense."

Bianca crossed her arms, and for someone who didn't perform she sure preened under the attention. "I can do sound, too, if it's soft enough. Anyone around me will still hear something, but I can morph it to be a sound that isn't out of place."

Olive rested her hands on her hips, evidently not as impressed as Duncan. "So you can go invisible. That's cool if you want to steal something, but how's it going to help us?" She jutted out her chin, her body stiff and protective at Duncan's side, as if she were the only person protecting the old man. "We can steal stuff on our own."

Bianca twisted her hand in a circular motion, and though nothing seemed different to me, it was quickly apparent that something had changed for Olive. Her eyes grew big as she looked around, her bangs swinging. "What did you do with them?" A brief flicker of panic fluttered across Olive's face. "I can't smell them," she said. "I can always smell them. Ikka? Sid?" There was more fear in her voice and in the clenched shiver of her body now than there had been when we fought the vodyanoy.

"We're still here," Ikka said, but Olive obviously didn't hear her.

"Cut it out," Sid said. "You're scaring her."

Bianca reversed the hand motion, and Olive threw herself against Sid's side, keeping the caulbearer in sight. I don't think Olive underestimated people very often; that's what seemed to have scared her more than anything. She'd written Bianca off, and if it had happened out in the real world in a combat situation, Olive would have lost.

Bianca didn't apologize for scaring Olive, but the aggression left her voice and she softened into her chair. "Now you see the applications?"

Olive leaned her face into Sid's side, and he squeezed her close. "You could hide an army," she said.

"Not an army, I don't think. But a large raiding party, definitely," Bianca answered, her lips a smug line. "With me, you regain the element of surprise."

Alistair held his arms out like a game-show host or a televangelist. These prizes could all be ours, he seemed to say, if only we played the game. I gave him a small nod even though it was unnecessary. He already knew he had us.

"Power, muscle, and stealth," he said, rubbing it in.

"And in exchange you get a kingdom," I said. "We get it, Alistair."

Duncan flicked his knife closed before stowing it in some unseen pocket. The fox and bear vanished in similar fashion. "Time to get moving," he said. And just like that, the meeting was over. Alistair and I might have played at it, but Duncan was really in charge while we were still in his cabin. Besides having the entire drove at his back, the quiet authority with which he dispatched orders announced exactly where he stood. No wonder Venus wanted him dead. She ruled through established cruelty and fearmongering. All Duncan would have to do was walk in and use that tone he had—the entire Coterie would be jumping to, ready to sacrifice themselves out of devotion. Out of loyalty. I couldn't tell which method was scarier. But then, why choose? It made me wonder who would really be in charge if we managed to pull this off. Lock handed me my stocking cap, whistling softly. It took me a second to realize it was a tune from *The Wizard of Oz*. The part that goes "We're off to see the wizard."

"For some reason, I have a hard time picturing Venus offering us a hot-air-balloon ride," I said, tugging my hat down over my ears, hearing Cade's voice in my mind lecturing me about the necessity of covered ears and the amount of body heat lost through your head.

"No," Lock said, reaching down to adjust my hat. "More like a field of poppies. But if you picture Owen as a flying monkey, things get real interesting."

17

SLOW BURN

SEVERAL HOURS LATER, we were settled in a skiff, and as I looked behind me all I could see were rowboats, kayaks, canoes, and other small boats spread like a wave. They cut through a layer of lobster-trap buoys so thick you could almost walk across it. Our craft was out in front, Bianca at its prow, her pale skin practically glowing in the darkness, her voice a floating whisper assuring us that no one from the island could see us approach. And that's where we were heading—a tiny private island off the Maine coast.

It was a smart move on Venus's part. Remote, quiet, no one to ask awkward questions. Hard to sneak up on, and even harder to escape from. Plus, it irritated me. I'm not a fan of being isolated by water. Sure, once I hit the island I'd be fine and dandy and ready to go, but the trip over was unnerving me. It set me on edge. I would be rattled before I even showed up. Venus never did things accidentally—even on the fly, she would be thinking and rethinking approaches. So this emotional upset was definitely planned. It served as a subtle warning: *This is just the beginning*, it said. *See how well I know you? How much I can anticipate your reactions? Better just pack it in now, child.* I could almost hear her obnoxious voice in my head.

I looked over at Parkin, encased in a life jacket and holding on to one of those little lifesaver rings. Apparently he couldn't swim and he sank like a freaking rock. Yup, we sure looked scary. Feel our impending wrath, Venus, you frosty bitch.

As we got closer, Bianca pushed her veil back so that it covered all the boats but ours. After all, it would look awfully suspicious if I appeared out of nowhere. So my boat was filled with the small team that Venus would see—Sid, Ikka, Lock, Bianca, Ezra, and me. The faces of my companions were drawn, tired, and wary. I was struck suddenly by how *young* we all looked. Yeah, everyone in the boat was older than me, if only by a few years, but compared with Venus we were practically fetuses.

Disembarking was done in relative silence. We didn't want to overload Bianca by creating more noise for her to morph than necessary. I may not have liked the caulbearer much, but even I had to admit she was dead useful.

Lock and Ikka yanked the skiff onto land, grinding the hull against the rocks. Sid winced at the sound. "Be gentle, you brutes. I told Lonnie I'd get it back in one piece."

"Don't worry, we won't hurt Lonnie's baby," Ikka said.

"Yeah," Lock said. "We need it to get home."

We should have laughed at Lock's lame joke, but the comment sank down into the ground, dragging us with it. There was a good chance none of us would need the skiff, and we all knew it. And it wasn't because we were going to suddenly grow wings and fly.

The beach didn't last very long—without much transition, it abruptly became forest. The trees jutted up, a black outline of spruce and pine clearly visible against the bright dusting of stars. The drove tied lines and did their last-minute preparations, all of them probably wondering if it was necessary or if, come morning, someone was going to discover a lot of abandoned boats along the shoreline of a deserted island.

For now, Bianca would keep all but our skiff hidden. She'd assured us in that huffy way of hers that she could maintain the veil after we left the beach. We were going to have to trust that she was right about her abilities and wouldn't accidentally slip and reveal our numbers to Venus.

My team lined up next to me, their eyes on the trees. All except Bianca, who was turned and watching everyone else. I could feel Lock's warmth at my back before I felt his shoulder bump mine.

"Lock," I said, not looking behind me. "Do me a favor?" When he murmured assent, I said, "If I don't survive, make sure Cade and Ryan do." I reached back and grabbed his hand. "Don't argue. Just say you'll do it."

He snorted. "Don't be stupid—of course I would. Even Ryan, if only so Ez and I can thrash him properly. But you need to stop listening to it."

"Listening to what?"

It was Sid who answered. "The forest," he said. "It's too quiet. No owls. No bugs. No bats. They've all gone a-hiding. A predator is in residence."

Lock laced his fingers into mine, getting a firmer grip on my hand. "You're picking up on it. The fear will start chipping away at you before you even catch sight of Venus."

I breathed in deeply through my nose and let it out my mouth. I hate psychological warfare. Give me a good ol' brawl any day—vicious and over quickly. Much more my style.

"I think we're ready," Bianca whispered. There were probably thirty drove members grouped behind us—a motley crew, but all standing with silent uniformity that told me they were used to working as a team. Les, Duncan, Alistair, and Parkin were leading small groups. Bianca was right: we were as ready as we were going to get. I took one last look at Olive, her tiny form standing next to Les. Somewhere deep in the pit of me, I said a tiny prayer and threw it out into the night. I'm not sure who or what I was saying it to, but the instinct was there. *Please. Let us make it out. Let me have this.* I wanted those boats just as full when we left as when we arrived.

But even as I prayed I knew it wouldn't happen. Coups were bought with blood. And no whispered entreaty to nameless deities would change that.

Ezra dropped a small cloth bag onto the ground. There was a muted *clank* when it hit. Knowing Ez, it was probably a set of throwing knives. He stripped off his clothes and didn't even strut, which showed how serious things had become. Ez shifted, and Olive picked up his clothes, then put them in the boat. The fox picked up the bag in his mouth, and with a twitch of his black ears he melted into the forest.

I let go of Lock and flicked my hands out, setting off sparks. To anyone watching from inside the woods it would look like a nervous gesture. But to everyone lined up on the beach, it was a signal. Almost as one we surged forward, ready to meet whatever was waiting for us.

Naturally, my foot slipped on a wet rock as soon as we moved, completely ruining the image. Lock caught me before I slipped too far. "That's what I love about you, cupcake. Your natural grace and class."

"I'll show you grace and class," I said as I gave him the finger. With a soft laugh he pulled ahead, leading us into the forest. It was dark and I didn't want to ruin our night vision with a fireball. Of course, the darkness didn't bother the hares much because they see better at night than people do, and Lock would be fine because the forest would probably speak to him or some such nonsense. But Bianca and I were blind as bats.

She surged forward, latching on to Lock's arm so he could lead her. Of course we were supposed to grab on to one of them so we wouldn't trip, but I suspected that she had specifically picked Lock even though Ikka was closer to her. If we hadn't needed Bianca, I'd have tripped her.

Sid's hand snagged mine, palm to palm, dragging me closer to him. It dwarfed my hand, and I could feel his callused fingers.

"Pay attention," Sid said, his voice a natural murmur of the forest, like the wing beat of an owl. I wished I had somewhere I fit in like this—the forest was so obviously his element. "Seriously, Ava—these trees have an extensive root system and I'm afraid you're going to trip."

Which, of course, I did. I had to clutch his arm with my other hand.

"See? The epitome of grace," Lock whispered.

The forest remained unnaturally quiet as we moved through

it, the half moon doing nothing to light our path. The trees were too thick for that. I still stumbled a little, but not nearly as much as I would have if Sid hadn't been leading me. Bianca didn't falter once, but then again, I thought Lock might be cheating and asking things to move out of the way.

Ezra darted from the woods and gave a soft *yip*. He hopped in place until Ikka moved closer, examining the thing he was dancing around.

"What is it?" Sid whispered.

Ikka picked up a rock the size of a cantaloupe and dropped it onto the ground while Ezra disappeared back into the undergrowth. There was a flash followed by a loud *snap*. "Bear traps," Ikka said, hefting the neutralized trap for us to see, then dropping it with a hiss. "With a high silver content." I couldn't see it, but from the *thump* that followed, I assumed that Ikka had tapped the ground with her foot. Olive appeared and Ikka showed her the trap. "Carefully go down the line and spread the word." Olive left without a sound.

We walked for a few more minutes before we crested a gentle slope. The trees ended at the top, leaving a man-made clearing ahead of us. Light flared, and my eyes stung at the sudden shift from pitch-black to bonfire glow. I let go of Sid's hand so I could wipe my eyes. The flare had caused them to water. When my vision cleared, I could see three large bonfires, maybe ten feet tall, and wide enough that my team could have grabbed hands and danced around each one. It was all very dramatic, but then, Venus has always been flamboyant.

They were spaced evenly throughout the clearing, and I could see people's darkened silhouettes in front of the middle one. As we walked slowly closer, I could make out Venus and

Owen, the bound and kneeling figure of Cade, and the very unbound figure of Ryan behind Venus. Warm anger flared in my chest at seeing Cade treated like that, burning hotter when I set my sights on Ryan. There was no question now. There he stood, willing, unhurt, right behind Venus. So much of this stemmed from Ryan's betrayal. Venus would have probably found another way to engineer things, but I'd never be positive. I'd never know how events would have played out if I'd just stayed away from Ryan James.

We had to get in range so that we could draw Venus and Owen away from Cade. Ryan could get his own ass home. Whether he was ignorant or not, I couldn't argue for his safety while looking at Cade bound at Venus's feet like an animal.

We got close enough that I could see Venus's amused smile. Her blond hair was twisted into an updo, the sparkle of diamond pins winking whenever she moved, like tiny floating sparks. She appeared to be wearing some sort of white leather body suit with boots, as if someone had dipped her in white chocolate. Typical. Her fashion version of a big middle finger. We were all dressed in dark colors—muted browns, dark greens, blacks—the better to blend into the night, not to mention that it made it easier for Bianca to push and pull reality around us.

But Venus was a creepy angelic vision next to the bonfire. No matter where she moved, she'd stand out. Clearly she thought this fight had a foregone conclusion. I can't say I didn't see her point. I knew that, even though I could only see her and a small handful of people, the woods were full.

Next to me, Lock had his head cocked, listening to the trees and plant life. "Thirty to the left," he whispered, and it was passed on with more of the drove's flashing hand signals, down to the end of the ranks. "Forty behind, fanned out. About twenty-five on the right...." He tipped his head again. "And about fifteen or so creeping up behind us. We're being surrounded, Aves."

We had guessed as much, so no surprise there. That was why small teams of were-hares had been slipping away as we'd crept closer. Eventually we'd be ringed like a bull's-eye, with Venus in the center. It didn't really matter, though. In the end it would come down to Venus and me. I was sure of that.

"Just remember," Alistair whispered off to my left, "try not to kill too many of my future employees. A kingdom without serfs is pure nonsense."

"Hard to argue with that," I mumbled.

"Ava, my darling," Venus called out. Her voice was clarion. It trumpeted over the hush of the woods, and it was obvious how much she was enjoying herself. Owen offered her his arm and she took it. Queen and king of Crazytown. This was how Venus had fun.

Personally, I prefer board games.

I stepped closer, my few visible reinforcements doing the same. We were fully in the clearing now, only twenty or so feet between us and my least favorite creatures on the planet. But also closer to my very favorite person in the entire universe. Cade had looked up when Venus said my name, but his face was in shadow so I couldn't tell how he was doing. Ryan was turned enough toward the firelight that I could see that his eyes, those same sweet hazel orbs that used to be all for me—that I now wanted to poke out—were for Venus. His hands hovered around her, hungry to touch, but waiting for permission. Watching me, Venus reached out and stroked his cheek. Ryan shuddered slightly, his body on bliss overload.

My heart wrenched. I couldn't tell what I was more disgusted at—Ryan or the fact that seeing him was upsetting me. I let my anger burn away the residuals of any other feeling for him. No more pity, love, jealousy; nothing. Just anger. Just hate. It was all he deserved.

Venus looked at my reinforcements, and I could see some genuinely amused surprise there. "I thought you'd bring more friends to the party," she said.

"Less is more," I said. "Wouldn't want to be gaudy, would we?" I crossed my arms. "Besides, this is supposed to be a friendly trade-off." My tone was flat and dry. Yeah, right. Still, I had to try to get her hostage clear. Maybe that would make me feel less emotional about it—if Cade were simply a hostage. "So how about you send Cade over and once I make sure he's okay, I'll come to you."

Venus trailed a hand down Ryan's cheek. "What, you don't want your little friend anymore? I thought he was part of the deal."

It was all I could do to keep from gritting my teeth. "He was never mine, Venus. He was always yours. Let's get this over with."

Venus's grin was a flash in the firelight. "Come, now, Ava. I didn't fall off the turnip truck this morning." I had a sudden image of Venus, her hair done up and full of diamonds, her white leather smudged and dirty from sitting on bags of turnips in the back of a rusted-out pickup. It was an image I'd definitely have to save for later.

"Fine," I said, walking forward, my arms held out, wrists together, like I was waiting to be trussed up. "I'll go first." I stopped halfway between Venus and my team. "This is what

285

you wanted. I'm offering myself up to your mercy. So here's the part where you live up to your promise and fulfill your end of the deal. Hand him over. Let Cade walk away unharmed, and it will all be over."

Venus stared at me for a few quiet breaths. The bonfires crackled, but that was the only other noise. She cocked her head, then signaled Owen curtly with one hand. "I truly thought you'd put up more of a fight, Ava. I believe I'm a little disappointed in you."

I gave a one-shouldered shrug as Owen grabbed my wrists. "I know when I'm beat, Venus." I could tell they weren't quite buying this but didn't know what to make of it either. I wasn't struggling. My arms were still while Owen strapped cuffs on each one, wards branded into the leather. A similar cuff would go around my neck and waist. They'd all be linked in the back by a chain. The contraption was meant to restrict my spark. The rest of me wasn't considered that dangerous.

While the cuffs were on, I wouldn't be able to light so much as a candle without a match.

Owen was almost finished binding me now, and I could tell that, the further into it he got, the more confused and worried Venus was becoming. She didn't understand what game I was playing and it was getting to her. Good.

Soon I was bound and trussed like a Thanksgiving turkey, and probably less dangerous than one. I'd only pissed Venus off enough to get bound like this a few times. It's terribly disorienting—like how I imagine phantom-limb syndrome would feel. I think my spark is there, but when I actually try to wiggle it—nothing.

I let Owen lead me to Venus. She snapped her fingers, and

a flunky hoisted Cade to a standing position. He was bleeding and wobbly on his feet. Even in the light of the bonfire I could see he had one hell of a shiner, but all in all he looked intact.

The flunky shoved him over to Lock. Cade stumbled, then stopped halfway. "Go," I told him firmly. I could tell he didn't want to, but Cade trusted me. He hesitated only a short minute before moving over to the relative safety of my team.

Venus held a hand up, and Ryan practically tripped over himself to nuzzle up against it. The sight was absolutely pathetic. "You sure you don't want this one?"

"I'd rather eat glass, thanks." I said. "But if you're dead set on discussing it . . ." I trailed off like I might be considering her offer. With the exception of vengeance, I no longer had any interest in Ryan, but I was interested in stalling. I was waiting for a sign. I just had to hope that the negotiation game was intriguing enough to keep Venus busy.

Somewhere, from the depths of the woods, came the sound of a woman's scream. My arms broke out in goose bumps as I recognized Ezra's call. Venus's crew were all looking around, trying to pinpoint the sound and figure out what it was. Before they knew what was happening, I threw myself into Owen, my shoulder leading the assault. I barreled into him, and he never had time to react. He crumpled into himself with a whoosh, his oxygen spent, before we both tumbled to the ground. There was a dull crack as his head struck a rock. His eyes glazed. I scrambled to my feet and was just looking up when Bianca dropped the caul.

There was a blink when nobody stirred. The world held its breath, and we all hung there, suspended, completely at Bianca's will. And then everything moved at once.

The scene became very jumbled, my vision coming in strange, surreal flashes. I felt like someone had spiked my drink and then pushed me into a room lit only by a strobe light. This was partially due to the fires, but mostly due to Alistair's lightning.

Alistair stood his ground as his lightning crashed around him. Rain poured from clouds, instantly drenching us all. Wind whipped around us, bringing its own unique howl. It was disorienting. Small, tussling factions began to slip and slide in the mud. People who got too close to Alistair instantly regretted it.

Alistair's main job, however, was neutralizing Owen. It would take a lot to get flame going in this madness. Sure, it negated me as well, but that was okay. That part of me had already been taken out of the equation. But I could still fight.

The ground rumbled under my feet. At first I thought it was thunder, but then I saw Parkin, or the rhinoceros formerly known as Parkin, come stampeding past. He bowled over several of Venus's lackeys before sliding into a turn and hitting a tree sidelong. The tree toppled over, breaking up more fights as people scurried away. Parkin shook his head, his gray hide catching the light. It was like watching a giant pinball.

And the hares. They were *everywhere*. I don't think they were much bigger than normal hares, but it didn't seem to matter. They fought like furry land piranhas. They ran in small schools, leaping as one onto an assailant, and I watched as each person went down in a fuzzy wave of death.

A man came running toward me, his face twisted into a grimace. Before I could blink, he was knocked down by a bear. The creature was an odd color—I could tell that even in the low light. Oddly, I felt no fear as I watched it roar into my assailant's face. I peered closely at it and saw the swirl and grain of wood. When I found Duncan in the fray, I understood. As I watched he flung his carvings into the air. They expanded, quickly unfolding so that by the time they hit the ground, they were real. Life-size.

I'd known what Duncan could do. I'd seen him bring his carvings to life several times over the years. But I hadn't known he could make them bigger. The possibilities of that gift were staggering. No wonder they'd wanted him to head the Coterie. Duncan was the only golem maker I'd ever met, and he was obviously damn powerful. A wooden lumberjack went by, his ax cleaving chunks out of people as he moved.

I suddenly understood why Venus was so attracted to firebugs. We'd be especially good at protecting her from someone who threw deadly wooden golems at her. Someone like Duncan. If he could do this, what would stop him from making something that shot big wooden stakes? They didn't make a ward to stop that. She must have been dreading this confrontation ever since she took over the Coterie in his stead. It had probably never occurred to her that she hadn't won out over him—that he'd stepped down. Not desiring power wouldn't make sense to a mind like Venus's.

It was then that I realized I couldn't see Venus anywhere. I laced my way through the tumult, searching this way and that. Everyone seemed too busy to notice the girl in chains.

Eventually, Venus found me. I felt someone grab me from behind. Strong arms wrapped around me and hauled me to a stop. Underneath various new and strange smells—probably Venus's perfume—was a smell I recognized. Ryan.

He said nothing as he held me. Venus paraded into my vision, her head high despite her lessened appearance—she wasn't looking as untouched and resplendent as before. Mud and blood splattered her outfit. Her hair was undone, loose, her shiny diamond pins long gone, and she had a cut on her temple. It was healing even as I watched, but that didn't matter. I stared at that cut and felt better. Venus could bleed. Someone had managed to get close to her—to injure her. If that was true, then it wasn't hopeless. If it can bleed, it can die. Simple as that.

I kicked out at her and she jumped back, gloating. Child's play for a vampire, I'm sure. For once there was no evil mono-loguing or theatrics. She simply hit me. Then she hit me again. My face felt pulpy and raw already, the rain stinging as it landed. Venus might have been able to restrain herself from her usual hoopla, but she couldn't help toying with me.

She struck me again, this time in the gut. I collapsed to the ground, wheezing, and Ryan let me fall. My knees hit the ground hard. I gagged, my hands buried in the cold sludge as I tried to breathe again. *It's easy*, I told my lungs. *Expand, contract, repeat.* They said, *Yeah? If it's so easy, why don't you do it?*

A cold hand dug into my hair and yanked me to my feet. There was nothing I could do but shiver as Venus pulled me to her, one arm snaked around my middle, gripping me with all the give of concrete reinforced with rebar, the other hand still fisted in my hair as she yanked my head to the side, exposing my neck.

Then the tearing sensation of pain. It hurt more than I felt it had a right to.

My next conscious thought was that someone was

breathing too fast. That was followed by the realization that the someone was me. My limbs felt cold and heavy, and I was drenched in sweat. But at least Venus wasn't holding me anymore.

Someone was picking me up by the shoulders, though. My head kept lolling around like my neck was all skin and tissue but no bone. Lightning flashed and I saw bare legs next to mine. Whoever held me was naked. He pulled me snug against his frame.

"Normally I'd at least take you to dinner before a naked cuddle, but needs must and all," Sid whispered. If I'd had the energy, I would have sobbed with relief. I could just make out Venus in front of me. She was being restrained by something. Ryan was digging at whatever it was, his hands bloody, his whimpering taking on a frantic keening tone.

Ezra, also completely naked except for the throwing knives in his hands, tackled Ryan to the ground. You would think after years of working with Ezra I'd be used to watching naked guys fight, but really, it never stops being weird.

Lock dipped one hand into Venus's pockets while she struggled in vain, and I realized that she was being held by a tree. It wasn't so much that the limbs were holding her—more like someone had shoved her partially into the trunk itself. As if she'd stood still as the tree grew around her. Even that wouldn't hold her forever, though. Especially with the transfusion I'd just given her. Lock lifted up a hand in triumph. Whatever he'd been looking for, he'd found it.

Sid spun me in his arms until I was facing him. He looked down at me with a smile. "Fancy meeting you here."

"Perv," I slurred, but his smile widened.

291

"I think she's okay," he said. "You found the key?"

Lock grunted, his hands on my chains. "What makes you say she's okay?"

"She just called me a perv."

I heard the tiny click of a lock opening, and my chains loosened. "I'm pretty sure she'd do that with her dying breath, so I wouldn't put too much stock in it."

Lock didn't get any further. Sid shouted something as Lock went down. I was set gently, if hastily, onto the ground as Sid ran over to pull Ryan off my fallen friend. Ryan was fighting like a frenzied, mad thing. *Ez*, I thought. *Where's Ez?*

Sid had the disadvantage of not actually wanting to hurt Ryan, at least not permanently. Ryan was lucky Sid was dealing with him. He wasn't nearly as attached to me as the others were and didn't know what Ryan had been accused of. I was alive enough to enjoy watching Sid move, the tone of his lanky frame, his speed as he dodged, but even I could tell he was pulling his punches. His style was defensive. Then Sid slammed Ryan into a tree. Hard. Maybe Lock and Ezra had been sharing tales after all.

Leaning against a trunk, I pulled myself up slowly. My limbs felt like dead weight as I stumbled over to Venus. I was cold and shaky. My brain calmly told me I was probably in shock from blood loss, but I couldn't really drag up enough energy to care.

Venus was a sight. Bands of wood encircled her chest and stomach, but I could hear them creak as she struggled. Lock was distracted, which I'm sure was her aim. If he didn't get a hold of the tree again soon, she'd be free. What wasn't covered by bark was an unholy mess of mud, ripped white leather, and blood—mostly mine. It was smeared around her mouth, and some of her hair was sticking to it.

I was really no match for Venus right then. I knew that. Almost all my energy was being used to keep me vertical. Lock hadn't removed my chains, so I had no fire, which was probably good. In that state using my fire would probably have killed me.

My best bet would have been to sit down and hope one of my friends helped me soon. Logically, I knew that. I wasn't surprised to see one of my chains in my hands, though. It was a little awkward, but it would do the job.

"Even unlocked," Venus gasped, "you still need help...to get...them off." Her voice was raspy but satisfied.

I pushed the length of chain held tight between my fists against Venus's exposed throat. Her eyes widened. I felt the give as her trachea collapsed. Tears sprang to my eyes, and I just kept pushing, some small strength coming from nowhere. "Hubris," I said, and I could tell she didn't get it. So I told her something she would understand. "This is for my mom, and Cade—" My voice gave out. I was so tired. The list was so very long. And really, it all came down to one thing for me, anyway. In my mind, I saw the photo of me, Cade, and Lilia in front of Duncan's fire pit. How many of those photos would there have been without Venus around to ruin everything? "You took my life from me," I said. I pushed the chain harder.

LOCK FOUND ME viciously strangling Venus. I didn't know how long I'd been doing it. The thing about vampires? If you don't burn them to a crisp, if you don't destroy the heart and remove the head, they just keep coming back to life. Their stupid bodies won't quit. I'd lost track of how many times I'd killed

Venus. Every time her body gave out, I'd slacken my pressure enough to let her throat rebuild, and then I'd begin again.

Lock pulled me back. Venus was unconscious, but I hadn't managed to kill her yet this time.

"We'll handle this, Aves. We've got it."

I shook my head, like a terrier with a tasty soup bone. He pulled me close and whispered in my ear. "Cupcake, you can barely stand. You've got nothing left. Let us help."

Let us save you from having to do this is what he really meant. Lock had been along with me on so many of my assignments. He'd watched me go through myriad reactions to what I had to do, from the physical to the emotional, and he'd stood by me. He'd picked me up, carried me, and been my friend. My best friend. And he wanted to step in and save me from this stain.

But this was one I wanted. I'd heard the argument about an eye for an eye making the whole world blind, and in general I believed it. Vengeance purely for the sake of vengeance isn't a good idea. Anyone who's read Shakespeare knows that. And, yeah, I wanted revenge. I needed it. But there was more to it. Venus was like a sociopathic kid with a stick. She was poking out a whole lot of eyes. I may have had a lot of anger and disgust directed at myself for what she made me do, but I had even more for Venus. Exponentially more.

"Please," I said, and it was a whisper. "I have enough for this. *I can do this.*"

"Ava," he begged.

I tipped my head against his and squeezed the arm that was around me. Even I could feel how weak that squeeze was. "Lock." And I felt him sag with defeat under all the argument

I put into that one word. I stared at Venus as she coughed up a little blood. Her throat was rebuilding itself again, the fine silver chain of her ward pushed up by the flesh. "You'll stop me," I said. "You won't let me go nova. I know you won't. Because Cade would never forgive you, and you'd be left alone with Ezra."

He laughed, but it sounded painful and wet, like he was trying not to cry. Then he held me away with one hand while he used the other to touch part of the tree. Bark melted back, revealing stained white leather. There was the whisper of a zipper before Venus's leather jacket fell open. Lock gingerly reached in and pulled out her long silver chain. I could see it glisten in the faint moonlight right before he unceremoniously ripped it from her neck. He handed it to me. Moving quickly but thoroughly, he searched Venus, removing backup wards from an ankle, a wrist, and her waist. Then, with an arm supporting me, he clumsily removed my chains. I heard them hit the ground. I looked around to make sure nothing would interrupt me this time. In the darkness I could barely make out Sid's shadowed form holding Ryan like a baby. By the way Ryan lay, I could tell he was unconscious. No sign of Ezra. I desperately hoped my friend was okay.

Lock supported me with both arms now, keeping me steady as I peered at Venus. I was suddenly so tired. I wanted nothing more than to go to sleep. To collapse where I was and let Lock handle the rest. But it wasn't his job.

It was mine.

"Just one last time, cupcake," he whispered, his lips moving against my cheek.

"Pull the tree back," I said, my words thick and slow. I

could do this. Oh how I hoped I could do this. Because if I went nova, I was taking everyone here with me. But I trusted Lock. I had to. This was going to end tonight—I'd promised myself that earlier.

The tree released her, and Venus was coherent enough to catch herself on her hands and knees. So I knew she was awake. I knew she felt it when I started.

The flame was slow. I was fighting exhaustion, wind, and soggy tinder, after all. That didn't stop it; at this point nothing short of my death would stop it. This fire had been a long time coming. I kept seeing flashes of memory—the bloodied back seat of a car, the chant of cicadas as my mom fought for her life, the warmth of her lap when she held me. Her laughter. Her voice as she told me stories while we hid in cheap motel rooms. The way she looked when she saw Cade, like she was lit up from the inside, not like a candle but a beacon, a lighthouse, the blaze of a forest fire.

I thought of these things and I burned. Venus screamed. I'm positive. But that wouldn't save her. Nothing would. Like I said, that flame was a long time coming.

It was the kind of spark that you put so much of yourself into that you lose control. If Lock hadn't been there, I really would've gone nova. There would have been nothing left of half the damn island, probably.

But Lock was there. And the flame didn't stop until I heard his voice, soft in my ear.

"Enough, Aves. Enough."

18

SCORCHED EARTH

THE TRIP off the island is only snapshots—short flashes of vision sandwiched between long stretches of darkness. The jarring, rocking motion of being carried as someone ran. The blackness of trees outlined against a red sky. The charcoal and earth smell of a forest fire. Then rain. So much rain. Me shivering from the cold of it.

Then nothing for a long time.

I WOKE UP in Grandma Rose's cabin, which is not really where I expected to wake up. I'd rated a bed this time, a somewhat dubious honor. Across from me, a battered and bruised Cade slept. I felt the tension in me ease at the sight. A rather scruffy Lock dozed in a chair by the window. He snored softly, and I smiled. I sobered when I saw who was perched on the end of my bed, glowering at me.

"Hello, Angela," I said warily. "To what do I owe this honor?" My voice rasped, dry from abuse.

Lock's mom was the only one who hadn't been beat with the exhaustion stick. She sat there, goddesslike, and examined me. Her lips were pursed, and I don't think she liked what she saw. "You could have killed him, you know. If things hadn't gone well."

"I know." I wasn't sure what else to say, so I sat there. The silence stretched between us, getting thinner by the second. Was I supposed to apologize? It would come out false. I felt bad for endangering my friends, but given the same situation, the same choice, I'd do it again in a fast minute.

"You nearly killed yourself." She gestured toward me. "As it is we had to borrow clothes from one of the girls to fit you, you lost so much weight." Her disapproval was almost palpable.

"Thank her for me."

She folded her hands primly in her lap. "There's no way to get you to understand the magnitude of what just happened, is there? To get you to realize how close you all were to destruction? The fox hasn't even regained consciousness yet."

"What happened to Ezra?" My voice cracked. "Is he going to be okay?"

She poured me a small glass of water. "Rose says so, and I trust her judgment. He'll have a long road ahead of him. With proper care..." She trailed off.

"Proper care? He's a were-fox. Why would he need proper care?"

"He stepped in a trap with a high silver content. The silver is slowing the healing process. We had to cut away some of his calf—the silver had turned the flesh necrotic. We're not sure how long he was in that trap before Ikka and Olive pulled him free, but he'd lost a great deal of blood. He's quite lucky he didn't lose his leg. He'll have a scar, but he'll regain use of the leg if he listens to Rose."

I closed my eyes. "Poor Ez." I tried propping myself up on some pillows, noticing as I did that Angela was right—I had lost a lot of weight. I could feel my hip bones through the thin blanket. "You accuse me of not getting it," I said as I struggled, "but I think *you* don't get it."

"What don't I understand?" she said, her hands returned to her lap, her face clearly set to "humor the patient" position. "Pray, enlighten me."

"You think I wasn't aware of what the risks were—that I'm still not. But I was fully aware of my chances."

"And you did it anyway?" she said, a faint hint of disgust apparent in her curled lip.

"Yup." All my wiggling made my pillow fall off the bed. Damn.

She threw her hands up in frustration before getting up and snagging my pillow from the floor. "Here, let me help you. You're just making things worse." She pushed me forward and jammed the pillow behind me before sitting on the bed, this time closer to me. She reached over to adjust my pillow and pull my blanket up.

"Let me make this clear, then. I take protecting my family very seriously. You endanger it again, and trust me, it won't end with a nice, friendly chat."

This was her version of friendly? I didn't want to see her furious, then. I crossed my arms and sank back into my pillow. "I take protecting my family seriously too." My voice softened, whether with weariness or residual fear, I'm not sure. "Venus would have killed Lock eventually, you know," I said. I was sure of that. He wouldn't have remained in Venus's employ unscathed for much longer. He was too soft. Too nice. She saw that as weakness. I didn't remind Angela that Lock had become a tithe to spare her and the other dryads. Maybe she was fine with playing dirty, but I saw no reason to do so.

But even though I was talking about her son, trying to appeal to her maternal side—the part of her maternal side that didn't want to eviscerate me like the right hand of Shiva—she looked at Cade instead. Her face lost its angry hardness. Her lip uncurled and her posture relaxed.

"I suppose saving your father was as important to you as my son is to me. In my anger I forgot that you had family at stake as well." She gave a long sigh. "And my son no doubt chose to throw himself into the fray with you." She smiled softly. "He's like his father in that way. Never could pass up a damsel in distress. You know, when we met—"

"Guardian," I said, smoothing the blanket over my lap.

"Excuse me?" she said, startled by the interruption.

"You said 'saving your father' just now. Cade is my guardian. Family, yes. Related, no."

We stared at each other; Lock muttering in his sleep was the only sound in the room. And she just kept *staring*.

My stomach plummeted. "He's not my father," I said. "He's just . . . Cade."

She rested a hand over one of mine and the image of her was suddenly blurry as my eyes welled. "You didn't know?" she asked.

I couldn't take the gentleness in her voice. Suddenly I wanted her to go back to being overprotective and rude. That I could handle.

"He's not my father," I said again. "It's not possible. I've done the math—my mom wasn't anywhere near Cade for at least a year before she had me."

She patted my hand. "And who gave you that time line?"

"My mom. Cade."

"And who told Cade?"

I didn't think it was possible, but my throat became ever drier. "Mom."

"And who told you when your birthday was? Humans like to give out those little pieces of paper when their babies are born. We had to get one for Lock so he could go to school. Do you have one of those?"

"A birth certificate," I said. Angela helped me take a sip of water. "I don't have one."

"So really," she concluded, putting the glass down, "all you have is your mother's word for it."

I could feel the tears falling as I shook my head. "No," I said. But in my mind I was already tallying evidence in favor of her statement. I'd always wanted Cade to be my dad, but as I grew older I was sure my mother would have told me if he was.

I mean, why wouldn't she?

And then it hit me: She'd lied to us for the same reason she'd left him. To protect him, of course. Even from me. Because if we'd ever been captured, my mom couldn't trust a child not to tell. And what you didn't know, you couldn't be tortured for. She was trying to protect both of us—I knew that. But it still felt like a stab in my chest.

"It's in the little pieces—but then, when isn't it? The shape of your chin, your nose. Over the years, I've become quite good at these things. May the rot take me if I'm wrong, but I'm not.

301

That man is your father as sure as the oak grows." She tilted her head the way a curious squirrel does sometimes. "Neither of you guessed?"

I shook my head. At least, I didn't think Cade had guessed, and I was positive my mom hadn't told him. If she had told him, he wouldn't have stood back and let her run on her own. Not Cade. He would have taken on the entire Coterie for us without even thinking about it. So, of course, she'd lied to him. She would have done so easily—anything to keep him safe.

I sobbed then, and Lock's mom, who mere moments before had wanted to throttle me, held me while I cried.

WE STAYED at Grandma Rose's for a few days. Most of our injuries would heal on their own, but we needed the rest. Ezra soon woke, asking for food and demanding that all of us do his bidding. He had color in his cheeks and he looked better, but he still couldn't walk without help. Ryan was also a wreck. Venus had held him in thrall for several days, and she'd really done a number on him. Rose said it was like watching someone come down off of heroin. He was shaky. Sick. Sometimes screaming. I sat there and listened to it, even though it hurt.

I was only allowed to see Ryan once after he woke up, before Sid and Ikka took him home. Ryan had missed some school and he'd probably get into trouble, but at least he was alive. I kept telling myself that as I stared at him. I wasn't the only one who'd lost weight. Venus had obviously been feeding off him, and I'm not sure she'd been doing a good job of making sure he ate too.

Deep, poisonous-looking bruises bloomed under his eyes.

Someone had brushed his hair and cleaned him up, but you could tell he didn't care.

"Why?" I asked. "I want to ask if it was all a lie, if you ever liked me at all—but that might sound pathetic, and really, you won't be honest anyway."

"Ava—" he said, reaching a hand out. When I made no move to take it, he dropped his hand into his lap.

"So I'm just going to stick to 'why' and leave it at that. I don't think it's asking much after what you put me through."

He looked away, the walls suddenly becoming really interesting. "My biological mom's a selkie," he said. "She got her skin back and left a long time ago. My mom, the one I call my mom, is actually my dad's second wife."

Growing up, Lilia had told me stories about selkies. They looked like seals but could strip their skins and become human. In a lot of those stories, someone managed to steal the skin and hide it, trapping the selkie. Someone like Ryan's dad, apparently.

"I've only seen her once since she left. She walked out of the water, took one look at me, and realized that I take after my dad. Human," he spat. "She told me I was suited for land and had to stay where I was. Then she left. No apology, no tears, nothing. She just swam away." He looked down at his hands as if he could change them if he stared long enough. "I wanted what you have."

Creatures bred with humans—it was generally frowned upon, but it happened. Sometimes the child took after the human parent. While I hated what being a firebug had done to my life, how would things have been if I had taken after my human parent? Knowing about a world, being able to see and touch it, but never being part of it. I'm not sure how I would have felt. I would be normal, but not like my mom. Sometimes it felt like my sparks were all I had left of her.

"A couple months ago, I heard about the Coterie from another kid like me—another dud half-breed. And I went to them," Ryan continued, snapping me out of my reverie. "When I said where I was from, Venus told me about you. What you were."

Venus must have felt like she'd struck the jackpot. A pretty human boy offering himself to her, the perfect bait for her wayward firebug. "So I was your ticket in?"

He curled his fingers, making loose fists. "I was supposed to watch you," he said.

"Spy, you mean."

He shrugged, as if one word were exactly like the other.

"If you were just supposed to spy, why take me to the Inferno? Why drug me?"

"Venus changed her mind—wanted me to bring you in unprepared. I thought maybe if I could give her more, it would speed up my initiation, so I said sure. Then everything went sideways, and I was supposed to help salvage it. Get you drunk. Make you more compliant and bring you back down to fix things. Only you don't drink. There was no way to get you to drink." He wrapped his hands around his shins, using his knees as a pillow. "And you kept trying to leave," he said, his voice quiet.

"So drugs seemed like a good solution."

"You were leaving! And you wouldn't listen! Wouldn't do what I said." His voice got louder with each statement.

I closed my eyes, like somehow that would stop the answer coming next. "The earrings? Were they bugged?"

"Brittany's idea. She's like me. Her dad's an incubus, but she bred human." The room fell silent as we studied each other. "We thought things would go better if we worked together."

"Well, you wanted to be a monster, Ryan. I'd say mission accomplished." I cupped my hands in front of me and called a spark, willing Ryan to not notice how it sputtered when it came to life. I was still worn thin from Venus.

"I almost lost everyone I love just so you could join the supersecret clubhouse." My flame got bigger. "You . . ." I shook my head. "You know what? I'm not going to waste my breath on you." I made the flame shift hotter so that he could feel the warmth of it, even curled in the corner of his bed. "Except to say this: If you ever come near me or mine again, I'll make you understand exactly how human you are. Understand?"

He didn't answer. He just closed his eyes and turned his face away from me. I'd made my point, so I let the flame go out. I wondered if he'd ever be close to the old Ryan again, or at least what I thought of as the old Ryan. Who knew what he was actually like. No matter what, he'd never be the same. He'd have nights where he'd wake up in a cold sweat, screaming. He'd dream of fire. Of blood. Venus would be the goddess she was named after. I'd be the dark thing trying to pull him into the cellar.

Ryan was tainted now.

I made for the door, but the sound of his voice made me turn back to him.

"He'll come for me."

"Who?" I asked, my hand on the knob.

"Owen. He'll come for me." Ryan wrapped his arms around himself and hugged tight. "Owen will take me to her. I won't go back. Not to my father's. I can't."

A chill crept through the room. "She's dead, Ryan. Venus is dead." So was Owen. I didn't have the heart to tell him that. Not yet. He wouldn't believe me anyway. "And you are going home. Back to where you belong."

When Lock carried me out of the forest that night, I'd seen the bright orange blaze in the sky. I hadn't realized what it meant at the time: Owen had gone nova. Venus's death was too much for him. He'd been her pet, and without his master, he'd skipped the slow-pining-to-death thing and gone straight to self-immolation.

Owen hadn't had a Lock to stop him. There had only been Alistair to put out the flames before the whole island went. A wave of gratitude for my friends welled up in me. My new ones. My old ones. My oldest one. I would be dead without them all. I guess sometimes it pays to let people get close to you.

But, then, sometimes it doesn't. I left Ryan mumbling to himself in Grandma Rose's bedroom. I didn't know who he was talking to, but it wasn't me. It would never be me again.

I got all the way outside before I realized that he'd never once said he was sorry. It was probably the most honest conversation we'd ever had.

19

THE MORE THINGS CHANGE . . .

ALISTAIR GAVE ME a whole week off to recuperate. I guess almost dying doesn't buy you much time in the Coterie. I'd thought my part in the organization was done. No Venus, no pact. But I was wrong.

At the end of the week I received a summons from Alistair. My presence was requested at the Inferno. I thought about ignoring it, but then I remembered how Alistair had looked walking across that clearing, storm clouds building up behind him, his short hair whipping in the wind as lightning flashed and thunder roared.

Ignoring him probably wouldn't work out well. Cade drove me down in the pickup. Angela had told him that he was my dad before we left her forest. We'd been sort of dancing around each other all week. We hadn't been able to talk about it yet. I think we were still processing. All those years I had wanted to meet my dad, and now here he was and I didn't know what to do. And knowing each other so well was actually making it more awkward. We already had a set relationship—a nice, comfortable one—and now that had suddenly shifted. And since there was no bookshop to go to anymore, there was nothing to get between the awkwardness and us.

I suppose I should have just been happy that my dad wasn't Darth Vader.

The Inferno looked exactly the same. I don't know why I expected it to look different, but I did. Someone should at least have put up an UNDER NEW MANAGEMENT sign or something. Ezra met us at the door. For once he didn't pick me up and whirl me around—the crutches got in the way of that. But he managed to kiss me on the cheek, and then he told me I owed him towing fees for his car.

"Take a gander at the staff," he said. "Recognize anyone?"

I did. I recognized some people from the battle—people who had fought on our side. And there were others, staff I knew by face and not by name, who were conspicuously absent.

"Regime change," Ezra said. "Alistair is cleaning house. Speaking of which . . ." He turned to lead, giving Cade and me a little come-hither crook with his hand. Out of habit, I'd been heading toward the elevators, down into the pits, so to speak. But that wasn't where Ezra was taking me. He was leading me through the maze of the restaurant, weaving around tables like walking with crutches was second nature. Cade and I were led to a secluded booth in the back of Purgatory. Alistair sat alone on one side of it, his sleeves rolled up, his hair slightly ruffled like he'd been running his hands through it. Papers covered the table. A few stacks had begun to emerge, but it appeared that Alistair was still sorting the majority of it.

"Venus apparently didn't even have an office," he said

without looking up. "What a ridiculous way to run an empire. Luckily, what with your handiwork marring much of the downstairs, I need to remodel anyway."

"It's not like it's a regular company," I said. "It's the Coterie." I felt like those three words answered a lot of questions. But maybe they meant something different now. Something better.

Alistair waved Ezra away. "Tell someone to bring us food. Not you. You go get off that leg." He waited until Ezra complied before continuing. "The Coterie is more like a giant corporation, and as such, organization is even more necessary. The head of the Coterie is basically the CEO of a company that owns several other businesses."

"To me the head of the Coterie has always seemed more like a deranged despot covered in the blood of her own people than a stiff in a suit."

"Despot, CEO, there are a lot of similarities." Alistair finally looked up. He stared at Cade and me, his hands folded together, the fingers loosely interlocking. He leaned into his folded hands so all I could see was the top half of his face as he peered at us. "How are you feeling, Mr. Halloway? Better, I hope?"

"Much better." Cade fingered a bruised spot on his ribs, unconsciously, I think. "I'd like to thank you for your part in my rescue. Things would have ended poorly without your aid, I understand."

I winced inwardly at his choice of words. Yes, of course Alistair's role was pivotal, but you don't admit to the head of the Coterie that you're indebted to him. It's about as safe as filling your pants full of chum and jumping into shark-infested water.

Alistair waved it away like it was nothing. "Forget it. Let us not hamper our new relationship with such debts and tallies."

Warning bells chimed in my ears. "New relationship?"

Alistair leaned back into the booth. I didn't like the expression on his face.

"No relationship," I said firmly, my hands gripping the edge of the table. "My pact was with Venus. She's gone. Therefore, so is my pact."

Alistair pulled a file out of one of the neat stacks and tossed it in front of me. "Your paperwork clearly states that you belong to the Coterie. Read it, if you like."

"I do like," I said, opening the file. Cade leaned over to read it as well, even though we'd been over it a hundred times. I'd always assumed that Venus was the Coterie, that the pact was null and void without her. A stomach-twisting shudder went through me as I read. I didn't have to search for long. Alistair had highlighted all the relevant bits, which I felt was very organized of him.

"As you are no doubt discovering, your pact clearly says you belong to this organization, which I now embody." He spoke calmly, still comfortably at ease on his side of the booth. I wanted to smack his serene face.

My hands were shaking as I handed the papers to Cade. "I guess I always thought Venus and the Coterie were one and the same."

"Yes and no," Alistair said. "Like I said, she was the CEO—or the despot." He smiled a tight-lipped smile. "But the company doesn't lose its assets when the CEO steps down, just as the country doesn't lose its resources when a despot has been tumbled." A waiter appeared with a basket of rolls and drinks, earning a smile from Alistair for his effort. "To be completely honest, your pact paperwork is littered with vague terminology like this. Had we met prior to you signing it, I would have recommended a lawyer. I'm assuming you didn't have anyone look at it?"

I shook my head.

"All the local nonhuman lawyers are Coterie owned," Cade said.

Alistair nodded sympathetically. "Look, I feel bad for you two—obviously you were bullied into an unfair arrangement." He pulled a piping hot roll out of the basket. "But I would be stupid not to make use of all my assets." He tore the bread slowly before buttering it. "I am not stupid," he said, his gaze meeting mine. "Ava, I'm sure you came in here thinking you were a free bug, and I do apologize for crushing that dream, but I'm afraid that I'm not in the position to be magnanimous about this. So far things have been going smoothly, but as word gets out, that will change. The head of the Coterie is a tempting position, and many will try their luck and come at me. Things will get messy. I need to be prepared for that."

I opened my mouth to argue, but Alistair stayed me with a hand. "We're still in the early days." He tapped one of the larger stacks of paper next to him. "I am, as Ezra might have mentioned, cleaning house. Despite her . . . charms . . . Venus had some very loyal followers. I'm giving some of them a chance to switch alliances. A few of them will refuse. Still more of them are too dangerous and unstable to even consider."

My blood chilled as I anticipated where he was going with this. "You want me to burn out the rats."

"Yes," he said, his eyes dark. He sighed and pushed the

basket of bread toward me, but I didn't feel hungry anymore. Not that it mattered. I would need to eat anyway. "I know you won't believe me, but I will be a different leader than Venus."

"Different isn't always better," Cade said.

"No, it's not," Alistair said, his uneaten roll resting on a plate in front of him. "But I feel I have things to offer you that she would not."

"Like?" Cade asked. My throat felt thick, making talking difficult.

"Ava, you and your team have received back pay for your services—don't argue," he said, before I could even open my mouth. It was going to be hard to get a word in edgewise with Alistair. "It's your money. You've more than earned it, and you will continue to draw a paycheck while you remain in the Coterie. What you do with it now doesn't concern me. Burn it if you wish, though I think that would be a tremendous waste, and it certainly wouldn't change how you earned it. And wasting the money won't bring those creatures back, Ava. It won't assuage any guilt you have festering in the corners of your soul. I suggest you use it to rebuild your bookstore. Even with good coverage, insurance won't handle everything. If that doesn't appeal to you, you can donate it wherever you see fit. That's all I will say on the matter."

He handed me another file.

I didn't open it—I was afraid to see what was inside.

"It won't bite, Ava. It's not an assignment."

"What is it, then?" I asked.

"Think of it as an offering—a little something to try to make up for not releasing you from your pact."

"I don't want it," I said automatically.

I got an amused twist of lips and a single raised eyebrow. "Not taking it will do nothing to me, Ava. It won't change your situation. Taking it won't make you more indebted to me or the Coterie. Take it or don't. Simple as that."

Yeah, right. I opened the folder. Alistair was telling the truth—it wasn't an assignment. I picked up a battered and worn piece of paper that looked like it had been folded, stored, shoved into pockets—all the things you do with paperwork that you have to carry your whole life. It was a birth certificate, and whoever forged it had been smart enough to make it look like it had seventeen years of wear.

"I used the birthday Lock gave me. From what I've been told that probably isn't the real one, and if you wish, I will try to discover what the proper one is. Someone had to deliver you, Ava. There were witnesses."

It was weird suddenly not knowing when I was born. When was my real birthday? Logically, I didn't think it mattered, but logic and people don't always mix. For some reason not knowing my birthday made me feel a little unfinished. I pushed the birth certificate aside until I could deal with it later. Underneath that was a passport, a driver's license, a social security card... and they all had my name on them. And underneath it all were a few pamphlets for college.

"It's only been a *week*," I said. "How did you do all this?"

"Strings, Ava. I've been doing some major marionette work."

"Why?"

He smiled and took a bite of his roll. "One reason would be to keep you happy. I realize I can't buy your loyalty, Ava. Our short time together has told me that. However, I would like to keep you from actively trying to sabotage things."

The waiter returned with our food, setting a thick steak in front of me, and I took a moment to put my napkin in my lap while I thought through what Alistair said.

"There are other ways for you to accomplish such things," I said.

Alistair was straightening his own napkin. "I need you legal—it makes you less noticeable and situations largely less sticky if you have all the trappings of a regular human. As for college, education is something I prize. My employees are encouraged to better themselves. I know you won't believe I'm doing it for altruistic reasons, so I will tell you that doing so will only improve my assets. I don't want pawns, Ava, I want a well-organized, functioning machine."

"You want samurais, not farmers playing soldiers."

Cade snorted and Alistair nodded. "Exactly." He looked down the aisle, and when I followed his gaze I saw Lock. My friend had a few battle wounds of his own, but he still looked pretty good. As he got closer, the air shivered and Bianca appeared. She was holding on to Lock's arm in a possessive manner that I didn't quite like. I attacked my steak with the knife. I was too forceful, and some of the vegetables slid over the lip of the plate and onto the tabletop. Smooth.

Bianca leaned up on her toes and kissed Lock on the cheek. He seemed surprised, but pleasantly. Alistair made no move to slide into the booth, so Bianca stole a chair from another table and pulled it over to us. Lock stood rather awkwardly near the table for a moment, clearly unsure as to whether he should leave or not. He wouldn't look at me. When Ezra shouted for him, he fled in obvious relief.

Alistair picked up a knife and fork and sliced into his steak

314

in a genteel fashion. I was not surprised to see that it was rare. "I won't pretend that you're not an important part of my new world order here, Ava. Nor am I going to pretend that you'll love me every second of the day. I'm your boss. Such feelings are natural. But I will ask that you at least pretend compliance when you're around."

"I'm pretty sure my paperwork does not say that I have to play nice."

"No," Alistair said, "it doesn't. But the more you play along, the less you actually have to work."

I popped a piece of broccoli in my mouth while I mulled that over. Cade, apparently making intuitive leaps that I couldn't, pieced it together before I could.

"Bait and switch," he said.

Alistair gave him a small smile. "Bravo."

When it was apparent to them that I was still in the dark, Alistair pointed at the caulbearer with his steak knife. "Bianca."

I stared at Bianca, and I think I can honestly say that she would have happily kicked me in the shins if we'd been alone. The feeling was more than mutual.

"Everyone will expect him to make you his Owen," Cade explained. "So he's going to pretend that's the case, but really it will be Bianca."

I tilted my head, trying to envision Bianca as Owen. It was a strange visual. Bianca seemed like an odd choice to me. She didn't seem on par with Owen—she wasn't scary. Which I guess was the point of hiding her. I would look scary, while she did the . . . what exactly would she do?

"I don't understand the subterfuge. If you need a heavy because Bianca isn't up to it, why not simply pick one?" Bianca stiffened, but I ignored her. "Why make everyone think it's me?"

"Man, you're thick," Bianca mumbled.

"What I need right now is loyalty. No one besides the drove and a few others know what Bianca can do—think of all the meetings she can sit in on, all the information she can gather. Unseen. Unnoticed. I have enough enforcers. What I need is someone to suss out the people who won't try to stab me the minute I turn around. You can't do it—you're too young, no one will trust you, and you have all the subtlety of an ox in an opera house."

"Harsh," Bianca said. "Can firebugs burn, Ava? Because that was definitely a burn."

I flipped her the finger. Everyone ignored us.

"You will work as a distraction because Venus has been using you as punishment for years. Your team has a reputation, and people are already scared of you. It makes more sense to trade on that than wait for people to be afraid of Bianca, which would undoubtedly take more effort and violence than is strictly necessary."

"Yeah, no one's going to be scared of her," I said. "She looks like a damn pixie."

Bianca flapped her hands like tiny wings. If I hadn't disliked her so much, I would have found it funny. Okay, it was still funny. Damn.

I took a bite of my roll. "So you want me to be a veil for the veil?"

"Yes. There will still be blood loss—there's nothing I can do about that. The least I can do is make it necessary. This is the best-case scenario." Alistair poked the file containing my paperwork with an index finger. "When the time comes, pick whichever college strikes your fancy. I chose options that are close so you can stay at home with minimal commute. Most of them also have online options. I will cover your books and tuition. I will also check your transcripts and get updates from your professors. You will maintain a 3.0 GPA at the very least— though I expect more of you—and you will supply me with your schedule so we can do our best to accommodate it. I don't like to be disappointed, Ava." He slipped a red strip of beef into his mouth, chewed, then swallowed. "Now, I recommend that you eat your steak before it gets cold."

The conversation was clearly over.

I LEFT Cade at the table with Alistair and Bianca. I might not entirely trust them yet, but I didn't think they'd do anything to Cade, since Alistair clearly wanted me on his side. Besides, I needed to talk to Lock alone. I cornered him in an empty hallway. He was leaning against the wall close to the men's room door, looking good, if a bit tired and scuffed up in his Purgatory uniform.

He picked at his shirt. "I guess this is the last week I'll have to wear this," he said. "With us getting back pay and actual wages, I won't need the extra job."

"That's definitely looking at the bright side of being hired thugs." I held up my hand to stop his lecture before it started. I didn't need it. Not today. "Why are you hanging out in a hallway?"

"Just in case Ez needs help. I'm supposed to stay nearby, but he doesn't want me to go into the actual bathroom with him. As if I haven't already seen everything."

"We should still have some boundaries," Ezra shouted through the door.

I wanted to pull Lock away from the bathroom, but knew from past experience that Ezra would still be able to hear us anyway. "I never got a chance to thank you," I said. Sparks flew from my fingers and drifted down toward the floor. I stomped them out. "You know, for that saving-my-life business and stuff."

Lock rested his head on the wall, his gray eyes assessing. "You are really bad at this."

"I really am. Can we fast forward past the part where we talk about squishy feelings?"

"No," he said. "Not this time. I told you, you can't always skip to the end."

"But I really want to."

"I know you do." He reached up and tucked a strand of hair behind my ear, a strangely intimate gesture. "Sometimes we have to do the hard stuff."

"You sound like Cade."

"There are worse things." He ran a hand nervously through his own hair. "So, Ezra and I were talking, and since we don't have to work in the restaurant anymore, we were thinking about moving out by you guys."

"I haven't agreed to anything!" Ezra shouted. "I don't know if I can give up my city-boy lifestyle."

Lock ignored him. "We'd help out with the bookshop rebuild. Hang out more. Maybe a lot more." Lock looked at me expectantly and I froze. I've never felt more like a deer in headlights watching an eighteen-wheeler as it barrels down at me.

I needed to say something. My brain remained an extremely helpful blank.

Ezra continued to shout through the door even though we weren't acknowledging him. "For the love of all that is—you're both ridiculous, you know. Absolutely ridiculous. Ava, Lock is asking you out on a date. Now tell him yes so I can stop listening to this awkward mating ritual of a conversation."

We remained silent, stuck in the moment. It was still my turn to say something, and I couldn't seem to make words happen. This conversation wasn't going the way I had planned *at all*.

"Wow," Lock said. "Speechless. That's not good." He drew away. "Forget it. All of it. Everything I've said since you entered this hallway."

There was a clatter from the bathroom. "Damn it!"

"I've got to go," Lock said, pushing away from the wall. "You're going to have to help Ezra."

I grabbed Lock's arm. "No, wait. Lock, I'm sorry. It's just... I can't—"

He cut me off before I could find coherency. "Please don't. You're making it worse." He gently pried my hand off his arm. "It's my turn to skip to the end on this one, Ava."

No Aves. Ava. Shit.

He let go of my hand and walked away. My heart didn't just break, it imploded into dust. Ezra tumbled through the door, his crutches tangled. I helped him sort things out. When everything was straightened, Ezra tucked his crutches under his arms and put his hands on my shoulders. "I want you to listen very carefully. I love you, my little dumpling, but you are as dumb as a sack of hammers sometimes."

"I learned it from watching you," I said.

"Shut up—I'm serious." He let go of my shoulder to point at his face. "This is my serious face."

"Ezra, I'm not in the mood. . . ."

"I don't care what mood you're in. You just crushed our best friend. Pulverized. Mashed. Eviscerated."

"Hey!"

"Ava, you let Ryan take you on a date. Ryan, who is surely in the running for the Biggest Scumbag on the Planet award, but you shut down the one person who for whatever reason loves us and puts up with our preposterous shit. That man dug glass out of my back. He makes us hot cocoa when we're all tired as hell, and he almost never complains about it. He risked his life for us, and you sat there like a lump."

"I really handled that badly, didn't I?"

"'Badly' doesn't even cover it, darling." He let go of me and got a better grip on his crutches. "You are officially the *Hindenburg* of the dating world." He reached out and brushed a tear off my cheek. I hadn't even realized I was crying.

"I can't lose him, Ez. I can't."

"And you think that will happen if you go out on a date?"

I nodded, not trusting myself to speak.

"You realize that this course of action might have worse results? One bad date you could have moved past, but this?" Ezra shook his head. "And you know what the worst part is? You're absolutely nuts for him." He gripped his crutches and started to move down the hallway. "Don't bother arguing. I know it's true even if you don't. C'mon, then. Let's see if the kitchen has pie."

I followed him down the hallway and wondered if there

was any way I was ever going to be able to fix this. For a fleeting second, I almost wished things could go back to the way they were a week ago. Ryan wouldn't be a traitor, and Lock would still be my best friend.

I'd thought Venus's death would be the end to my problems. If that was true, how come my life was still such a mess?

20

SPIRIT FINGERS

CADE WAS POPPING popcorn while I stood on the porch talking to Duncan. He'd ostensibly stopped by to drop off some things, but Cade decided we needed to chat and left us on the porch together. I didn't want to talk to Duncan. My feelings about him were mixed. On one hand, he'd helped me save Cade's life. On the other, he'd endangered it in the first place, even if he didn't do it on purpose.

So far we hadn't managed to say much to each other. I caught a whiff of skunk on the breeze.

"Must be spring," Duncan joked. "The skunks are out."

"I just need to know," I said, thinking back to our planning session in Duncan's kitchen. How sure and commanding he'd been. "Who's head of the Coterie now? Alistair or you?"

Duncan took out his pipe and tapped it on the porch railing. "I never lied to you, Ava. I might have kept some of my personal life to myself, but that is my prerogative. I meant it when I said I was tired." He stuffed his pipe with tobacco, the scent rich and earthy. "I don't want to lead." He dug a matchbook out of his pocket. "I just didn't want Venus to lead either." Duncan lit his pipe and stared intently in the window at Cade, who was pouring the popped corn from the pot into a bowl. "I don't have any children of my own, Ava. Cade is it. And I couldn't be prouder of him if he was my own flesh and blood. Sooner or later, either to spur you or punish you, she would have killed him." He blew a smoke ring out into the night. "I think you can understand why I made my choices."

I did, because it sounded eerily like what I'd said to Lock's mom. Duncan had to protect his family. When I didn't say anything, he nodded. Then he tipped his weather-beaten hat at me and left.

I wanted to be furious with him for being one of the small cogs that set the machine of fate into motion, but I couldn't. In his place, I would have made the same choices.

I'D PICKED *Summer Stock* as the night's movie, because I wanted dance numbers and romance. I wanted humor and Judy Garland and Gene Kelly dancing into the sunset. After that, I was going to watch *Little Shop of Horrors*, because I needed to see people eaten by plants. I made Cade rent the funny version, though. The one where Rick Moranis gets the girl. In the original everyone dies, and I just wasn't up for so much misery. Cade had explained that the original was more Faustian and much more powerful, but I didn't want Faustian. I wanted the good guy to win. And I wanted dance numbers. So help me, I wanted jazz hands. I *needed* spirit fingers.

I was still calling Cade by his first name. No need to get the townsfolk talkin'. Not that I cared about that. The real reason was that it was weird to look at Cade and use the words *father* or *dad*. Maybe I could call him Big Papa? No matter what, it all sounded funny in my head. I'd been calling him Cade my whole life. It wasn't easy to make a quick transition like that. He hadn't brought up those words either, so I think he was having similar issues.

I shoved a handful of popcorn into my mouth.

"Chew, Rat. You're going to choke like that." Cade joined me on the couch, setting his own bowl on the coffee table.

I said, "I'm chewing!" but what came out was "Mm-chumging" and a few stray popcorn bits. I sighed and grabbed a napkin.

"No Lock tonight?" Cade asked, looking into his bowl.

"He's busy" is what I said. *He's on a date with* Bianca, *the sullen brat*, is what I meant.

"I see." Cade glanced at me, and I got the feeling that he'd heard both versions. He grabbed the popcorn bowl and tipped some of his into mine, because I'd already eaten half in some sort of popcorn-induced fugue state. "And this bothers you because you don't want to share your best friend, or because you're not on the date?"

I threw a piece of popcorn at him. "I don't want to talk about it," I answered. "It's weird."

"We've always talked about everything," he said.

I poked my popcorn, pushing it around the bowl, hoping it might form a pattern, like tea leaves, and tell me the answers. All I got was salt under my nails. "I don't know what I want to say yet. Besides, what with ... stuff ... and things ... isn't it kind of strange now?"

"Because I'm your dad?" Now Cade was examining his

popcorn for all it was worth. "Does it really upset you that much?"

I could hear the brittle edge in his voice, the pain, and I knew I'd caused it.

Damn.

Ezra and Lock were right. I suck at this.

"It's not—I just." I sighed. "I used to hope, you know? That you and Mom . . . The happy ending and all that." But that hope had died along with most childhood dreams. "It's not bad, it's just surreal. I've thought of you one way for so long that it's hard to make the shift."

"I still can't believe she lied to me," Cade said, his voice thick. "Lilia never lied to me. Not once. She might have hidden things, but she never out-and-out lied. We don't know your birthday. . . . You might even be eighteen now. An adult. I just can't believe it."

"People do all kinds of strange things to protect the ones they love," I said.

He reached an arm around me and squeezed me close, kissing the top of my head. I tried to imagine for a moment a life without him in it, and I couldn't.

"Sometimes transition happens and it's hard, and it can hurt, but it can also be good, reevaluating someone." He rubbed my arm. "You might want to consider it with Lock."

I mock punched him. "I told you I didn't want to talk about it."

"I'm your dad," he says. "We'll talk about these things until you get really uncomfortable and never want to look at a boy again. It's a great tactic, actually. Works wonders."

I burst into laughter then, and it seemed to cause the

325

pressure to lift. While not totally back to normal, it felt like things might be closer to okay again. I could get used to this.

Sometime later, after both movies and a lengthy discussion of why Gene Kelly was so damn amazing, I was walking up the stairs to my loft when I heard Cade pause.

"Rat?"

"Yeah?"

"I used to hope too." And then, much softer and almost to himself, he said, "All the time."

"I know you did, Dad," I said, my voice barely audible, my throat was so tight.

He stared up at me for a moment before he smiled, and it was so open, so happy, that I knew this was the smile my mom fell in love with.

"Good night, Rat," he said. Then he clicked off the light and went to his room.

I was in my loft before I realized that I'd said "Dad" instead of "Cade." And I was all the way under my covers when I figured out that was what had caused the smile. I reached one hand up, pointed my index finger, and called a blue flame to the tip of it. I traced three words in the air, over and over until they were burned into my retinas. Then I closed my eyes and could clearly see *Cade + Lilia = Ava.*

Best. Equation. Ever.

I grinned, then wondered whose smile I had. Maybe in the morning I'd ask my dad.

ACKNOWLEDGMENTS

There comes a time in every book where I think: "This is it—this time it's just not going to come together." But it inevitably does, and mostly that has to do with a very large group of people. So special thanks to superstar editor Noa Wheeler and everyone under the Macmillan Kids umbrella, of course. Jason Anthony, my agent, who puts up with a great deal, and everyone at Lippincott, Massie, McQuilkin. Also Jill Gillet, Sylvie Rabineau, and the RWSG agency for all their hard work. Many thanks to Maria Massie for getting my book translated into languages I can't read—which I still think is really cool. Thanks to April Ward for the amazing book cover—it makes my heart explode with joy.

To Darin and Serafina Carlucci for reading several drafts and pointing out all the things I got wrong when it comes to the great state of Maine. Huge thanks to Cindy Pon for last-minute support. To my Fierce Reads ladies—Jennifer Bosworth, Leigh Bardugo, Marissa Meyer, Emmy Laybourne, Ann Aguirre, and Elizabeth Fama. You have all been a great support team and extremely patient with my whining. Thanks especially to Ann for all the title help and beta reading and Marissa (and Gennifer Albin!) for writing dates. You ladies are the best. To Martha Brockenbrough for laser targeted edits, thoughts, and brainstorming. Kelly Jones for wonderful notes and beta reads. Juliet Swann and the rest of team Scotland for reading, thoughtful notes, and support. Everyone at Third Place Books and 826 Seattle for the support over the years (and of course Team Honey Bear—how could I forget you?). You've all been wonderful to my little books and to me and I am a grateful Lish.

Thanks to Vlad Verano for excellent design work and book swag, as well as Erika and Eric at Imaginary Trends for continuing to make the best T-shirts EVER. Aaron Carlton continues to rule my Web page with an iron fist (along with Bradley Bleeker's artwork) and for that I am indebted. Brenda Winter-Hansen, Brent McKnight, Melissa Warner for writing dates. To Porkchop and Henry "Hank" Miles Leinonen for sharing an Ezra-worthy anecdote. And of course, all the usual suspects like friends, family, and Team Parkview. To the librarians, booksellers, bloggers, and readers out there who have read and loved and shared my books—I hug you. A lot.

There are, naturally, too many people to mention, and my memory is faulty and sad, so if I forgot you or didn't mention you and you helped me along the way, please know that you are appreciated.

Thanks, team. I can't believe we made it to another one.